D0874100

INK AND DAGGERS

ALSO AVAILABLE FROM TITAN BOOKS

edited by

MAXIM JAKUBOWSKI

INK AND DAGGERS

19 AWARD-WINNING STORIES FROM

NEIL GAIMAN

VAL McDERMID

ANN CLEEVES

PETER ROBINSON

KEVIN WIGNALL

GEORGE PELECANOS

CHRISTOPHER FOWLER

VICTORIA SELMAN

CHRIS SIMMS

JAMES SALLIS

AND MANY MORE!

TITAN BOOKS

Ink and Daggers
Print edition ISBN: 9781803363202
E-book edition ISBN: 9781803363219

Published by Titan Books
A division of Titan Publishing Group Ltd
144 Southwark Street, London SE1 0UP
www.titanbooks.com

First edition: September 2023
10 9 8 7 6 5 4 3 2 1

This is a work of fiction. All of the characters, organizations, and events
portrayed in this novel are either products of the author's imagination or
are used fictitiously. Any resemblance to actual persons, living or dead
(except for satirical purposes), is entirely coincidental.

A CIP catalogue record for this title is available from the British Library.

Printed and bound by CPI Group (UK) Ltd, Croydon CR0 4YY.

TABLE OF CONTENTS

INTRODUCTION

MAXIM JAKUBOWSKI

A couple of years ago, it occurred to me that no one had ever collected the wonderful short stories that had over the course of several previous decades won the prestigious Dagger award under one single cover. As I was about to become the Chair of the Crime Writers' Association, who happen to run the Daggers, the solution was an obvious one and the result was DAGGERS DRAWN, which featured nineteen such past winners; winners all!

It has been a great personal satisfaction that the book, both in the UK and the USA, has been well received both commercially and critically, and brought new attention to some wonderful tales and reminded many a reader of how good a well-crafted crime and mystery short story can prove in the hands of expert writers, both well-known or, in some cases, unjustly forgotten.

So, I have returned to that well of plenty.

Every year, an panel of independent judges, drawn from reviewers, readers, booksellers, academics and other writers, convenes to read what has been published in the UK during the course of the previous calendar year and comes up with a long list, which is then whittled down to a short list and, in due course, a winner. None of the judges can sit for more than three years, so that there is an ever-changing balance of views and opinions. This actually applies to all the categories in which the CWA presents Daggers.

As much as we are proud of all our past winners, there are years – in fact, every single year – when the competition is intense and the choices to be made excruciating and some wonderful books and stories are inevitably not rewarded by a Dagger and remain, for posterity, on the short list. Which does not mean they are inferior in any way. Paradoxically, there are probably more well-known crime writers who have gone no further than the short list than those who actually won the award, which suggested a second volume of stories drawn from the Daggers archives was a must.

Judging what is best between stories (and novels) that sometimes have very little in common beyond their criminous nature is always a subjective choice and depends a lot on the personalities of the judges involved, but I would confidently venture to state that looking back at the Daggers, ever since they were created, the standards have been immaculate and that the CWA has not missed out on any of the big names and books in the field in their choices. And so many authors who were still an unknown quantity when they won a Dagger have gone on to even greater fame since!

So here are a further nineteen outstanding stories, drawn on this occasion from the Short Story Dagger shortlists and I believe they are as dazzling as those I had the privilege to reprint in our first instalment. Again, there were instances when the writer has appeared on the short list on more than one occasion (twice: Peter Lovesey, Ken Bruen, three times: Peter Robinson) in which case I asked them to chose which of their stories they wished to be featured.

Puzzles, dramas, twists, blood, poison, murder, death, whodunits and whydunits: all human life is here as our metaphorical daggers dig deep into the dark side of life.

Savour slowly.

MJ

THE CONSOLATION BLONDE

VAL McDERMID

Awards are meaningless, right? They're always political, they're forgotten two days later and they always go to the wrong book, right? Well, that's what we all say when the prize goes somewhere else. Of course, it's a different story when it's our turn to stand at the podium and thank our agents, our partners and our pets. Then, naturally enough, it's an honor and a thrill.

That's what I was hoping I'd be doing that October night in New York. I had been nominated for Best Novel in the Speculative Fiction category of the US Book Awards, the national literary prizes that carry not only prestige but also a $50,000 check for the winners. *Termagant Fire*, the concluding novel in my *King's Infidel* trilogy, had broken all records for a fantasy novel. More weeks in the *New York Times* bestseller list than King, Grisham and Cornwell put together. And the reviews had been breathtaking, referring to *Termagant Fire* as 'the first novel since Tolkien to make fantasy respectable.' Fans and booksellers alike had voted it their book of the year. Serious literary critics had examined the parallels between my fantasy universe and America in the defining epoch of the 60s. Now all I was waiting for was the imprimatur of the judges in the nation's foremost literary prize.

Not that I was taking it for granted. I know how fickle judges can be, how much they hate being told what to think by the rest of the world. I understood only too well that the *succes d'estime* the book had enjoyed could be the very factor that would snatch my moment of glory from my grasp. I had already given myself a stiff talking-to in my hotel bathroom mirror, reminding myself of the dangers of hubris. I needed to keep my feet on the ground, and maybe failing to win the golden prize would be the best thing that could happen to me. At least it would be one less thing to have to live up to with the next book.

But on the night, I took it as a good sign that my publisher's table at the awards dinner was right down at the front of the room, smack bang up against the podium. They never like the winners being seated too far from the stage just in case the applause doesn't last long enough for them to make it up there ahead of the silence.

My award was third from last in the litany of winners. That meant a long time sitting still and looking interested. But I could only cling on to the fragile conviction that it was all going to be worth it in the end. Eventually, the knowing Virginia drawl of the MC, a middle-ranking news anchorman, got us there. I arranged my face in a suitably bland expression, which I was glad of seconds later when the name he announced was not mine. There followed a short, stunned silence, then, with more eyes on me than on her, the victor weaved her way to the front of the room to a shadow of the applause previous winners had garnered.

I have no idea what graceful acceptance speech she came out with. I couldn't tell you who won the remaining two categories. All my energy was channeled into not showing the rage and pain churning inside me. No matter how much I told myself I had prepared for this, the reality was horrible.

At the end of the apparently interminable ceremony, I got to my feet like an automaton. My team formed a sort of flying wedge around me; editor ahead of me, publicist to one side, publisher to the other. 'Let's get you out of here. We don't need pity,' my publisher growled, head down, broad shoulders a challenge to anyone who wanted to offer condolences.

By the time we made it to the bar, we'd acquired a small support crew, ones I had indicated were acceptable by a nod or a word. There was Robert, my first mentor and oldest buddy in the business; Shula, an English sf writer who had become a close friend; Shula's girlfriend Caroline, and Cassie, the manager of the city's premier sf and fantasy bookstore. That's what you need at a time like this, people around who won't ever hold it against you that you vented your spleen in an unseemly way at the moment when your dream turned to ashes. Fuck nobility. I wanted to break something.

But I didn't have the appetite for serious drinking, especially when my vanquisher arrived in the same bar with her celebration in tow. I finished my Jack Daniels and pushed off from the enveloping sofa. 'I'm not much in the mood,' I said. 'I think I'll just head back to my hotel.'

'You're at the InterCon, right?' Cassie asked.

'Yeah.'

'I'll walk with you, I'm going that way.'

'Don't you want to join the winning team?' I asked, jerking my head towards the barks of laughter by the bar.

Cassie put her hand on my arm. 'You wrote the best book, John. That's victory enough for me.'

I made my excuses and we walked into a ridiculously balmy New York evening. I wanted snow and ice to match my mood, and said as much to Cassie.

Her laugh was low. 'The pathetic fallacy,' she said. 'You writers just never got over that, did you? Well, John, if you're going to cling to that notion, you better change your mood to match the weather.'

I snorted. 'Easier said than done.'

'Not really,' said Cassie. 'Look, we're almost at the InterCon. Let's have a drink'

'OK.'

'On one condition. We don't talk about the award, we don't talk about the asshole who won it, we don't talk about how wonderful your book is and how it should have been recognized tonight.'

I grinned. 'Cassie, I'm a writer. If I can't talk about me, what the hell else does that leave?'

She shrugged and steered me into the lobby. 'Gardening? Gourmet food? Favorite sexual positions? Music?'

We settled in a corner of the bar, me with Jack on the rocks, she with a Cosmopolitan. We ended up talking about movies, past and present, finding to our surprise that in spite of our affiliation to the sf and fantasy world, what we both actually loved most was film noir. Listening to Cassie talk, watching her push her blonde hair back from her eyes, enjoying the sly smiles that crept out when she said something witty or sardonic, I forgot the slings and arrows and enjoyed myself.

When they announced last call at midnight, I didn't want it to end. It seemed natural enough to invite her up to my room to continue the conversation. Sure, at the back of my mind was the possibility that it might end with those long legs wrapped around mine, but that really wasn't the most important thing. What mattered was that Cassie had taken my mind off what ailed me. She had already provided consolation enough, and I wanted it to go on. I didn't want to be left alone with my rancor and self-pity or any of the other uglinesses that were fighting for space inside me.

She sprawled on the bed. It was that or an armchair which offered little prospect of comfort. I mixed drinks, finding it hard not to imagine sliding those tight black trousers over her hips or running my hands under that black silk tee, or pushing the long shimmering overblouse off her shoulders so I could cover them with kisses.

I took the drinks over and she sat up, crossing her legs in a full lotus and straightening her spine. 'I thought you were really dignified tonight,' she said.

'Didn't we have a deal? That tonight was off limits?' I lay on my side, carefully not touching her at any point.

'That was in the bar. You did well, sticking to it. Think you earned a reward?'

'What kind of reward?'

'I give a mean backrub,' she said, looking at me over the rims of her glasses. 'And you look tense.'

'A backrub would be... very acceptable,' I said.

Cassie unfolded her legs and stood up. 'OK. I'll go into the bathroom and give you some privacy to get undressed. Oh, and John – strip right down to the skin. I can't do your lower back properly if I have to fuck about with waistbands and stuff.'

I couldn't quite believe how fast things were moving. We hadn't been in the room ten minutes, and here was Cassie instructing me to strip for her. OK, it wasn't quite like that sounds, but it was equally a perfectly legitimate description of events. The sort of thing you could say to the guys and they would make a set of assumptions from. If, of course, you were the sort of sad asshole who felt the need to validate himself like that.

I took my clothes off, draping them over the armchair without actually folding them, then lay face down on the bed. I wished I'd spent more of the spring working out than I had writing. But I knew my shoulders were still respectable, my legs strong and hard, even if I was carrying a few more pounds around the waist than I would have liked.

I heard the bathroom door open and Cassie say, 'You ready, John?'

I was very, very ready. Somehow, it wasn't entirely a surprise that it wasn't just the skin of her hands that I felt against mine.

How did I know it had to be her? I dreamed her hands. Nothing slushy or sentimental; just her honest hands with their strong square fingers, the palms slightly callused from the daily shunting of books from carton to shelf, the play of muscle and skin over blood and bone. I dreamed her hands and woke with tears on my face. That was the day I called Cassie and said I had to see her again.

'I don't think so.' Her voice was cautious, and not, I believed, simply because she was standing behind the counter in the bookstore.

'Why not? I thought you enjoyed it,' I said. 'Did you think it was just a one-night stand?'

'Why would I imagine it could be more? You're a married man, you live in Denver, you're good-looking and successful. Why on earth would I set myself up for a let-down by expecting a repeat performance? John, I am so not in the business of being the Other Woman. A one-night stand is just fine, but I don't do affairs.'

'I'm not married.' It was the first thing I could think of to say. That it was the truth was simply a bonus.

'What do you mean, you're not married? It says so on your book jackets. You mention her in interviews.' Now there was an edge of anger, a 'don't fuck with me' note in her voice.

'I've never been married. I lied about it.'

A long pause. 'Why would you lie about being married?' she demanded.

'Cassie, you're in the store, right? Look around you. Scope out the women in there. Now, I hate to hurt people's feelings. Do you see why I might lie about my marital status?'

I could hear the gurgle of laughter swelling and bursting down the telephone line. 'John, you are a bastard, you know that? A charming bastard, but a bastard nevertheless. You mean that? About never having been married?'

'There is no moral impediment to you and me fucking each other's brains out as often as we choose to. Unless, of course, there's someone lurking at home waiting for you?' I tried to keep my voice light. I'd been torturing myself with that idea every since our night together. She'd woken me with soft kisses just after five, saying she had to go. By the time we'd said our farewells, it had been nearer six and she'd finally scrambled away from me, saying she had to get home and change before she went in to open the store. It had made sense, but so too did the possibility of her sneaking back in to the cold side of a double bed somewhere down in Chelsea or SoHo.

Now, she calmed my twittering heart. 'There's nobody. Hasn't been for over a year now. I'm free as you, by the sounds of it.'

'I can be in New York at the weekend,' I said. 'Can I stay?'

'Sure,' Cassie said, her voice somehow promising much more than a simple word.

That was the start of something unique in my experience. With Cassie, I found a sense of completeness I'd never known before. I'd always scoffed at terms like 'soulmate', but Cassie forced me to eat the words baked in a humble pie. We matched. It was as simple as that. She compensated for my lacks, she allowed me space to demonstrate my strengths. She made me feel like the finest lover who had ever laid hands on her. She was also the first woman I'd ever had a relationship with who miraculously never complained that the writing got in the way. With Cassie, everything was possible and life seemed remarkably straightforward.

She gave me all the space I needed, never minding that my fantasy world sometimes seemed more real to me than what was for dinner. And I did the same for her, I thought. I didn't dog her steps at the store, turning up for every event like an autograph hunter. I only came along to see writers I would have gone to see anyway; old friends, new kids on the block who were doing interesting work, visiting foreign names. I encouraged her to keep up her girls' nights out, barely registering when she rolled home in the small hours smelling of smoke and tasting of Triple Sec.

She didn't mind that I refused to attempt her other love, rock climbing; forty year old knees can't learn that sort of new trick. But equally, I never expected her to give it up for me, and even though she usually scheduled her overnight climbing trips for when I was out of town on book business, that was her choice rather than my demand. Bless her, she never tried taking advantage of our relationship to nail down better discount deals with my publishers, and I respected her even more for that.

Commuting between Denver and New York lasted all of two months. Then in the same week, I sold my house and my agent sold the *King's Infidel* trilogy to Oliver Stone's company for enough money for me actually to be able to buy a Manhattan apartment that was big enough for both of us and our several thousand books. I loved, and felt loved in return. It was as if I was leading a charmed life.

I should have known better. I am, after all, an adherent of the genre of fiction where pride always, always, always comes before a very nasty fall.

We'd been living together in the kind of bliss that makes one's friends gag and one's enemies weep for almost a year when the accident happened. I know that Freudians claim there is never any such thing as accident, but it's hard to see how anyone's subconscious could have felt the world would end up a better or more moral place because of this particular mishap.

My agent was in the middle of a very tricky negotiation with my publisher over my next deal. They were horse-trading and haggling hard over the money on the table, and my agent was naturally copying me in on the emails. One morning, I logged on to find that day's update had a file attachment with it. 'Hi, John,' the e-mail read. 'You might be interested to see that they're getting so nitty-gritty about this deal that they're actually discussing your last year's touring and miscellaneous expenses. Of course, I wasn't supposed to see this attachment, but we all know what an idiot Tom is when it comes to electronics. Great editor, cyber-idiot. Anyway, I thought you might find it amusing to see how much they reckon they spent on you. See how it tallies with your recollections...'

I wasn't much drawn to the idea, but since the attachment was there, I thought I might as well take a look. It never hurts to get a little righteous indignation going about how much hotels end up billing for a one-night stay. It's the supplementaries that are the killers. $15 for a bottle of water was the best I came across on last year's tour. Needless to say, I stuck a glass under the tap. Even when it's someone else's dime, I hate to encourage the robber barons who masquerade as hoteliers.

I was drifting down through the list when I ran into something out of the basic rhythm of hotels, taxis, air fares, author escorts. *Consolation Blonde, $500*, I read.

I knew what the words meant, but I didn't understand their linkage. Especially not on my expense list. If I'd spent it, you'd think I'd know what it was.

Then I saw the date.

My stomach did a back flip. Some dates you never forget. Like the US Book Awards dinner.

I didn't want to believe it, but I had to be certain. I called Shula's girlfriend Caroline, herself an editor of mystery fiction in one of the big London houses. Once we'd got the small talk out of the way, I cut to the chase. 'Caroline, have you ever heard the term "consolation blonde" in publishing circles?'

'Where did you hear that, John?' she asked, answering the question inadvertently.

'I overheard it in one of those chi-chi midtown bars where literary publishers hang out. I was waiting to meet my agent, and I heard one guy say to the other, "He was OK after the consolation blonde." I wasn't sure what it meant but I thought it sounded like a great title for a short story.'

Caroline gave that well-bred middle-class Englishwoman's giggle. 'I suppose you could be right. What can I say here, John? This really is one of publishing's tackier areas. Basically, it's what you lay on for an author who's having a bad time. Maybe they didn't win an award they thought was in the bag, maybe their book has bombed, maybe they're having a really bad tour. So you lay on a girl, a nice girl. A fan, a groupie, a publicity girlie, bookseller, whatever. Somebody on the fringes, not a hooker as such. Tell them how nice it would be for poor old what's-his-name to have a good time. So the sad boy gets the consolation blonde and the consolation blonde gets a nice boost to her bank account plus the bonus of being able to boast about shagging a name. Even if it's a name that nobody else in the pub has ever heard before.'

I felt I'd lost the power of speech. I mumbled something and managed to end the call without screaming my anguish at Caroline. In the background, I could hear Bob Dylan singing *Idiot Wind*. Cassie had set the CD playing on repeat before she'd left for work and now the words mocked me for the idiot I was.

Cassie was my Consolation Blonde.

I wondered how many other disappointed men had been lifted up by the power of her fingers and made to feel strong again? I wondered whether she'd have stuck around for more than that one-night stand if I'd been a poor man. I wondered how many times she'd slid into bed with me after a night out, not with the girls, but wearing the mantle of the Consolation Blonde. I wondered whether pity was still the primary emotion that moved her when she moaned and arched her spine for me.

I wanted to break something. And this time, I wasn't going to be diverted.

I've made a lot of money for my publisher over the years. So when I show up to see my editor, Tom, without an appointment, he makes space and time for me.

That day, I could tell inside a minute that he wished for once he'd made an exception. He looked like he wasn't sure whether he should just cut out the middle man and throw himself out of the twenty-third floor window. 'I don't know what you're talking about,' he yelped in response to my single phrase.

'Bullshit,' I yelled. 'You hired Cassie to be my consolation blonde. There's no point in denying it, I've seen the paperwork.'

'You're mistaken, John,' Tom said desperately, his alarmed chipmunk eyes widening in dilemma.

'No. Cassie was my consolation blonde for the US Book Awards. You didn't know I was going to lose, so you must have set her up in advance, as a stand-by. Which means you must have used her before.'

'I swear, John, I swear to God, I don't know…' Whatever Tom was going to say got cut off by me grabbing his stupid preppie tie and yanking him out of his chair.

'Tell me the truth,' I growled, dragging him towards the window. 'It's not like it can be worse than I've imagined. How many of my friends has she fucked? How many five hundred buck one-night stands have you pimped for my girlfriend since we got together? How many times have you and your buddies laughed behind my back because the woman I love is playing consolation blonde to somebody else? Tell me, Tom. Tell me the truth before I throw you out of this fucking window. Because I don't have any more to lose.'

'It's not like that,' he gibbered. I smelled piss and felt a warm dampness against my knee. His humiliation was sweet, though it was a poor second to what he'd done to me.

'Stop lying,' I screamed. He flinched as my spittle spattered his face. I shook him like a terrier with a rat.

'OK, OK,' he sobbed. 'Yes, Cassie was a consolation blonde. Yes, I hired her last year for you at the awards banquet. But I swear, that was the last time. She wrote me a letter, said after she met you she couldn't do this again. John, the letter's in my files. She never cashed the check for being with you. You have to believe me. She fell in love with you that first night and she never did it again.'

The worst of it was, I could tell he wasn't lying. But still, I hauled him over to the filing cabinets and made him produce his evidence. The letter was everything he'd promised. It was dated the day after our first encounter, two whole days before I called her to ask if I could see her again. *Dear Tom, I'm returning your $500 cheque. It's not appropriate for me to accept it this time. I won't be available to do close author escort work in future. Meeting John Treadgold has changed things for me. I can't thank you enough for introducing us. Good luck. Cassie White.*

I stood there, reading her words, every one cutting me like the wounds I'd carved into her body the night before.

I guess they don't have awards ceremonies in prison. Which is probably just as well, given what a bad loser I turned out to be.

THE CASE OF DEATH AND HONEY

NEIL GAIMAN

It was a mystery in those parts for years what had happened to the old white ghost man, the barbarian with his huge shoulder-bag. There were some who supposed him to have been murdered, and, later, they dug up the floor of Old Gao's little shack high on the hillside, looking for treasure, but they found nothing but ash and fire-blackened tin trays.

This was after Old Gao himself had vanished, you understand, and before his son came back from Lijiang to take over the beehives on the hill.

⁓

This is the problem, *wrote Holmes in 1899* : Ennui. And lack of interest. Or rather, it all becomes too easy. When the joy of solving crimes is the challenge, the possibility that you cannot, why then the crimes have something to hold your attention. But when each crime is soluble, and so easily soluble at that, why then there is no point in solving them.

25

Look: this man has been murdered. Well then, someone murdered him. He was murdered for one or more of a tiny handful of reasons: he inconvenienced someone, or he had something that someone wanted, or he had angered someone. Where is the challenge in that?

I would read in the dailies an account of a crime that had the police baffled, and I would find that I had solved it, in broad strokes if not in detail, before I had finished the article. Crime is too soluble. It dissolves. Why call the police and tell them the answers to their mysteries? I leave it, over and over again, as a challenge for them, as it is no challenge for me.

I am only alive when I perceive a challenge.

⌇

The bees of the misty hills, hills so high that they were sometimes called a mountain, were humming in the pale summer sun as they moved from spring flower to spring flower on the slope. Old Gao listened to them without pleasure. His cousin, in the village across the valley, had many dozens of hives, all of them already filling with honey, even this early in the year; also, the honey was as white as snow-jade. Old Gao did not believe that the white honey tasted any better than the yellow or light-brown honey that his own bees produced, although his bees produced it in meagre quantities, but his cousin could sell his white honey for twice what Old Gao could get for the best honey he had.

On his cousin's side of the hill, the bees were earnest, hard-working, golden-brown workers, who brought pollen and nectar back to the hives in enormous quantities. Old Gao's bees were ill-tempered and black, shiny as bullets, who produced as much honey as they needed to get through the winter and only a little more: enough for Old Gao to sell from door to door, to his fellow villagers, one small lump of honeycomb at a time. He would charge more for the brood-comb, filled with bee-larvae, sweet-tasting morsels of protein, when he had brood-comb to sell, which was rarely, for the bees were angry and sullen and everything they did, they did as little as possible, including make more bees, and Old Gao was always aware that each piece of brood-comb he sold were bees he would not have to make honey for him to sell later in the year.

Old Gao was as sullen and as sharp as his bees. He had had a wife once, but she had died in childbirth. The son who had killed her lived for a week, then died himself. There would be nobody to say the funeral rites for Old Gao, no-one to clean his grave for festivals or to put offerings upon it. He would die unremembered, as unremarkable and as unremarked as his bees.

The old white stranger came over the mountains in late spring of that year, as soon as the roads were passable, with a huge brown bag strapped to his shoulders. Old Gao heard about him before he met him.

"There is a barbarian who is looking at bees," said his cousin.

Old Gao said nothing. He had gone to his cousin to buy a pailful of second rate comb, damaged or uncapped and liable soon to spoil. He bought it cheaply to feed to his own bees, and if he sold some of it in his own village, no-one was any the wiser. The two men were drinking tea in Gao's cousin's hut on the hillside. From late spring, when the first honey started to flow, until first frost, Gao's cousin left his house in the village and went to live in the hut on the hillside, to live and to sleep beside his beehives, for fear of thieves. His wife and his children would take the honeycomb and the bottles of snow-white honey down the hill to sell.

Old Gao was not afraid of thieves. The shiny black bees of Old Gao's hives would have no mercy on anyone who disturbed them. He slept in his village, unless it was time to collect the honey.

"I will send him to you," said Gao's cousin. "Answer his questions, show him your bees and he will pay you."

"He speaks our tongue?"

"His dialect is atrocious. He said he learned to speak from sailors, and they were mostly Cantonese. But he learns fast, although he is old."

Old Gao grunted, uninterested in sailors. It was late in the morning, and there was still four hours walking across the valley to his village, in the heat of the day. He finished his tea. His cousin drank finer tea than Old Gao had ever been able to afford.

He reached his hives while it was still light, put the majority of the uncapped honey into his weakest hives. He had eleven hives. His cousin had over a hundred. Old Gao was stung twice doing this, on the back of the hand and the back of the neck. He had been stung over a thousand times in his life. He could not have told you how many times. He barely noticed the stings of other bees, but the stings of his own black bees always hurt, even if they no longer swelled or burned.

The next day a boy came to Old Gao's house in the village, to tell him that there was someone – and that the someone was a giant foreigner – who was asking for him. Old Gao simply grunted. He walked across the village with the boy at his steady pace, while the boy ran ahead, and soon was lost to sight.

Old Gao found the stranger sitting drinking tea on the porch of the Widow Zhang's house. Old Gao had known the Widow Zhang's mother, fifty years, ago. She had been a friend of his wife. Now she was long dead. He did not believe anyone who had known his wife still lived. The Widow Zhang fetched Old Gao tea, introduced him to the elderly barbarian, who had removed his bag and sat beside the small table.

They sipped their tea. The barbarian said, "I wish to see your bees."

Mycroft's death was the end of Empire, and no-one knew it but the two of us. He lay in that pale room, his only covering a thin white sheet, as if he were already becoming a ghost from the popular imagination, and needed only eye-holes in the sheet to finish the impression.

I had imagined that his illness might have wasted him away, but he seemed huger than ever, his fingers swollen into white suet sausages.

I said, "Good evening Mycroft. Doctor Hopkins tells me you have two weeks to live, and stated that I was under no circumstances to inform you of this."

"The man's a dunderhead," said Mycroft, his breath coming in huge wheezes between the words. "I will not make it to Friday."

"Saturday at least," I said.

"You always were an optimist. No, Thursday evening and then I shall be nothing more than an exercise in practical geometry for Hopkins and the funeral directors at Snigsby and Malterson, who will have the challenge, given the narrowness of the doors and corridors, of getting my carcass out of this room and out of the building."

"I had wondered," I said. "Particularly given the staircase. But they will take out the window-frame and lower you to the street like a grand piano."

Mycroft snorted at that. Then, "I am forty-nine years old, Sherlock. In my head is the British Government. Not the ballot and hustings nonsense, but the business of the thing. There is no-one else knows what the troop movements in the hills of Afghanistan have to do with the desolate shores of North Wales, no-one else who sees the whole picture. Can you imagine the mess that this lot and their children will make of Indian Independence?"

I had not previously given any thought to the matter. "*Will* it become independent?"

"Inevitably. In thirty years, at the outside. I have written several recent memoranda on the topic. As I have on so many other subjects. There are memoranda on the Russian Revolution – that'll be along within the decade I'll wager – and on the German problem and… oh, so many others. Not that I expect them to be read or understood." Another wheeze. My brother's lungs rattled like the windows in an empty house. "You know, if I were to live, the British Empire might last another thousand years, bringing peace and improvement to the world."

In the past, especially when I was a boy, whenever I heard Mycroft make a grandiose pronouncement like that I would say something to bait him. But not now, not on his deathbed. And also I was certain that he was not speaking of the Empire as it was, a flawed and fallible construct of flawed and fallible people, but of a British Empire that existed only in his head, a glorious force for civilisation and universal prosperity.

I do not, and did not, believe in Empires. But I believed in Mycroft.

Mycroft Holmes. Nine and forty years of age. He had seen in the new century but the Queen would still outlive him by several months. She was more than thirty years older than he was, and in every way a tough old bird. I wondered to myself whether this unfortunate end might have been avoided.

Mycroft said, "You are right of course, Sherlock. Had I forced myself to exercise. Had I lived on birdseed and cabbages instead of porterhouse steak. Had I taken up country dancing along with a wife and a puppy and in all other ways behaved contrary to my nature, I might have bought myself another dozen or so years. But what is that in the scheme of things? Little enough. And sooner or later, I would enter my dotage. No. I am of the opinion that it would take two hundred years to train a functioning Civil Service, let alone a secret service…"

I had said nothing.

The pale room had no decorations on the wall of any kind. None of Mycroft's citations. No illustrations, photographs or paintings. I compared his austere digs to my own cluttered rooms in Baker Street and I wondered, not for the first time, at Mycroft's mind. He needed nothing on the outside, for it was all on the inside – everything he had seen, everything he had experienced, everything he had read. He could close his eyes and walk through the National Gallery, or browse the British Museum Reading Room – or, more likely, compare intelligence reports from the edge of the Empire with the price of wool in Wigan and the unemployment statistics in Hove, and then, from this and only this, order a man promoted or a traitor's quiet death.

Mycroft wheezed enormously, and then he said, "It is a crime, Sherlock."

"I beg your pardon?"

"A crime. It is a crime, my brother, as heinous and as monstrous as any of the penny dreadful massacres you have investigated. A crime against the world, against nature, against order."

"I must confess, my dear fellow, that I do not entirely follow you. What is a crime?"

"My death," said Mycroft, "in the specific. And Death in general." He looked into my eyes. "I mean it," he said. "Now isn't *that* a crime worth investigating, Sherlock, old fellow? One that might keep your attention for longer than it will take you to establish that the poor fellow who used to conduct the brass band in Hyde Park was murdered by the third cornet using a preparation of strychnine."

"Arsenic," I corrected him, almost automatically.

"I think you will find," wheezed Mycroft, "that the arsenic, while present, had in fact fallen in flakes from the green-painted bandstand itself onto his supper. Symptoms of arsenical poison a complete red-herring. No, it was strychnine that did for the poor fellow."

Mycroft said no more to me that day or ever. He breathed his last the following Thursday, late in the afternoon, and on the Friday the worthies of Snigsby and Malterson removed the casing from the window of the pale room, and lowered my brother's remains into the street, like a grand piano.

His funeral service was attended by me, by my friend Watson, by our cousin Harriet and, in accordance with Mycroft's express wishes – by no-one else. The Civil Service, the Foreign Office, even the Diogenes Club – these institutions and their representatives were absent. Mycroft had been reclusive in life; he was to be equally as reclusive in death. So it was the three of us, and the parson, who had not known my brother, and had no conception that it was the more omniscient arm of the British Government itself that he was consigning to the grave.

Four burly men held fast to the ropes and lowered my brother's remains to their final resting place, and did, I daresay, their utmost not to curse at the weight of the thing. I tipped each of them half a crown.

Mycroft was dead at forty-nine, and, as they lowered him into his grave, in my imagination I could still hear his clipped, grey, wheeze as he seemed to be saying, "Now *there* is a crime worth investigating."

The stranger's accent was not too bad, although his vocabulary seemed limited, but he seemed to be talking in the local dialect, or something near to it. He was a fast learner. Old Gao hawked and spat into the dust of the street. He said nothing. He did not wish to take the stranger up the hillside; he did not wish to disturb his bees. In Old Gao's experience, the less he bothered his bees, the better they did. And if they stung the barbarian, what then?

The stranger's hair was silver-white, and sparse; his nose, the first barbarian nose that Old Gao had seen, was huge and curved and put Old Gao in mind of the beak of an eagle; his skin was tanned the same colour as Old Gao's own, and was lined deeply. Old Gao was not certain that he could read a barbarian's face as he could read the face of a person, but he thought the man seemed most serious and, perhaps, unhappy.

"Why?"

"I study bees. Your brother tells me you have big black bees here. Unusual bees."

Old Gao shrugged. He did not correct the man on the relationship with his cousin.

The stranger asked Old Gao if he had eaten, and when Gao said that he had not the stranger asked the Widow Zhang to bring them soup and rice and whatever was good that she had in her kitchen, which turned out to be a stew of black tree-fungus and vegetables and tiny transparent river-fish, little bigger than tadpoles. The two men ate in silence. When they had finished eating, the stranger said, "I would be honoured if you would show me your bees."

Old Gao said nothing, but the stranger paid Widow Zhang well and he put his bag on his back. Then he waited, and, when Old Gao began to walk, the stranger followed him. He carried his bag as if it weighed nothing to him. He was strong for an old man, thought Old Gao, and wondered whether all such barbarians were so strong.

"Where are you from?"

"England," said the stranger.

Old Gao remembered his father telling him about a war with the English, over trade and over opium, but that was long ago.

They walked up the hillside, that was, perhaps, a mountainside. It was steep, and the hillside was too rocky to be cut into fields. Old Gao tested the stranger's pace, walking faster than usual, and the stranger kept up with him, with his pack on his back.

The stranger stopped several times, however. He stopped to examine flowers – the small white flowers that bloomed in early spring elsewhere in the valley, but in late spring here on the side of the hill. There was a bee on one of the flowers, and the stranger knelt and observed it. Then he reached into his pocket, produced a large magnifying glass and examined the bee through it, and made notes in a small pocket notebook, in an incomprehensible writing.

Old Gao had never seen a magnifying glass before, and he leaned in to look at the bee, so black and so strong and so very different from the bees elsewhere in that valley.

"One of your bees?"

"Yes," said Old Gao. "Or one like it."

"Then we shall let her find her own way home," said the stranger, and he did not disturb the bee, and he put away the magnifying glass.

꩜

The Croft
East Dene, Sussex
August 11th, 1919

My dear Watson,

I have taken our discussion of this afternoon to heart, considered it carefully, and am prepared to modify my previous opinions.

I am amenable to your publishing your account of the incidents of 1903, specifically of the final case before my retirement, with the following provisions.

In addition to the usual changes that you would make to disguise actual people and places, I would suggest that you replace the entire scenario we encountered (I speak of Professor Presbury's garden. I shall not write of it further here) with monkey glands, or some such extract from the testes of an ape or lemur, sent by some foreign mystery-man. Perhaps the monkey-extract could have the effect of making Professor Presbury move like an ape – he could be some kind of "creeping man", perhaps? – or possibly make him able to clamber up the sides of buildings and up trees. Perhaps he could grow a tail, but this might be too fanciful even for you, Watson, although no more fanciful than many of the rococo additions you have made in your histories to otherwise humdrum events in my life and work.

In addition, I have written the following speech, to be delivered by myself, at the end of your narrative. Please make certain that something much like this is there, in which I inveigh against living too long, and the foolish urges that push foolish people to do foolish things to prolong their foolish lives.

> *There is a very real danger to humanity. If one could live for ever, if youth were simply there for the taking, that the material, the sensual, the worldly would all prolong their worthless lives. The spiritual would not avoid the call to something higher. It would be the survival of the least fit. What sort of cesspool may not our poor world become?*

Something along those lines, I fancy, would set my mind at rest.

Let me see the finished article, please, before you submit it to be published.

I remain, old friend, your most obedient servant,
Sherlock Holmes

∽

They reached Old Gao's bees late in the afternoon. The beehives were grey, wooden boxes piled behind a structure so simple it could barely be called a shack. Four posts, a roof, and hangings of oiled cloth that served to keep out the worst of the spring rains and the summer storms. A small charcoal brazier served for warmth, if you placed a blanket over it and yourself, and to cook upon; a wooden palette in the centre of the structure, with an ancient ceramic pillow, served as a bed on the occasions that Old Gao slept up on the mountainside with the bees, particularly in the autumn, when he harvested most of the honey. There was little enough of it compared to the output of his cousin's hives, but it was enough that he would sometimes spend two or three days waiting for the comb that he had crushed and stirred into a slurry to drain through the cloth into the buckets and pots that he had carried up the mountainside. Then he would melt the remainder, the sticky wax and bits of pollen and dirt and bee slurry, in a pot, to extract the beeswax, and he would give the sweet water back to the bees. Then he would carry the honey and the wax blocks down the hill to the village to sell.

He showed the barbarian stranger the eleven hives, watched impassively as the stranger put on a veil and opened a hive, examining first the bees, then the contents of a brood box, and finally the queen, through his magnifying glass. He showed no fear, no discomfort: in everything he did the stranger's movements were gentle and slow, and he was not stung, nor did he crush or hurt a single bee. This impressed Old Gao. He had assumed that barbarians were inscrutable, unreadable, mysterious creatures, but this man seemed overjoyed to have encountered Gao's bees. His eyes were shining.

Old Gao fired up the brazier, to boil some water. Long before the charcoal was hot, however, the stranger had removed from his bag a contraption of glass and metal. He had filled the upper half of it with water from the stream, lit a flame, and soon a kettleful of water was steaming and bubbling. Then the stranger took two tin mugs from his bag, and some green tea leaves wrapped in paper, and dropped the leaves into the mug, and poured on the water.

It was the finest tea that Old Gao had ever drunk: better by far than his cousin's tea. They drank it cross-legged on the floor.

"I would like to stay here for the summer, in this house," said the stranger.

"Here? This is not even a house," said Old Gao. "Stay down in the village. Widow Zhang has a room."

"I will stay here," said the stranger. "Also I would like to rent one of your beehives."

Old Gao had not laughed in years. There were those in the village who would have thought such a thing impossible. But still, he laughed then, a guffaw of surprise and amusement that seemed to have been jerked out of him.

"I am serious," said the stranger. He placed four silver coins on the ground between them. Old Gao had not seen where he got them from: three silver Mexican Pesos, a coin that had become popular in China years before, and a large silver yuan. It was as much money as Old Gao might see in a year of selling honey. "For this money," said the stranger, "I would like someone to bring me food: every three days should suffice."

Old Gao said nothing. He finished his tea and stood up. He pushed through the oiled cloth to the clearing high on the hillside. He walked over to the eleven hives: each consisted of two brood boxes with one, two, three or, in one case, even four boxes above that. He took the stranger to the hive with four boxes above it, each box filled with frames of comb.

"This hive is yours," he said.

They were plant extracts. That was obvious. They worked, in their way, for a limited time, but they were also extremely poisonous. But watching poor Professor Pillsbury during those final days – his skin, his eyes, his gait – had convinced me that he had not been on entirely the wrong path.

I took his case of seeds, of pods, of roots, and of dried extracts and I thought. I pondered. I cogitated. I reflected. It was an intellectual problem, and could be solved, as my old maths tutor had always sought to demonstrate to me, by intellect.

They were plant extracts, and they were lethal.

Methods I used to render them non-lethal rendered them quite ineffective.

It was not a three-pipe problem. I suspect it was something approaching a three-hundred-pipe problem before I hit upon an initial idea – a notion perhaps – of a way of processing the plants that might allow them to be ingested by human beings.

It was not a line of investigation that could easily be followed in Baker Street. So it was, in the autumn of 1903, that I moved to Sussex, and spent the winter reading every book and pamphlet and monograph so far published, I fancy, upon the care and keeping of bees. And so it was that in early April of 1904, armed only with theoretical knowledge, that I took delivery from a local farmer of my first package of bees.

I wonder, sometimes, that Watson did not suspect anything. Then again, Watson's glorious obtuseness has never ceased to surprise me, and sometimes, indeed, I had relied upon it. Still, he knew what I was like when I had no work to occupy my mind, no case to solve. He knew my lassitude, my black moods when I had no case to occupy me.

So how could he believe that I had truly retired? He knew my methods.

Indeed, Watson was there when I took receipt of my first bees. He watched, from a safe distance, as I poured the bees from the package into the empty, waiting hive, like slow, humming, gentle treacle.

He saw my excitement, and he saw nothing.

And the years passed, and we watched the Empire crumble, we watched the government unable to govern, we watched those poor heroic boys sent to the trenches of Flanders to die, all these things confirmed me in my opinions. I was not doing the right thing. I was doing the only thing.

As my face grew unfamiliar, and my finger-joints swelled and ached (not so much as they might have done, though, which I attributed to the many bee-stings I had received in my first few years as an investigative apiarist) and as Watson, dear, brave, obtuse, Watson, faded with time and paled and shrank, his skin becoming greyer, his moustache becoming the same shade of grey, my resolve to conclude my researches did not diminish. If anything, it increased.

So: my initial hypotheses were tested upon the South Downs,

in an apiary of my own devising, each hive modelled upon Langstroth's. I do believe that I made every mistake that ever a novice beekeeper could or has ever made, and in addition, due to my investigations, an entire hiveful of mistakes that no beekeeper has ever made before, or shall, I trust, ever make again. *The Case of the Poisoned Beehive,* Watson might have called many of them, although *The Mystery of The Transfixed Women's Institute* would have drawn more attention to my researches, had anyone been interested enough to investigate. (As it was, I chided Mrs Telford for simply taking a jar of honey from the shelves here without consulting me, and I ensured that, in the future, she was given several jars for her cooking from the more regular hives, and that honey from the experimental hives was locked away once it had been collected. I do not believe that this ever drew comment.)

I experimented with Dutch Bees, with German Bees and with Italians, with Carniolans and Caucasians. I regretted the loss of our British Bees to blight and, even where they had survived, to interbreeding, although I found and worked with a small hive I purchased and grew up from a frame of brood and a queen cell, from an old Abbey in St. Albans, which seemed to me to be original British breeding stock.

I experimented for the best part of two decades, before I concluded that the bees that I sought, if they existed, were not to be found in England, and would not survive the distances they would need to travel to reach me by international parcel post. I needed to examine bees in India. I needed to travel perhaps further afield than that.

I have a smattering of languages.

I had my flower seeds, and my extracts and tinctures in syrup. I needed nothing more.

I packed them up, arranged for the cottage on the Downs to be cleaned and aired once a week, and for Master Wilkins – to whom I am afraid I had developed the habit of referring, to his obvious distress, as "Young Villikins" – to inspect the beehives, and to harvest and sell surplus honey in Eastbourne market, and to prepare the hives for winter.

I told them I did not know when I should be back.

I am an old man. Perhaps they did not expect me to return.

And, if this was indeed the case, they would, strictly speaking, have been right.

Old Gao was impressed, despite himself. He had lived his life among bees. Still, watching the stranger shake the bees from the boxes, with a practised flick of his wrist, so cleanly and so sharply that the black bees seemed more surprised than angered, and simply flew or crawled back into their hive, was remarkable. The stranger then stacked the boxes filled with comb on top of one of the weaker hives, so Old Gao would still have the honey from the hive the stranger was renting.

So it was that Old Gao gained a lodger.

Old Gao gave the Widow Zhang's granddaughter a few coins to take the stranger food three times a week – mostly rice and vegetables, along with an earthenware pot filled, when she left at least, with boiling soup.

Every ten days Old Gao would walk up the hill himself. He went initially to check on the hives, but soon discovered that under the stranger's care all eleven hives were thriving as they had never thrived before. And indeed, there was now a twelfth hive, from a captured swarm of the black bees the stranger had encountered while on a walk along the hill.

Old Gao brought wood, the next time he came up to the shack, and he and the stranger spent several afternoons wordlessly working together, making extra boxes to go on the hives, building frames to fill the boxes.

One evening the stranger told Old Gao that the frames they were making had been invented by an American, only seventy years before. This seemed like nonsense to Old Gao, who made frames as his father had, and as they did across the valley, and as, he was certain, his grandfather and his grandfather's grandfather had, but he said nothing.

He enjoyed the stranger's company. They made hives together, and Old Gao wished that the stranger was a younger man. Then he would stay there for a long time, and Old Gao would have someone to leave his beehives to, when he died. But they were two old men, nailing boxes together, with thin frosty hair and old faces, and neither of them would see another dozen winters.

Old Gao noticed that the stranger had planted a small, neat garden beside the hive that he had claimed as his own, which he had moved away from the rest of the hives. He had covered it with a net. He had also created a "back door" to the hive, so that the only bees that could reach the plants came from the hive that he was renting. Old Gao also observed that, beneath the netting, there were several trays filled with what appeared to be sugar solution of some kind, one coloured bright red, one green, one a startling blue, one yellow. He pointed to them, but all the stranger did was nod and smile.

The bees were lapping up the syrups, though, clustering and crowding on the sides of the tin dishes with their tongues down, eating until they could eat no more, and then returning to the hive.

The stranger had made sketches of Old Gao's bees. He showed the sketches to Old Gao, tried to explain the ways that Old Gao's bees differed from other honeybees, talked of ancient bees preserved in stone for millions of years, but here the stranger's Chinese failed him, and, truthfully, Old Gao was not interested. They were his bees, until he died, and after that, they were the bees of the mountainside. He had brought other bees here, but they had sickened and died, or been killed in raids by the black bees, who took their honey and left them to starve.

The last of these visits was in late summer. Old Gao went down the mountainside. He did not see the stranger again.

It is done.

It works. Already I feel a strange combination of triumph and of disappointment, as if of defeat, or of distant storm-clouds teasing at my senses.

It is strange to look at my hands and to see, not my hands as I know them, but the hands I remember from my younger days: knuckles unswollen, dark hairs, not snow-white, on the backs.

It was a quest that had defeated so many, a problem with no apparent solution. The first Emperor of China died and nearly destroyed his empire is pursuit of it, three thousand years ago, and all it took me was, what, twenty years?

I do not know if I did the right thing or not (although any "retirement" without such an occupation would have been, literally, maddening). I took the commission from Mycroft. I investigated the problem. I arrived, inevitably, at the solution.

Will I tell the world? I will not.

And yet, I have half a pot of dark brown honey remaining in my bag; a half a pot of honey that is worth more than nations. (I was tempted to write, *worth more than all the tea in China*, perhaps because of my current situation, but fear that even Watson would deride it as cliché.)

And speaking of Watson...

There is one thing left to do. My only remaining goal, and it is small enough. I shall make my way to Shanghai, and from there I shall take ship to Southhampton, a half a world away.

And once I am there, I shall seek out Watson, if he still lives – and I fancy he does. It is irrational, I know, and yet I am certain that I would know, somehow, had Watson passed beyond the veil.

I shall buy theatrical make-up, disguise myself as an old man, so as not to startle him, and I shall invite my old friend over for tea.

There will be honey on buttered toast served for tea that afternoon, I fancy.

There were tales of a barbarian who passed through the village on his way east, but the people who told Old Gao this did not believe that it could have been the same man who had lived in Gao's shack. This one was young and proud, and his hair was dark. It was not the old man who had walked through those parts in the spring, although, one person told Gao, the bag was similar.

Old Gao walked up the mountainside to investigate, although he suspected what he would find before he got there.

The stranger was gone, and the stranger's bag.

There had been much burning, though. That was clear. Papers had been burnt – Old Gao recognised the edge of a drawing the stranger had made of one of his bees, but the rest of the papers were ash, or blackened beyond recognition, even had Old Gao been able to read barbarian writing. The papers were not the only things to have been burnt; parts of the hive that stranger had rented were now only twisted ash; there were blackened, twisted, strips of tin that might once have contained brightly coloured syrups.

The colour was added to the syrups, the stranger had told him once, so that he could tell them apart, although for what purpose Old Gao had never enquired.

He examined the shack like a detective, searching for a clue as to the stranger's nature or his whereabouts. On the ceramic pillow four silver coins had been left for him to find – two yuan coins and two silver pesos – and he put them away.

Behind the shack he found a heap of used slurry, with the last bees of the day still crawling upon it, tasting whatever sweetness was still on the surface of the still-sticky wax.

Old Gao thought long and hard before he gathered up the slurry, wrapped it loosely in cloth, and put it in a pot, which he filled with water. He heated the water on the brazier, but did not let it boil. Soon enough the wax floated to the surface, leaving the dead bees and the dirt and the pollen and the propolis inside the cloth.

He let it cool.

Then he walked outside, and he stared up at the moon. It was almost full.

He wondered how many villagers knew that his son had died as a baby. He remembered his wife, but her face was distant, and he had no portraits or photographs of her. He thought that there was nothing he was so suited for on the face of the earth as to keep the black, bullet-like bees on the side of this high, high hill. There was no other man who knew their temperament as he did.

The water had cooled. He lifted the now solid block of beeswax out of the water, placed it on the boards of the bed to finish cooling. Then he took the cloth filled with dirt and impurities out of the pot. And then, because he too was, in his way, a detective, and once you have eliminated the impossible whatever remains, however unlikely, must be the truth, he drank the sweet water in the pot. There is a lot of honey in slurry, after all, even after the majority of it has dripped through a cloth and been purified. The water tasted of honey, but not a honey that Gao had ever tasted before. It tasted of smoke, and metal, and strange flowers, and odd perfumes. It tasted, Gao thought, a little like sex.

He drank it all down, and then he slept, with his head on the ceramic pillow.

When he woke, he thought, he would decide how to deal with his cousin, who would expect to inherit the twelve hives on the hill when Old Gao went missing.

He would be an illegitimate son, perhaps, the young man who would return in the days to come. Or perhaps a son. Young Gao. Who would remember, now? It did not matter.

He would go to the city and then he would return, and he would keep the black bees on the side of the mountain for as long as days and circumstances would allow.

THE DEAD THEIR EYES IMPLORE US

GEORGE PELECANOS

Someday I'm gonna write all this down. But I don't write so good in English yet, see? So I'm just gonna think it out loud.

Last night I had a dream.

In my dream, I was a kid, back in the village. My friends and family from the *chorio*, they were there, all of us standing around the square. My father, he had strung a lamb up on a pole. It was making a noise, like a scream, and its eyes were wild and afraid. My father handed me my Italian switch knife, the one he gave me before I came over. I cut into the lamb's throat and opened it up wide. The lamb's warm blood spilled onto my hands.

My mother told me once: Every time you dream something, it's got to be a reason.

I'm not no kid anymore. I'm twenty-eight years old. It's early in June, Nineteen Hundred and Thirty Three. The temperature got up to one hundred degrees today. I read in the *Tribune*, some old people died from the heat.

Let me try to paint a picture, so you can see in your head the way it is for me right now. I got this little one-room place I rent from some old lady. A Murphy bed and a table, an icebox and a stove. I got a radio I bought for a dollar and ninety-nine. I wash my clothes in a tub, and afterwards I hang the *roocha* on a cord I stretched across the room. There's a bunch of clothes, *pantalonia* and one of my work shirts and my *vrakia* and socks, on there now. I'm sitting here at the table in my union suit. I'm smoking a Fatima and drinking a cold bottle of Abner Drury beer. I'm looking at my hands. I got blood underneath my fingernails. I washed real good but it was hard to get it all.

It's five, five-thirty in the morning. Let me go back some, to show how I got to where I am tonight.

What's it been, four years since I came over? The boat ride was a boat ride so I'll skip that part. I'll start in America.

When I got to Ellis Island I came straight down to Washington to stay with my cousin Toula and her husband Aris. Aris had a fruit cart down on Pennsylvania Avenue, around 17th. Toula's father owed my father some *lefta* from back in the village, so it was all set up. She offered me a room until I could get on my feet. Aris wasn't happy about it but I didn't give a good goddamn what he was happy about. Toula's father should have paid his debt.

Toula and Aris had a place in Chinatown. It wasn't just for Chinese. Italians, Irish, Polacks and Greeks lived there, too. Everyone was poor except the criminals. The Chinamen controlled the gambling, the whores, and the opium. All the business got done in the back of laundries and in the restaurants. The Chinks didn't bother no one if they didn't get bothered themselves.

Toula's apartment was in a house right on H Street. You had to walk up three floors to get to it. I didn't mind it. The milkman did it every day and the old Jew who collected the rent managed to do it, too. I figured, so could I.

My room was small, so small you couldn't shut the door all the way when the bed was down. There was only one toilet in the place, and they had put a curtain by it, the kind you hang on a shower. You had to close it around you when you wanted to shit. Like I say, it wasn't a nice place or nothing like it, but it was okay. It was free.

But nothing's free, my father always said. Toula's husband Aris made me pay from the first day I moved in. Never had a good word to say to me, never mentioned me to no one for a job. He was a sonofabitch, that one.

Dark, with a hook in his nose, looked like he had some Turkish blood in him. I wouldn't be surprised if the *gamoto* was a Turk. I didn't like the way he talked to my cousin, either, 'specially when he drank. And this *malaka* drank every night. I'd sit in my room and listen to him raise his voice at her, and then later I could hear him fucking her on their bed. I couldn't stand it, I'm telling you, and me without a woman myself. I didn't have no job then so I couldn't even buy a whore. I thought I was gonna go nuts.

Then one day I was talking to this guy, Dimitri Karras, lived in the 606 building on H. He told me about a janitor's job opened up at St. Mary's, the church where his son *Panayoti* and most of the neighborhood kids went to Catholic school. I put some Wildroot tonic in my hair, walked over to the church, and talked to the head nun. I don't know, she musta liked me or something, 'cause I got the job. I had to lie a little about being a handyman. I wasn't no engineer, but I figured, what the hell, the furnace goes out you light it again, goddamn.

My deal was simple. I got a room in the basement and a coupla meals a day. Pennies other than that, but I didn't mind, not then. Hell, it was better than living in some Hoover Hotel. And it got me away from that bastard Aris. Toula cried when I left, so I gave her a hug. I didn't say nothing to Aris.

I worked at St. Mary's about two years. The work was never hard. I knew the kids and most of their fathers: Karras, Angelos, Nicodemus, Recevo, Damiano, Carchedi. I watched the boys grow. I didn't look the nuns in the eyes when I talked to them so they wouldn't get the wrong idea. Once or twice I treated myself to one of the whores over at the Eastern House. Mostly, down in the basement, I played with my *pootso*. I put it out of my mind that I was jerking off in church.

Meanwhile, I tried to make myself better. I took English classes at St. Sophia, the Greek Orthodox church on 8th and L. I bought a blue serge suit at Harry Kaufman's on 7th Street, on sale for eleven dollars and seventy-five. The Jew tailor let me pay for it a little bit at a time. Now when I went to St. Sophia for the Sunday service I wouldn't be ashamed.

I liked to go to church. Not for religion, nothing like that. Sure, I wear a *stavro*, but everyone wears a cross. That's just superstition. I don't love God, but I'm afraid of him. So I went to church just in case, and also to look at the girls. I liked to see 'em all dressed up.

There was this one *koritsi*, not older than sixteen when I first saw her, who was special. I knew just where she was gonna be, with her mother, on the side of the church where the women sat separate from the men. I made sure I got a good view of her on Sundays. Her name was Irene, I asked around. I could tell she was clean. By that I mean she was a virgin. That's the kind of girl you're gonna marry. My plan was to wait till I got some money in my pocket before I talked to her, but not too long so she got snatched up. A girl like that is not gonna stay single forever.

Work and church was for the daytime. At night I went to the coffeehouses down by the Navy Yard in Southeast. One of them was owned by a hardworking guy from the neighborhood, Angelos, lived at the 703 building on 6th. That's the *cafeneion* I went to most. You played cards and dice there if that's what you wanted to do, but mostly you could be yourself. It was all Greeks.

That's where I met Nick Stefanos one night, at the Angelos place. Meeting him is what put another change in my life. Stefanos was a Spartan with an easy way, had a scar on his cheek. You knew he was tough but he didn't have to prove it. I heard he got the scar running protection for a hooch truck in upstate New York. Heard a cheap *pistola* blew up in his face. It was his business, what happened, none of mine.

We got to talking that night. He was the head busman down at some fancy hotel on 15th and Penn, but he was leaving to open his own place. His friend Costa, another *Spartiati*, worked there and he was gonna leave with him. Stefanos asked me if I wanted to take Costa's place. He said he could set it up. The pay was only a little more than what I was making, a dollar-fifty a week with extras, but a little more was a lot. Hell, I wanted to make better like anyone else. I thanked Nick Stefanos and asked him when I could start.

I started the next week, soon as I got my room where I am now. You had to pay management for your bus uniform, black pants and a white shirt and short black vest, so I didn't make nothing for awhile. Some of the waiters tipped the busmen heavy, and some tipped nothing at all. For the ones who tipped nothing you cleared their tables slower, and last. I caught on quick.

The hotel was pretty fancy and its dining room, up on the top floor, was fancy, too. The china was real, the crystal sang when you flicked a finger at it, and the silver was heavy. It was hard times, but you'd never know it from the way the tables filled up at night. I figured I'd stay there a coupla years, learn the operation, and go out on my own like Stefanos. That was one smart guy.

The way they had it set up was, Americans had the waiter jobs, and the Greeks and Filipinos bused the tables. The coloreds, they stayed back in the kitchen. Everybody in the restaurant was in the same order that they were out on the street: the whites were up top and the Greeks were in the middle; the *mavri* were at the bottom. Except if someone was your own kind, you didn't make much small talk with the other guys unless it had something to do with work. I didn't have nothing against anyone, not even the coloreds. You didn't talk to them, that's all. That's just the way it was.

The waiters, they thought they were better than the rest of us. But there was this one American, a young guy named John Petersen, who was all right. Petersen had brown eyes and wavy brown hair that he wore kinda long. It was his eyes that you remembered. Smart and serious, but gentle at the same time.

Petersen was different than the other waiters, who wouldn't lift a finger to help you even when they weren't busy. John would pitch in and bus my tables for me when I got in a jam. He'd jump in with the dishes, too, back in the kitchen, when the dining room was running low on silver, and like I say, those were coloreds back there. I even saw him talking with those guys sometimes like they were pals. It was like he came from someplace where that was okay. John was just one of those who made friends easy,

I guess. I can't think of no one who didn't like him. Well, there musta been one person, at least. I'm gonna come to that later on.

Me and John went out for a beer one night after work, to a saloon he knew. I wasn't comfortable because it was all Americans and I didn't see no one who looked like me. But John made me feel okay and after two beers I forgot. He talked to me about the job and the pennies me and the colored guys in the kitchen were making, and how it wasn't right. He talked about some changes that were coming to make it better for us, but he didn't say what they were.

"I'm happy," I said, as I drank off the beer in my mug. "I got a job, what the hell."

"You want to make more money don't you?" he said. "You'd like to have a day off once in a while, wouldn't you?"

"Goddamn right. But I take off a day, I'm not gonna get paid."

"It doesn't have to be like that, friend."

"Yeah, okay."

"Do you know what 'strength in numbers' means?"

I looked around for the bartender 'cause I didn't know what the hell John was talking about and I didn't know what to say.

John put his hand around my arm. "I'm putting together a meeting. I'm hoping some of the busmen and the kitchen guys will make it. Do you think you can come?"

"What we gonna meet for, huh?"

"We're going to talk about those changes I been telling you about. Together, we're going to make a plan."

"I don't want to go to no meeting. I want a day off, I'm just gonna go ask for it, eh?"

"You don't understand." John put his face close to mine. "The workers are being exploited."

"I work and they pay me," I said with a shrug. "That's all I know. Other than that? I don't give a damn nothing." I pulled my arm away but I smiled when I did it. I didn't want to join no group, but I wanted him to know we were still pals. "C'mon, John, let's drink."

I needed that job. But I felt bad, turning him down about that meeting. You could see it meant something to him, whatever the hell he was talking about, and I liked him. He was the only American in the restaurant who treated me like we were both the same. You know, man to man.

Well, he wasn't the only American who made me feel like a man. There was this woman, name of Laura, a hostess who also made change from the bills. She bought her dresses too small and had hair bleached white, like Jean Harlow. She was about two years and ten pounds away from the end of her looks. Laura wasn't pretty but her ass could bring tears to your eyes. Also, she had huge tits.

I caught her giving me the eye the first night I worked there. By the third night she said something to me about my broad chest as I was walking by her. I nodded and smiled, but I kept walking 'cause I was carrying a heavy tray. When I looked back she gave me a wink. She was a real whore, that one. I knew right then I was gonna fuck her. At the end of the night I asked her if she would go to the pictures with me sometime. "I'm free tomorrow," she says. I acted like it was an honor and a big surprise.

I worked every night, so we had to make it a matinee. We took the streetcar down to the Earle, on 13th Street, down below F. I wore my blue serge suit and high button shoes. I looked like I had a little bit of money, but we still got the fisheye, walking down the street. A blonde and a Greek with dark skin and a heavy black moustache. I couldn't hide that I wasn't too long off the boat.

The Earle had a stage show before the picture. A guy named William Demarest and some dancers who Laura said were like the Rockettes. What the hell did I know, I was just looking at their legs. After the coming attractions and the short subject the picture came on: "Gold Diggers of 1933." The man dancers looked like cocksuckers to me. I liked Westerns better, but it was all right. Fifteen cents for each of us. It was cheaper than taking her to a saloon.

Afterwards, we went to her place, an apartment in a rowhouse off H in Northeast. I used the bathroom and saw a Barnards Shaving Cream and other man things in there, but I didn't ask her nothing about it when I came back out. I found her in the bedroom. She had poured us a couple of rye whiskies and drawn the curtains so it felt like the night. A radio played something she called "jug band"; it sounded like colored music to me. She asked me, did I want to dance. I shrugged and tossed back all the rye in my glass and pulled her to me rough. We moved slow, even though the music was fast.

"Bill?" she said, looking up at me. She had painted her eyes with something and there was a black mark next to one of them were the paint had come off.

"Uh," I said.

"What do they call you where you're from?"

"*Vasili.*"

I kissed her warm lips. She bit mine and drew a little blood. I pushed myself against her to let her know what I had.

"Why, Va-silly," she said. "You are like a horse, aren't you?"

I just kinda nodded and smiled. She stepped back and got out of her dress and her slip, and then undid her brassiere. She did it slow.

"*Ella,*" I said.

"What does that mean?"

"Hurry it up," I said, with a little motion of my hand. Laura laughed.

She pulled the bra off and her tits bounced. They were everything I thought they would be. She came to me and unbuckled my belt, pulling at it clumsy, and her breath was hot on my face. By then, God, I was ready.

I sat her on the edge of the bed, put one of her legs up on my shoulder, and gave it to her. I heard a woman having a baby in the village once, and those were the same kinda sounds that Laura made. There was spit dripping out the side of her mouth as I slammed myself into her over and over again. I'm telling you, her bed took some plaster off the wall that day.

After I blew my load into her I climbed off. I didn't say nice things to her or nothing like that. She got what she wanted and so did I. Laura smoked a cigarette and watched me get dressed. The whole room smelled like pussy. She didn't look so good to me no more. I couldn't wait to get out of there and breathe fresh air.

We didn't see each other again outside of work. She only stayed at the restaurant a coupla more weeks, and then she disappeared. I guess the man who owned the shaving cream told her it was time to quit.

For awhile there nothing happened and I just kept working hard. John didn't mention no meetings again though he was just as nice as before. I slept late and bused the tables at night. Life wasn't fun or bad. It was just ordinary. Then that bastard Wesley Schmidt came to work and everything changed.

Schmidt was a tall young guy with a thin moustache, big in the shoulders, big hands. He kept his hair slicked back. His eyes were real blue, like water under ice. He had a row of big straight teeth. He smiled all the time, but the smile, it didn't make you feel good.

Schmidt got hired as a waiter, but he wasn't any good at it. He got tangled up fast when the place got busy. He served food to the wrong tables all the time, and he spilled plenty of drinks. It didn't seem like he'd ever done that kind of work before.

No one liked him, but he was one of those guys, he didn't know it, or maybe he knew and didn't care. He laughed and told jokes and slapped the busmen on the back like we were his friends. He treated the kitchen guys like dogs when he was tangled up, raising his voice at them when the food didn't come up as fast as he liked it. Then he tried to be nice to them later.

One time he really screamed at Raymond, the head cook on the line, called him a "lazy shine" on this night when the place was packed. When the dining room cleared up Schmidt walked back into the kitchen and told Raymond in a soft voice that he didn't mean nothing by it, giving him that smile of his and patting his arm. Raymond just nodded real slow. Schmidt told me later, "That's all you got to do, is scold 'em and then talk real sweet to 'em later. That's how they learn. 'Cause they're like children. Right, Bill?" He meant coloreds, I guess. By the way he talked to me, real slow the way you would to a kid, I could tell he thought I was a colored guy, too.

At the end of the night the waiters always sat in the dining room and ate a stew or something that the kitchen had prepared. The busmen, we served it to the waiters. I was running dinner out to one of them and forgot something back in the kitchen. When I went back to get it, I saw Raymond, spitting into a plate of stew. The other colored guys in the kitchen were standing in a circle around Raymond, watching him do it. They all looked over at me when I walked in. It was real quiet and I guess they were waiting to see what I was gonna do.

"Who's that for?" I said. "Eh?"

"Schmidt," said Raymond.

I walked over to where they were. I brought up a bunch of stuff from deep down in my throat and spit real good into that plate. Raymond put a spoon in the stew and stirred it up.

"I better take it out to him," I said, "before it gets cold."

"Don't forget the garnish," said Raymond.

He put a flower of parsley on the plate, turning it a little so it looked nice. I took the stew out and served it to Schmidt. I watched him take the first bite and nod his head like it was good. None of the colored guys said nothing to me about it again.

I got drunk with John Petersen in a saloon a coupla nights after and told him what I'd done. I thought he'd a get a good laugh out of it, but instead he got serious. He put his hand on my arm the way he did when he wanted me to listen.

"Stay out of Schmidt's way," said John.

"Ah," I said, with a wave of my hand. "He gives me any trouble, I'm gonna punch him in the kisser." The beer was making me brave.

"Just stay out of his way."

"I look afraid to you?"

"I'm telling you, Schmidt is no waiter."

"I know it. He's the worst goddamn waiter I ever seen. Maybe you ought to have one of those meetings of yours and see if you can get him thrown out."

"Don't ever mention those meetings again, to anyone," said John, and he squeezed my arm tight. I tried to pull it away from him but he held his grip. "Bill, do you know what a Pinkerton man is?"

"What the hell?"

"Never mind. You just keep to yourself, and don't talk about those meetings, hear?"

I had to look away from his eyes. "Sure, sure."

"Okay, friend." John let go of my arm. "Let's have another beer."

A week later John Petersen didn't show up for work. And a week after that the cops found him floating down river in the Potomac. I read about it in the *Tribune*. It was just a short notice, and it didn't say nothing else.

A cop in a suit came to the restaurant and asked us some questions. A couple of the waiters said that John probably had some bad hootch and fell into the drink. I didn't know what to think. When it got around to the rest of the crew, everyone kinda got quiet, if you know what I mean. Even that bastard Wesley didn't make no jokes. I guess we were all thinking about John in our own way. Me, I wanted to throw up. I'm telling you, thinking about John in that river, it made me sick.

John didn't ever talk about no family and nobody knew nothing about a funeral. After a few days, it seemed like everybody in the restaurant forgot about him. But me, I couldn't forget.

One night I walked into Chinatown. It wasn't far from my new place. There was this kid from St. Mary's, Billy Nicodemus, whose father worked at the city morgue. Nicodemus wasn't no doctor or nothing, he washed off the slabs and cleaned the place, like that. He was known as a hard drinker, maybe because of what he saw every day, and maybe just because he liked the taste. I knew where he liked to drink.

I found him in a non-name restaurant on the Hip-Sing side of Chinatown. He was in a booth by himself, drinking something from a teacup. I crossed the room, walking through the cigarette smoke, passing the whores and the skinny Chink gangsters in their too-big suits and the cops who were taking money from the Chinks to look the other way. I stood over Nicodemus and told him who I was. I told him I knew his kid, told him his kid was good. Nicodemus motioned for me to have a seat.

A waiter brought me an empty cup. I poured myself some gin from the teapot on the table. We tapped cups and drank. Nicodemus had straight black hair wetted down and a big mole with hair coming out of it on one of his cheeks. He talked better than I did. We said some things that were about nothing and then I asked him some questions about John. The gin had loosened his tongue.

"Yeah, I remember him," said Nicodemus, after thinking about it for a short while. He gave me the once-over and leaned forward. "This was your friend?"

"Yes."

"They found a bullet in the back of his head. A twenty-two."

I nodded and turned the teacup in small circles on the table. "The *Tribune* didn't say nothing about that."

"The papers don't always say. The police cover it up while they look for who did it. But that boy didn't drown. He was murdered first, then dropped in the drink."

"You saw him?" I said.

Nicodemus shrugged. "Sure."

"What'd he look like?"

"You really wanna know?"

"Yeah."

"He was all gray and blown up, like a balloon. The gas does that to 'em, when they been in the water."

"What about his eyes?"

"They were open. Pleading."

"Huh?"

"His eyes. It was like they were sayin' please."

I needed a drink. I had some gin.

"You ever heard of a Pinkerton man?" I said.

"Sure," said Nicodemus. "A detective."

"Like the police?"

"No."

"*What*, then?"

"They go to work with other guys and pretend they're one of them.

"They find out who's stealing. Or they find out who's trying to make trouble for the boss. Like the ones who want to make a strike."

"You mean, like if a guy wants to get the workers together and make things better?"

"Yeah. Have meetings and all that. The guys who want to start a union. Pinkertons look for those guys."

We drank the rest of the gin. We talked about his kid. We talked about Schmeling and Baer, and the wrestling match that was coming up between Londos and George Zaharias at Griffith Stadium. I got up from my seat, shook Nicodemus's hand, and thanked him for the conversation.

"*Efcharisto, patrioti.*"

"*Yasou, Vasili.*"

I walked back to my place and had a beer I didn't need. I was drunk and more confused than I had been before. I kept hearing John's voice, the way he called me "friend." I saw his eyes saying please. I kept thinking, I should have gone to his goddamn meeting, if that was gonna make him happy. I kept thinking I had let him down. While I was thinking, I sharpened the blade of my Italian switch knife on a stone.

The next night, last night, I was serving Wesley Schmidt his dinner after we closed. He was sitting by himself like he always did. I dropped the plate down in front of him.

"You got a minute to talk?" I said.

"Go ahead and talk," he said, putting the spoon to his stew and stirring it around.

"I wanna be a Pinkerton man," I said.

Schmidt stopped stirring his stew and looked up my way. He smiled, showing me his white teeth. Still, his eyes were cold.

"That's nice. But why are you telling me this?"

"I wanna be a Pinkerton, just like you."

Schmidt pushed his stew plate away from him and looked around the dining room to make sure no one could hear us. He studied my face. I guess I was sweating. Hell, I *know* I was. I could feel it dripping on my back.

"You look upset," said Schmidt, his voice real soft, like music. "You look like you could use a friend."

"I just wanna talk."

"Okay. You feel like having a beer, something like that?"

"Sure, I could use a beer."

"I finish eating, I'll go down and get my car. I'll meet you in the alley out back. Don't tell anyone, hear, because then they might want to come along. And we wouldn't have the chance to talk."

"I'm not gonna tell no one. We just drive around, eh? I'm too dirty to go to a saloon."

"That's swell," said Schmidt. "We'll just drive around."

I went out to the alley were Schmidt was parked. Nobody saw me get into his car. It was a blue, '31 Dodge coupe with wire wheels, a rumble seat, and a trunk rack. A five hundred dollar car if it was dime.

"Pretty," I said, as I got in beside him. There were hand-tailored slipcovers on the seats.

"I like nice things," said Schmidt.

He was wearing his suit jacket, and it had to be eighty degrees. I could see a lump under the jacket. I figured, the bastard is carrying a gun.

We drove up to Colvin's, on 14th Street. Schmidt went in and returned with a bag of loose bottles of beer. There must have been a half dozen Schlitz's in the bag. Him making waiter's pay, and the fancy car and the high-priced beer.

He opened a coupla beers and handed me one. The bottle was ice cold. Hot as the night was, the beer tasted good.

We drove around for a while. We went down to Hanes Point. Schmidt parked the Dodge facing the Washington Channel. Across the channel, the lights from the fish vendors on Maine Avenue threw color on the water. We drank another beer. He gave me one of his tailor-mades and we had a couple smokes. He talked about the Senators and the Yankees, and how Baer had taken Schmeling out with a right in the tenth. Schmidt didn't want to talk about nothing serious yet. He was waiting for the beer to work on me, I knew.

"Goddamn heat," I said. "Let's drive around some, get some air moving."

Schmidt started the coupe. "Where to?"

"I'm gonna show you a whorehouse. Best secret in town."

Schmidt looked me over and laughed. The way you laugh at a clown.

I gave Schmidt some directions. We drove some, away from the park and the monuments to where people lived. We went through a little tunnel and crossed into Southwest. Most of the streetlamps were broke here. The rowhouses were shabby, and you could see shacks in the alleys and clothes hanging on lines outside the shacks. It was late, long time past midnight. There weren't many people out. The ones that were out were coloreds. We were in a place called Bloodfield.

"Pull over there," I said, pointing to a spot along the curb where there wasn't no light. "I wanna show you the place I'm talking about."

Schmidt did it and cut the engine. Across the street were some houses. All except one of them was dark. From the lighted one came fast music, like the colored music Laura had played in her room.

"There it is right there," I said, meaning the house with the light. I was lying through my teeth. I didn't know who lived there and I sure didn't know if that house had whores. I had never been down here before.

Schmidt turned his head to look at the rowhouse. I slipped my switch knife out of my right pocket and laid it flat against my right leg.

When he turned back to face me he wasn't smiling no more. He had heard about Bloodfield and he knew he was in it. I think he was scared.

"You bring me down to niggertown, for *what*?" he said. "To show me a whorehouse?"

"I thought you're gonna like it."

"Do I look like a man who'd pay to fuck a nigger? *Do* I? You don't know anything about me."

He was showing his true self now. He was nervous as a cat. My nerves were bad, too. I was sweating through my shirt. I could smell my own stink in the car.

"I know plenty," I said.

"Yeah? *What* do you know?"

"Pretty car, pretty suits…top shelf beer. How you get all this, huh?"

"I earned it."

"As a Pinkerton, eh?"

Schmidt blinked real slow and shook his head. He looked out his window, looking at nothing, wasting time while he decided what he was gonna do. I found the raised button on the pearl handle of my knife. I pushed the button. The blade flicked open and barely made a sound. I held the knife against my leg and turned it so the blade was pointing back.

Sweat rolled down my neck as I looked around. There wasn't nobody out on the street.

Schmidt turned his head. He gripped the steering wheel with his right hand and straightened his arm.

"What do you want?" he said.

"I just wanna know what happened to John."

Schmidt smiled. All those white teeth. I could see him with his mouth open, his lips stretched, those teeth showing. They way an animal looks after you kill it. Him lying on his back on a slab.

"I heard he drowned," said Schmidt.

"You think so, eh?"

"Yeah. I guess he couldn't swim."

"Pretty hard to swim, you got a bullet in your head."

Schmidt's smile turned down. "Can *you* swim, Bill?"

I brought the knife across real fast and buried it into his armpit. I sunk the blade all the way to the handle. He lost his breath and made a short scream. I twisted the knife. His blood came out like someone was pouring it from a jug. It was warm and it splashed on to my hands. I pulled the knife out and while he was kicking at the floorboards I stabbed him a coupla more times in the chest. I musta hit his heart or something because all the sudden there was plenty of blood all over the car. I'm telling you, the seats were slippery with it. He stopped moving. His eyes were open and they were dead.

I didn't get tangled up about it or nothing like that. I wasn't scared. I opened up his suit jacket and saw a steel revolver with wood grips holstered there. It was small caliber. I didn't touch the gun. I took his wallet out of his trousers, pulled the bills out of it, wiped off the wallet with my shirttail, and threw the empty wallet on the ground. I put the money in my shoe. I fit the blade back into the handle of my switch knife and slipped the knife into my pocket. I put all the empty beer bottles together with the full ones in the paper bag and took the bag with me as I got out of the car. I closed the door soft and wiped off the handle and walked down the street.

I didn't see no one for a couple of blocks. I came to a sewer and I put the bag down the hole. The next block I came to another sewer and I took off my bloody shirt and threw it down the hole of that one. I was wearing an undershirt, didn't have no sleeves. My pants were black so you couldn't see the blood. I kept walking towards Northwest.

Someone laughed from deep in an alley and I kept on.

Another block or so I came up on a group of *mavri* standing around the steps of a house. They were smoking cigarettes and drinking from bottles of beer. I wasn't gonna run or nothing. I had to go by them to get home. They stopped talking and gave me hard eyes as I got near them. That's when I saw that one of them was the cook, Raymond, from the kitchen. Our eyes kind of came together but neither one of us said a word or smiled or even made a nod.

One of the coloreds started to come towards me and Raymond stopped him with the flat of his palm. I walked on.

I walked for a couple of hours, I guess. Somewhere in Northwest I dropped my switch knife down another sewer. When I heard it hit the sewer bottom I started to cry. I wasn't crying 'cause I had killed Schmidt. I didn't give a damn nothing about him. I was crying 'cause my father had given me that knife, and now it was gone. I guess I knew I was gonna be in America forever, and I wasn't never going back to Greece. I'd never see my home or my parents again.

When I got back to my place I washed my hands real good. I opened up a bottle of Abner Drury and put fire to a Fatima and had myself a seat at the table.

This is where I am right now.

Maybe I'm gonna get caught and maybe I'm not. They're gonna find Schmidt in that neighborhood and they're gonna figure a colored guy killed him for his money. The cops, they're gonna turn Bloodfield upside down. If Raymond tells them he saw me I'm gonna get the chair. If he doesn't, I'm gonna be free. Either way, what the hell, I can't do nothing about it now.

I'll work at the hotel, get some experience and some money, then open my own place, like Nick Stefanos. Maybe if I can find two nickels to rub together, I'm gonna go to church and talk to that girl, Irene, see if she wants to be my wife. I'm not gonna wait too long. She's clean as a whistle, that one.

I've had my eye on her for some time.

HUNTED

VICTORIA SELMAN

'*R*un *for your life... I mean everything I've said...*'
    That creepy Beatles song is a soundtrack in my head as I stumble, tripping against a rock half hidden in the undergrowth. I stub my toe, twist my ankle, curse softly beneath my breath. No way I want to draw attention to myself out here. No way I want to advertise my injury to him.

I push myself up, quick as I can, ignoring the throbbing in my ankle. There's blood on my jeans, so much blood. Brown and crusted. Seeing it makes my heart beat faster. If that's possible.

Where is he?

I listen for a giveaway sound; acorns crunching, the rustle of leaves. A clue as to where he might be hiding. My head's cocked, my eyes darting. Every muscle taut and primed. Yet it's difficult to hear anything over the sound of my kettledrum heart, my ragged breath.

I run every day, always follow the same ritual. Hydrate, stretches and then I'm off; all the way down to Christmas Common and back again.

There was no time for a warm-up routine this morning though, and I've run a hell of lot further than I normally do.

The sweat is dripping between my breasts and shoulder blades. My mouth is dry, a stabbing pain under my ribcage. No amount of training could have prepared me for this. For what's at stake.

Where is he?

I'm panting, flooded with adrenaline, as the wind hisses and the bony oaks watch on. Spectators to the fight.

I twist my head, left then right. I can't see him but I know he's out here. Old Crazy Eyes, so like my father with his red lumberjack shirt, bruised fists and bloodshot peepers. A drunk. A sadist.

He's hiding, lurking, waiting for his chance. Waiting to…

Crack.

A twig snaps, followed by the unmistakable gallop of feet. The sound reverberates through the forest, bouncing off the worn and weathered bark.

A rush of heat surges through me and I'm off again. I'm exhausted, wounded, and yet the need to survive pushes me on. I can't let him get…

As I tear through the trees, I think of the past week, the cabin I was confined to. The torture chamber.

I see again the wooden table in the centre of the room, blotchy with old blood; the brown patches forming interconnected shapes like countries on a map. Countries no-one in their right mind would want to visit.

I see the knives and saws and hatchets hanging on ceiling hooks. The blades polished, sharp, glinting in the light. A threat. A promise.

I see the green surgeon's apron with its long elasticated sleeves. The mask. The blue latex gloves.

And I see his wide wild eyes, inches from mine. I smell his dirty pork breath. His stale sweat.

The rattle of the hooks as the first knife is chosen, then…

My muscles tighten. An electric charge shoots down my spine. My already thundering heart doubles its efforts, smashing against my chest; a break for freedom.

He's close. I must hurry.

Hopeless, says the voice inside my head. *No point fighting it…*

His voice.

How many times did he say those words? How many times did he raise his fist, his knife?

Stop it, I tell myself. *Don't think of that now.*

If only I knew where he was.

I keep running.

Thorny bushes reach out their arms to block my path. Hidden roots trip me up.

My face is scratched, my throat parched. When the rain comes, cold and heavy, I stick out my tongue but it doesn't quench my thirst. The water will have to wait.

Where is he?

Chest heaving, I scan the area.

An animal flits out of the bushes. For a moment I think it's him. And then I see a flash of colour through the leaves. His shirt, the same red-orange hue as fresh blood.

He's off again and so am I; breathing air in through my nose and out through my mouth, arching my toes up towards my shins to quicken my cadence. Lengthening my strides.

The gap between us starts to narrow. I can actually smell him now, an animal scent. Vulpine. Foul. He looks over his shoulder and stumbles, and I think it's going to be okay. That this is my chance.

I'm wrong.

We've reached a road. How did I not see that?

The light is different here, the shadows have melted away. And then I hear it; the unmistakable rumble of an approaching engine.

My throat closes up. My veins fill with lead.

Of all the miserable luck!

A police car, can you believe? Decked out with tinsel, Christmas carols blasting out the open window.

It's slowing. My quarry's waving the driver down, arms moving as if wiping steam from a mirror.

The car stops. A copper gets out, puts his hand on Crazy Eyes' shoulder, his own eyes widening in horror as the bastard tells his tale.

It won't take them long to find the cabin. The chamber where I was tortured as a child and where I now torture men who remind me of my abuser. Stand-ins for the monster death stole from me. My father. The devil.

They'll find the cabin first. And then the graves. All six of them.

But will they find me?

In an instant the game has changed.

I take one last look at the car then bolt.

Now it's me running for my life.

EAST OF SUEZ, WEST OF CHARING CROSS ROAD

JOHN LAWTON

Unhappiness does not fall on a man from the sky like a branch struck by lightning, it is more like rising damp. It creeps up day by day, unfelt or ignored until it is too late. And if it's true that each unhappy family is unhappy in its own way, then the whole must be greater than the sum of the parts in Tolstoy's equation, because George Horsfield was unhappy in a way that could only be described as commonplace. He had married young and he had not married well.

In 1948 he had answered the call to arms. At the age of eighteen he hadn't much choice. National Service – the Draft – the only occasion in its thousand-year history that England had had peacetime conscription. It was considered a necessary precaution in a world in which, to quote the US Secretary of State, England had lost an empire and not yet found a role. Not that England knew this – England's attitude was that we had crushed old Adolf and we'd be buggered if we'd now lose an empire – it would take more than little brown men in loincloths… OK so we lost India… or Johnny Arab with a couple of petrol bombs or those bolshy Jews in their damn kibbutzes – OK, so we'd cut and run in Palestine, but dammit man, one has to draw the line somewhere. And the line was east of Suez, somewhere east of Suez, anywhere east of Suez – a sort of moveable feast really.

George had expected to do his two years square-bashing or polishing coal. Instead, to both his surprise and pleasure, he was considered officer material by the War Office Selection Board. Not too short in the leg, no dropped aitches, a passing knowledge of the proper use of a knife and fork and no pretensions to be an intellectual. He was offered a short-service commission, rapidly trained at Eaton Hall in Cheshire – a beggarman's Sandhurst – and put back on the parade ground not as a private but as 2nd Lt H.G. Horsfield RAOC.

Why RAOC? Because the light of ambition had flickered in George's poorly exercised mind – he meant to turn this short-service commission into a career – and he had worked out that promotion was faster in the technical corps than in the infantry regiments and he had chosen the Royal Army Ordnance Corps, the 'suppliers', whose most dangerous activity was that they supplied some of the chaps who took apart unexploded bombs, but, that allowed for, an outfit in which one was unlikely to get blown up, shot at or otherwise injured in anything resembling combat.

George's efforts notwithstanding, England did lose an empire, and the bits it didn't lose England gave away with bad grace. By the end of the next decade a British prime minister could stand up in front of audience of white South Africans, until that moment regarded as our 'kith and kin', and inform them that 'a wind of change is blowing through the continent'. He meant 'the black man will take charge', but as ever with Mr Macmillan, it was too subtle a remark to be effective. Like his 'you've never had it so good' it was much quoted and little understood.

George did not have it so good. In fact the 1950s were little else but a disappointment to him. He seemed to be festering in the backwaters of England – Nottingham, Bicester – postings only relieved, if at all, by interludes in the backwater of Europe known as Belgium. The second pip on his shoulder grew so slowly it was tempting to force it under a bucket like rhubarb. It was 1953 before the pip bore fruit. Just in time for the coronation.

They gave him a few years to get used to his promotion – he boxed the compass of obscure English bases – then Lt Horsfield was delighted with the prospect of a posting to Libya, at least until he got there. He had thought of it in terms of the campaigns of the Second World War that he'd followed with newspaper clippings, a large cork board and drawing pins when he was a boy – Monty, the eccentric, lisping Englishman versus Rommel, the old Desert Fox, the romantic, halfway-decent German. Benghazi, Tobruk, El Alamein – the first land victory of the war. The first real action since the Battle of Britain.

There was plenty of evidence of the war around Fort Kasala (known to the British as 595 Ordnance Depot, but built by the Italians during their brief, barmy empire in Africa). Mostly it was scrap metal. Bits of tanks and artillery half-buried in the sand. A sort of modern version of the legs of Ozymandias. And the fort itself looked as though it had taken a bit of a bashing in its time. But the action had long since settled down to the slow-motion favoured by camels and even more so by donkeys. It took less than a week for it to dawn on George that he had once more drawn the short straw. There was only one word for the Kingdom of Libya – boring. A realm of sand and camel shit.

He found he could get through a day's paper work by about eleven in the morning. He found that his clerk-corporal could get through it by ten, and since it was received wisdom in Her Majesty's Forces that the devil made work for idle hands, he enquired politely of Corporal Ollerenshaw, 'What do you do with the rest of the day?'

Ollerenshaw, not having bothered either to stand or salute, on the arrival of an officer was still behind his desk. He held up the book he had been reading – *Teach Yourself Italian*.

"*Come sta?*"

"Sorry, Corporal, I don't quite...."

"It means how are you, sir? In Italian. I'm studying for my O level exam in Italian."

"Really?"

"Yes, sir. I do a couple of exams a year. Helps to pass the time. I've got Maths, English, History, Physics, Biology, French, German and Russian – this year I'll take Italian and Art History."

"Good Lord, how long have you been here?"

"Four years sir. I think it was a curse from the bad fairy at my christening. I would either sleep for a century until kissed by a prince or get four years in fuckin' Libya. Scuse my French, sir."

Ollerenshaw rooted around in his desk drawer and took out two books – *Teach Yourself Russian* and a *Russian-English, English-Russian Dictionary*.

"Why don't you give it a whirl sir, it's better than goin' bonkers or shaggin' camels."

George took the books and for a week or more they sat unopened on his desk.

It was hearing Ollerenshaw through the partition – '*Una bottiglia di vino rosso, per favore*' – '*Mia moglie vorrebbe gli spaghetti alle vongole*' – that finally prompted him to open them. The alphabet was a surprise, so odd it might as well have been Greek, and as he read on he realised it was Greek and he learnt the story of how two Orthodox priests from Greece had created the world's first artificial alphabet for a previously illiterate culture by adapting their own to the needs of the Russian language. And from that moment George was hooked.

Two years later, and the end of George's tour of duty in sight, he had passed his O level and A level Russian and was passing fluent – passing only in that he had just Ollerenshaw to converse with in Russian and might, should he meet a real Russki for a bit of a chat, be found to be unequivocally fluent.

Most afternoons the two of them would sit in George's office in sanctioned idleness talking Russian, addressing each other as comrade and drinking strong black tea to get into the spirit of things Russian.

"Tell me, *tovarich*," Ollerenshaw said. "Why have you just stuck with Russian. While you've been teaching yourself Russian I've passed Italian, Art History, Swedish and Technical Drawing."

George had a ready answer for this.

"Libya suits you. You're happy doing nothing at the bumhole of nowhere. Nobody to pester you but me – a weekly wage and all found – petrol you can flog to the wogs – you're in lazy bugger's heaven. You've got skiving down to a fine art. And I wish you well of it. But I want more. I don't want to be a lieutenant all my life and I certainly don't want to be pushing around dockets for pith helmets, army boots and jerry cans for much longer. Russian is what will get me out of it."

"How do'you reckon that?"

"I've applied for a transfer to Military Intelligence."

"Fuck me! You mean MI5 and all them spooks an' that?"

"They need Russian speakers. Russian is my ticket."

MI5 did not want George. His next home posting, still a lowly First Lieutenant at the age of twenty-nine, was to Command Ordnance Depot Upton Bassett on the coast of Lincolnshire – flat, sandy, cold and miserable. The only possible connection with things Russian was that the wind which blew bitterly off the North Sea all year round probably started off somewhere in the Urals.

He hated it.

The saving grace was that a decent-but-dull old bloke – Major Denis Cockburn, a veteran of WW2, with a good track record in bomb disposal took him up.

"We can always use a fourth at bridge."

George came from a family that thought three-card brag was the height of sophistication but readily turned his hand to the pseudo-intellectual pastime of the upper classes.

He partnered the Major's wife, Sylvia – the Major usually partnered Sylvia's unmarried sister, Grace.

George, far from being the most perceptive of men, at least deduced that a slow process of matchmaking had been begun. He didn't want this. Grace was at least ten years older than him and far and away the less attractive of the two sisters. The Major had got the pick of the bunch, but that wasn't saying much.

George pretended to be blind to hints and deaf to suggestions. Evenings with the Cockburns were just about the only damn thing that stopped him from leaving all his clothes on a beach and disappearing into the North Sea forever. He'd hang on to them. He'd ignore anything that changed the status quo.

Alas, he could not ignore death.

When the Major died of a sudden and unexpected heart attack in September 1959, seemingly devoid of any family but Sylvia and Grace, it fell to George to have the grieving widow on his arm at the funeral.

"You were his best friend," Sylvia told him.

No, thought George, I was his only friend and that's not the same thing at all.

A string of unwilling subalterns were dragooned into replacing Denis at the bridge table. George continued to do his bit. After all it was scarcely any hardship, he was fond of Sylvia in his way, and it could not be long before red tape broke up bridge nights forever when the Army asked for the house back and shuffled her off somewhere with a pension.

But the break-up came in the most unanticipated way. He'd seen off Grace with a practised display of indifference, but it had not occurred to him that he might need to see off Sylvia too.

On February 29 1960, she sat him down on the flowery sofa in the boxy sitting room of her standard army house, told him how grateful she had been for his care and company since the death of her husband, and George, not seeing where this was leading, said that he had grown fond of her and was happy to do anything for her.

It was then that she proposed to him.

She was, he thought about forty-five or six, although she looked older, and whilst a bit broad in the beam was not unattractive.

This had little to do with his acceptance. It was not her body that tipped the balance, it was her character. Sylvia could be a bit of a dragon when she wanted, and George was simply too scared to say no. He could have said something about haste or mourning or with real wit have quoted Hamlet saying that the 'funeral baked meats did coldly furnish forth the marriage table'. But he didn't.

"I'm not a young thing any more," she said. "It need not be a marriage of passion. There's much to be said for companionship."

George was not well-acquainted with passion. There'd been the odd dusky prostitute out in Libya, a one-night fling with a NAAFI woman in Aldershot... but little else. He had not given up on passion because he did not consider that he had yet begun with it.

They were married as soon as the banns had been read, and he walked out of church under a tunnel of swords in his blue dress uniform, the Madame Bovary of Upton Bassett, down a path that led to twin beds, Ovaltine and hairnets worn overnight. He had not given up on passion, but it was beginning to look as though passion had given up on him.

Six weeks later, desperation led him to act irrationally. Against all better judgement he asked once more to be transferred to Intelligence and was gobsmacked to find himself summoned to an interview at the War Office in London. London... Whitehall... the hub of the universe.

Simply stepping out of a cab so close to the Cenotaph – England's memorial to her dead, at least her own, white dead, of countless

Imperial ventures – gave him a thrill. It was all he could do not to salute.

Down all the corridors and in the right door to face a Lt Colonel, then he saluted. But, he could not fail to notice, he was saluting not some secret agent in civilian dress, not Bulldog Drummond or James Bond, but another Ordnance officer just like himself.

"You've been hiding your light under a bushel, haven't you?" Lt Colonel Breen said when they'd zipped through the introductions.

"I have?"

Breen flourished a sheet of smudgy-carbonned typed paper.

"Your old CO in Tripoli tells me you did a first class job running the mess. And I think you're just the chap we need here."

Silence being the better part of discretion and discretion being the better part of an old cliché, George said nothing and let Breen amble to his point.

"A good man is hard to find."

Well – he knew that, he just wasn't wholly certain he'd ever qualified as a 'good man'. It went with 'first class mind' (said of eggheads) or 'very able' (said of politicians) and was the vocabulary of a world he moved in without ever touching.

"And we need a good man right here."

Oh Christ – they weren't making him mess officer? Not again!

"Er… actually sir, I was under the impression that I was being interviewed for a post in Intelligence."

"Eh? What?"

"I have fluent Russian sir, and I…"

"Well you won't be needing it here… ha… ha… ha!"

"Mess Officer?"

Breen seemed momentarily baffled.

"Mess Officer? Mess Officer? Oh I get it. Yes, I suppose you will be in a way, it's just that the mess you'll be supplying will be the entire British Army 'East of Suez'. And you'll get your third pip. Congratulations, Captain."

Intelligence was not mentioned again except as an abstract quality that went along with 'good man' and 'first class mind'.

Sylvia would not hear of living in Hendon or Finchley. The army had houses in north London, but she would not even look. So they moved to West Byfleet in Surrey, onto an hermetically sealed Army estate of identical houses, and as far as George could see, identical wives, attending identical coffee mornings.

"Even the bloody furniture's identical!"

"It's what one knows," she said. "And it's a fair and decent world without envy. After all the thing about the forces is that everyone knows what everyone else earns. Goes with the rank, you can look it up in an almanac if you want. It takes the bitterness out of life."

George thought of all those endless pink gins he and Ollerenshaw had knocked back out in Libya, and how what had made them palatable was the bitters.

George hung up his uniform went into plain clothes, War Office Staff Captain (Ord) General Stores, let his hair grow a little longer and became a commuter – the 7.57 a.m. to Waterloo, and the 5.27 p.m. back again. It was far from Russia.

Many of his colleagues played poker on the train, many more did crosswords and a few read. George read, he got through most of Dostoevsky in the original, the books disguised with the dust jacket from a Harold Robbins or an Irwin Shaw, and when he wasn't reading stared out of the window at the suburbs of south

London – Streatham, Tooting, Wimbledon – and posh 'villages' of Surrey – Surbiton, Esher, Weybridge – and imagined them all blown to buggery.

The only break in the routine was getting rat-arsed at the office party a few days before Christmas 1962, falling asleep on the train and being woken by a cleaner to find himself in a railway siding in Guildford at dawn the next morning.

It didn't feel foolish – it felt raffish, almost daring, a touch of Errol Flynn debauchery, but as 1963 dawned England was becoming a much more raffish and daring place – and Errol Flynn would soon come to seem like the role model for an entire nation.

It was all down to one person really – a nineteen-year-old named Christine Keeler. Miss Keeler had had an affair with George's boss, the top man, the Minister of War, the Rt. Hon. John (Umpteenth Baron) Profumo (of Italy) MP (Stratford-on-Avon, Con.), OBE. Miss Keeler had simultaneously had an affair with Yevgeny Ivanov, an 'attaché of the Soviet Embassy' (newspeak for spy) – and the ensuing scandal had rocked Britain, come close to toppling the government, led to a trumped-up prosecution (for pimping) of a society doctor, his subsequent suicide and the resignation of the afore-mentioned John Profumo.

At the War Office, there were two notable reactions. Alarm that the class divide had been dropped long enough to allow a toff like Profumo to take up with a girl of neither breeding nor education, whose parents lived in a converted wooden railway carriage, that a great party (Conservative) could be brought down by a woman of easy virtue (Keeler) – and paranoia that the Russians could get that close.

For a while Christine Keeler was regarded as the most dangerous woman in England. George adored her. If he thought he'd get away with it he'd have pinned her picture to his office wall.

It was possible that his lust for a pin-up girl he had never met was what led him into folly.

The dust had scarcely settled on the Profumo Affair. Lord Denning had published his report entitled unambiguously 'Lord Denning's Report' and found himself an unwitting bestseller when it sold 4000 copies in the first hour and the queues outside Her Majesty's Stationery Office in Kingsway stretched around the block and into Drury Lane, and the country had a new prime minister in the cadaverous shape of Sir Alec Douglas-Home, who had resigned an earldom for the chance to live at No. 10.

George coveted a copy of the Denning Report but it was understood to be very bad form for a serving officer, let alone one at the Ministry that had been if not at the heart of the scandal then most certainly close to the liver and kidneys, to be seen in the queue.

His friend Ted – Captain Edward Ffyffe-Robertson RAOC – got him a copy and George refrained from asking how. It was better than any novel – a marvellous tale of pot-smoking West Indians, masked men, naked orgies, beautiful, available women and high society. He read it and re-read it, and since he and Sylvia had now taken not only separate beds but also separate rooms, slept with it under his pillow.

About six months later Ted was propping up the wall in George's office, having nothing better to do than jingle the coins in his pocket or play pocket billiards whilst making the smallest of small talk.

Elsie the tea lady parked her trolley by the open door.

"You're early," Ted said.

"Ain't even started on teas yet. They got me 'anding out the post while old Albert's orf sick. What a diabolical bleedin' liberty. Ain't they never 'eard of demarcation? Lucky I don't have the union on 'em."

Then she slung a single, large brown envelope onto George's desk.

"I see you got yer promotion then, Mr 'Orsefiddle. Alright for some."

She pushed her trolley on. George looked at the envelope.

'Lt Colonel H.G. Horsfield.'

"It's got to be a mistake, surely?"

Ted peered over.

"It is, old man. Hugh Horsfield. Half-colonel in Artillery. He's on the fourth floor. Daft old Elsie's given you his post."

"There's another Horsfield?"

"Yep. Been here about six weeks. Surprised you haven't met him. He's certainly made his presence felt."

With hindsight George ought to have asked what Ted's last remark meant.

Instead, later the same day, he went in search of Lt Col Horsfield, out of nothing more than curiosity and a sense of fellow-feeling.

He tapped on the open door. A big bloke with salt and pepper hair and a spiky little moustache, looked up from his desk.

George beamed at him.

"Lt Col H.G. Horsfield? I'm Captain H.G. Horsfield."

His alter ego got up and walked across to the door and with a single utterance of "Fascinating" swung it to in George's face.

Later, Ted said. "I did try to warn you old man. He's got a fierce reputation."

"As what?"

"He's the sort of bloke who gets described as not suffering fools gladly."

"Are you saying I'm a fool?"

"Oh, the things only your best friend will tell. Like using the right brand of bath soap. No, I'm not saying that."

"Then what are you saying?"

"I'm saying that to a high flyer like Hugh Horsfield, blokes like us who keep our boys in pots and pans and socks and blankets are merely the also-rans of the British Army. He deals with the big stuff. He's artillery after all."

"Big stuff? What big stuff?"

"Well, we're none of us supposed to say are we. But here's a hint. Think back to August 1945 and those mushroom-shaped clouds over Japan."

"Oh. I see. Bloody hell!"

"Bloody hell indeed."

"Anything else?"

"I do hear that he's more than a bit of a ladies' man. In the first month alone he's supposed to have shagged half the women on the fourth floor. And you know that blonde in the typing pool we all nicknamed the Jayne Mansfield of Muswell Hill?"

"Not her too? I thought she didn't look at anything below a full colonel?"

"Well, if the grapevine has it aright she dropped her knickers to half-mast for this half-colonel."

What a bastard.

George hated his namesake.

George envied his namesake.

૮૦

It was someone's birthday. Some bloke on the floor below, whom, he didn't know particularly well but Ted did. A whole crowd of them, serving soldiers in civvies, literally and metaphorically letting their hair down, followed up cake and coffee in the office with a mob-handed invasion of a night club in Greek Street, Soho. Soho – a ten minute walk from the War Office, the nearest thing London had to a red-light district, occupying a maze of narrow little streets east of the elegant Regent Street, south of the increasingly vulgar Oxford Street, north of the bright lights of Shaftesbury Avenue and west of the bookshops of the Charing Cross Road. It was home to the Marquee music club, the Flamingo, also a music club, the private boozing club known as the Colony Room, the scurrilous magazine *Private Eye*, the Gay Hussar restaurant, the Coach and Horses pub (and too many other pubs ever to mention) a host of odd little shops where a nod and a wink might get you into the back room for purchase of a faintly pornographic film, a plethora of strip clubs and the occasional and more-than-occasional prostitute.

He'd be late home. So what? They'd all be late home.

They moved rapidly on to Frith Street and street by street and club by club worked their way across towards Wardour Street. The intention George was sure was to end up in a strip joint. He hoped to slip away before they reached The Silver Tit or The Golden Arse and the embarrassing farce of watching a woman wearing only a G-string and pasties jiggle all that would jiggle in front a bunch of pissed and paunchy, middle-aged men who confused titillation with satisfaction.

He'd been aware of Lt Col Horsfield's presence from the first – the upper class bray of a bar-room bore could cut through any amount of noise. He knew H.G.'s type. Minor public school, too idle for university, but snapped up by Sandhurst because he cut a decent figure on the parade ground. Indeed, he rather thought the only reason the Army had picked him for Eaton Hall was that he too looked the officer type at a handsome 5ft 11 inches.

As they reached Dean Street George stepped off the pavement meaning to head south and catch a bus to Waterloo, but Ted had him by one arm.

"Not so fast, old son. The night is yet young."

"If it's all the same to you, Ted, I'd just as soon go home. I can't abide strippers, and H.G. is really beginning to get on my tits if not on theirs."

"Nonsense, you're one of us. And we won't be going to a titty bar for at least an hour. Come and have drink with your mates and ignore H.G. He'll be off as soon as the first prozzie flashes a bit of cleavage at him."

"He doesn't?"

"He does. Sooner or later everybody does. Haven't you?"

"Well... yes... out in Benghazi... before I was married... but not..."

"It's OK, old son. Not compulsory. I'll just be having a couple of jars myself then I'll be home to Mill Hill and the missis."

It was a miserable half hour. He retreated to a booth on his own, nursing a pink gin he'd didn't much want. He'd no idea how long she'd been sitting there. He just looked up from pink reflections and there she was. Petite, dark, twenty-ish and looking uncannily like the dangerous woman of his dreams; the almost pencil-thin eyebrows, the swept back chestnut hair, the almond eyes, the pout of slightly prominent front teeth and the cheekbones from heaven or Hollywood.

"Buy a girl a drink?"

This was what hostesses did. Plonked themselves down, got you to buy them a drink and then ordered house 'champagne' at a price that dwarfed the national debt. George wasn't falling for that.

"Have mine," he said, pushing the pink gin across the table. "I haven't touched it."

"Thanks love."

He realised at once that she wasn't a hostess. No hostess would have taken the drink.

"You're not working here, are you?"

"Nah. But…"

"But what?"

"But I am… working."

The penny dropped, clunking down inside him, rattling around in the rusty pinball machine of the soul.

"And you think I…"

"You look as though you could do with something. I could… make you happy… just for a while I could make you happy."

George heard a voice very like his own say, "How much?"

"Not up front, love. That's just vulgar."

"I haven't got a lot of cash on me."

"S'OK. I take cheques."

She had a room three flights up in Bridle Lane. Clothed she was gorgeous, naked she was irresistible. If George died on the train home he would die happy.

She had one hand on his balls and was kissing him in one ear – he was priapic as Punch. He was on the edge, seconds away from entry, sheathed in a Frenchie, when the door burst open, his head turned sharply and a flash bulb went off in his eyes.

When the stars cleared he found himself facing a big bloke in a dark suit, clutching a Polaroid camera and smiling smugly at him.

"Get dressed Mr Horsfield. Meet me in the Stork Café in Berwick Street. You're not there in fifteen minutes this goes to your wife."

The square cardboard plate shot from the base of the camera and took form before his eyes.

He fell back on the pillow and groaned. He'd know a Russian accent anywhere. He'd been set up – trussed up like a turkey.

"Oh… shit."

"Sorry, love. But, y'know. It's a job. Gotta make a livin' somehow."

George's wits were gathering slowly cohering into a fuzzy knot of meaning.

"You mean they pay you to… frame blokes like me?"

"Fraid so. Prozzyin' ain't what it used to be."

The knot pulled tight.

"You take money for this!?!"

"O'course. I'm no Commie. It's a job. I get paid. Up front."

He had a memory somewhere of her telling him that was vulgar, but he sidestepped it.

"Paid to get you out of yer trousers, into bed, do what I do till Boris gets here."

"What you do?"

"You know, love… the other."

"You mean sex?"

"If it gets that far. He was a bit early tonight."

A light shone in George's mind. The knot slackened off and the life began to crawl back into his startled groin.

"You've been paid to... fuck me?"

"Language, love. But yeah."

"Would you mind awfully if we... er... finished the job?"

She thought for a moment.

"Why not? Least I can do. Besides, I like you. And old Boris is hardly going to bugger off after fifteen minutes. He needs you. He'll wait till dawn if he has to."

Walking to Berwick Street, along the Whore's Paradise of Meard Street, apprehension mingled with bliss. It was like that moment in Tobruk when Johnny Arab had stuck a pipe of super-strength hashish in front of him and he had looked askance at it but inhaled all the same. The headiness never quite offset and overwhelmed the sheer oddness of the situation.

In the caff a few late night 'beatniks' (scruffbags, Sylvia would have called them) spun out cups of frothy coffee as long as they could and put the world to rights – while Boris, if that really was his name, sat alone at a table next to the lavatory door.

George was at least half an hour late. Boris glanced at his watch but said nothing about it. Silently he slid the finished polaroid – congealed as George thought of it – across the table, his finger never quite letting go of it.

"This type of camera only takes these shots. No negative. Hard to copy and I won't even try unless you make me. Do what we ask Mr Horsfield and you will not find us unreasonable people. Give us what we want and when we have it, you can have this. Frame it, burn it I don't care – but if we get what we want you can be assured this will be the only copy and your wife need never know."

George didn't even look at the photo. It might ruin a precious memory.

"What is it you want?"

Boris all but whispered, "Everything you're sending East of Suez."

"I see," said George utterly baffled by this.

"Be here one week tonight. Nine o' clock. You bring evidence of something you've shipped out – show willing as you people say – and we'll brief you on what to look for next. In fact we'll give you a shopping list."

Boris stood up. A bigger bugger in a black suit came over and stood next to him. George hadn't even noticed this one was in the room.

"Well?" he said in Russian.

"A pushover," Boris replied.

The other man picked up the photo, glimmed it and said, "When did he shave off the moustache?"

"Who cares?" Boris replied.

Then he switched to English, said, "Next week" to George and they left.

George sat there. He'd learnt two things. They didn't know he spoke Russian, and they had the wrong Horsfield. George felt like laughing. It really was very funny – but it didn't let him off the hook… whatever they called him, Henry George Horsfield RAOC or Hugh George Horsfield RA… they had still had a photograph of him in bed with a whore. It might end up in the hands of the right wife or the wrong wife, but he had no doubts it would all end up on a desk at the War Office if he screwed up now.

∽

He got bugger all work done the next day. He had sneaked in to home very late, left a note for Sylvia saying he would be out early, caught the 7.01 train and sneaked into the office very early. He could not face her across the breakfast table. He couldn't face anyone. He closed his office door, but after ten minutes decided that that was a dead giveaway and opened it again. He hoped Ted did not want to chat. He hoped Daft Elsie had no gossip as she brought round the tea.

At 5.30 in the evening he took his briefcase and sought out a caff in Soho. He sat in Old Compton Street staring into his deflating frothy coffee much as he had stared into his pink gin the night before. Oddly, most oddly, the same thing happened. He looked up from his cup and there she was. Right opposite him. A vision of beauty and betrayal.

"I was just passin'. Honest. And I saw you sittin' in the window."

"You're wasting your time. I haven't got the money and after last night…"

"I'm not on the pull. It's six o' clock and broad bleedin' daylight. I… I… I thought you looked lonely."

"I'm always lonely," he replied, surprised at his own honesty. "But what you see now is misery of your own making."

"You'll be fine. Just give old Boris what he wants."

"Has it occurred to you that that might be treason?"

"Nah… it's not as if you're John Profumo or I'm Christine Keeler. We're small fry we are."

Oh God, if only she knew.

"I can't give him what he wants. He wants secrets."

"Don't you know any?"

"Of course I do… everything's a sodding secret. But… but… I'm RAOC. Do you know what that stands for?"

"Nah. Rags And Old Clothes?"

"Close. Our nickname is The Rag And Oil Company. Royal Army Ordnance Corps. I keep the British Army in saucepans and socks!"

"Ah."

"You begin to see? Boris will want secrets about weapons."

"O' course he will. How long have you got?"

"I really ought to be on a train by nine."

"Well… you come home with me. We'll have a bit of a think."

"I'm not sure I could face that room again."

"You silly bugger. I don't work from home, do I? Nah. I got a place in Henrietta Street. Let's nip along and put the kettle on. It's cosy. Really it is. Ever so."

How Sylvia would have despised the 'ever so'. It would be 'common'.

Over tea and ginger biscuits she heard him out – the confusion of two Horsfields and how he really had nothing that Boris would ever want.

She said, "You gotta laugh aint' yer?"

And they did.

She thought while they fucked – he could see in her eyes that she wasn't quite with him, but he didn't much mind.

Afterwards, she said, "You gotta do what I have to do."

"What's that?"

"Fake it."

George took this on board with a certain solemnity and doubt. She shook him by the arm vigorously.

"Leave it out, Captain. I'd never fake one with you."

∽

The best part of a week passed. He was due to meet Boris that evening and sat at his desk in the day trying to do what the nameless whore had suggested. Fake it.

He had in front of him a 'Shipping Docket' for frying pans.

"FP1 Titanium Range 12 inch. Maximum heat dispersal. 116 units."

It was typical army-speak that the docket didn't actually say they were frying pans. The docket was an FP1 and that was only used for frying pans, so the bloke on the receiving end in Singapore would just look at the code and know what was in the crate. There was a certain logic to it. Fewer things got stolen this way. He'd once shipped thirty-two kettles to Cyprus and somehow the word had 'kettle' had ended up on the docket and only ten ever arrived at their destination.

He could see possibilities in this. All he needed was a jar of that new-fangled American stuff, 'Liquid Paper', which he bought out of his own money from an import shop in the Charing Cross Road, a bit of jiggery pokery and access to the equally new-fangled, equally American, Xerox machine. Uncle Sam had finally given the world something useful. It almost made up for popcorn and Rock'n'Roll.

Caution stepped in. He practised first on an inter-office memo. Just as well, he made a hash of it. 'Staff Canteen Menu, Changes to: Sub-section Potato, Mashed: WD414' would never be the same again. No matter, if one of these yards of bumff dropped onto his desk in the course of a day, then so did a dozen more. He'd even seen one headed 'War Office Gravy, Lumps in'.

He found the best technique was to thin the Liquid Paper as far as it would go, and then treat it like ink. Fortunately, the empire had only just died – or committed hara-kiri – and he had in his desk drawer two or three dip pens, with nibs, and a dry, clean, cutglass inkwell that might have graced the desk of the Ass't Commissioner Eastern Nigeria in 1910.

And – practise does make perfect. And a copy of a copy of a copy – three passes on the Xerox – makes the perfect into a pleasing blur.

Titanium was fairly easily altered to Plutonium.

A full stop was added before Range.

12 Inch became 120 miles.

He stared, willing something to come to him about Maximum heat dispersal and when nothing did concluded it was fine as it was. And 116 units sounded spot on. A good healthy number, divisible by nothing.

He looked over his handywork. It would do. It would... pass muster, that was the phrase. And it was pleasingly ambiguous.

"FP1 Plutonium. Range 120 miles. Maximum heat dispersal. 116 units."

But what if Boris asked what they were?

Boris did, but by then George was ready for him.

"FP means Field Personnel. And I'm sure you know what Plutonium is."

"You cheeky bugger. You think I'm just some dumb Russki? The point is to what aspect of Field Personnel does this document refer?"

George looked him in the eye, said, "Just put it all together. Add up the parts and get to the sum."

Boris looked down at the paper and then up at George.

Whatever penny dropped George would roll with it.

"My God. I don't believe it. You bastards are upping the ante on us. You're putting tactical nuclear weapons into Singapore!"

"Well," George replied in all honesty. "You said it, I didn't."

"And they shipped in January. My God they're already there!"

George was emboldened.

"And why not – things are hotting up in Viet Nam. Or did you think that after Cuba we'd just roll over and die?"

And then he kicked himself. Was Viet Nam, either bit of it, within 120 miles of Singapore? He hadn't a clue.

Mouth, big, shut.

But Boris didn't seem to know either.

He pushed the polaroid across the table to him. This time he took his hand off it.

"You will understand. We keep our word."

George doubted this.

And then Boris reached into his pocket, pulled out a white envelope and pushed that to George.

"And I am to give you this."

"What is it?"

"Five hundred pounds. I believe you call it a monkey."

Good God – here he was betraying his country's canteen secrets and the bastards were actually going to pay him for it.

He took it round to Henrietta Street.

He didn't mention it until after they'd made love.

And she said, "Bloody hell. That's more'n I make in a month," and George said, "It's more than I make in three months."

They agreed. They'd stash it in the bottom of her wardrobe and think what they might do with it some other time.

As he was leaving for Waterloo, George said, "Do you realise, I don't know your name?"

"You din ask. And it's Donna."

"Is that your real name?'

"Nah. S'my workin' name. Goes with my surname. Needham. It's like a joke. Donna Needham. Gettit?"

"Yes. I get it. You're referring to men."

"Yeah, but you can call me Janet if you like. That's me real name."

"I think I prefer Donna."

It became part of the summer. Part of the summer's new routine.

He would ring home about once a week and tell Sylvia he would be working late.

"The DDT to the DFC's in town. The brass want me in a meeting, Sorry, old thing."

Considering that she had been married to a serving Army Officer for twenty years before she met George, Sylvia had never bothered to learn any Army jargon. She expected men to talk bollocks and she paid it no mind. She accepted it and dismissed it simultaneously.

George would then keep an appointment with Boris in the Berwick Street caff, sell his country up the Swannee, and then go round to the flat in Henrietta Street.

Even as his conscience atrophied, or quite possibly because it atrophied, love blossomed. He was absolutely potty about Donna and told her so every time he saw her.

Boris didn't use the Berwick Street café every time, and it suited both to meet at Kempton Park racecourse on the occasional Saturday particularly if Sylvia had gone to a whist drive or taken herself off shopping in Kingston-upon-Thames. Five bob each way on the favourite was George's limit. Boris played long shots and made more than he lost. It was, George thought, a fair reflection on both their characters and their trades.

As the weeks passed, George doctored more dockets, pocketed more cash – although he never again collected £500 in one go (Boris explained that this had been merely to get his attention), every meeting resulted in his treachery being rewarded with a hundred or two hundred pounds.

Some deceptions required a bit of thought.

For example he found himself staring at a docket for saucepans he had shipped to Hong Kong from the makers in Lancashire.

SP3 PRESTIGE Copper-topped 6 inch. 250 units.

Prestige was probably the best-known maker of saucepans in the country. He couldn't leave the word intact – it was just possible that even old Boris had heard of them.

But once contemplated, his liar's muse came to his rescue and it was easily altered to read...

FP3 P F T Cobalt-tipped 6 inch. 250 units.

He'd no idea what this might mean, but, once in the caff with two cups of frothy coffee in front of them, as ever, Boris filled in most of the blanks.

Yes. FP meant what it had always meant. He struggled a little with P F T, and George waited patiently as Boris steered himself in the direction of Personal Field Tactical, and as he put that together with cobalt-tipped his great Russian self-righteousness surfaced with a bang.

"You really are a bunch of bastards aren't you? You're fitting hand-held rocket launchers with missiles coated with spent uranium!"

Oh was that it? George knew cobalt had something to do with radioactivity, but quite what was beyond him.

"Armour-piercing cobalt-tipped shells? You bastards. You utter fockin bastards. Queensberry Rules, my Bolshevik arse!"

Ah… armour-piercing, that was what they were for. George hadn't a clue and would have guessed blindly had Boris asked.

"Bastards!"

After which outburst Boris slipped him a hundred quid and called it a long un.

Midsummer, George got lucky. He was running out of ideas, and somebody mentioned that the Army had American-built ground-to-air missiles deployed with NATO forces in Europe. A truck-mounted launcher that went by the code-name of *Honest John*. It wasn't exactly a secret and there was every chance Boris knew what *Honest John* was.

It rang a bell in the great canteen of the mind. A while back, he was almost certain, he had shipped fifty large stewpots out to Aden, bought from a firm in Waterford called Honett Iron. It was the shortest alteration he ever made, and lit the shortest fuse in Boris.

"Bastards!" he said yet again.

And then he paused and in thinking came close to unravelling George's skein of lies. George had thought to impress Boris with a fake docket for a missile that really existed, and it was about to blow up in his face.

"Just a minute. I know this thing, it only has a range of 15 miles.

Who can you nuke from Aden? It doesn't make sense. Every other country is more than fifteen miles away. There's nothing but fockin dyesert within 15 miles of Aden."

George was stuck. To say anything would be wrong, but this was one gap Boris's fertile imagination didn't seem willing to plug.

"Er... that depends," said George.

"On what?"

"Er... on... on what you think is going on in the er... 'fockin dyesert'."

Boris stared at him.

A silence screaming to be filled.

And Boris wasn't going to fill it.

George risked all.

"After all, I mean... you either have spyplanes or you don't."

It was enigmatic.

George had no idea whether the Russians had spyplanes. The Americans did. One had been shot down over the Soviet Union in 1960, resulting in egg-on-face as the Russians paraded the unfortunate pilot alive before the world's press. So much for the cyanide capsule.

It was enigmatic. Enigmatic to the point of meaninglessness but it did the trick. It turned Boris's enquiries inward. Meanwhile George had scared himself shitless. He'd got cocky and he'd nearly paid the price.

He lobbed another envelope of money into the bottom of Donna's wardrobe. He hadn't counted it and neither of them had spent any of it, but he reckoned they must have about £2000 in there.

"I have to stop," he said. "Boris damn near caught me tonight."

⌒

Two days later, George opened his copy of the Daily Telegraph on the train to work and page one chilled him to the briefcase.

'RUSSIAN SPY PLANE SHOT DOWN OVER ADEN'

He had reached Waterloo and was crossing the Hungerford Footbridge to the Victoria Embankment before he managed to reassure himself with the notion that because it had been shot down, the USSR still didn't know what was (not) going on in the 'fockin dyesert'.

He told Donna, the next time they met, the next time they made love. He lay back in the afterglow and felt anxiety awaken from its erotically induced slumber.

"You see," he said. "I had to tell Boris something. There's nothing going on in the 'fockin dyesert'. But the Russians launched a spyplane to find out. On Boris's say so. On my say so. I mean, for all I know the Viet Cong are deploying more troops along the DMZ, the Chinese might be massing their millions at the border with Hong Kong... this is all getting... out of hand."

Donna ran her fingers through his hair, brought her lips close to his ear, with that touch of moist breath that drove him wild.

"Y'know Georgie, you been luckier than you know."

"How so?"

"Supposin' there really had been something going on out in the 'fockin dyesert'?"

"Oh Christ."

"Don't bear thinkin' about do it? But you're right. This is all gettin' outa hand. We need to so something."

"Such as?"

"Dunno. But, let me think. I'm better at it than you are."

"Could you think quickly. Before I start World War III."

"Sssh, Georgie. Donna's thinkin'."

"It's like this," she said. "You want out, but the Russkis have enough on you to fit you up for treason, and then there's the polaroid of you an' me in bed an' your wife to think about."

"I got the polaroid back months ago."

"You did? Good. Now… thing is, as I see it, they got you for selling them our secrets 'bout rockets an' 'at out East. Only you gave 'em saucepans and tea urns. So, what have they really got?"

"Me. They've got me, because saucepans and tea urns are just as secret as nukes. I'm still a traitor. I'll be the Klaus Fuchs of kitchenware."

"No. You're not. The other Horsfield is, 'cos that's who they think they're dealing with."

George could not see where this was headed.

"We gotta do two things, see off old Boris and put the other Horsfield in the frame. Give 'em the Horsfield they wanted in the first place."

"Oh God."

"No… listen… Boris thinks he's been dealing with Lt Col Horsfield. What we gotta do is make the Colonel think he's dealing with Boris… swap him for you and then blow the whistle."

"Or let the whistle blow," said George.

"How do you mean?"

"If I understand that cunning little mind of yours aright you mean to try and frame Horsfield."

"S'right."

"I know H.G. He's a total bastard, but he can't be scared or intimidated. We make any move against him, he catches even a whiff of Russian involvement he'll blow the whistle himself."

"Y'know. That's even more than I hoped for. Let me try for the full house then. Is he what you might call a ladies' man?"

"How do you mean?"

"Well, no offence Georgie, but you was easy to pull. If I was to try and pull H.G. what would he do?"

"Oh, I see. Well if office gossip is to be believed he'd paint his arse blue and shag you under a lamp-post in Soho Square."

"Bingo," said Donna. "Bingo bloody bingo!"

They dipped into the wardrobe money for the first time.

"I can't do this myself, and I can't use the room in Bridle Lane. I'll pay a mate to do H.G., and I know a house in Marshall Street that's going under the wrecking ball any day now. It'll be perfect. I get a room kitted out so it looks like a regular pad and then we just abandon it. The grey area is knowing when we might get to H.G."

"It's Ted's birthday next week. Bound to be a pub and club crawl. I could even predict that at some point we'll all be in the same club you found me in."

"What would be H.G.'s type?"

"Now you mention it… not you. He goes for blondes, blondes with big…"

"Tits?"

"Quite."

"OK, that narrows it down. I'll have to ask Judy. She'll want a ton for the job and another for the risk, but she'll do it."

Ted's birthday bash coincided with George's Boris night at the Berwick Street caff. Something was going right. God knows, they might even get away with this. 'This' – he wasn't at all sure what 'this' was. He knew his own part in this, but the initiative had now passed to Donna. She had planned the night's activity like a film script.

He slipped away early from Ted's party. Ted was three sheets to the wind anyway. H.G. was in full flight with a string of smutty stories and the only risk was that he might get off with some woman before Judy pulled him. As he was leaving, a tall, busty blonde, another Jayne Mansfield or Diana Dors, cantilevered by state-of-the-art bra mechanics into a pink lambswool sweater that showed plenty of cleavage and looked as solid as Everest, came into the club. She winked at George, and carried on down the stairs without a word.

George went round to Bridle Lane.

It was a tale of two wigs.

Donna had a wig ready for him.

"You and Boris are about the same size. It's just a matter of hair colour. Besides, it's not as if H.G. will get a good look at you."

And a wig ready for herself. She was transformed into a pocket Marilyn Monroe.

He hated the waiting. They stood at the corner of Foubert's Place, looking down the length of Marshall Street. It was past nine when a staggering, three-quarters pissed H.G. appeared on the arm of a very steady Judy. They stopped under a lamp-post. He didn't paint his arse blue, but he groped her in public, his hand on her backside, his face half-buried in her cleavage.

George watched Judy gently reposition his hand at her waist and heard her say, "Not so fast, soldier, we're almost there."

"We are? Bloody good show."

George hated H.G.

George hated H.G. for being so predictable.

Donna whispered.

"Ten minutes at the most. Judy'll pull a curtain to, when he's got his kit off. Now, are you sure you know how to work it?"

"It's just a camera like any other, Donna."

"Georgie – we only got one chance."

"Yes. I know how to work it."

When the curtain moved, George tip-toed up the stairs, imagining Boris doing the same thing all those months ago as he prepared to spring the honeytrap.

At the bedroom door he could hear the baritone rumble of H.G.'s drunken sweet nothings.

"S'wonderful. S'bloody amazing. Tits. Marvellous things. If I had tits… bloody hell… I'd play with them all day."

Then, kick, flash, bang, wallop… and H.G. was sprawled where he had been and he was uttering Boris's lines in the best Russian accent he could muster.

"You have ten minutes, Colonel Horsfield. You fail to meet me in the Penguin Café in Kingly Street, this goes to your wife."

He was impressed by his own timing. The polariod shot out of the bottom of the camera just as he said 'wife'.

H.G. was staring at him glassy-eyed. Judy grabbed her clothes and ran past him hell-for-leather. Still, H.G. stared. Perhaps he was too drunk to understand what was happening.

"You have ten minutes, Colonel. Penguin Café, Kingly Street. *Das vidanye.*"

He'd no idea why he'd thrown in the '*das vidanye*' – perhaps a desperate urge to sound more Russian than he had.

H.G. said, "I'll be there… you Commie fucking bastard. I'll be there."

Much to George's alarm he got up from the bed, seemingly less drunk, bollock-naked, stiff cock swaying in its Frenchie, and came towards him.

George fled. It was what Donna had told him to do.

Down in the street, George arrived just in time to see Judy pulling on her stilletoes and heading off towards Beak Street. Donna took the polaroid from him, waved it in the air and looked for the image.

"Gottim," she said.

George looked at his watch. Didn't dare to raise his voice much above a whisper.

"I must hurry. I have to meet Boris."

"No. No, you don't. You leave Boris to me."

This wasn't part of the plan. This had never been mentioned.

"What?"

"Go back to the party."

"I don't…"

"Find your mates. They must be in a club somewhere near. You know the pattern, booze, booze, strippers. Find 'em. Ditch the wig. Ditch the camera. Go back and make yourself seen."

She kissed him.

"And don't go down Berwick Street."

∽

Donna stood awhile on the next corner, watched as H.G. emerged and saw him rumble off in the direction of Kingly Street. Then she went the other way, towards Berwick Street and stood behind one of the market stalls that were scattered along the right-hand side.

She could see Boris. He was reading a newspaper, letting his coffee go cold and occasionally glancing at his watch. He was almost taking George's arrival for granted, but not quite.

She was reassured when he finally gave and stood a moment on the pavement outside the caff, looking up at the stars and muttering something Russian. Really, he wasn't any taller than George, just a bit bigger in the chest and shoulders. What with the wig and flashbulb going off, all H.G. was likely to say was 'some big bugger, sort of darkish, in a dark suit, didn't really get a good look I'm afraid.'

That was old Boris, a big, dark bugger in a dark suit.

Her only worry was that if Boris flagged a cab and there wasn't one close behind, she'd lose him. But it was a warm summer evening, Boris had decided to walk. He set off westward, in the direction of the Soviet Embassy. Perhaps he needed to think? Was he going to shop George for one no-show or was he going to roll with it, string it and George out in the hope of keeping the stream of information flowing?

Boris crossed Regent Street into Mayfair, and headed south towards Piccadilly. He seemed to be in no hurry and paid no attention to cabs or buses. Indeed, he seemed to pay no attention to anything, as though he was deep in thought.

She matched her pace to his, trying to stay in shadow, but Boris never looked back. In Shepherd Market he turned into one of those tiny alleys that dot the northern side of Piccadilly and she quickened her step to get to the corner.

The light vanished. A hand grabbed her by the jacket and pulled her into the alley. The other hand pulled off her wig, and Boris's voice said, "Don't take me for a fockin fool. Horsfield doesn't show and then you appear in a silly wig, trailing after me like a third-rate gumshoe. What the fock are you playing at?"

It was better than she'd dared hope for. She'd been foxed all along to work out how to get him alone, this close, in a dark alley. And now he'd done it for her.

She pressed her gun to his heart and shot him dead.

Then she leant down, tucked the polaroid into his inside pocket, put her wig back on, walked down to Piccadilly and caught a number 38 bus home.

The first George heard was from Daft Elsie, pushing her trolley round just after 11 the next morning.

"Can't get on the fourth floor. Buggers won't let me. Some sort of argy-bargy going on. I ask yer. Spooks and spies. Gotta be a load of old bollocks, ain't it?"

"Two sugars, please," said George.

"And I got these 'ere jam don'uts special for that Colonel 'Orsepiddle. 'Ere love, you have one."

"So," he tried to sound casual. "It all revolves around the good colonel does it?"

"Let's put it this way love. "E's doin' a lot of shoutin'. An' it's not as if he whispers at the best of times."

So – H.G. wasn't so much blowing the whistle as shouting the odds.

After lunch Ted dropped in, dropped the latest, not-yet-late-final-but-almost edition of the *London Evening Standard* onto his desk.

George pulled it towards him.

"Soviet Embassy Attaché Shot Dead in Mayfair."

George said nothing.

Ted said, "Could be an interesting few weeks. Russkis play hell. Possibly bump off one of ours. A few expulsions, followed by retaliatory expulsions… God I'd hate to be in Moscow right now."

"What makes you think we did it? I mean, do we shoot foreign agents in the street?"

"Not as a rule. But boldness was our friend. I gather from a mate at Scotland Yard that they're clueless. No one saw or heard a damn thing. Any way… change the subject… what was up with you last night? Throwing up in the bogs for an hour. Not like you, old son."

"Change it back – does this have anything to do with the hoo ha going on on the fourth floor?"

"Well. Let me put it this way. Be a striking bloody coincidence if it didn't."

It became received wisdom in the office that the Russians had tried to set up H.G. and that he would have none of it. Less received, but much bandied, was the theory that rather than keep the meeting with the man attempting blackmail, H.G. had simply rang MI5 who had bumped off the unfortunate Russki on his way across Mayfair. That one Boris Alexandrovich Bulganov was found dead within a few yards of MI5 HQ in Curzon Street added to the veracity, as did a rumour that he'd had a photograph of H.G. in bed with a prozzie in his pocket. Some wag pinned a notice to the canteen message board offering £10 for a copy but found no takers.

Ted was profound upon the matter, "Always knew he'd end up in trouble if he let his dick do the thinking for him."

It became, almost at once, a diplomatic incident. Nothing on the scale of Profumo or the U2 spyplane, but the Russians accused the British of assassinating Boris, whom they described as a 'cultural attaché'. The British accused the Russians of attempting to blackmail H.G. Horsfield, whose name never graced the newspapers – merely 'unnamed high-ranking British officer' – and George could only conclude that neither one had put the dates together and worked out that they had been blackmailing *an* H.G. Horsfield for some time, but not *the* H.G. Horsfield. If they'd swapped information, George would have been sunk. But, of course, they'd never do that.

H.G.'s 'reward' was to be made a full colonel and posted to the Bahamas. Anywhere out of the way. Why the Bahamas might need a tactical nuclear weapons expert was neither here nor there nor anywhere.

George never heard from the Russians again. He expected to. Every day for six months he expected to. But he didn't.

Six months on Boris's death was eclipsed.

George arrived home in West Byfleet to find an ambulance and a crowd of neighbours outside his house.

Mrs Wallace, wife of Jack Wallace, lieutenant in REME – George thought her name might be Betty – came up oozing an alarming mixture of tears and sympathy.

"Oh, Captain Horsfield... I don't know what to..."

George pushed past her to the ambulancemen. A covered stretcher was already in the back of the ambulance and he knew the worst at once.

"How?" he asked simply.

"She took a tumble, sir. Top o'the stairs to the bottom. Broken neck. Never knew what hit her."

George spent an evening alone with a bottle of scotch, ignoring the ringing phone. He hadn't loved Sylvia. He had never loved Sylvia. He had been fond of her. She was too young, a rotten age to go… and then he realised he didn't actually know how old Sylvia was. He might find out only when they chipped it on her tombstone.

Grief was nothing, guilt was everything.

Decorum ruled.

He did not go to Henrietta Street for the best part of a month.

He wrote to Donna, much as he wrote to many of his friends, knowing that the done thing was the notice in the *Times*, but that few of his friends read the *Times* and that the *Daily Mail* didn't bother with a *Deaths* column.

When he did go to Henrietta Street, he cut through Covent Garden, fifty yards to the north and bought a bouquet of flowers.

"You never brought me flowers before."

"I've never asked you to marry me before."

"Wot? Marriage? Me an' you?"

"I can't think that 'marry me' would imply anything else."

And having read the odd bit of Shakespeare in the interim, George quoted an approximation of Hamlet on the matter of baked meats, funerals and wedding feasts.

"Sometimes, Georgie, I can't understand a word you say."

She was hesitant. The last thing he had wanted, though he had troubled himself to imagine it. She said she'd 'just put the kettle on', and when she had seemed to perch on the edge of the sofa without a muscle in her body relaxing.

"What's the matter?"

"If… if we was to get married… what would we do? I mean we carried on… once we got shot of the Russians, we just carried on… as normal. Only there weren't no normal."

George knew exactly what she meant, but said nothing.

"I mean… oh… bloody nora… I don't know what I mean."

"You mean that serving army officers don't marry prostitutes."

"Yeah… something like that."

"I have thought of leaving the Army. There are opportunities in supply management, and the Army is one of the best references a chap could have."

The kettle whistled. She turned it off but made no move towards making tea.

"Where would we live?"

"Anywhere. Where are you from?"

"Colchester."

Colchester was the biggest military prison in the country – the glasshouse, England's Leavenworth. Considered the worst posting a man could get. He'd never shake off the feel of the Army in Colchester.

"OK. Well… perhaps not Colchester…"

"I always wanted to live up north."

"What? Manchester? Leeds?"

"Nah… 'Ampstead. I'd never want to leave London… specially now it's started to… wotchercallit? … swing."

"Hampstead won't be cheap."

"I saved over three thousand quid from the game."

"I have about a thousand in savings, and I inherited more from Sylvia. In fact about seven-and-a-half thousand pounds. Not inconsiderable."

Not inconsiderable – a lifetime of saving roughly equivalent to a couple of years on 'the game'.

"And of course, I'll get a pension. I've done sixteen years and a bit. I'll get part of a pension now, more if I leave it, and at thirty-five I'm young enough to put twenty or more years into another career."

"And there's the money in the bottom of the wardrobe."

"I hadn't forgotten."

"I counted it. Just the other day I counted it. We got seventeen-hundred-and-thirty-two pounds. O'course there been expenses."

Donna was skirting the edge of a taboo subject. George was in two minds as to whether let her plunge in. Who knows? It might clear the air.

"I give Judy two hundred. And there was money for the room… an 'at."

George bit, appropriately, on the bullet.

"And how much did the gun cost you?"

There was a very long pause.

"Did you always know?"

"Yes."

"It didn't come cheap. Fifty quid."

In for a penny, in for a pound.

Marry without secrets.

George cleared his throat.

"And of course, there's the cost of your return ticket to West Byfleet last month, isn't there?"

He could see her go rigid, a ramrod to her spine, a crab-claw grip to her fingers on the arm of the sofa.

He hoped she'd speak first, but after an age it seemed to him she might never speak again.

"I don't care," he said softly. "Really I don't."

She would not look at him.

"Donna. Please say yes. Please tell me you'll marry me."

Donna said nothing.

George got up and made tea, hoping he would be making tea for two for the rest of their lives.

MOTHER'S MILK

CHRIS SIMMS

One glimpse across the graveyard and he knew that milking her dry would pose no problem at all.

To an ordinary person she was a sad-looking woman in her forties, fat thighs bulging as she bent towards the headstone to replace the dying flowers with a fresh bouquet.

But to Daniel Norris she stank of need. The need for company. The need for human warmth. The need for someone on which to lavish kindness. So acute was his ability to sniff out and exploit vulnerability, she may as well have held a loudhailer to her lips and announced to the bleak cemetery: 'Dear God, this lonely life is killing me.'

He slid into the shadow of a moss-furred crypt and waited for her to pass. As he stood there out of the weak October sun, a breeze whispered between the graves. The cold air seemed to catch in his throat, provoking another bout of painful coughing that he fought hard to suppress. Soon, he heard the crunch of gravel as her stout legs took her back towards the gates. She moved across his field of vision, hair dull and brown, head held up. An attempt to bravely face the grey afternoon.

The moment she was out of sight, he hurried over to the grave she had just left. The headstone was new. He sneered at her tacky taste. Shiny black marble topped by two maudlin cherubs, both trumpeting a silent lament to an unhearing God. His eyes scanned quickly over the inscription, letters chiselled out then painted with a layer of fake gold. Something pathetic about her babies now being with the angels. His eyebrows raised in slight surprise: he had assumed it was a husband and not young ones she'd lost.

He studied the large and expensive bouquet. If this was the weekly ritual he suspected it was, she had plenty of cash to spare. He rubbed his hands together in the chill autumnal air.

Several days dragged by as he eked out an existence between dimly lit boozers and dingy bookies. A win on the dogs on Friday provided some much-needed cash for the weekend. He combed his grey-flecked hair and put his blazer on over his only decent shirt. Then he treated himself to twenty Bensons, leaving the dented tin of rolling tobacco in his hostel room before heading to the Tap and Spile.

During a visit earlier in the week, he'd read the small sign above the door and noted the licensee was a single woman. Jan Griffiths. He'd watched her through the window, noticing the lack of wedding ring as she pulled a pint while keeping up an easy flow of conversation with the customer. He'd liked her dyed blonde hair and sparkling blue eyes.

Now he walked into the pub with an easy roll in his step, one hand in his pocket. Confident and at ease with his place in the world. He slid his thin frame on to a bar stool, nodded at her with a wolfish half-smile then watched as she registered the expression. He knew it never failed to pique the interest of her type.

'You look like the cat who has got the cream,' she stated, a wary curiosity in her voice.

'Do I?' he said, taking the twenties from his pocket. 'Just got some good news on a business deal I'm in town for. A bottle of your best champagne please.'

Nothing ventured, nothing gained.

She smiled, pleased to be filling the till so early in the evening. 'I'll need to get it from upstairs. How many glasses would you like?' Her eyes moved to the empty bar beside him.

'Well, I'm hoping you won't make me drink it alone. So two please.'

She smiled again, turning on her heel and looking back at him over her shoulder. 'Never can say no to a bit of bubbly,' she said archly, hips swinging slightly as she headed for the stairs.

He looked around the cosy pub at the scattering of drinkers quietly sipping their pints. A warm glow spread across his chest. 'Nice place,' he said to himself, thinking he could get used to it.

She re-appeared a minute later, a bottle of Moët standing upright in the ice bucket in her hands. 'One bottle of bubbly.'

He handed two twenties over then watched as she took the foil off and expertly prised the cork loose with a soft pop. A small gush of foam emerged and his eyes wandered to her generous cleavage.

'So what's the business deal?'

He glanced up, realising she'd seen exactly where his eyes had strayed. She didn't seem bothered. 'Oh, a new retail development in the town centre,' he replied. During his first recce round town he'd spotted a large commercial property for sale. 'The one next to that big Barclays.'

'On Prince's Street?' She sounded impressed. 'That's massive. Have you bought it?'

'I wish,' he said with a smile. 'I'm just the middleman between the vendor and the buyers. Venture capitalists from the Middle East. Still, I get my commission as a result.' As she placed two glasses on the bar, he nodded at them. 'Will you be mum?'

'With pleasure.' She poured them both a drink and handed a glass to him. 'Well, here's to your deal.'

'Thanks.'

They clinked glasses and he took a large sip, briefly savouring the sensation of bubbles popping against the roof of his mouth before swallowing it down. 'Delicious.'

'So where are you from?' she asked.

'Wherever business takes me,' he replied. 'I'll be in town for a while yet, tying up the loose ends of this deal, sorting out planning permission for the shops.'

'It's going to be a shopping centre then?'

'That's the intention. My clients want retail units put in then they'll offer out the space to the usual suspects. Boots, Topshop, Subway and the like.'

He took another sip, aware of her eyes assessing him and he realised she'd have heard countless tales of bullshit across the bar.

'So how long have you been in the pub game?' he asked casually.

'Donkey's years,' she laughed. 'It's all I know.'

'You run a nice place here,' he said, glancing over his shoulder.

She gave a small smile. 'It's not bad. Business wise, I mean. The big pubs they've opened in the centre have taken away a few customers, but mainly younger drinkers. I prefer a quieter crowd.'

He refilled their glasses. 'Absolutely. Not enough places like these left.'

She moved away to serve another customer and he almost drained his glass, wondering how quickly she'd come back to him. To his satisfaction, it was almost straight away. The allure of strangers. Deciding not to push things too early, he finished his drink and patted the tops of his thighs. 'Well, I'd better be off. My clients are taking me to dinner at seven o'clock.'

Her eyes went to the unfinished bottle. 'What about your champagne?'

'If it would keep, I'd say put it behind the bar for tomorrow,' he replied, hinting at his return. 'You have it. My treat.'

'Well... thanks,' she answered uncertainly, wrong-footed by his sudden departure.

He returned to the cemetery exactly a week after he first saw her. Earlier in the morning he'd picked up a drab suit in a charity shop, pairing it with his oldest shirt and tie. Finally, he'd put on a pair of battered leather shoes, pleased with the look of someone down on their luck but determined to keep up appearances nonetheless.

She appeared at eleven o'clock, making her way straight to the same grave, another large bouquet in her arms. He made a rip in the paper that wrapped his bunch of cheap chrysanthemums, watching as she plucked a couple of weeds from the bed of marble chippings in front of the headstone before exchanging fresh flowers for the wilted. After standing in sad contemplation for a good five minutes, she started to turn around.

He trampled over a couple of graves to make it onto the path that would intersect hers. Two lost souls, drifting alone in the world.

As he walked with head bowed, he tried to drag up any memories that might bring tears to his eyes. God knew he'd been witness to enough pain and distress. But the anguished weeping of so many women had all been his doing; and the images of their distraught faces did nothing to stir his heart.

She was now less than twenty feet from his side. He caught his foot in a non-existent crack and stumbled forwards, flowers cascading to the ground as the wrapping tore completely. Regaining his balance, he stooped forwards as if to start picking them up. But then he placed his hands on his knees and let out an anguished sob. Her footsteps stopped beside him and, knowing that it would clinch his act, the tears he'd been failing to summon suddenly appeared.

A hand was placed on his shoulder and he looked up at her face as it wavered and shifted through the liquid that filled his eyes.

'There, there,' she murmured, pressing his head to her bosom.

Within four days he had packed his few possessions, moved out of the hostel and was sleeping in her spare room. She'd lapped up his story of a childhood spent in care homes, adult years wasted in a directionless drift, not anchored by family to any area. Then the long search for his real mother – a search that had finally ended in the town's cemetery.

She brought her blubbering under control by clucking and fussing around him. Then she bustled about in the kitchen, carrying through dinner on a tray as he sat dejected on her sofa, his eyes furtively searching the room while she'd cooked his food.

Every night she'd conclude her nursing routine by bringing him a mug of Ovaltine. Creamy, smooth and comforting, it was a taste he began looking forward to.

'That's because I make it with milk, the proper way,' she'd smile, her look of pleasure increasing with his every sip.

But the need to get to a pub and enjoy a cigarette and a drink was steadily growing. So he began to recover from his feigned despondency, apparently revived by the succession of meals she so lovingly prepared. One day, he announced that it was time he sorted himself out, found a job and a place of his own.

Her eyes had widened in alarm at his mention of moving out. 'Stay as long as you like. The house is too big for just me. I like you being here. Please.'

The desperation in her voice surprised him. It was going to be so easy cleaning her out of everything.

He pondered her words, thinking of the three bedrooms upstairs. The spare room he slept in, her pink nightmare and the locked door with the nursery placard on it. He'd peeped through the keyhole at the first opportunity and was just able to make out babyish wall paper and some cuddly toys on a chest of drawers. Three bedrooms and a decent garden. Worth what? Three hundred grand, minimum.

'What happened to your family Marjorie? What happened to your babies?' he whispered, curious that, apart from her creepy shrine, all trace of them had been removed from the house.

The question obviously distressed her and she waved it away with an agitated flutter of her hands. 'I really can't speak about it. Not yet. I'm sorry, it's still all too… raw,' she said, fingers grasping at the crucifix around her neck.

He nodded. 'I understand Marjorie, I understand. But I must repay your kindness somehow. Let me pay you some rent at least.'

She shook her head. 'Really, I don't need it.'

He paused, always amazed at his ability to bring out the maternal instincts of women. 'Think of it for me. For my self-respect if nothing else. There's a job I spotted when I first arrived here. A salesman for those industrial vacuums they use in pubs and restaurants. It's something I've done before. They'd take me on, I just need to brush up a bit...' His words died away and his eyes dropped to his scuffed old shoes.

She sprang to her feet. 'You need proper work clothes.' She crossed to the dresser in the corner, took out a file from the top drawer and extracted several twenty-pound notes from inside. 'Here, take this. Buy yourself a nice new suit.'

'No Marjorie, I couldn't,' he protested, holding up his hands while making a mental note of the file's whereabouts.

'Then take it as a loan,' she insisted.

'OK,' he agreed reluctantly. 'And I'm paying you back every penny, understand?'

He scoured the shops for a sale. After finding one and then mercilessly bargaining down the young assistant, he picked up a suit, three shirts and a pair of shoes for a steal. The deal left him with over eighty pounds in change. He headed straight for the nearest pub with a copy of the *Racing Post*, where he picked his runners over a couple of pints and several cigarettes.

When he set off back to Marjorie's at five o'clock that afternoon he was fifty quid and several more pints up. As he ambled happily along, he wondered how to explain the state he was in. She opened the door to find him swaying on her doorstep, shopping bag hanging from one arm.

'I rang them. I've got an interview tomorrow,' he sighed.

'Well… that's good news, isn't it?' she said, confused by the look of sadness on his face.

'But then I went back to my mother's grave. Oh Marjorie, if I hadn't dithered for so long before tracing her, I might have spoken to her before she died. I'm afraid I've had a few drinks.'

'Come here,' she said, arms outstretched.

He slipped inside and endured a suffocating hug.

'You mustn't punish yourself. Now take that jacket off and sit down.' She led him to the sofa in the immaculate front room. 'I'm making tea. Is beef casserole all right?'

'Great, thanks,' he replied with a weak smile.

She sniffed at his jacket. 'This reeks of cigarettes. You really shouldn't smoke.'

'I know. It's only when I'm stressed.'

She nodded. 'Well, I'll give it a good airing on the washing line.'

'Thank you,' he said, reaching for the TV's remote control as soon as she was out of the room.

He woke with a sore throat and cursed himself for smoking so heavily the day before. The previous evening, she'd washed and ironed his shirts. He walked down the stairs straightening his tie.

'Oh Daniel. You look the perfect gentleman.' She moved across the kitchen, encroaching on his personal space. 'Stand still, you've got a stray strand of hair.'

He fought the urge to slap her hand away, gratefully smiling as she smoothed it into place.

'Perfect,' she said, standing back. 'I've ordered you a cab. We don't want you going by bus and getting to your interview late.'

He sat down and waited for her to cook him breakfast.

'Just here's fine mate,' he leaned over from the rear of the taxi.

'The betting office?' the driver replied, confused. Hadn't his passenger said to the pudgy woman that he needed a fare to the far side of town?

'Yeah, here will do.'

'That's four eighty then, please.'

He counted out the exact money. A bout of coughing caught him by surprise as he walked towards the bookie's, and he lit a cigarette to quell the itch in his throat.

The morning was spent working out his bets. He rang Marjorie at midday. 'I've got the job. Can you believe it?'

'Daniel, that's brilliant! I'll cook something special for tea.'

'They want me to start straightaway. I've got a sales patch right in the centre of town. Mainly pubs, so I'll probably end up smelling of cigarettes each day.'

'Never mind. Did they say what they'll pay you?'

'It's commission only, but the vacuum is a great product. I'm sure I'll sell loads. I've got to demo it to prospective customers. They're dropping me off and have given me a special trolley to wheel it around on.'

'They're making you carry one around town?'

'Yes. And I have to drop it back off at the factory at the end of each day.'

'That's ridiculous. You need a car.'

He smiled to himself. 'I'll manage somehow. Now I've got to go. See you later.'

He hung up and then walked over to the Tap and Spile. 'Hello there,' he said, taking the same stool at the bar, straightening a pristine shirt cuff.

Jan Griffiths looked up, a tea towel in her hand, eyes passing briefly over his new suit. 'Hello again. Thanks for the champagne the other night.'

'My pleasure,' he replied.

'How's business going?'

'OK,' he said. 'There's a few question marks over the rates the council wants to charge. I'm arguing it's a multi-let property, so not subject to the standard commercial tariffs they'd levy if...' He paused. 'Sorry, that's probably more of an answer than you were expecting. How about you?'

She surveyed the deserted pub. 'Lunches tend to be quiet. But I'm not giving up the bar meals. Every decent pub should offer them.'

He picked up a menu. 'What do you recommend, then?'

'I don't know,' she said, polishing another glass. 'The chicken pie is good.'

'Home-made too, I see.'

'Of course.'

'Is it breast or leg?' he asked provocatively.

'You'll have to see,' she replied, one eyebrow lifting.

'Fine with me. I love both.'

He walked back to the bookies a couple of hours later, stopping at a newsagent's to buy some Rennie for the burning ache at the back of his throat. Things were looking good. Marjorie was proving as easy as he knew she would be and it was going better than he dared hope with Jan. So good in fact, he'd asked her out to dinner on Sunday night. He pictured her face, her cleavage, and realised she was really growing on him. If his plans for Marjorie worked out, he and Jan could look forward to some fun times together.

The next morning he woke with a headache and a metallic taste in his mouth. He struggled out of bed, a bout of coughs racking his chest. God he felt awful. He counted back the number of drinks he'd got through in the pub. Not enough to warrant a hang over like this. He'd have to have a word with Jan about how often she cleaned the pipes in her pub.

'Morning,' he said dully, shuffling into the kitchen in a bathrobe and slippers.

'Daniel, are you all right?' Marjorie said, lines of concern across her forehead.

'Not so good actually. I'm glad it's Saturday. I don't think I could have faced working today. Have you got any aspirin?'

'Yes,' she said, immediately opening a cupboard and reaching for the top shelf. He watched the flesh wobbling under her thick upper-arms with disgust.

'Here we are. Now you go and sit on the sofa. Can you manage some tea and toast? I'll bring everything through.'

She bustled in with a blanket shortly after, tucking it around him before carrying through a tray piled with toast, a pot of tea, a glass of milk and two aspirin in a little pot.

'Thanks, could you pass me the remote?'

She appeared again a couple of hours later, hovering by the sofa and aggravating him with her presence. 'I'm going to the cemetery today. I always take flowers for my babies on a Saturday. Do you feel up to coming? We could take some for your mother too.'

Her and those bloody babies he thought, dragging his eyes from the TV screen. Normally a lie would appear instantly on his lips, but his mind seemed to be working sluggishly. 'Erm, no. No thanks.'

'No to coming with me?'

'Yes, I still feel terrible.'

'How about I take some flowers for your mother? You'll need to tell me exactly where her grave is.'

He raised his fingers to his temples and shut his eyes. 'No, don't worry. I'd feel guilty if you took flowers for me. It's something I'd prefer to do myself.'

'OK then. Would you like more tea? Or an Ovaltine perhaps?'

He looked at the huge pot, still half full. 'Yes, an Ovaltine sounds good. And a couple more aspirin please.'

Once she'd gone, he sat sipping his drink, swallowing down the aspirin with the last gulp. Then he kicked off the blanket, walked over to the front window, lifted the net curtain and peered down the street. No sign of her. His temples were thudding and he realised his heart was racing uncomfortably fast as he turned to the top drawer of the dresser and took the file out.

Everything was there. Details of several savings accounts, bank cards, cheque books, even the deeds to the house. He flicked through to the back of the file, grunting incredulously when he found the sheet of paper with all her passwords neatly written out. Stupid, stupid bitch.

He thought forward to his meal with Jan the following evening. If it went smoothly, he'd start draining Marjorie's accounts dry the next day. Then he could invite Jan on a luxury cruise and be out of this horrible house within a week.

He turned to the envelope at the front and counted the cash inside. Almost four hundred quid. Taking the phone back to the sofa, he called the bookies where he'd become a regular. 'Hi George, it's Dan Norris here. Can I place a few phone bets?'

A couple of hours later, the keys clicked in the front door and she walked into the front room, a rosy flush on her chubby cheeks. 'How are you feeling?'

'Rotten,' he said, shifting on the sofa. 'My throat feels so sore.'

'Poor baby,' she said, shrugging off her coat and pressing her fingertips to his brow. 'Perhaps I should take your temperature. You could be coming down with the flu. It's that time of year.'

'You might be right. My joints are starting to ache too.'

She brought the thermometer through from the kitchen, perched on the edge of the sofa and popped it in his mouth. As they waited, he was aware of her large buttocks pressing against him. Fat cow. After three minutes she took it out and tilted it towards the window. 'It's a bit up.'

'Maybe I should have some fresh air,' he said, needing a cigarette and wanting to get away from her cloying company. But when he tried to stand the blood surged in his head and red clouds suddenly filled the room.

When he came to, he was stretched out on the sofa once more, the blanket tucked up to his chin. She was sitting on the arm, looking down at him, her bloated face filling his vision. 'You fainted, you poor dear. It's lucky you hadn't got to your feet.'

Feeling weak as a child, he shut his eyes again. 'My head's pounding. I need more aspirin.'

She instantly stood. 'Of course. I think you're dehydrated, I'll get you a drink, too.'

Returning a minute later he saw she was carrying a steaming mug and small bottle. 'I've made you some more Ovaltine. I'm afraid you've had all the aspirin. But I've got some Calpol.'

'Calpol? Isn't that for toddlers?'

'Yes. It was for...' Tears brimmed in her eyes. 'We'll give you an extra big dose.'

Too exhausted to protest, he watched as she poured out a tablespoon of the red liquid. Once he'd swallowed it, she placed the mug of Ovaltine in his hands. 'Now drink up. We can't have you like this, can we?'

He spent the rest of the afternoon lying on the sofa, listlessly watching the telly as his pulse rose and fell again and again. At seven o'clock she came over and stood in front of the sofa. 'I think it's beddy-bed time. Shall I help you up?'

Irritated by her patronising choice of words, he waved her away. 'I'm fine here. I'll go up later.'

'Head still bad?'

He nodded once. 'If there's no improvement by tomorrow I think we'd better call for a doctor.'

She found him there the next morning. He was lying on his back, a shallow pant coming from his slightly parted lips.

'Oh dear, still feeling poorly?'

His eyelids fluttered and he looked at her from the corner of his eye. 'I'm more than poorly. I need a bloody doctor.' He gestured weakly to the phone's handset. 'Can you pass it to me? I've been trying to reach it, but I can hardly move.' He needed to call Jan to cancel their dinner date.

'Let me get you a drink, your throat sounds awfully dry.'

'OK. Yes, a drink would be good.'

She returned a minute later with a mug in her hands. Kneeling in front of the sofa, she reached an arm round his neck and lifted his head off the cushions.

'What's this? More bloody Ovaltine? I just want water.'

'Now, now,' she clucked. 'I've made it with milk, exactly how you like it. Take a sip, it's not too hot.'

With a reluctant sigh, he did as he was told. Once it was finished, she lay his head back down.

The Ovaltine seemed to have made everything worse. 'Please, will you just call me a doctor? I'm seriously ill here.'

She picked up the handset and returned it to its stand on the far side of the room. 'Silly thing. We don't need a doctor. I'm here to take care of you.'

A surge of self-pitying anger made the dull thump in his head more pronounced. 'Listen, I need more than cups of shitty Ovaltine. I need medical help. Call me a fucking doctor.'

She held a finger up. 'Any more language like that and I'll wash your mouth out with soap. Now let's get you upstairs, you need to be in bed.'

He tried to shrug off her arm as it slid round his neck. 'Give me the phone,' he gasped thinking of Jan, the only person in the world he could turn to for help. Not caring if it meant revealing the truth about himself to her.

Ignoring his demand, she pulled him into a sitting position then draped one of his arms round her shoulders.

'Get your hands off me,' he protested feebly, trying to disentangle himself. Her grip was so strong.

'OK,' she said brusquely. 'One, two, three, up!' She hoisted him to his feet and his vision swirled and faded.

'What are you doing?' he mumbled helplessly, unsure if they were actually moving until he felt the edges of the stairs banging against his shins. 'I need the toilet.'

'There, there. Everything will be OK,' she grunted, half carrying him up to the landing.

His vision cleared a little and he realised they'd stopped outside the door marked nursery. She took a key from her pocket. His head lolled forward as she unlocked the door. The room had the letters of the alphabet running below the picture rail. The blind was down and a mobile of toy animals hung over an enormous cot in the corner.

'What... what is this?' he said, trying to focus.

'Don't you worry, I'm here to take care of you.' She lowered the bars of the cot and lay him down.

'I need the toilet. I have to go to the toilet.' He started to cry.

'That's fine,' she said, stripping off his pyjamas and taking a pair of incontinence pants from a drawer.

He felt her slipping them on and he looked at the photos lined up on the shelf to his side. Framed photos of gaunt-faced men, all lying in the cot he now found himself in.

'Who... who are they?' he whispered.

'My babies of course,' she answered brightly, picking up each picture to kiss it. 'All dead now. All dead.' She looked down at him, a smile on her face. 'My babies always die. It's what God wants.'

He stared up at her with horror, remembering the inscription in the cemetery about her babies being with angels. There were no actual names listed on the gravestone.

'Now, it's time for your next feed. Mummy will get it.' She raised the bars back up and he heard her go downstairs. He had to get out.

Sobbing with exertion, he tried to get a forearm over the top of the bars. He was only able to lift a hand just clear of the knitted blanket.

When she returned, she was carrying a large baby bottle. She teased a drip onto her upturned wrist. 'Just right.'

He tried to shy away from her as she bent over him. But she firmly cupped his cheek and turned his face towards her.

'What's in that? What is it?' he said through gritted teeth as the teat was forced between his lips.

'Mother's milk, my sweet one. Mother's milk.'

LOVE

MARTYN WAITES

LOVE IT. FUCKIN LOVE IT. No other feelin in the world like it.

Better than sex. Better than anythin.

There we was, right, an there they was. Just before the Dagenham local elections. Outside the community centre. Community centre, you're avina laugh. Asylum seeker central, more like. Somali centre.

June, a warm night, if you're interested.

Anyway, we'd had our meetin, makin our plan for the comin election, mobilisin the locals off the estate, we come outside, an there they was. The Pakis. The Anti Nazis. Shoutin, chantin – Nazi Scum, BNP Cunts. So we joined in gave it back with Wogs Out an that, Seig Heillin all over the place. Pakis in their casual leathers, Anti Nazis in their sloppy uni denims, us lookin sharp in bombers an eighteen holers. Muscles like taut metal rope under skin-tight T-shirts an jeans, heads hard an shiny. Tattoos: dark ink makin white skin whiter.

Just waitin.

Our eyes; burnin with hate.

Their eyes; burnin with hate. Directed at us like laser death beams.

Anticipation like a big hard python coiled in me guts, waitin to get released an spread terror. A big hard-on waitin to come.

Buildin, gettin higher:

Nazi Scum BNP Cunts

Wogs Out Seig Heil

Buildin, gettin higher –

Then it came. No more verbals, no more posin. Adrenalin pumped right up, bell ringin, red light on. The charge.

The python's out, the hard-on spurts.

Both sides together, two wallsa sound clashin intaya. A big, sonic tidal wave ready to engulf you in violence, carry you under with fists an boots an sticks.

Engage. An in.

Fists an boots an sticks. I take. I give back double. I twist an thrash. Like swimmin in anger. I come up for air an dive back in again, lungs full. I scream the screams, chant the chants.

Wogs out Seig Heil

Then I'm not swimmin. Liquid solidifies round me. An I'm part of a huge machine. A muscle an bone an blood machine. A shoutin, chantin cog in a huge hurtin machine. Arms windmillin. Boots kickin. Fuelled on violence. Driven by rage.

Lost to it. No me. Just the machine. An I've never felt more alive. Love it. Fuckin love it.

I see their eyes. See the fear an hate an blood in their eyes.

I feed on it.

Hate matches hate. Hate gives as good as hate gets.

Gives better. The machine's too good for them.

The machine wins. Cogs an clangs an fists an hammers. The machine always wins.

Or would, if the pigs hadn't arrived.

Up they come, sticks out. Right lads, you've had your fun. Time for us to have a bit. Waitin till both sides had tired, pickin easy targets.

The machine falls apart; I become meself again. I think an feel for meself. I think it's time to run.

I run.

We all do; laughin an limpin, knowin we'd won.

Knowin our hate was stronger than theirs. Knowin they were thinkin the same thing.

Run. Back where we came from, back to our lives. Our selves.

Rememberin that moment when we became somethin more.

Cherishin it.

I smiled.

LOVED IT.

D'you wanna name? Call me Jez. I've been called worse.

You want me life story? You sound like a copper. Or a fuckin social worker. Fuckin borin, but here it is. I live on the Chatsworth Estate in Dagenham. The borders of east London/Essex. You'll have heard of it. It's a dump. Or rather a dumpin ground. For problem families at first, but now for Somalis an Kosovans that have just got off the lorry. It never used to be like that. It used to be a good place where you could be proud to live. But then so did Dagenham. So did this country.

There's my dad sittin on the settee watchin *Tricia* in his vest, rollin a fag. I suppose you could say he was typical of this estate (an of Dagenham an the country). He used to have a job, a good one. At the

Ford plant. Knew the place, knew the system, knew how to work it. But his job went when they changed the plant. His job an thousands of others. Now it's a centre of excellence for diesel engines. An he can't get a job there. He says the Pakis took it from him. They got HNDs an degrees. He had an apprenticeship for a job that don't exist no more. No one wants that now. No one wants him now. He's tried. Hard. Honest. So he sits in his vest, rollin fags, watchin *Tricia*.

There's Tom, me brother, too. He's probably still in bed. He's got the monkey on his back. Allsorts, really, but mostly heroin. He used to be a good lad, did well at school an that, but when our fat slag bitch of a mother walked out all that had to stop. We had to get jobs. Or try. I got a job doin tarmacin an roofin. He got a heroin habit. Sad. Fuckin sad. Makes you really angry.

Tarmacin an roofin. Off the books, cash in hand. With Barry the Roofer. Baz. Only when I'm needed, though, or seasonal, when the weather's good, but it's somethin. Just don't tell the dole. I'd lose me Jobseeker's Allowance.

It's not seasonal at the moment. But it's June. So it will be soon.

So that's me. It's not who I am. But it's not WHAT I AM.

I'm a Knight of St George. An proud of it. A True Believer. A soldier for truth.

This used to be a land fit for heroes, when Englishmen were kings an their houses castles. A land where me dad had a job, me brother was doin well at school an me fat slag bitch of a mother hadn't run off to Gillingham in Kent with a Paki postman. Well, he's Greek, actually, but you know what I mean. They're all Pakis, really.

An that's the problem. Derek (I'll come to him in a minute) said the Chatsworth Estate is like this country in miniature. It used to be a good place where families could live in harmony and everyone knew everyone else. But now it's a run-down shithole full of undesirables an people who've given up tryin to get out. No pride anymore. No self respect. Our heritage sold to Pakis who've just pissed on us. Love your country like it used to be, says Derek, but hate it like it is now.

And I do. Both. With all my heart.

Because it's comin back, he says. One day, sooner rather than later, we'll reclaim it. Make this land a proud place to be again. A land fit for heroes once more. And you, my lovely boys, will be the ones to do it. The footsoldiers of the revolution. Remember it word for word. Makes me all over again when I think of it.

An I think of it a lot. Whenever some Paki's got in me face, whenever some stuck up cunt's had a go at the way I've done his drive or roof, whenever I look in me dad's eyes an see that all his hope belongs to yesterday, I think of those words. I think of my place in the great scheme, at the forefront of the revolution. An I smile. I don't get angry. Because I know what they don't.

That's me. That's WHAT I AM.

But I can't tell you about me without tellin you about Derek Midgely. Great, great man. The man who showed me the way an the truth. The man who's been more of a father to me than me real dad. He's been described as the demigog of Dagenham. I don't know what a demigog is, but if it means someone who KNOWS THE TRUTH an TELLS IT LIKE IT IS, then that's him.

But I'm gettin ahead. First I have to tell you about Ian.

Ian. He recruited me. Showed me that way.

I met him the shopping centre. I was sittin around one day wonderin what to, when he came up to me.

I know what you need, he said.

I looked up. An there was a god. Shaved head, eighteen holers, jeans an T-shirt so tight I could make out the curves an contours of his muscled body. An he looked so relaxed, so in control. He had his jacket off an I could see the tats over his forearms an biceps. Some pro ones like the flag of St George, some done himself like Skins Foreva. He looked perfect.

An I knew there an then, I wanted what he had. He was right. He did know what I needed.

He got talkin to me. Asked me questions. Gave me answers. Told me who was to blame for my dad not havin a job. Who was to blame for my brother's habit. For my fat slag bitch mother runnin off to Gillingham. Put it all in context with the global Zionist conspiracy. Put it closer to home with pictures I could understand: the Pakis. The niggers. The asylum seekers.

I looked round Dagenham. Saw crumbling concrete, depressed whites, smug Pakis. The indiginous population overrun. Then back at Ian. An with him lookin down at me an the sun behind his head lookin like some kind of halo, it made perfect sense.

I feel your anger, he said, understand your hate.

The way he said hate. Sounded just right.

He knew some others that felt the same. Why didn't I come along later an meet them?

I did.

An never looked back.

Ian's gone now. After what happened.

For a time it got nasty. I mean REALLY nasty. Body in the concrete foundations of the London Gateway nasty.

I blamed Ian. All the way. I had to.

Luckily, Derek agreed.

Derek Midgely. A great man, like I said. He's made the St George pub on the estate his base. It's where we have our meetins. He sits there in his suit with his gin an tonic in front of him hair slicked back, an we gather round, waitin for him to give us some pearls of wisdom, or tell us the latest instalment of his masterplan. It's brilliant, just to be near him. Like I said, a great, great man.

I went there along with everyone else the night after the community centre ruck. I mean meetin. There was the usuals. Derek, of course, holdin court, the footsoldiers of which I can proudly number myself, people off the estate (what Derek calls the concerned populace), some girls, Adrian an Steve. They need a bit of explainin. Adrian is what you'd call an intellectual. He wears glasses an a duffelcoat all year round. Always carryin a canvas bag over his shoulder. Greasy black hair. Expression like he's somewhere else. Laughin at a joke only he can hear. Don't know what he does. Know he surfs the internet, gets things off that. Shows them to Derek. Derek nods, makes sure none of us have seen them. Steve is the local councillor. Our great white hope. Our great fat whale, as he's known out of Derek's earshot. Used to be Labour until, as he says, saw the light. Or until they found all the fiddled expenses sheets an Nazi flags up in his living room an Labour threw him out. Still, he's a tru man of the people.

Derek was talkin. What you did last night, he says, was a great and glorious thing. And I'm proud of each and every one of you.

We all smiled.

However, Derek went on, I want you to keep a low profile between now and Thursday. Voting day. Let's see some of the other members of our party do their bit. We all have a part to play.

He told us that the concerned populace would go leafletin and canvassin in their suits an best clothes, Steve walkin round an all. He could spin a good yarn, Steve. How he'd left Labour in disgust because they were the Paki's friend, the asylum seeker's safe haven. How they they invited them over to use our National Heath Service, run drugs an prostitution rings. He would tell that to everyone he met, try an make them vote for him. Derek said it was playin on their legitimate fears but to me it just sounded so RIGHT. Let him play on whatever he wanted.

He went on. We listened. I felt like I belonged. Like I was wanted, VALUED. Meetins always felt the same.

LIKE I'D COME HOME.

The meetin broke up. Everyone started drinkin.

Courtney, one of the girls, came up to me, asked if I was stayin on. She's short with a soft barrel body an hard eyes. She's fucked nearly all the footsoldiers. Sometimes more than once, sometimes a few at a time. Calls it her patriotic duty. Hard eyes, but a good heart. I went along with them once. I had to. All the lads did. But I didn't do much. Just sat there, watched most of the time. Looked at them. Didn't really go near her.

Anyway, she gave me that look. Rubbed up against me. Let me see the tops of her tits down the front of her low cut T-shirt. Made me blush. Then made me angry cos I blushed. I told her I had to go, that I couldn't afford a drink. My Jobseeker's Allowance was gone an Baz hadn't come up with any work for me.

She said that she was gettin together with a few of the lads after the pub. Was I interested?

I said no. And went home.

Well not straight home. There was somethin I had to do first. Somethin I couldn't tell the rest of them about.

There's a part of the estate you just DON'T GO. At least not by yourself. Not after dark. Unless you were tooled up. Unless you want somethin. An I wanted somethin.

It was dark there. Shadows on shadows. Hip hop an reggae came from open windows. The square was deserted. I walked, crunched on gravel, broken glass. I felt eyes watchin me. Unseen ones. Wished I'd brought my blade. Still, I had my muscles. I'd worked on my body since I joined the party, got good an strong. I was never like that at school. Always the weak one. Not any more.

I was kind of safe, I knew that. As long as I did what I was here to do I wouldn't get attacked. Because this was where the niggers lived.

I went to the usual corner an waited. I heard him before I saw him. Comin out of the dark, along the alleyway, takin his time, baggy jeans slung low on his hips, Calvins showin at the top. Vest hangin loose. Body ripped an buff.

Aaron. The Ebony Warrior.

Aaron. Drug dealer.

I swallowed hard.

He came up close, looked at me. The usual look, smilin, like he knows somethin I don't. Eye to eye. I could smell his warm breath on my cheek. I felt uneasy. The way I always do with him.

Jez, he said slowly, an held his arms out. See anythin you want?

I swallowed hard again. My throat was really dry.

You know what I want. My voice sounded ragged.

He laughed his private laugh. I know exactly, he said, an waited.

His breath was all sweet with spliff an alcohol. He kept starin at me. I dug my hand into my jacket pocket. Brought out money. Nearly the last I had, but he didn't know that.

He shook his head, brought out a clingfilm wrap from his back pocket.

Enjoy, he said.

It's not for me an you know it.

He smiled again. Wanna try some? Some skunk, maybe? Now? With me?

I don't do drugs. I hardly drink. An he knows it. He was tauntin me. He knew what my answer would be.

Whatever, he said. Off you go then, back to your little Hitler world.

I said nothing. I never could when he talked to me.

Then he did somethin he'd never done before. He touched my arm.

You shouldn't hate, he said. Life too short for that, y'get me?

I looked down at his fingers. The first black fingers I'd ever had on my body. I should have thrown them off. Told him not to touch me, called him a filthy nigger. Hit him.

But I didn't. His fingers felt warm. And strong.

What should I do, then? I could hardly hear my own voice.

Love, he said.

I turned round, walked away.

I heard his laugh behind me.

At home, dad was asleep on the sofa. Snorin an fartin. I went into Tom's room. Empty. I left the bundle by his bedside an went out.

I hadn't been lyin to Courtney. It was nearly the last of me money. I didn't like buyin stuff for Tom, but what could I do? It was either that or he went out on the street to sell somethin, himself even, to get money for stuff. I had no choice.

I went to bed but couldn't sleep. Things on me mind but I didn't know what. Must be the elections. That was it. I lay starin a the ceilin, then realised me cock was hard. I took it in me hand. This'll get me to sleep, I thought. I thought hard about Courtney. An all those lads.

That did the trick.

The next few days were a bit blurry. Nothin much happened. It was all waitin. For the election. For Baz to find me some more work. For Tom to run out of heroin again an need another hit.

Eventuallly Thursday rolled round and it was election day. I went proudly off to the pollin station at the school I used to go to. Looked at the kids' names on the walls. Hardly one of them fuckin English. Made me do that cross all the more harder.

I stayed up all night watchin the election. Tom was out, me dad fell asleep.

Steve got in.

I went fuckin mental.

I'd been savin some cans for a celebration an I went at them. I wished I could have been in the St George with the rest but I knew us footsoldiers couldn't. But, God, how I WANTED TO. That was where I should have been. Who I should have been with. That was where I BELONGED.

But I waited. My time would come.

I stayed in all the next day. Lost track of time.

Put the telly on. Local news. They reported what had happened. Interviewed some Paki. Called himself a community leader. Said he couldn't be held responsible if members of his community armed themselves and roamed the streets in gangs looking for BNP members. His people had a right to protect themselves.

They switched to the studio. An there was Derek. Arguin with some cunt from Cambridge. Least that's what he looked like. Funny, I thought people were supposed to look bigger on TV. Derek just looked smaller. Greasy hair. Fat face. Big nose. Almost like a Jew, I thought. Then felt guilty for thinkin it.

It's what the people want, he said, the people have spoken. They're sick an tired of a government that is ignorin the views of the common man and woman. An the common man an woman have spoken. We are not extremists. We are representin what the average, decent person in this country thinks but doesn't dare say because of political correctness. Because of what they fear will happen to them.

I felt better hearin him say that. Then they turned to the Cambridge cunt. He was a psychologist or psychiatrist or sociologist or somethin. I thought here it comes. He's gonna start arguin back an then Derek's gonna go for him. But he didn't. This sociologist just looked calm. Smiled, almost.

It's sad, he said. It's sad so few people realise. As a society it seems we base our responses on either love or hate, thinking they're opposites. But they're not. They're the same. The opposite of love is not hate. It's indifference.

They looked at him.

People only hate what they fear within themselves. What they fear themselves becoming. What they secretly love. A fascist – he gestured to Derek – will hate democracy. Plurality. Anything else – he shrugged – is indifference.

I would have laughed out loud if there had been anyone else there with me.

But there wasn't. So I said nothing.

A weekend of lyin low. Difficult, but had to be done. Don't give them a target, Derek had said. Don't give them an excuse.

By Monday I was rarin to get out the flat. I was even lookin forward to goin to work.

First I went down the shoppin centre. Wearin me best skinhead gear. Don't know what I expected, the whole world to have changed or somethin, but it was the same as it had been. I walked round proudly, an I could feel people lookin at me. I smiled. They knew. Who I was. What I stood for. They were the people who'd voted.

There was love in their eyes. I was sure of it.

At least, that's what it felt like.

Still in a good mood, I went to see Baz. Ready to start work.

An he dropped a bombshell.

Sorry mate, I can't use you no more.

Why not?

He just looked at me like the answer was obvious. When I looked like I didn't understand, he had to explain it to me.

Cos of what's happened. Cos of what you believe in. No don't get me wrong, he said, you know me. I agree, there's too many Pakis an asylum seekers over here. But a lot of those Pakis are my customers. An, well, look at you. I can hardly bring you along to some Paki's house an let you work for him, could I?

So sorry, mate, that's that.

I was gutted. I walked out of there knowin I had no money. Knowin that, once again, the Pakis had taken it from me.

I looked around the shoppin centre. I didn't see love any more. I saw headlines on the papers:

RACIST COUNCILLOR VOTED IN TO DAGENHAM

Then underneath:

KICK THIS SCUM OUT

I couldn't believe it. They should be welcomin us with open arms. This was supposed to be the start of the revolution. Instead it was the usual shit. I just knew the Pakis were behind it. An the Jews. They own all the newspapers.

I had nowhere to go. I went to the St George but this was early mornin an there was no one in. None of my people.

So I just walked round all day. Thinkin. Not gettin anythin straight. Gettin everythin more twisted.

I thought of goin to the St George. They'd be there. Celebratin. Then there was goin to be a late-night march round the streets. Let the residents, the concerned populace, know they were safe in their houses. Let everyone know who ruled the streets.

But I didn't feel like it.

So I went home.

An wished I hadn't.

Tom was there. He looked like shit. Curled up on his bed. He'd been sick. Shit himself.

Whassamatter? I said. D'you wanna doctor?

He managed to shake his head. No.

What then?

Gear. Cold turkey. Cramps.

An he was sick again.

I stood back, not wantin it to go on me.

Please, he gasped, you've got to get us some gear… please…

I've got no money, I said.

Please…

An his eyes, pleadin with me. What could I do? He was my brother. My flesh an blood. An you look after your own.

I'll not be long, I said.

I left the house.

Down to the part of the estate where you don't go. I walked quickly, went to the usual spot. Waited.

Eventually he came. Stood before me.

Back so soon? Aaron said. Then smiled. Can't keep away, can you?

I need some gear, I said.

Aaron waited.

But I've got no money.

Aaron chuckled. Then no sale.

Please. It's for… it's urgent.

Aaron looked around. There was that smile again.

How much d'you want it? he said.

I looked at him.

How much? he said again. An put his hand on my arm.

He moved in closer to me. His mouth right by my ear. He whispered, tickling me. My heart was beatin fit to burst. My legs felt shaky.

You're like me, he said.

I tried to speak. It took me two attempts. No I'm not, I said.

Oh yes you are. We do what our society says we have to do. Behave like we're supposed to. Hide our true feelings. What we really are.

I tried to shake my head. But I couldn't.

You know you are. He got closer. You know I am.

An kissed me. Full on the mouth.

I didn't throw him off. Didn't call him a filthy nigger. Didn't hit him. I kissed him back.

Then it was hands all over each other. I wanted to touch him, feel his body, his beautiful, black body. Feel his cock. He did the same to me. That python was inside me, ready to come out. I loved the feeling.

I thought of school. How I was made to feel different. Hated them for it. Thought of Ian. What we had got up to. I had loved him. With all my heart. An he loved me. But we got found out. An that kind of thing is frowned upon, to say the least. So I had to save my life. Pretend it was all his doing. I gave him up. I never saw him again. I never stopped loving him.

I loved what Aaron was doing to me now. It felt wrong. But it felt so right.

I had him in my hand, wanted him in my body. Was ready to take him.

When there was a noise.

We had been so into each other we hadn't heard them approach.

So this is where you are, they said. Fuckin a filthy nigger when you should be with us.

The footsoldiers. On patrol. An tooled up.

I looked at Aaron. He looked terrified.

Look, I said, it was his fault. I had to get some gear for my brother...

They weren't listening. They were starin at us. Hate in their eyes. As far as they were concerned I was no longer one of them. I was the enemy now.

You wanna run nigger lover? Or you wanna stay here an take your beatin with your boyfriend? The words spat out.

I zipped up my jeans. Looked at Aaron.

They caught the look.

Now run, the machine said, hate in its eyes. But from now on, you're no better than a nigger or a Paki.

I ran.

Behind me, heard them layin into Aaron.

I kept running.

I couldn't go home. I had no gear for Tom. I couldn't stay where I was. I might not be so lucky next time.

So I ran.

I don't know where.

After a while I couldn't run any more. I slowed down, tried to get me breath back. Too tired to run anymore. To fight back.

I knew who I was. Finally. I knew WHAT I WAS.

An it was a painful truth. It hurt.

Then from the end of the street I saw them. Pakis. A gang of them. Out protecting their own community. They saw me. Started running.

I was too tired. I couldn't outrun them. I stood up, waited for them. I wanted to tell them I wasn't a threat, that I didn't hate them.

But they were screaming, shouting, hate in their eyes.

A machine. Cogs an clangs an fists an hammers.

I waited, smiled.

Love shining in my own eyes.

RETROSPECTIVE

KEVIN WIGNALL

There was more death and misery in this room than was fit for any civilised place. Mutilated bodies, the diseased and the starving, the fearful and the grief-stricken and all those empty eyes, the haunted and expressionless faces – it was all here, and it was all his.

Tomorrow night, the Dorchester Street Gallery would open its doors and the celebrities and art world players would get their vicarious thrills as they socialised and flirted and exchanged business cards over wine and morsels amid the horror of his life's work.

Most of his life's work, at any rate; the landscape photographs of recent years had been shunted off into one small side gallery. He didn't mind that, either, conscious of the fact that the landscapes hadn't earned him this retrospective.

When people thought of Jonathan Hoyle, they thought of the images that had been used to fill both the two large gallery spaces and the big fat accompanying catalogue. For nearly twenty years, he'd produced these iconic photographs of the world's war zones and he suspected he was alone in seeing what he'd done. Far from exposing the truth, he'd reduced human tragedy to the level of pornography, or worse, for pornographers were at least honest.

He heard a noise behind him and turned to see the young gallery assistant approaching. Her name was Sophie, he thought, and she looked pretty and mousy in the moneyed way of gallery assistants. If he were a different type of photographer, he'd be trying to seduce her into sitting for him.

'Having a final look around, Mr Hoyle?'

He wasn't sure how to respond, so he said, 'Please, call me Jon.'

'Thank you.' She blushed, and again, he thought maybe he should move from his current obsession to the landscape of the female body. 'It's a bit cheeky of me, I know, but do you think you could sign my copy of the catalogue?'

He looked at the catalogue in her hand and his thoughts crumbled into dust. There was the dead Palestinian boy whose picture had once appeared on newspaper front pages the world over. The gallery had offered him a choice of two photographs for the cover and he'd opted for this one without a second thought, but it still depressed him to see it.

'Of course.' He took the catalogue and the pen she proffered. 'It's Sophie, isn't it?' She nodded and he wrote a simple inscription, thanking her for all her help.

She studied it, apparently happy with the personal touch, then looked at the cover and said, 'It's such a beautiful picture, incredibly moving.' She looked up at him again and said, 'Why did you stop... I mean, why didn't you take anymore war photography after this one?'

He sighed. These questions would always haunt him. The life he'd lived, the person he'd been, out there on the ragged edges of the world, it would always get in the way of the simpler things. You're a pretty girl, he wanted to say, I'd like to go for a drink with you and talk about art, and I'd like to see you naked. But she was right, the Palestinian boy had been the last.

'I stopped because I'd finally captured the truth; there was nothing left to say after that.'

She smiled, uncertain, as if she feared he might be teasing her. 'But your photographs are *all* about the truth.'

'Are they?' She didn't know how to respond. 'Goodnight, Sophie, I'll see you tomorrow evening.' He drifted towards the door, enigma intact, almost self-satisfied.

It was already dark and there was a cold wind picking up, but he decided to walk back to the hotel, wanting to clear his head out there on the streets. As he stepped outside though, he was faced with a black Range Rover, tinted windows, a young guy in a suit waiting by one of the rear doors.

'Evening, Mr Hoyle. Your car.' He was Australian, like most of the people keeping London's service economy afloat. The guy opened the door in readiness for him.

Jon was about to tell him that he felt like walking, but stopped himself and said, 'My car? No one ordered a car for me.'

If he'd had a moment longer he might have figured that the guy's suit was a little too expensive to suggest a chauffeur. He didn't have time though. Before he'd even finished speaking, the guy had produced a gun from somewhere, a silencer already attached. He was pointing it at Jon, but holding it in a casual, almost non-threatening way.

'Get in the car, mate. I don't wanna have to kill you here, but I will.'

The thought of running had died even before it was fully formed. He remembered seeing that French journalist getting shot in Somalia, remembered how sudden and arbitrary it had been – one minute talking to the soldiers, the next crumpled in the dust, oozing blood. There was no running, and he felt bad because, right at this moment, he couldn't remember that French journalist's name, even though he'd drunk with him a couple of times.

Jon got in the back of the Range Rover and the young guy got in after him, closing the door.

'Okay, let's go.' Another guy was in the driving seat but it was soon clear the car belonged to the gunman. They lurched forwards, nearly clipping another parked car, and the Australian said, 'Mate, if you scratch my bloody paintwork!' He turned to Jon then and said, 'Gotta blindfold you.' He put the blindfold on, tying it behind Jon's head, surprisingly gentle. 'How's that feel?'

'Okay, I suppose, under the circumstances.'

'Yeah, sorry about that. The name's Dan, Dan Borowski.' Bizarrely, Jon felt him take his hand and shake it like he was introducing himself to a blind man. And it was bizarre mainly because he knew this was it; whoever they were, they were going to kill him.

I don't wanna have to kill you here, that's what the guy had said, and he'd given his full name, which meant he saw no danger because he was talking to a dead man. He couldn't help but be amused by the irony of it, that he'd travelled unscathed through every impression of hell the world had to offer, only to die in London.

'You're gonna kill me.'

He waited for the voice, and when it came it was a little regretful. 'Yeah. Client wants to meet you first, but your number's up. I'm sorry.'

'Why? I mean, why does he want me dead?'

'Didn't say.' His tone was casual again. 'Gotta be something to do with your work though, don't you think?'

Jon nodded. He was surprised how calm he felt. He wondered if experienced pilots felt like this when their planes finally took a nosedive, if they serenely embraced the void, knowing they'd defied it too long already.

Jon didn't want pain, but he could imagine this guy, Dan, making it easy for him anyway; he was clearly a professional killer, not like some of the monstrous amateurs he'd seen parading around in their makeshift uniforms. He didn't want to die either, but he'd tap-danced around death for so long, he could hardly complain now as it reached out to rest its hand upon his shoulder.

He was curious though, trying to think which aspect of his work had angered someone so much that, even now, a few years after he'd stopped being a war photographer, they were still determined to kill him for it. It couldn't be for offending some cause or other.

He could only imagine this being a personal bitterness, the result of a photograph that had so intruded on someone else's grief or suffering that this seemed a justifiable retribution. That ruled out the landscapes, but not much else.

He supposed a lot of the people who knew and loved the subjects of his photographs would have killed him if they'd had the means. The fact that this person clearly had been able to hire a contract killer perhaps narrowed it down a little further. It made the Balkans, the Middle East and Central America more likely as the source. It hardly mattered though; whoever it was, whichever photograph, they were striking a blow for all the unknown families.

'You *are* a contract killer, I take it.'

'Among other things,' said Dan.

Jon was already getting attuned to having no visuals to fall back on, and although Dan had fallen silent again, he could sense that he had more to say. Sure enough, after a couple more beats, a stop at traffic lights, a left turn, Dan spoke again.

'You know, in a way, you and I are a lot alike. Our jobs, anyway.'

Jon laughed and said, 'I'm cynical about the work I do, but that's a bit rich. I photograph death. In a strange way, I think I sanitise it, but at least I can hold my hands up and say I've never caused it.'

There was a slight pause, during which Jon realised he'd talked in the present tense, even though it was a while now since he'd photographed the overspill of war. Dan seemed fixed on something else, the distraction audible in his voice as he said, 'I'm picking up some negative vibes here, like you're dismissing the work you've produced. I've gotta tell you, Jon, you're wrong about that. You're a great photographer, and it's a document of our times, good or bad.'

'Well, we'll have to agree to differ on that.'

'No way!' He laughed as if they were old friends disagreeing over favorite teams or dream dates. 'Seriously, I'm such a fan of your work. I've even got the book of landscapes. It was one of the reasons I agreed to this job.'

It was Jon's turn to laugh. 'You agreed to kill me for money because you're such a fan of my work! Well thanks, I'm touched.'

Another pause, and Dan's response was subdued, even a little hurt, 'The contract would have gone to someone else, anyway. I took the job because I wanted to meet you, and I wanted to make sure it was done right.'

He couldn't ignore the final point because it was what he'd hoped for, that he wouldn't let him suffer. And maybe another man, certainly one in another profession, wouldn't have looked at his own killer's intentions in quite the same way, but Jon *was* touched by the sentiment now that he thought about it.

'Thanks, Dan. I do appreciate that, and I know if it hadn't been you, it would have been someone else.'

'Yeah, it's too bad.'

'You didn't say how we were similar.'

He was relaxed again, almost cheery as he said, 'I just meant the way we go into areas, not just geographical areas, you know, areas of the human condition that most people don't ever experience. We drop in, I do what I've been paid to do, you get your picture, and we're back out again, onto the next little screw-up.'

'I still don't see it. From my point of view, you're part of the problem. I may not be part of the solution, but at least I'm letting the world know what's really happening.'

Dan laughed and said, 'See, we're already getting somewhere; you're looking at your own work in a more positive light.' The car stopped and the engine was turned off. For the first time, Jon felt a nervous twitching in his stomach. 'We're here.'

Dan helped him out of the car, a brief reminder of the cold night air, a coldness he wanted to savour, to fill his lungs with it like he was about to swim underwater for a long time. They walked through a door and it was still cold but no longer fresh, then up several flights of stone steps.

At the top, they walked through another door and then Dan took off the blindfold. They were in a large loft which looked as if it had only recently stopped being used as a factory or workspace.

No doubt its next reincarnation would be as a couple of fabulous apartments, and neither of the new owners would ever imagine that it had been the scene of an execution.

There were two chairs in the middle of the floor, facing each other, a few yards apart. He noticed too, over to one side, what looked like a picture under a sheet, resting against a pillar. Jon wondered if that was it, the evidence of his crime, the photograph that had cost him his life.

He'd seen that happen to other photographers, their determination to get the ultimate shot drawing them too far into the open. It felt now like a stray bullet had hit him sometime in the last twenty years, the day he'd taken that picture, whatever it was, and ever since, he'd simply been waiting to fall.

'Take a seat. We shouldn't have to wait long.'

'Will you do it here?' Dan looked around the room as if weighing up its suitability. He nodded. Jon pointed at the picture under the sheet. 'Is that the photograph under there? Is that why he wants me dead?'

'I don't know, but you'll find out soon enough. Best you just sit down.'

Dan sat on one of the chairs so Jon took the other. He took a good look at Dan now. He looked young but he was probably thirty, maybe older, good-looking in that healthy Australian way, and his face was familiar somehow, but then, Jon had seen so many faces in his life, they all ended up looking a little familiar.

Suddenly, he thought of the blindfold. He had no idea which part of London they were in, though they hadn't driven far. But if he was definitely to be killed, he couldn't understand why he'd had to be blindfolded.

'Does this guy definitely want me dead? There's no way out of it?'

Dan shook his head regretfully and said, 'Why do you ask?'

'The blindfold. If he definitely wants me dead, I can't understand why I had to be blindfolded.'

'He's just really cautious. And he doesn't know that when I bring someone in, they stay in.'

'How much is he paying you?' Dan smiled and offered the briefest shake of his head.

He stared at Jon for a while then, still smiling, intrigued, and finally said, 'I don't suppose you recognise me?'

'Your face is vaguely familiar, but I don't know where from.'

'You took my picture once.' He could see the look of surprise on Jon's face and waited for it to sink in before adding, 'Not only that – it's in the exhibition.'

'I... I don't remember.'

'Yes you do. Near the Congo-Rwandan border. You were taking pictures of the refugees escaping the fighting. Remember, there were thousands of them, just this silent broken river of people pouring over the border. I walked past you, didn't think anything of it. Then I see the picture, all those refugees walking towards the camera, me walking away from it.'

Jon shook his head, astonished, because he did remember now. He'd been taking shots for an hour or more, never quite feeling he'd captured what he was after. Then a Western soldier had walked past him in black combats, heavily-armed but still looking suicidally ill-equipped for where he was heading, a war zone of mind-altering barbarity. That was his picture, another one which had been dubbed iconic.

And the amazing thing was, he'd seen him again, five days later, back in the hotel. He'd recognized him just from the easy confident gait of his walk, from his build, the cut of his hair. Jon had asked someone who he was and he'd been told he was a mercenary, that he'd gone in for the German government and brought out some aid workers who'd been taken by the guerrillas. It had always intrigued him, that a man could walk so casually into hell and still come back.

'You saved those German aid workers.'

Dan shrugged and said, 'I saved three of them. One had already been killed by the time I got there. Another died on the way out.'

'I've always wondered about that. Weren't you scared at all, going in there, knowing what was happening?'

'No,' he said, smiling dismissively.

'I've been to some pretty freaky places, but I would have been scared going in there.'

'That's because you only had a camera. I was armed; I knew I could handle it. I didn't know I could get them out alive, I was nervous about that, but I knew I could handle a few drug-crazed guerrillas.'

'So you're not just a contract killer.'

'No, like I said, I do all kinds of stuff. But don't paint me like Mother Teresa – I got paid more for bringing those people out of the jungle than you probably got paid in five years.'

'At least you brought them out. You saved someone; it's more than I ever did.'

'It wasn't your job to save people.'

'It wasn't my job, but it was my duty as a human being. I used to look at some of these people and think they were savages, and yet I'd watch people dying and worry about things like light and exposure.' Dan was shaking his head, the blanket disagreement of a true fan. 'Tell me something, if you'd been in the jungle and stumbled across those hostages, would you have left them there to die? It wouldn't have been your job to save them, no payment, but would you?'

'Yeah, I probably would have had a go.'

'That's the difference, Dan. You may be a cold-blooded killer, but you're still human. I never saved anyone.'

Dan seemed to turn it over for a few seconds and then said, 'You know, certain times of year, if a croc finds a baby turtle on the river bank, it'll scoop it up in its mouth, take it down to the water and let it go. See, they're programmed to help newly hatched crocs, so they just help anything small that's moving towards the water. Six months later, that croc, he'll still kill that turtle.'

Jon wondered if that was true, but was struck then by something else. 'I don't follow. What's your point?'

Dan laughed and said, 'I have absolutely no bloody idea!'

Jon laughed too and then they were both silenced as the street door down below opened and closed and heavy steps worked laboriously towards them. Jon expected to feel nervous again, but if anything, their conversation had left him even more prepared. Maybe the nerves would come again later, but with any luck, he wouldn't have too long to think about it.

Dan stood up now, but gestured for Jon to stay where he was, and as if the approaching man were already in earshot, he said quietly, 'You know, if there'd been any other way...'

'Don't. And I'm glad I met you, too. I was always curious about the guy in that photograph.'

Dan nodded and walked over to the door as it opened and a heavy-set guy in his fifties walked in. He was balding, wearing an expensive grey suit, an open collar. At first, Jon had him down as an Eastern European, but he quickly realised the guy was an Arab.

The guy looked across, a mixture of disdain and satisfaction, but spoke to Dan for a minute or two in hushed tones. Their conversation seemed relaxed, as if they were filling each other in on what had happened recently, and when it was over, Dan nodded and left.

The client walked across the room without looking at him, picked up the picture under its sheet and placed it on the chair facing Jon. He walked around the chair and stood behind it, finally allowing himself to make eye contact.

'You are Jonathan Hoyle.' His voice was deep, the accent giving it an added gravitas. 'May I call you Jonathan?'

'People call me Jon.'

He gave a little nod and said, 'So, Jon, do you know anyone called Nabil?' Jon shook his head. 'It's my name. I am Nabil. It was also my son's name. I know you don't have children, so I also know that you don't understand what it is to lose a child. And I know you don't understand what it is for your dead child's photograph to be made into a piece of art, bought and sold, put on the covers of books. I know you don't understand any of this.' There was no anger in his words; they were no more than statements of fact. And Jon couldn't question them so he remained silent. 'That is what I know about you. And this is what I know about me. I know that killing you tonight will not bring my son back and will not ease my pain. Indeed, the pain may become worse because your death will bring even more interest to your work, but still, I must insist on your death. First, I want you to look again at my son's photograph, knowing his name, knowing...'

He stopped, suddenly overcome, and took a deep breath. Jon lowered his gaze slightly, not wanting to stare at this man who was still so visibly torn by grief. He heard the sheet being pulled away, saw it drop to the floor, and a part of him didn't want to look up, because he had a feeling he knew which picture it would be, and the memory of it was already making him feel sick.

'Look at my son, Mr Hoyle. Jon, look at my son.'

He looked up. There was the print of the Palestinian boy, blown-up life-size. His name had been Nabil and he'd been fourteen years old and now Jon could think of no good reason why he shouldn't die tonight.

The boy's father wasn't crying but he had the look of a man who had no more tears left, a man who'd been beaten by life and was spent. Jon thought of all the times over the last four years that this man had chanced upon that picture and had the wound torn afresh.

Jon knew something of that, because he'd experienced it too. He'd seen the picture pulled from image libraries and used to illustrate newspaper and magazine stories – no context, no explanation, just a cynical, exploitative pathos.

He'd been fêted for that photograph and yet as ambivalent as he'd been about it, as much as its appearance had made jagged shards of his memory, he'd never once given thought to the boy's family. He could see it now, of course, how they'd probably come to hate him even more than the unknown Israeli soldier whose bullet had killed Nabil that day in Gaza.

'Do you have anything to say?'

'That was the last photograph I ever took in a war zone.'

Nabil laughed a little, incredulous as he said, 'That's not much of a defence.'

'I don't have any defence. It isn't right for you to kill me, but I can make no sound argument for sparing me. If it means anything, if it offers any comfort, I'm sorry.'

Nabil nodded once, almost like a bow of his head. Jon wanted it over with now, he wanted Dan to come back into the room and end it, but Nabil looked contemplative, as if he was still dwelling upon something and wanted to ask another question. He suddenly became grim and determined though, and started towards the door.

Jon felt his stomach tighten into a spasm, his blood spinning out of control with adrenaline, a mixture of fear and of self-loathing, knowing that it was wrong to leave it like this, without at least telling him the truth. 'Nabil.' Nabil stopped and turned to look at him. Jon felt ashamed because he knew it looked like he was stalling, and he wasn't; his nerves were for something else, for the things he wanted to say for the first time. He wanted to offer this man something more than a trite apology, and he wanted to get something off his own conscience before he died. 'Before you call Dan back in, I want to tell you something about the day your son died. It won't change anything, but I want to tell you anyway.'

Nabil's expression was unyielding, but he walked back towards the chair and stood a few paces behind it. 'Go on.'

Jon took a couple of deep breaths, looked at the photograph again, then at Nabil. 'I took a lot of good photographs that day, and in the days before. You remember how volatile it was at that time, almost like there was something unstable in the air.'

'I remember.'

'So I was there, and there were Palestinian boys, young men, throwing stones at an Israeli patrol. I saw your son.'

Nabil prickled defensively and said, 'Yet you have no pictures of him throwing stones.'

'Because he wasn't throwing stones. Like a lot of people those days, he was just trying to get from one place to another without getting caught up in it. He didn't look scared, he just looked like a kid who was used to it, confident, almost carefree.' He looked at the photograph in front of him and wished as he had many times, that he'd captured that carefree face as a counterpoint. 'I wasn't even wasting film at that point. Stone throwing, that was just becoming routine. Then someone started firing on the soldiers and one of them got hit. They fired back and one of the stone throwers took a bullet in the shoulder. I got some good pictures of his friends helping him, this hive of activity and this dazed, strangely calm kid in the middle of it all. There were a couple of other photographers with me. And within another ten minutes it was all over. I was walking away on my own when I saw blood on the floor. I walked around the corner, into the yard of a house that had been bombed the week before, and I saw the body lying there. I recognised him right away, the kid I'd seen earlier. I guessed he'd been hit by a stray bullet, had managed to drag himself into the yard. He looked so young, and all the clichés were there – he looked peaceful, his face angelic, and the only thing that went through my mind at that moment, was that I knew this photograph would make front pages all around the world. I took it, just one shot, and I knew I'd got it, the bloody hole in the side of his chest, the angelic face. I felt satisfied. I'm ashamed to say that, but I did, I felt like I'd found that day's star prize. And then the strangest thing happened. I kept looking through the lens, looking at his face, and I just knew something wasn't right, somehow. It took a moment, but I saw it in the end.' He got up out of his chair and walked towards the picture. Nabil glanced at the door, as if ready to shout, but Jon kept his course. He picked up the picture and turned it for Nabil to see. 'This is the truest photograph I ever took, and it's a fake. It shows a dead Palestinian boy, your son, but when this photograph was taken, the boy wasn't dead.'

Nabil looked at him, surprised and yet wary, as if suspecting an attempt to earn his forgiveness. Jon didn't want that though, and wasn't even sure whether it was in this Nabil's power to grant it. He wanted only to tell the truth of how this photograph had been taken.

'Remember, I told you this won't change anything. The circumstances matter to me, but it doesn't change a thing.'

'Please, continue.'

Jon nodded and said, 'I knelt down beside him and checked for a pulse, but I didn't need to. As soon as my hand touched his neck, his eyes opened, and he started to mutter something, very quietly, like he was afraid we'd be overheard. I knew he was really bad.' Jon shook his head, the memory of his own helplessness briefly overpowering him again. 'I just didn't know what to do, and in the distance I could hear the Israeli armored cars and I thought, if I could just get out to them, they'd have a medic with them, or there might be an ambulance. I put my camera down and I went to leave, but he grabbed my arm and I couldn't understand what he was saying but I could see it in his face, that he didn't want me to go, and I knew he was dying and there was nothing I could do. The injury was bad. He'd lost a lot of blood. And he looked so alone – I'd never noticed that before. So I just held his hand and I looked at him. I was muttering back to him, telling him I was still there.' Jon could feel tears in his eyes, but they weren't stacked up enough to run down onto his cheeks, and he didn't want them to because he didn't want any sympathy. 'I couldn't save him. All the horrors I've witnessed, all the death and mutilation, but I didn't know how to save that boy.'

Nabil was staring at him blankly, overcome with the onslaught of new information about his son's death.

'You stayed with him? Till he died?'

'It wasn't long after that. It was almost like he'd been waiting for someone to find him, so that he didn't die alone. And he didn't die alone, I gave him that much, but another person could have saved him, I'm sure of it. That's why I stopped being a war photographer.'

'Because you watched my son die?'

'I've seen plenty of kids die. No, it was because I had the illusion of detachment snatched away from me, and once you've lost that, you never get it back.' Jon put the picture back on the chair and took one last look at it. He was glad it was over. 'You can call Dan in now. I'm ready.'

Without looking at him, Nabil walked across to the door and opened it. Jon could see Dan sitting on the top step outside. He jumped up and by the time he came into the room, his gun was already in his hand. It would be quick, Jon told himself, and it would be done.

Dan looked at Nabil, surprised that he was still there, and said, 'Wouldn't you prefer to leave first?'

'No, but there's no need for the gun. You can take him back.'

Dan shrugged, expressing no emotional response, no disappointment, no relief, and said simply, 'You do realise this doesn't change anything?'

He was talking about the fee and Nabil nodded and said, 'Of course, and I'm sorry if I've wasted your time.'

'Time's never wasted,' said Dan, smiling.

Nabil finally looked at Jon again. 'It's some comfort that you were with my son in his final moments, but that isn't why I'm sparing you. I was determined to kill the man who took that picture because I knew he had absolutely no understanding of what he'd done by taking it. I was wrong. I see now, you did understand.'

'That once, I understood. But there are thousands of mothers and fathers out there to whom I could offer no answers, none at all.'

The grieving father in front of him said no more. He offered Jon his hand, and when he shook it, he was surprised to find his own palm clammy and Nabil's dry as parchment. Nabil must have given some slight signal then, because Dan touched Jon on the elbow and the two of them left.

He looked back before descending the stairs. Nabil was sitting in the chair he'd occupied himself, and he was staring at the picture of his son, broken, the universe refusing to reform itself around him. Jon wished he could go back in there and say something else to comfort him, but he'd already given him everything he had.

The driver had gone, and Dan drove back with Jon in the passenger street. He still didn't recognize this part of London. At first neither of them spoke, but after a few minutes, Dan said, 'What the bloody hell happened back there?'

'I don't know.' Jon tried to think back, but all he could think of was Dan coming in with his gun already drawn, then his insistence on getting his fee. 'You would have killed me, wouldn't you? I mean, you wouldn't have given it a second thought.'

'Of course. But I thought I explained all of that. I wouldn't have been killing *you*, Jonathan Hoyle, I just would have been hitting a target.'

Jon smiled. He could imagine this guy being completely untroubled by what he did, sleeping well, walking lightly through the world. He'd been like that himself once, and maybe Dan's moment would also come, but he doubted it somehow.

He'd killed people, he'd saved people, he'd inhabited the same world as Jon, and on at least one occasion, they'd even crossed paths. But Dan Borowski was a natural in that world, someone who wore death easily and saw it for what it was.

No doubt if Dan had found the young Nabil dying in the ruins, he'd have known what to do. If the boy could have been saved, Dan would have left him and gone for help. If he couldn't, Dan would have stayed with him, just as Jon had, but when it was all done, he'd have left it behind.

'When you were talking earlier, about our jobs being similar, you missed something.'

Dan glanced over, casually curious, and said, 'What's that?'

'The need to detach what you're doing from the individual on the end of it – your target, my subject.'

Dan nodded, and at first it didn't look like he'd respond further, but then he said, 'I wonder how many people around the world have died since I picked you up earlier. Hundreds? Thousands? It doesn't matter. None of those lives matter to us. If I'd killed you tonight, the vast majority of the world's population wouldn't have even known about it. If I die tomorrow, it won't matter to anyone. So you see, it's just not worth thinking about. I live well, and that's enough for me. Should be enough for you too.'

Jon nodded, even though he felt like he needed a few minutes to work out what Dan had just said – on first pass, it wasn't much clearer than the crocodile story. Then he realised that they'd turned into Dorchester Street and a moment later Dan had pulled up outside the gallery.

'Oh, God, sorry mate, I've brought you back to the gallery. I'll take you to the hotel.'

'No, this is fine, really. After everything that's happened, I could use the fresh air.'

Dan laughed and said, 'I bet!' He looked serious then as he added, 'It's been a pleasure, Jon, and for what it's worth, I think you handled yourself really bloody well. Not many people would've stayed calm like that.'

'I had nothing to lose.' He smiled and said, 'So long, Dan.'

'You take care now.'

Jon got out of the car and watched as Dan pulled away. He heard his name then and turned to see Sophie coming out of the gallery, her coat on, bag over her shoulder, catalogue under one arm. She managed to lock the door without putting anything on the floor, then walked over to him.

'Hi, what are you still doing here?'

'Long story. I was somewhere else, and then I got dropped off here by mistake.' She smiled, showing interest, the slightly awkward way people did when they felt they had to be interested but weren't really. 'Sorry, don't let me keep you. I'm sure you wanna get home.'

'No, it's fine. I don't have anything to rush back for.' Maybe he needed to go back to photographing people in some form or other because it seemed he'd read her completely wrong.

'Well, I'm only heading back to the hotel – would you like to come back for dinner?'

She looked staggered, maybe even suspecting he wasn't serious, as she said, 'I'd love to, but do you mind? The general word is that you don't care for company.'

'I never used to.'

They started to walk and he couldn't help but smile. A contract killer named Dan Borowski had shot him in the head this evening, a death he'd accepted, even embraced – from now on, everything else was a gift.

BAG MAN

LAVIE TIDHAR

1.

'How come you never got married, Max?'

He was sitting on the edge of the bed putting on his socks and shoes. Marina reclined in the bed. The street light outside the window cast her face in a yellow glow.

'Who says I didn't?'

He pulled up his trousers and buckled his belt and smoothed the crease in his trousers and put on his gun. He had one strapped to his leg and another under the coat and he also had a knife, just in case. The briefcase was on the floor beside the bed.

'I never figured you for the marrying kind.'

Marina had been a working girl in the past but now she ran a flower shop and she and Max had an understanding. And he didn't normally say any damn thing so why was he being chatty tonight? He thought of Sylvie in Marseilles and the boy, who might even have grown-up children of his own by now, it had been nearly forty years since he'd gone and left them. When he came to Israel he joined the army, full of enthusiasm, a patriotism he'd never quite lost. Never quite lost the accent, either.

These days he barely remembered what she had looked like, even her smell. He wondered vaguely if she was still alive. But he'd done what was best.

'It wouldn't be fair,' he said. 'Considering.'

You can't lose what you never had, he thought. Put on his wristwatch. Sat down again and ran his hand along Marina's smooth leg, fondly. 'I have to go,' he said.

'You always have to go,' she said.

Max shrugged. Picked up the briefcase and went to the door. 'A man's got to work,' he said.

'And you're more honest than most,' she said, and laughed, showing small white teeth. 'What's in the case, Max? Guns? Money? Pills?'

'I don't know,' he said. He really didn't, and he didn't care. 'I just know where to pick it up and where to drop it off.'

Truth was Benny was keeping him mostly on ice for a few months after that job in the Negev went bad. A Bedouin clan had been muscling in on some of Benny's southern territory and he'd sent Max to take care of things, and Max did, he'd left two bodies behind him in Rahat but they caught up with him as he was driving back along the lonely desert road and they filled his rented car with bullets. He was lucky to still be alive, he'd run into one of the dry wadis and before they could come after him a border police patrol showed up and the Bedouins made themselves scarce. But it had been close and he wasn't getting any younger, sixty was coming up on him like a brick wall.

He tried to remember what it felt like, the pursuit and running through the dry riverbed, thinking they were coming behind with their AKs. For a moment it felt like being a kid again, playing cowboys and Indians. It should have been horrifying: instead it was a rush.

He smiled at Marina as he left. Went down the stairs with the briefcase in his hand. A kiddie job. He hummed a song, something even older than himself. Opened the door to the street and stepped outside still humming.

2.

'On the *ground*, motherfucker,' Pinky said. Pinky was hopped up on speed and he felt like he was flying. He perched on the seat of his bicycle and aimed the gun at the old man with the briefcase.

There were four of them on bicycles, training guns on the old dude. They'd waited outside in the shadows until the light came on in the upstairs apartment where that old Russian whore lived. It was so easy it was laughable. He wanted to laugh. His teeth were chattering from the speed and he couldn't make them stop. 'Hand over the briefcase, slowly.'

The old man didn't put up a fight. He looked very calm, which annoyed Pinky. Pinky was seventeen and he didn't like old people, with the exception of his grandmother, who let him stay with her and sometimes cooked him roast chicken with paprika in the oven, which he loved, but who most of the time just sat by the window with a sad, resigned look on her face.

Apart from old people, Pinky didn't like African refugees, Filipino workers, Russian immigrants in general, beggars, teachers, fat people, stuck-up girls who wouldn't talk to him, Arabs (obviously),

Orthodox Jews (obviously), social workers and, of course, the police.

He hefted the briefcase in his hand wondering what was in it. It felt light but not too light. He grinned like a maniac and his teeth chattered. 'That's it,' he said. 'Stay on the ground, old man.'

The old man didn't say anything, just lay there, looking up at Pinky like he was memorising his face.

'Did I say you can look at me!' Pinky screamed. The window overhead opened and the Russian whore stuck her ugly face out and Pinky raised the gun and she quickly withdrew.

'Come on, Pinky, let's go,' Bilbo said. They called him Bilbo because he was small and hairy. It was either that or, sometimes, Toilet Brush.

'Shut up!' Pinky said. 'I said no names!'

'Sorry, Pinky. I mean—'

'You want me to shoot you myself?' Pinky waved the gun at Bilbo.

'I'm sorry, I'm sorry,' Bilbo said. His real name was Chaim, which was even worse than Toilet Brush, or at least that's what Pinky always figured.

'Take the case and go,' the old man said. His tone annoyed Pinky. He climbed off the bike.

'I already did,' he said.

'Good for you,' the old man said.

'Fuck you!' Pinky said, and he kicked the old man viciously in the ribs. The old man grunted but didn't say a thing.

'Come on, man!' Rambo said. Rambo was big and stupid but he was loyal. Pinky hawked up phlegm and spat on the old man but missed him and the spit landed on the pavement near the old man's face. Pinky got back on the bike and then, just to prove he could, he aimed the gun up at the sky and squeezed off a shot. It inadvertently hit the street light, which exploded loudly, startling all of them and scattering glass on the ground.

'Shit!' Rambo said. Pinky's heart was beating to a drum and bass track. They got on their bikes and pedalled away as quickly as they could, whooping into the night.

3.

Max got up and brushed glass shards off his trousers. Marina stuck her head out of the window, and he could see her in silhouette against the light of the moon. 'Get back inside,' he said, gently.

For a moment there he thought that punk kid was going to shoot him. What a way to go, he thought. Shot by some kid on a dirty street in the old bus station area. They didn't even pat him down for his guns.

He didn't really care who they were, but he wanted to know who had employed them to rob him.

He began to walk, humming softly to himself. At this time of night the old bus station area was coming alive as its residents, mostly foreign migrant workers and refugees, returned home to their slum-like apartments. The bars and shebeens, always open, became busier. The junkies, who came from all over the city, congregated on the burnt remains of the old terminal building, and the sex shops and what was left of the brothels welcomed their furtive johns with tired indifference.

But there was beauty here, too, Max thought, passing a stall selling flowers, roses and chrysanthemums, anemones, poppies.

They scented the air, joining the smells from the nearby shawarma stand where suicide bombers twice blew themselves up, the smell of cumin and garlic and lamb fat. Two Filipino kids, up late, played football by a butcher stall, where a man in a stained apron methodically cut chops out of the carcass of a pig, using the cleaver with a proficiency Max admired.

He wove his way deeper into the maze of narrow streets, crumbling building fronts, faded shop signs. A young white girl with needle marks on her arms tried to entice him into a dark hallway, lethargically. He waved her away. The night was still young and boys will be boys, but he had a feeling it won't be as easy as that. He reached the front of a store that said *Bookshop* overhead. Dusty textbooks in the window, geography books by the long-deceased Y. Paporish with maps that showed countries which no longer existed. Max let himself in.

A bell dinged as he stepped through. The shop was dark and dusty, with books piled everywhere, paperbacks in English and French, forgotten Hebrew novels and ancient comics hung up by a string, their pages fluttering sadly like the wings of dead butterflies.

Hanging on the wall was a detailed artist's illustration of the imagined future of Tel Aviv's central bus station. It showed a graceful tower rising into the sky, a sort of 1950s retrofuturistic construction decorated with spiral bridgeways and floating flower gardens, and showed happy, well-fed, well-dressed residents, the men in suits and ties and the women in floral dresses, all smiling and holding hands as they beheld this miracle of engineering.

'Makes you cry, doesn't it?' a voice said. Max turned and saw Mr Bentovich, the ancient proprietor, a small pale man who always seemed to Max to resemble a particularly inedible and quite likely poisonous mushroom.

'Didn't see you there, Bento.'

'You're being familiar again, Max. I don't like people being familiar.'

'Sorry, Mr Bentovich.'

They shook hands. Bento's was moist and cold. His touch made Max shudder. They stood there and admired the artist's impression of what the future most decidedly did not look like. 'To what do I owe the pleasure, Max? You're not here to do me in, are you?'

Bento laughed, the sound a dry cough in the dusty air of the bookshop. 'Don't get me wrong,' he said. 'If anyone's to do it, I'd rather it was you, Max.'

'I'm flattered.'

'What do you want?' Bento said. 'I'm up on my payments to Benny.' He went behind the counter and when Max looked at him he knew Bento had his hand, under the desk, on the butt of a gun. He shook his head, raised his hands. 'I come in peace,' he said.

'I hate this place,' Bento said. His little wizened face looked like it would cry. 'I used to sell books, Max. Books!'

'I know, Bent—Mr Bentovich. I know. How's business, though?'

Bento shrugged. 'Alright,' he said. He pushed a hidden button on the desk and the top sprung open and he swept his hand majestically as if to say, Take your pick.

The desk was divided into compartments and in each one Max saw dried fungus, cubes of hashish, pre-rolled joints, moist cannabis sativa, pills, more pills, even more pills, and a bag of mints – 'For my throat,' Bento said when he saw Max's look.

'Sell to kids, much?'

'From where I'm standing,' Bento said, morosely, 'everyone's a kid, Max. Even you.'

'I'm looking for one kid in particular,' Max said. 'About seventeen, pre-army. A little shit.'

'They're *all* little shits, Max. Can I offer you anything? On the house. You need some Viagra? Cialis? Something to keep your pecker up?'

'I need what you know, Bento,' Max said, and the friendliness was gone from his voice, and this time Bento didn't correct him on the use of his name. 'About a little shit called Pinky, who has three friends even stupider than he is.'

'Pinky, Pinky,' the old bookseller said, 'now, why would I know a Pinky?'

'Because he was as high as a kite the last time I saw him,' Max said, 'which was not that long ago, Bento. Not that long ago at all. You sell diet pills?'

'I sell everything, Max,' Bento said, reproachfully. 'You mean amphetamines?'

'Why are you fucking with me, Bento?' Max said. 'You know who I'm after. So why are we playing games? What are you after?'

'I'll tell you what I'm not after, Max. I'm not after any trouble.'

'And why would there be trouble?'

Bento just shrugged, which made Max wary.

'Who is this kid?' he said.

'He's just a punk,' Bento said.

'Who is he working for?'

Bento laughed. 'Working for?' he said. 'Who'd employ a moron like that.'

'I don't know, Bento,' Max said, patiently. 'That's why I asked.'

'Why the interest, anyway?' Bento said.

'Do you always answer a question with a question?'

'Do you?'

Max sighed and pulled out his gun and put the muzzle against Bento's forehead. Bento stood very still and his eyes were large and jumped around too much: they were the only animated feature of his face. 'You dip into your own merchandise?' Max said.

'You try being stuck in here all day dealing with scum,' Bento said. 'Those kids would be the death of me one day. You know someone got done just outside my front door? The other side of the road. Eritrean or Somali, one of those guys.'

'I'm sorry for your loss,' Max said.

'Wise guy,' Bento said. 'Can you take the gun away, please?'

'Since you said please,' Max said. 'No. Tell me where I can find Pinky.'

Bento's face twisted in a sudden grimace of hatred, but whether it was of Max, of the kids, or of the circumstances that led him here, to this dismal bookshop in the modern ghetto of the old bus station of Tel Aviv, Max couldn't say.

'He and his little friends squat in an abandoned flat on Wolfson,' Bento said.

'Yes?'

Bento gave him the address. Max made the gun disappear. When Max was at the door Bento said, 'Max?' and Max said, 'Yes?' turning around to face him.

'Don't come back here,' Bento said.

'I hope I don't have to,' Max said, and he saw the old bookseller scowl.

4.

He had the feeling he was being watched as he walked to the address Bento gave him. A vague sense of unease that grew with each step, but he could see no one, could only trust his instinct, and he thought, they will come in good time. First he had his business to take care of.

It was a rundown building on a rundown street and it didn't take much to break the lock on the downstairs door. The stairwell was unlit and smelled of piss and as he climbed the floors he saw four pairs of bicycles chained to the railings. He reached the third floor and an unpainted door and kicked it open and walked inside with his gun drawn.

Five pairs of eyes turned to stare at him in mute shock. They were sitting on a couple of couches rescued from a dumpster and the air was thick with the smell of Bento's dope.

'Hello, Pinky.'

'What the fuck.' Pinky reached under the cushion for a gun. Max fired, once, the bullet sinking into the dirty stuffing of the couch, sending up a plume of dust and crumbly foam.

'Shit, man,' Pinky said. His movements were jerky, delayed with shock and drugs.

'The next one will be in your brains,' Max said, 'if you had any.'

The short fat kid started to laugh.

'Shut the fuck up, Bilbo,' Pinky said.

There were four boys and a girl. She looked up at Max with stoned, uncurious eyes.

'Get out,' he said. He motioned with his gun.

'Me, mister?'

'You. Leave.'

'But I only just got here.'

'Do I have to ask you twice?'

'Can I at least take the dope?' the girl said.

Max shrugged. 'Why not,' he said.

'Hey!' Bilbo said.

'Shut up, Bilbo,' Max said.

The girl went through the boys' effects and pocketed weed, pills and money.

'Bitch,' Pinky said. She stuck her tongue at him.

'Are you going to shoot them, mister?' she said when she was almost at the door.

'I don't know,' Max said, 'what do you think?'

She shrugged. 'It's a free country,' she said.

She disappeared outside and Max returned to the business at hand. 'Where is my briefcase?' he said.

'Look, we didn't mean nothing, it was just—'

Max shot Pinky in the knee.

The boy screamed, a high-pitched cry that filled the room and leaked like snot to the street outside. The other boys huddled in their seats, staring at Max with frightened stoned eyes.

'Where's my briefcase?'

'It's not here!' It was the fat kid, Bilbo. 'We didn't have nothing to do with it, honestly, mister, it was just a job! He said it was nothing, just taking something from an old guy and—'

'He?' Max said.

'Bogdan,' Pinky said, crying. He was going into shock. 'It was Bogdan, it was Bogdan!'

'Ah,' Max said. He almost felt sorry for the kids.

Almost.

'You gave him the briefcase?'

'Soon as we left you. Then we scored some weed and came home.'

'We really didn't mean nothing, mister. We weren't going to really shoot you or anything.'

'I need a doctor! Call an ambulance!'

'You don't need an ambulance yet,' Max said. He surveyed the four boys. Shook his head. What was Bogdan thinking, using these clowns? They didn't even shave properly yet.

He said, 'Look, I'm going to give you a choice.'

They looked at him but didn't say anything. Good. Max said, 'I can either shoot you now—'

'Please don't!'

He waited for them to calm down. 'Or,' he said, waving the gun at the narrow balcony, 'you could take yourselves over there and jump.'

'You what?'

'Are you crazy, mister?'

'Or I could shoot you where you are.'

The boys looked at each other, pale and frightened. Pinky moaned softly, his hands round his ruined leg.

'You'd have to pick him up and throw him over,' Max said. 'I don't think he can make it on his own.'

'Please, mister!'

'It's not that far down,' Max said. 'I figure you'll probably break a few bones but you're young, your bodies are still flexible. You might live.'

He waved the gun. 'Come on,' he said. 'I haven't got all night to stay and chat.'

'Please! We'll get you back the case!'

'From Bogdan?'

They looked down at the floor.

'I'm going to count down from three,' Max said, 'starting with you,' he pointed at a big lump of a boy. 'What's your name?'

'Rambo,' the boy mumbled.

'Well, Rambo,' Max said. 'Help your friend Pinky there get to his feet. Three, two, one—'

'OK, alright! You don't have to count so quickly!' The boy jumped to his feet. He went over to Pinky.

'Come on, Pinky,' he said. He slung Pinky's arm over his shoulders and lifted him up. Pinky was crying, snot was running down the front of his shirt.

'You, Bilbo, and you, what's your name?'

'Danny?' the boy said.

'I don't know,' Max said. 'Is it?'

'What?'

'Just get over there,' Max said. The three boys and the wounded Pinky made their way slowly to the balcony. The balcony doors were open. A warm breeze wafted into the room and the marijuana smoke made its way out to the street.

'What's it going to be?' Max said.

The boys looked down to the street. Looked back at Max and his gun. He smiled at them without humour. 'Well?'

'Shit,' Rambo said. 'We just wanted to get high.' He picked up Pinky and before anyone could say anything to stop him he threw him over the railings.

Pinky disappeared over the balcony and dropped. There was a short scream and then a thud. They all looked over the balcony. Pinky lay on the asphalt with his leg at an angle and his head caved in.

'Doesn't look too bad,' Max said.

The small kid, Danny, panicked. He rushed Max, almost knocking him back, and made for the door. Max fired once, twice, and hit the kid in the back. Danny fell, his hand still on the door handle. He didn't get up.

Max stood up and looked at Bilbo and the big kid. 'Well?' he said.

'Please,' Rambo said. 'Please.'

Bilbo was crying.

Max said nothing.

The two boys held hands. They looked over the railing. 'Help me up,' Bilbo said. He was struggling to climb over the railing. Rambo made an impatient motion and pushed him, and Bilbo flapped his arms in the air as he lost his balance and then he, too, dropped with a high-pitched scream. Rambo was the last to go. He dove almost like an athlete, as if he were diving into a pool. Max looked down and saw that he'd landed on the fat kid's body.

Max pocketed the gun and stepped over the small kid's body and left the flat.

5.

When he left the building the stars had gone and he thought it was going to rain. Someone was screaming from an open window. The kids were lying on the ground where they fell like rain.

Max walked away from them when someone took a shot at him.

It had come from somewhere to his left ahead and he was already moving, taking the corner and seeing two dark figures holding guns both levelled at him. He fired and one went down and the other yelled something in Arabic and behind him Max heard running footsteps and he knew they'd finally caught up with him.

'Listen,' he said, 'it was just a job, it wasn't personal.'

The man had a gun to his face and behind him more men blocked the passageway. There was no way out. The man came out of the shadows. He was a thin young man in worn jeans and a chequered shirt, and he had deeply tanned skin. On his head he wore a red Bedouin keffiyeh.

'Shut up,' he said. He raised his gun and slapped Max hard with it. The pain seared through Max's head. He tasted blood. The man gestured. Max turned. Three other men stood there training guns on him.

'Start moving.'

If they wanted him dead he would already be dead, he thought. He followed them down the road. They left the one man's corpse behind them. A dusty jeep was parked by the side of the road.

'Get in.'

Max stopped and just stood there.

'Don't make me shoot you,' the man said. 'First I'll shoot you in the leg. You're not going to die yet. Not for a long time yet.'

The other men laughed and Max felt a cold fury rising in him. He heard police sirens in the distance. One of the neighbours would have rang up the emergency services by now, for the kids.

Max said, 'I can't.'

'What do you mean you can't?'

'I have a package to deliver.'

'What sort of package?'

'Drugs, money. I don't know. A kidney maybe.'

'You don't know.'

'I don't know. But I just killed at least two kids to keep it.'

He heard them conferring though he did not understand the words.

'Where is it?'

'Someone took it.'

'Who?'

'A guy called Bogdan.'

'Who does the package belong to?'

'Benny,' Max said. 'It belongs to Benny.'

He heard the man spit on the ground. 'Benny sent you? To kill my father?'

'He did.'

The Bedouin laughed. 'Then we will go get your package, Mr Max,' he said. 'And then we will pay Benny a visit.'

They shoved him into the back of the car. Piled in on either side of him, taciturn men with the warmth of the desert. 'What's your name?' Max said.

'Ashraf,' the man said. He was sitting up front in the passenger seat. Turned and scrutinised Max. 'Who is this Bogdan?' he said.

'He is a dangerous man in a world of dangerous men,' Max said, and Ashraf laughed, and the other men followed suit.

'What is he, *mafiya*?' Ashraf said.

Max nodded. Ashram studied him. Behind them police cars with flashing blue lights congregated on Wolfson. 'Not a friend of yours, then?'

'He and Benny had a disagreement,' Max said. He might as well be honest. He wasn't sure he was going to live through this, but losing the briefcase annoyed him all the same.

'I'm sorry about your father,' he said.

Ashraf slapped him. 'You're not worthy of saying his name,' he said. But Max had forgotten what the old Bedouin's name was.

He had come into the yard before the trailer, with a permanent fire burning in the yard and the skeleton of a Tel Aviv car suspended on a jack, stripped bare of its components, and two small children playing backgammon with an intensity that didn't allow them to even glance at him. He came in his car and the old man and two bodyguards stepped out with AKs and he shot before they had a chance to shoot him, putting down the old man with a bullet to the head and one bodyguard in the chest shot and the other with a gutshot. Then he drove away: the whole thing did not take a minute.

'You could have caught me sooner,' he said, thinking of the cars chasing him down the Arava road, and of his desperate dash into the dunes. 'If it wasn't for the border police.'

Ashraf laughed without humour. 'Well,' he said. 'We caught up with you now.'

He looked at Max with uncurious eyes. 'Where is this Bogdan?' he said.

So Max told him.

6.

It was a Bauhaus building on the edge of the old neighbourhood. It resembled a ship, with a rounded foredeck and small round porthole windows. It was two stories high and the paint job was peeling badly.

They watched it from the jeep. There were two bulky men outside, packing under their coats. The only door was reinforced steel. No one came in or out of the building.

The Bedouins were organising. Ashraf barked orders and the men disappeared from the car. One had a sniper rifle, Israeli military issue. Then it was just Ashraf and Max and the driver in the car.

'Remember,' Ashraf said, and smiled without humour. 'The first bullet's for you.'

'Yeah, yeah,' Max said. He stepped out of the car. He did not like the plan. Not that there really was a plan. He walked to the building's entrance.

'Stop right there.' They were two large Russians and now they brought up guns. Max stopped and raised his hands, palms forward. 'I'm not carrying,' he said.

'That's smart,' the one on the left said.

Max knew him slightly. 'Leonid,' he said, nodding.

'Max,' Leonid said. He smirked. The other one Max didn't know. 'You sore?'

'A little,' Max admitted. 'Sending *kids*?'

Leonid smirked wider. 'Boss wanted the package,' he said.

'What's *in* the package?' Max said. Leonid shrugged. 'What do I know,' he said. 'I just work here.'

'Can I see him?'

'Why? You want to ask for it back?'

Leonid said something in Russian and the other man laughed.

'I thought Bogdan and Benny had an understanding,' Max said. Leonid shrugged again. Opened his mouth to say something and never finished the thought.

There were two cracks in the night and Leonid's head disappeared. He crumpled by the door. The other man was down. Whoever Ashraf's shooter was, he was well-trained. The two other men ran crouching to the door and attached a small explosive device. Max flattened himself against the wall when the explosion came. It tore the door off its hinges and blasted it in. The Bedouins were already moving, Ashraf and two of his men, the unseen sniper still there, Max thought. Ashraf pushed Max roughly, first through the door. It was full of smoke and debris inside. It was hard to see, which was when Max elbowed Ashraf in the face, broke his nose, and reached for the man's gun hand. The gun fired but missed. Then Max broke two of Ashraf's fingers and took hold of the gun. He was going to shoot Ashraf but there was a blast of machine-gun fire and Max dropped to the ground. He crawled through smoke and the firefly flashes of tracer bullets. Soft grunts and the sound of falling bodies behind him. He saw the shooter through the smoke and raised Ashraf's gun and fired. The shooter fell back and suddenly there was silence. It hurt Max's ears. He stood cautiously and stepped forward.

'*Don't* fucking move, Max.'

'Bogdan.'

The gun was stuck in Max's ribs.

'Drop it, Max.'

'It wasn't my idea, Bogdan. It was these Bedouins.'

'I said drop it, Max.'

'Where's the briefcase, Bogdan?'

Bogdan laughed. 'I wish I could have seen your face when those kids robbed you,' he said.

'You can see my face now,' Max said. 'Am I laughing?'

'The gun, Max.'

Max dropped the gun.

'Good, good.'

The smoke was clearing. There were bodies on the ground.

Max said, 'There's still a sniper outside.'

Men were streaming past Max and Bogdan, heading outside. Max heard shots. Bogdan said, 'Not for much longer.'

'I just want the briefcase, Bogdan.'

'You have some nerve, Max. I'll give you that.'

'Hey, I was going to ask nicely.'

The gun didn't leave his side. Max took a deep breath, coughed. He said, 'Look what I've got.' Pulled back his coat. Showed Bogdan's the Bedouins' final joke.

'Fuck me, Max, when did you join the Palestinian resistance?' Bogdan said. He took a step back. They'd wired Max up with explosives and a dead man's switch.

'Drop the gun, Bogdan,' Max said. He bent down and picked up his own gun. There was no reason, he just felt more comfortable that way.

'Take it easy, Max,' Bogdan said. 'I can help you. I've got guys can disarm that thing in a minute if you let them.'

'And where will we be then, Bogdan?' Max said. 'No, I'll take my chances. Maybe I could go into business as a walking bomb.'

'Just don't try boarding a plane,' Bogdan said. 'You know how they are at the airport about these things.'

'And I was just thinking how nice it would be to take a holiday,' Max said. 'Where's the case, Bogdan?'

He sensed men behind him. Sensed guns trained on him. Smiled. Went to Bogdan and smashed him across the face with the gun. Bogdan stared up at him in hatred.

'This isn't over,' he said.

Max took Bogdan's gun and pocketed it. Stuck his own gun in Bogdan's ribs. Thought that every moment could be his last. Wondered how stable the explosives were.

'You're staying close to me,' he said.

'Isn't over,' Bogdan said. He led Max deeper into the building, into a room on the second floor. Bogdan's men followed silently but didn't fire. It was a regular office room with filing cabinets and a desk. There was a bottle of arak on the table. Max helped himself to the bottle, drank, the aniseed flavour smooth on his throat. The alcohol burned pleasantly. He figured he'd earned himself a drink.

Bogdan reached under the desk and brought out the case. Max ran his fingers on it. The lock was intact.

'You didn't open it?' he said.

'It isn't for me,' Bogdan said.

'Then who for?'

'For your mother, the whore,' Bogdan said.

Max sighed. 'Come on,' he said. He picked up the case. 'You go first.'

'You're mad if you think you can get away with it.'

'I'm just doing my job,' Max said. For the first time he felt his composure slipping. It's been a long night. '*You* robbed *me!*'

'If I knew you were going to be such a bitch about it I'd have just told those kids to shoot you.'

'We all make mistakes,' Max said.

He pushed Bogdan out the door and down the stairs. Bogdan's men parted silently before them. Max felt that every moment he could get a bullet in the back, but he didn't.

He pushed Bogdan past Ashraf's corpse and what remained of the door and then over Leonid. The Bedouins' jeep was still there, the driver slumped in the seat with his head at an unnatural angle. The windows were broken and the frame riddled with bullet holes but the wheels were intact. They went to the car and Max opened the door and pulled the driver's corpse out and climbed in. There was blood on the steering wheel. Max kept his gun trained on Bogdan's face.

'I'll be seeing you again, Max,' Bogdan said. 'Real soon.'

Max sighed. The key was in the ignition. He turned the key and the jeep came alive and he felt it buck and shudder beneath him.

'Oh, fuck it,' he said, and shot Bogdan in the face.

A storm of bullets started up as Bogdan fell; but Max's foot was already on the accelerator and he drove away, expecting to be blown up at every moment, bullets pinging into the chassis and the doors and he wondered what suicide bombers prayed to, the moment before they blew up.

But he got away and the gunfire receded behind him. One wheel was out but he didn't care, he manoeuvred the car away from Bogdan's Bauhaus building, away from the gunshots, all the dead men and the dead or dying Bogdan, who, even if he lived, would never smile again, if he ever did.

He ditched the car three blocks away, knowing they would come after him but he had the case, that was the important thing. He went into the night and the night's velvety darkness sang to him with the cry of the dead and the wail of police sirens.

7.

'Did you have any problems?' Benny said.

'Nothing I couldn't handle.'

It was the next day and he was at the Market Porter, an old, faded Persian restaurant Benny favoured as his informal office. Faded pictures on the walls of television actors famous three decades in the past. The smell of greasy lamb cooking on a spit.

He'd gone to see an old friend from the army who cut him out of the bomb vest and seemed happy to accept the explosives in lieu of payment. They would go on the open market and – who knew? – perhaps end up strapped to a genuine suicide bomber. There was always a market for explosives.

Max didn't care. He'd taken a room in a boarding house for the night and slept deeply and well and then went to see Benny in the morning.

'You're late,' Benny said.

Max put the briefcase on the table. 'I'm here, aren't I?' he said.

Benny pushed aside the newspaper he'd been reading. Dominating the front page was a picture of dead men in front of a Bauhaus building shaped like a ship and, at the bottom, a news item about the shocking torture meted out to a group of young thugs, three of whom were dead and one still in intensive care.

'I suppose you are,' Benny said. He took out a thick envelope and tossed it to Max, who caught it one handed.

'Thanks.'

'Don't mention it.' Benny stood up to go, picking up the briefcase. 'I might as well pull you off light duty,' he said. 'Seeing as you can't seem to keep away from trouble either way.'

Max smiled. As Benny went to leave he said, 'What's in the case?'

Benny turned by the restaurant door and looked back at him. 'Does it matter?' he said.

Max thought about it. Sunlight rippled through the windows into the gloom of the restaurant.

'No,' he said. 'I suppose not.'

THE WASHING

CHRISTOPHER FOWLER

The first time the bell rang, Linda was supervising the last of the crates. The front door of the flat was wedged open, so she was surprised that someone had bothered to ring at all. Spain, she thought, wiping her hands and heading along the corridor, they're more formal here than at home. Their circumstances are different.

The man standing before her was sixtyish, sturdy and balding, with a wart the size of a marrowfat pea on the side of his nose. He wore a dark grey suit with a formal waistcoat and a watch-chain, and must have been boiling. He regarded her over the top of his half-moon glasses and did not smile.

'You are new,' he said in heavily accented English. He pointed accusingly at the door. 'This is wrong.'

She looked at the wet paint in surprise. It was a warm brown, the colour you'd get if you mixed plums into chocolate.

'We just painted it,' she explained. 'It's the same as all the other doors in the building.'

He was taken aback by her English accent. 'It is not like the others at all, Madam. It is the wrong colour. It must be repainted at once.' He managed to suggest that there would be dire consequences if it wasn't.

'The painter assures me it will dry lighter,' she replied cheerfully.

'No no no.' He wagged a nicotine-stained finger at her. 'It is not right. Did you check your lease for the correct colour reference?'

'I don't think so.' Miguel had taken care of the rental agreement. She had not been shown the paperwork and knew there would be an argument if she asked to see it. The best thing with a husband, she found, was to give in and agree, then forget about it. It usually worked with Miguel.

'I'm sorry,' she said. 'I will have it repainted.'

He left without another word. Five minutes later, he returned to issue another statement. 'Your removal van is blocking my car.'

'I'm sorry,' she said again.

He pinned her with a gimlet stare. 'Two sorrys is two too many.' With that he turned and vanished into the gloom of the landing.

The stairwell was unlit. Already she had miscounted the steps and fallen both up and down them. The building was over a hundred years old. Even on the brightest summer day the flat was so dark that she had to put the lights on. The sun reached a peak of fierce intensity at 4 p.m., when the shops were only just opening after their siestas and the breeze from the sea had burned away, leaving hot dead air behind.

There were no cooling ceiling fans because they were not needed; the building's thick brick walls and lack of internal light kept it as cold as a larder. After the removal van had gone, she set about tidying up and putting away the crockery. Unwrapping her mother's coffee cups with great care, she set them out along the kitchen dresser. She had hoped Miguel would help with the unpacking, but he regarded the home as a woman's domain and avoided all forms of household maintenance, as if helping would somehow impugn his masculinity.

The days passed more slowly than they did in England, where the solstices offered less than five hours of daylight and five hours of darkness at their extremes. Here it always seemed to be a type of summer. 4 p.m. was the hour for staying out of the searing sunlight and tackling household chores as slowly as possible. Miguel did not get home until eight, which meant that the afternoons would become interminable if she failed to find a way of occupying the time.

When the bell rang she knew it was someone from within the building, because the inside door had an old-fashioned clockwork bell. There were twelve flats, but she had yet to meet anyone other than Carlos the janitor and Mr Two-Sorrys.

She opened the repainted door to a slender young woman with cropped hair, a long thin neck and slightly protuberant eyes. At least this one knew how to smile, and what a smile! Its corners seemed to reach her ears. 'I am Pippa and I am so sorry,' she began, darting forward to formally offer her hand. 'It is my fault. The baby's sock.'

Linda shook her hand. 'Please, come in.'

Pippa checked the threshold as one might look before crossing a road, then took an exaggerated step inside. 'Oh, this is nice, you have no walls. All this space! We have many more walls, for the children's bedrooms. I have two boys and a baby girl. You must hear them at night. I hope they don't disturb you too much.'

She headed straight for the open windows of the back bedroom. 'The clothesline,' she explained, pointing out and down. Each flat had a rack of three clotheslines outside, attached to the wall with rusted metal arms. A pulley allowed the clothes to be moved some ten feet along the side of the flat. Linda followed her neighbour's pointing finger. 'I live above you,' Pippa told her. 'I go to peg the baby's sock and poof – it fell down onto your line.'

A pink sock not much larger than a man's thumb had landed on one of her towels. Pippa snapped it up and came back inside.

Linda had heard that this technique was used whenever someone needed an excuse to visit a new neighbour. 'Would you like a coffee?' she asked.

Pippa threw up her hands in horror. 'No, no, I do not want to make you work.'

'I'm having one.'

'All right then, just for a moment.' She seated herself swiftly enough and looked around. 'It's nice. You are married?'

'My husband Miguel is from here,' she explained. 'We met in England. He came back to his old job. His company supplies military equipment.' She lit the kettle, glad of the company. The building was grave-silent during the day. At night she sometimes heard dinners being prepared on other floors, and tantalising smells of fried fish, pork stews and *albondigas* drifted up from the courtyard.

'And you, you could just leave everything and come here?' Pippa asked.

'I had to give up my job but yes, I'm afraid there's no arguing with Miguel. He can be very forceful.' She laughed a little too gaily.

'Have you met the others?'

'No, only a rude man who complained about the colour of our door.'

'Ah yes, he is the *prepotente*, you know this word? He thinks he is the boss, yes? Because his brother is a friend of the Generalissimo. I am no friend of Franco. One day he will be gone and then we will speak of better times. But the others here, they have been here since *la Guerra Civil*, they love our great leader so you must be careful what you say.'

'Oh, I am an outsider. I try not to get involved.' Linda liked her instantly. Pippa was open and honest, with an innocence that took risks by showing itself. 'Who else should I know in the building?' she asked.

'Come, come.' Pippa rose and headed back to the window. The building formed a large U shape. The other half was no more than twenty feet away. Twelve racks of washing lines extended from the rear windows. Some bore bedsheets. Others had rows of shorts arranged in ascending sizes. Not all of the lines were used.

'You must always look at these.' Pippa pointed to the racks. 'You may not see anyone on the stairs but you can tell who is in and what they are doing. Look, my two boys.' She pointed up at her own clothesline, upon which were strung two matching football shirts. 'And over there.'

The washing line opposite was full up with stockings, two red blouses, some pairs of frilly knickers, a pretty lace brassiere and a flared white dress covered in blue and yellow irises. Half a dozen paper windmills, red, orange, gold and silver, turned in a flowerpot hooked to the railing.

'That is the apartment of Maria. She is a dancer at *El Nacional*. She is so pretty.' She shook out her fingers at the thought. '*Muy bonita*. But very poor. She needs to find a husband but the attractive ones are also poor, I think.'

After coffee Linda thanked Pippa for coming down, and they agreed to meet again.

Miguel was nearly always late home. She had expected it would be like this at the start, but had hoped they might settle into more regular hours. After the flat had been decorated there was little else to do, and the streets were too hot to walk through on summer afternoons, so she seated herself by the open bedroom windows. They were shaded by four, so she could sit and read without having to fan herself. She was trying to revise her Spanish from a schoolbook but the effort invariably made her sleepy.

She hardly ever saw anyone on the gloomy central staircase. A couple of times an old lady passed her without saying a word. Pippa came down for coffee once or twice a week. At night Linda heard the squeaking of the pulleys, and knew that her neighbours were hanging out their clothes. Each day she found herself checking the washing lines to see who was in and who had been out the night before.

One afternoon she sat in the shade with a truncated paperback of Cervantes' *Don Quixote* in her lap, and her eyelids grew heavy. A squeak from the window directly opposite woke her. The floor-length glass was always heavily curtained and was never left open more than a few inches.

In place of the usual blouses and the iris dress was a long white cotton gown, a man's formal shirt and a pair of black socks. Down in the courtyard she could see pink and yellow specks of confetti.

'Who is Maria seeing?' she asked Pippa on their next coffee afternoon.

'Didn't I tell you?' Pippa dropped her jaw, appalled. 'She has married *El Prepotente*.'

'Mr Two-Sorrys? No!'

'Yes, very ugly but very powerful. His name is José Masvidal. He's in the military division, the one I told you about with the brother who knows Franco. I don't like him so I did not go to the wedding. Better to smile from a distance than lie close up.' Pippa pulled a face. She was full of peculiar sayings that probably had more impact in their original language. 'Now Maria is married he will never let her go anywhere. She is much younger. She is my friend. I say to her, come dancing with me, and now she is too scared to go.'

'So she's going to stay in all the time?' Linda asked.

'Oh yes, she will not be allowed out in the evenings. It is not respectful, it is *vergonzoso*. You know, shameful. Because she was a dancer and he is a good Catholic in the government.'

Summer turned to autumn. The shadows changed their angle but the temperature barely seemed to fall. She saw less of Pippa because her friend had taken a part-time job in the *mercat*, working in one of their grain stores.

Outside the building opposite, the washing on the line had changed.

Now there were always four large spotlessly white shirts, vests, an old man's drawers, black socks, a shapeless black shift dress and what she'd assumed was underwear belonging to an elderly lady; an arrangement of baggy, beige cotton sacks. The paper windmills had been removed from the flowerpot and a heavy lead crucifix had appeared on the back wall. The woman who passed through the shadows moved with a supple, fluid grace. *She's so young*, Linda thought. *Don't let that happen to me.*

∽

In the late afternoon the clock in the kitchen seemed to slow down. The sun took hours to set. It reached a low point in the reddening sky and just hung there without moving. When Miguel returned he asked her how her day had been, and proceeded to tell her about his without waiting for her reply.

'The man opposite has stopped his new wife from going out,' she said one evening over dinner. 'He's making her wear old lady clothes because they're more respectable.'

'A nightmare of a day today,' said her husband, looking around for his cigarettes. 'Put the radio on, will you?'

The clothes on the line opposite had changed from fancy to plain, from bright blue flowers to charcoal grey, from French scanties to beige drawers. How easy it was to dismantle a woman's personality and replace it with something that smothered and suffocated. In all this time she hardly ever saw the woman behind the washing. She heard the pulley squeak a little before midnight twice a week and always went to look, but it was too dark to see, so she waited until the next morning to look at the line.

One morning she caught a glimpse of Maria in full sunshine, going to the *mercat*. She was slender-waisted and had tumbling auburn hair that shone in the fresh early light. She walked happily, bouncing slightly, swinging her basket, glad to be free.

Linda waited for her return. As Maria approached the building with her groceries she looked apprehensive, as if all her fears were held inside its dark stone walls.

'Your friend doesn't dance anymore?' asked Linda casually over coffee.

Pippa stirred her cup thoughtfully. 'I asked her to come with me but she won't. Sometimes I go by her flat but she doesn't invite me in now.' She lowered her voice as if worried that someone might overhear them. 'It's the husband. He doesn't like me. He's had the walls repainted and has changed the furniture. All of her lovely bright things have gone. He moved in his grandmother's dresser and her armchairs. So dark and heavy. I saw them taking her lovely pink dressing table down the stairs. Such a waste.'

The rains came. Miguel had to travel on business. The trips could last up to a week. For the first time she wondered if she was like Maria, willing to clip her wings for the love of a man. Sometimes she watched Miguel dressing for work and wondered how well she really knew him.

When she went back to her seat by the window and looked across the courtyard on the next washday she was in for a surprise. Maria was at the window. She looked furtively behind her as if to make sure that she was alone, then hung out her old red panties and blouse, taking them in the second they were dry, which in the afternoon sun was only a matter of minutes. Linda wondered if she had taken to going out while her husband was away.

'I've met him a couple of times,' said Miguel over dinner one evening. 'José moves in high circles. He is greatly respected.'

'José from across the courtyard?' she said, surprised, her fork halfway to her mouth.

'He married the local beauty. A bit fast, by all accounts. He had to rein her in a bit.'

'Perhaps it was her job to let him out,' she said defensively.

'I don't know what you mean,' Miguel replied, placing his knife and fork together.

❧

There was now a pattern, she noted. Whenever there were no white shirts and black socks to hang out, her old clothes reappeared. José Masvidal's schedule was not unlike her husband's. He had to travel most at the weekends.

Christmas came and the flat was closed up while they visited each other's families. Pippa went home to see her mother. The building was mostly empty. In January the old pattern continued, but in the middle of February there was another change in the clothesline opposite. A man's shirt with bright blue stripes was hung out to dry beside Maria's sexiest items. José Masvidal would never wear such a shirt. As soon as the items were dry they were hurriedly taken indoors.

'It was a tiring journey,' said Miguel, settling into his armchair beside the radio. 'Across to Zaragoza, and on to a military facility outside Teruel. José was there. We had quite a talk. He's a very nice man.'

'How are things going with his "fast" wife?' she asked, keen for news. It seemed as if the men sometimes found out more than the women.

'He never mentions her,' Miguel admitted vaguely. 'José plays bowls and golf. He likes to tell me when he beats his rivals.'

'Does she go with him?'

'I can't imagine she'd want to watch a group of middle-aged men playing games.' Miguel carefully refolded his copy of *El País*. 'We're visiting military posts over the next four weekends. Make sure you go to church on Sunday mornings.' She studied his face to see if he was joking but found nothing.

All through March the brightly striped shirt appeared on the washing line. Sometimes it was accompanied by racy blue swimming trunks. One afternoon when Pippa came down, Linda asked her about the owner of the clothes.

Pippa's eyes widened. 'You mustn't say!' she cried, shocked. 'Do you know what would happen if he found out? Why, he would have her killed.'

It was Linda's turn to be shocked. 'You don't actually mean—'

'Do you have any idea what goes on when those men go out together? They're on military business.' Pippa pushed her coffee aside and leaned in closer. 'The noisy ones in the towns they visit just disappear. I'm not saying they don't bring it upon themselves but they're certainly sent away somewhere, and often they don't come back. A man is always a danger but like-minded men in a group – they can go too far.'

'Perhaps we should visit Maria to make sure she's okay,' Linda suggested.

'Trust me,' said Pippa, 'she's fine.' She held her painted nails level to the table top. 'So long as everything stays like this. No upsets. It's best for everyone. And it's best you don't know any more.' She flattened her red lips and held a finger against them. 'Yes? For all of us.' There was a bang on the ceiling and a slow rising wail. She listened for a moment, then shrugged. '*Los niños*. Always the boys. One day I swear they will kill each other.'

The flat was so silent at night that the sound of the key in the lock was enough to wake her. She turned on the bedside light and sat up. Miguel came in and set down his briefcase.

'You're back early,' she said. 'I wasn't expecting you for two more days.'

'The trip was cut short.' He unbuttoned his jacket with great concentration and hung it on a chair.

'Oh? Why?'

'It's complicated,' he said wearily. 'Do you really want me to try and explain?'

'Did you come back with your friend José?'

'It's because of him we came back.' He pulled off his shirt and threw it on the floor. 'I need to get some sleep. I'm in early tomorrow.'

By the time she awoke he had already left. She picked up his shirt, washed it and hung it out. The other washing line was empty, and the glass doors remained closed all day.

Later she sat in her seat by the window and read a trashy thriller. When her attention drifted she raised her head and looked across the narrow courtyard. The line was still empty. If José had come back, where were his shirts? She waited by the window, fully expecting that at any moment the glass door opposite would open and the washing would appear, but there was nothing. Miguel called to say he would be later than usual, so she ate alone, the sound of her cutlery ringing in the empty flat.

Just as she was climbing into bed, she heard the squeak of the pulley. She waited until it had finished turning and the door had shut, then crept over to the window without putting on the lights. The white shirts were back, four of them, with four pairs of black socks. And so were the beige old lady drawers. Maria ironed everything first; the creases in the shirts had perfect sharp edges.

The bright striped shirt had stopped appearing on Saturdays. The red blouses and lace underwear did not return. One afternoon the glass door was left open and she could see inside the apartment. It had been painted grey and was dominated by the lead crucifix on the back wall. Linda tried to imagine what had happened. Mr Masvidal had returned early and thrown out the lover. Now his flighty wife was being made to repent her ways. Maria never even went to the shops anymore. Twice a week a crate of groceries appeared outside the door of the Masvidal apartment.

Linda heard from her friends in England. When are you coming back? they asked, but she was unable to give them an answer. Miguel had been promoted and his prospects looked good. Her desire for a child returned, but the doctor had advised against trying again for the sake of her health, so she contented herself with looking after Pippa's boys from time to time.

She missed her old job in England. She had only been cataloguing records in a provincial newspaper office, but she had lost herself in the stories they told. The local library here had a pitiful selection of books in English, so she relied on her sister to send the latest novels from London. She wondered if she could write something herself, perhaps about the dancer who had married the military bureaucrat, hoping for a better life. She bought a notepad and a fountain pen, and sat by the open windows plotting.

The day she started writing, a new dress appeared on the line. It had a little colour, pale primroses around the hem, but its main feature was its size. It was a maternity smock.

Linda could not wait to take coffee with Pippa. 'How far gone is she?' she asked, setting out freshly made *coca de forner* in thick oily slices.

'Five months at least,' said Pippa excitedly. 'Even I didn't know. She's so skinny that she's only just started to put on weight. I thought, 'So, she's eaten a few cakes,' but no, she tells me just the other day.'

'You think this will bring her and José closer together?'

'How can a baby make that much difference? You know what they say: *Lavar cerdos con jabón es perder tiempo y jabón.* Washing pigs is a waste of time and soap.'

'I think it loses something in translation,' said Linda, pouring coffee.

Every Wednesday evening she attended a writing course run by the British Embassy from one of the chambers in their amber stone wedding cake of a building behind the main plaza. There she learned about murders and motives and mysteries with a handful of bewildered elderly ex-pats and a couple from Kenya who found sexual suggestion in every passing remark.

After her latest effort had been picked apart by a stern patrician from Henley-on-Thames who had never recovered from ending up here after failing to get his novel published in England, she went home and prepared dinner for Miguel. It seemed perverse to want to dash through the flat and check the back clotheslines for the latest update, but lately the washing had come to act as a lifeline to the world, a jungle telegraph that told her there were real emotions flailing behind closed curtains and shut windows. Tonight, though, there was nothing. The primrose maternity dress, which always made an appearance on Wednesday nights, failed to materialise.

'Terrible,' said Pippa, barely able to gasp in enough air with the shock of it all. She had brought their usual coffee hour forward to the morning, so desperate was she to share her news. 'She has lost the baby. That pig—' She went to spit but remembered where she was just in time. 'He kicked her. In here.' She waved a bony tanned had over her own non-existent stomach.

'Did Maria tell you that?' asked Linda, wide-eyed.

'No, of course not, she says she slipped on the stairs but I know it was him. She told me the baby was not planned and he has three of his own, from his first wife. I never tell you that?' She waved the missed information aside. 'So, she is in Our Lady of Grace, recovering. The most terrible bruises, right from here to here.'

'But if you think it was her husband something must be done,' said Linda firmly. She looked around the sombre room, trying to imagine a course of action. 'I can talk to my husband and ask him to find out the truth.'

'You must not do such a thing,' Pippa insisted. 'If you tell him then José will know it was me who told you. Promise me you will say nothing.'

Linda promised and the confidence was kept. But the windows opposite had taken on a sinister air that perversely drew her attention, because after Maria returned from the hospital, Linda noticed that something had changed.

Washdays still arrived twice a week and the shirts were pegged out as they always had been, but now they were badly ironed and no longer bleached to a fierce whiteness. The sleeves were grey and patchy, the collars washed without the studs being removed. Each one was hung with a single peg so that it creased badly as it dried. The maternity dress reappeared but had been taken in so that it

215

fitted tightly. Maria was not about to let her husband forget what had happened to their unborn child.

Summer arrived once more and the temperature soared back to its usual lethal intensity. The sky was so blue above the rooftops that it looked like the atmosphere was evaporating into space. Rectangles of fierce light slid slowly across the drawing room's polished floor and over the kitchen tiles, marking off the hours of the day.

One evening Miguel came home in a strangely sour mood. Whenever he was like this she knew it was better to keep away, but tonight there was something about his face that made her ask.

'They say he fell,' Miguel told her, half under his breath. 'The man was as strong as an ox. Every morning he lifted weights, even when we were away attending conferences. I refuse to believe it.'

'Who?' It was so rare that she asked questions, she wondered if she could still be heard. Perhaps her voice had shrivelled to nothing without her noticing.

'José Masvidal,' he snapped back at her, striding about the room. 'He was found at the bottom of the stairs with his head—' Miguel grimaced at the image that had formed inside his own head.

'You mean the marble stairs at the ministry?'

'No, our stairs – the stairs outside his own front door!' Miguel shouted.

Linda had experienced the treachery of the unlit staircase often enough, and wondered if accidents had occurred in the past. She had not ventured up the opposite staircase but could tell it was the same.

'They should put lights on them,' she said. 'The skylights need cleaning and hardly lets in anything. I've nearly fallen there myself. Who found him?'

'*She* did.' He could not bring himself to say her name. 'She says he left for work and something made her go back to the front door. He was lying with his head down, what was left of it. He'd fallen from the top to the bottom. A man like that, as strong as an *ox!*'

She went down and crossed the vestibule of cracked black and white tiles, heading for the other side of the building. As she climbed the darkened stairs she heard a metallic thump and a slide. Carlos the janitor was working his way across the landing with a galvanised bucket and a mop. Water flooded across the tiles.

She looked at the patch he was cleaning. The sticky dark stain on the lowest step was, she noted, roughly the shape of Spain. Carlos was mute, and as a consequence his features were highly expressive. He shrugged at her, rolling his eyes at the door above. He had successfully scrubbed away the marks on the landing. Now he tipped soapy water across the last step, dissolving the Spanish map.

Pippa was next, of course. As Linda started the coffee she stood in the doorway looking up at the ceiling, listening. 'They're asleep, thank goodness,' she said, coming in. 'I brought cake.' Her wide brown eyes spoke volumes. 'I shall be sent to Hell for saying it, but the answers to prayers come in many disguises. He beat her all the time and she did nothing. That was why she could never go out. Her body was black and blue.'

'Have you talked to her?' Linda asked. 'How is she? It must have been awful finding him there.'

'Yes, probably. She is at the police station.'

'Why?' Linda brought over cups and plates, setting them in their usual places. 'Surely they don't suspect her?'

'What, you think she bashed in his head and dragged him to the stairs? Where would she get such a weapon to do this?'

'You've thought it through, then,' Linda observed.

'She is at the police station because she must make a statement,' said Pippa, unwrapping the cake. 'After all, she found his body. I myself think she is in a dangerous situation. Her husband was friends with the captain of police.' She raised a knife over the cake and cut it. 'When Maria was younger and even prettier she was arrested. But the handsome young policemen did not press charges and let her come home.' She left the implication hanging in the air. 'Your husband is also friendly with the police, no?'

'Miguel? He never told me that.'

'There are many things he doesn't tell you, I think.'

'Is there anything we can do for Maria?' she asked, feeling as useless as all who merely observe. 'Perhaps we should go down there and vouch for her character.'

'And how can you do that when you have not properly met her? No, we must pray for her,' said Pippa with finality. 'That is all we can do. It is as my mother said; the men do the work and the women do the praying.'

An argument of such simplicity was hard to refute. They ate their slices of cake in silence and tried not to glance across at the washing line.

'At least she will be a rich widow,' said Pippa, munching. 'We have a saying: The new wife comes before the old children.'

The next afternoon, as Linda sat in her chair by the windows and read, Maria's glass door opened and sunlight suddenly fell into her room. The great lead crucifix had gone from the wall. There remained a single bare nail.

It was washday. She heard someone singing 'Bésame Mucho'. Maria sang as she hung out the washing. Linda tried to catch her eye but as usual the girl kept her head bowed modestly. The iris dress, white and blue, had reappeared. She hung it out and went back inside.

Linda wondered where the crucifix had gone.

The afternoon sank into a state of overheated enervation, but she found herself unable to settle. It felt as if a storm was breaking somewhere nearby. She read a few pages, then tried to plan the evening's meal, but found herself pacing back and forth across the drawing room.

At 5 p.m. a car pulled up in the street outside and two policemen got out. One of them was carrying a large wooden box with a leather handle. They looked up at the building, then went to the entrance. Linda knew who they had come for and why they were there; they would question Maria and examine the scene of the death. The box contained forensic equipment.

When she went to her chair by the open windows she glanced across and saw that the iris dress had gone, although the pegs were still in place. Leaning over the edge, she looked down. The dress had slipped free of its line and had fallen into the centre of the little stone courtyard.

Latching the door, she ran downstairs, carefully counting the steps as she went. At the bottom a small back door opened onto the outside area. She quickly gathered up the light cotton dress and took it upstairs to her flat. When she examined it in bright sunlight she saw that it was no longer just blue and white but had several irregular pink patches, including one geometric shape that to her mind resembled the upper half of a crucifix.

Maria had scrubbed the dress, but not with the right detergent. At the hem were several carmine spots she had completely missed in her panic.

Linda poured a solution of soap and bleach into her sink, adding boiling water. While the material was soaking she went to the windows and looked across once more. The men were pacing around Maria, asking her questions.

She acted quickly and without hesitation. Running back to the sink, Linda rinsed out the dress, noting with satisfaction that the fabric had been restored to its crisp white background. Even the hem was spotless. She squeezed out most of the water, but the dress was still damp and heavy. Laying it across her arms, she left the apartment and went across to Maria's building.

On the way, she stopped in the courtyard and dropped the dress back onto the dirty stone floor. Then she picked it back up and climbed the stairs. Carlos had made a good job of the stonework. The steps had already dried. Approaching the partially opened door, she could hear the detective's questions.

'One last thing, Mrs Masvidal. You were up and dressed when your husband left for work, yes? What were you wearing when you went to the front door and found he had fallen?'

She barged in, acting as though she had no idea that there was anyone else in the flat. She spoke loudly and confidently to cover her nervousness. 'Maria, darling, your lovely dress fell off the washing line. I'm afraid it will need another rinse.'

The astonished Maria accepted the wet dress from her.

'She washes her clothes every Thursday,' Linda explained to the severe-looking gentlemen. 'I see everything. I live in the flat directly opposite.' She turned her attention to Maria. 'One of your pegs broke. Such a pretty dress. I saw it fall from the line.' She gave everyone a nice friendly smile. 'Well, I can see you have friends over. Perhaps if you'd like to have coffee later?'

She smiled again and left them all standing there in the middle of the living room. When she reached her own flat, she put the coffee on. After a few minutes she heard the throaty ignition of a car engine, and got to the front window in time to see the police drive off.

Linda unlatched her front door, then made the coffee and set out three cups. She unwrapped some chocolate cake she had been saving, and cut three thick slices.

When she looked up, Maria and Pippa were standing in the open doorway, waiting to be invited in.

WEDNESDAY'S CHILD

KEN BRUEN

H ad.

Funny how vital that damn word had become in my life.

Had... An Irish mother. Had... Big plans.

Had... Serious rent due.

Had... To make one major score.

I'd washed up in Ireland almost a year ago. Let's just say I *had* to leave New York in a hurry.

Ireland seemed to be one of the last places on the planet to still love the good ol' USA.

And, they were under the very erroneous impression that we had money.

Of course, until very recently, they'd had buckets of the green, forgive the pun, themselves. But the recession had killed their Celtic Tiger.

I'd gone to Galway as it was my mother's hometown and was amazed to find an almost mini-USA. The teenagers all spoke like escapees from *The Hills*. Wore Converse, baseball T-shirts, chinos. It was like staggering onto a shoot for The Gap.

With my accent, winning smile, and risky credit cards, I'd rented an office in Woodquay, close to the very centre of the city. About a mugging away from the main street. I was supposedly a financial consultant but depending on the client, I could consult on any damn thing you needed. I managed to get the word around that I was an ex-military guy, and had a knack for making problems disappear.

And was not averse to skirting the legal line.

I was just about holding my head above water, but it was getting fraught.

So, yeah, I was open to possibilities.

How I met Sheridan.

I was having a pint of Guinness in McSwiggan's and no, I wasn't hallucinating but right in the centre of the pub is a tree.

I was wondering which came first when a guy slid onto the stool beside me. I say *slid* because that's exactly how he did it. Like a reptile, he just suddenly crept up on me.

I've been around as you've gathered and am always aware of exits and who is where, in relation to the danger quota.

I never saw him coming.

Should have taken that as an omen right then.

He said, "You'll be the Yank I hear about."

I turned to look at him. He had the appearance of a greyhound recovering from anorexia and a bad case of the speed jags. About thirty-five, with long greying hair, surprisingly unmarked face, not a line there, but the eyes were old.

Very.

He'd seen some bad stuff or caused it. How do I know?

I see the same look every morning in the mirror.

He was dressed in faded blue jeans, a T-shirt that proclaimed *Joey Ramone will never die* and a combat jacket that Jack Reacher would have been proud of. He put out a bony hand, all the veins prominent, and said, "I'm Sheridan, lemme buy you a pint."

I took his hand, surprisingly strong for such a wasted appearance, said, "Good to meet you, I'm Morgan."

Least that's what it said on the current credit cards.

He had, as he put it, a slight problem, a guy he owed money to and the how much would it cost to make the guy go away.

I laughed, said, "You're going to pay me to get rid of a guy who you owe money to? One, why would you think I can do it, and two, how will you pay me?"

He leaned closer, smelled of patchouli, did they still make that old hippy shit? Said, "You've got yerself a bit of a rep, Mr Morgan, and how would I pay you, oh, I'd pay you in friendship and trust me, I'm a good friend to have."

Maybe it was the early pint, or desperation or just for the hell of it, but I asked, "Who's the guy?"

He told me, gave me his name and address and leaned back; asked, "You think you can help me out here, Mr Morgan?"

I said, "Depends on whether you're buying me the pint you offered or not."

He did.

As we were leaving, I said, "I'll be here Friday night; maybe you can buy me another pint."

Like I said, I didn't have a whole lot going on so I checked out the guy who was leaning on Sheridan.

No biggie but on the Thursday, his car went into the docks and him in it.

Some skills you never forget.

Friday night. I was in McSwiggan's; Sheridan appeared as I ordered a pint and he said to the barman, "On me, Sean."

He gave me a huge smile; his right molar was gold and the rest of his teeth looked like they'd been filed down.

We took our drinks to a corner table and he slapped my shoulder, said, "Sweet fooking job, mate."

I spread my hands, said, "Bad brakes, what can I tell you."

He threw back his head, laughed out loud, a strange sound, like a rat being strangled, said, "I love it, bad break. You're priceless."

That was the real beginning of our relationship. Notice I don't say friendship.

I don't do friends.

And I very much doubt that anyone in their right mind would consider Sheridan a friend.

We did a lot of penny-ante stuff for the next few months, nothing to merit any undue attention but nothing either that was going to bankroll the kind of life I hoped for.

Which was

Sea

Sun

And knock-you-on-your-ass cash.

An oddity, and definitely something I should have paid real attention to. I'd pulled off a minor coup involving some credit cards I had to dump within twenty-four hours. With Sheridan's help, we scooped a neat five thousand dollars. And at the time when the dollar had finally kicked the Euro's ass.

See, I do love my country.

You're thinking, "Which one?"

Semper fi and all that good baloney. It pays the cash, it gets my allegiance.

So, we were having us a celebration; I split it down the middle with him, because I'm a decent guy. We *flashed* up as Sheridan termed it.

Bearing in mind that the Irish seven-course meal is a six pack and a potato, we went to McDonagh's, the fish-and-chipper, in Quay Street.

We sat outside in a rare hour of Galway Sun; Sheridan produced a flask of what he called Uisce Beatha, Holy Water. In other words, Irish Moonshine, Poteen.

Phew-oh, the stuff kicks like one mean-tempered mule.

Later, we wound up in Feeney's, one of the last great Irish pubs. Here's the thing: I'd sometimes wondered if Sheridan had a woman in his life. I didn't exactly give it a whole lot of thought, but it crossed my mind. As if he was reading my mind he said, "Morgan, what day were you born on?"

I was about to put it down to late night drink speak, but I was curious, asked, "That's a weird question, what day, how the hell would I know what day?"

He looked sheepish, and when you add that to his rodent appearance, it was some sight, he said, "See, my girl, she has this thing about the nursery rhyme, you know, Monday's child is fair of face and… Thursday's, is, yeah, has far to go, she judges people on what their day of birth is."

My girl!

I was so taken aback by that it took me a moment to ask, "What are you?"

No hesitation, "Thursday's child."

We laughed at that and I don't think either of us really knew why.

I asked, "Who is the girl, why haven't I met her?"

He looked furtive, hiding something but then, his whole life seemed to be about hiding stuff, he said, "She's shy, I mean, she knows we're mates and all, but she wants to know your birth day before she'll meet you."

I said, "Next time I talk to Mom, I'll ask her, OK?"

As Mom had been in the ground for at least five years, it wasn't likely to be any time soon.

Another round of drinks arrived and we moved on to important issues, like sport. Guy stuff, if ever you reach any sort of intimacy, move to sports, move way past that sucker, that intimacy crap.

I meant to look up the nursery rhyme but, as far as I got, was discovering I was born on a Wednesday.

Told Sheridan it was that day and he said, "I'll tell her."

He was distracted when I told him, the speed he took turning him this way and that, like a dead rose in a barren field.

I'd noticed he was becoming increasingly antsy, speed fiends, what can I tell you? But he was building up to something.

It finally came.

We were in Garavan's, on Shop Street; still has all the old stuff you associate with Ireland and even… whisper it, Irish staff.

And snugs.

Little portioned off cubicles where you can talk without interruption.

Sheridan was on Jameson; I stay away from spirits, too lethal. He was more feverish than usual; asked, "You up for the big one?"

I feigned ignorance; said, "We're doing OK."

He shook his head, looked at me, which is something he rarely did, his eyes usually focused on my forehead, but this was head on; said, "Morgan, we're alike, we want some serious money and I know how we can get it."

I waited.

He said, "Kidnapping."

Without a beat I said, "Fuck off, that is the dumbest crime on the slate."

He was electric, actually vibrating; said, "No, listen, this is perfect, we... well me really, snatch a girl, her old man is fooking loaded and you, as the consultant you are and known, as such, you're the go-between; we tell the rich bastard the kidnappers have selected you as the pick-up man, you get the cash, we let the girl go and hello, we're rich."

I picked up the remnants of my pint; said, "No. Kidnapping never works. Forget it."

He grabbed my arm, said, "Listen, this is the daughter of Jimmy Flaherty; he owns most of Galway; his daughter, Brona, is the light of his life and he has no love of the cops; he'll pay, thinking he'll find us later, but we'll be in the wind and with a Yank as a broker for the deal; he'll go along, he's a Bush admirer."

I let the Bush bit slide.

I acted like I was considering it, then said, "No, it's too... out there."

He let his head fall, dejection in neon, and said, "I've already got her."

It's hard to surprise me. You live purely on your wits and instincts as I've always done; you have envisioned most scenarios. This came out of left field.

I gasped. "You what?"

He gave me a defiant look, then, "I thought you might be reluctant and I already made the call to Flaherty, asked for one million and said I'd only use a neutral intermediary, and suggested that Yank consultant."

I was almost lost for words.

Almost.

Said, "So I'm already fucked; you've grabbed the girl and told her father I'm the messenger."

He smiled; said, "Morgan, it's perfect, you'll see."

I was suddenly tired; asked, "Where's the girl now?"

His smile got wider; he said, "I can't tell you, see, see the beauty of it, you really are the innocent party and… here's the lovely bit, he'll pay you for your help."

Before I could answer this he continued, "You'll get a call from him asking you to help, to be the bagman."

I asked, "What if I tell Mr Flaherty I want no part of this?"

He gave me that golden tooth smile; said, "Ah Morgan, nobody says no to that man; how he got so rich."

I left early, said to Sheridan, "I don't like this, not one bit."

He was still shouting encouragement to me as I left.

I waited outside, in the doorway of the Chinese café a ways along. Sheridan had never told me where he lived, and I figured it was time to find out.

It was an hour or so before he emerged and he'd obviously had a few more Jamesons. A slight stagger to his walk and certainly, he wasn't a hard mark to follow.

He finally made it to a house by the canal and went in and I waited until he'd turned on the lights.

And I called it a night.

Next morning, I was the right side of two decent coffees, the *Financial Times* thrown carelessly on my desk, my laptop feeding me information on Mr Flaherty when the door is pushed open.

A heavily built man in a very expensive suit, with hard features and two even heavier men behind him, strode in.

I didn't need Google search to tell me who this was.

He took the chair opposite me, sat down, opened his jacket, and looked round.

The heavies took position on each side of the desk.

He said, "What a shit hole."

I asked, "You have an appointment?"

He laughed in total merriment, and the two thugs gave tight smiles; said. "You don't seem overrun with business."

I tried. "Most of my business is conducted over the phone, for discretion's sake."

He mimicked, "Discretion... hmm. I like that."

Then suddenly he lunged across the desk, grabbed my tie, and pulled me halfway across, with one hand, I might add. He said, "I like Yanks. Otherwise, you'd be picking yer teeth off the floor right now."

Then he let go.

I managed to get back into my chair, all dignity out the window, and waited.

He said, "I'm Jimmy Flaherty and some bollix has snatched me only child; he wants a million in ransom and says you are to be the go-between."

He snapped his fingers and one of the thugs dropped a large briefcase on the desk.

He said, "That's a million."

I took his word for it.

He took out a large Havana and the other heavy moved to light it; he asked, "Mind if I smoke?"

He blew an almost perfect smoke ring and we watched it linger over the desk like a bird of ill omen till he said, "This fuckhead will contact you and you're to give him the money."

He reached in his pocket, tossed a mobile phone on the desk, said, "Soon as you can see my daughter is safe, you call that number and give every single detail of what you observe."

He stood up; said, "I'm not an unreasonable man, you get my daughter back, and the bastard who took her, I'll throw one hundred large in your direction."

He'd obviously watched far too many episodes of *The Sopranos* and I was tempted to add, "Capisce."

But reined it in.

I said, "I'll do my best, sir."

He rounded on me, near spat. "I said I liked Yanks, but you screw up, you're dead meat."

When he was gone, I opened my bottom drawer, took out the small stash, did a few lines, and finally mellowed out.

My mind was in hyper-drive.

I had the score.

One freaking million and all I had to do was... skedaddle.

Run like fuck.

Greed.

Greed is a bastard.

I was already thinking how I'd get that extra hundred-thousand and not have Flaherty looking for me.

That's the curse of coke, it makes you think you can do anything.

I locked the briefcase in my safe and moved to the bookshelf near the door.

It had impressive-looking books, all unread, and moving aside *Great Expectations,* I pulled out the SIG Sauer.

Tried and tested and of a certain sentimental value.

I'd finalised my divorce with it, so it had a warm history.

I headed for Sheridan's house on the canal, stopping en route to buy a cheap briefcase, and when the guy offered to remove all the paper padding they put in there, I said, no need.

I got to the house just after two in the afternoon and the curtains were still down.

Sheridan sleeping off the Jameson.

I went round the back and sure enough, the lock was a joke and I had that picked in thirty seconds.

Moved the SIG to the right-hand pocket of my jacket and ventured in. This was the kitchen. I stood for a moment and wondered if there was a basement, where Sheridan might have put the poor girl.

Heard hysterical laughter from upstairs and realised Sheridan was not alone.

"Way to go, lover," I muttered as I began to climb the stairs.

Sheridan as late afternoon lover had never entered my mind but what the hell, good for him.

I got to the bedroom and it sounded like a fine old time was being had by all.

Hated to interrupt, but business!

Opened the door and said, "Is this a bad time?"

Sheridan's head emerged from the sheets and he guffawed, said, "Fooking Morgan."

The woman, I have to admit, a looker, pulled herself upright, her breasts exposed, reached for a cigarette and said, "Is this the famous American?"

There was a half-empty bottle of Jameson on the table beside Sheridan and he reached for it, took a lethal slug, gagged; said, "Buddy, meet Brona."

She laughed as my jaw literally dropped.

She said, in not too bad an American pastiche, "He's joining the dots."

I put the briefcase on the floor and Sheridan roared, "Is that it, fook, is that the million?"

He didn't enjoy it too long; Brona shot him in the forehead; said, "You come too quick."

Turned the gun on me and was a little surprised to see my SIG leveled on her belly.

Nicely toned stomach, I'll admit.

She smiled, said, "Mexican standoff?"

In Galway.

I said, "You put yours on the bed, slowly, and I'll put mine on the floor, we have to be in harmony on this."

We were.

And did.

I asked, "Mind if I have a drink?"

She said, "I'll join you."

I got the bottle of Jameson and as she pushed a glass forward, I cracked her skull with it; said, "I think you came too quick."

I checked her pulse and as I'd hoped, she wasn't dead. But mainly, she wouldn't be talking for awhile.

I did the requisite cleaning up and now for the really tricky part.

Rang Flaherty.

First the good news.

I'd got his daughter back and alive.

Managed to kill one of the kidnappers.

Got shot myself in the cluster fuck.

The other kidnapper had gotten away.

And... with the money.

He and his crew were there in jig time.

The shot in my shoulder hurt like a bastard and I hated to part with the SIG, but what can you do.

Wrapped it in Sheridan's fingers.

I don't know how long we were there; Flaherty's men got Brona out of there right away and I had to tell my story to Flaherty about a dozen times.

I think two things saved my ass

1. ... His beloved daughter was safe.

2. ... One bad guy was dead.

And I could see him thinking, if I was involved?

Why was I shot?

Why hadn't I taken off?

I even provided a name for the other kidnapper, a shithead who'd dissed me way back.

He produced a fat envelope; said, "You earned it."

And was gone

Four days later, I was, as Sheridan said, "In the wind."

Gone.

A few months later, tanned, with a nice unostentatious villa in the south of Spain, a rather fetching beard coming in, as the Brits would say, and a nice señorita who seemed interested in the quiet English writer I'd now become; a sort of middle-list cozy author persona. I was as close to happy as it gets.

One evening, with a bag full of fresh-baked baguettes, some fine wine, and all the food for a masterful paella, I got back to the villa a little later than usual; I might even have been humming something from *Man of La Mancha*.

Opened the door and saw a woman in the corner, the late evening shadows washing over her; I asked, "Bonita?"

No.

Brona, with a sawn off in her lap.

I dropped the bags.

She asked, "What day were you born on?"

I said, "Wednesday."

She laughed; said, "Complete the rhyme…"

Jesus, what was it?

I acted like I was thinking seriously about that, but mainly I was thinking, how I'd get to the Walther PPK, in the press beside her.

Then she threw the said gun on the floor beside my wilted paella feast, smiled, said, "Here's a hint, Tuesday's child is full of Grace… so…"

Now she leveled the sawn off, cocked the hammer; said, "You get one guess."

ACCOUNTING FOR MURDER

CHRISTINE POULSON

ITEM # 1

'Say it with Cake'
Speciality Cakes for all Occasions
1 Market Square, Silverbridge
Prop. Magdalene Dyer

Iced Victoria sponge with inscription:
'To my darling wife Laura on our 20th'

To be collected by Mr Jolyon Sleep 6 pm 25 June.

£25 to be paid

ITEM # 2

The George and Vulture
2-6 Market Square, Silverbridge

Visa: xxxx xxxx xxxx 0307

Sale: 2 x 1 gin and tonic
          1 bottle Chardonnay

Amount: £28.16

19:24   25/6/2014

ITEM # 3

Blooming Lovely
17 Market Square
Framley

27 June 2012

12 red roses to be delivered to Miss Magdalene Dyer
at 1 Market Square, Silverbridge

Message: 'Enjoyed our drink. Lunch tomorrow? J'

£30
Paid in cash

ITEM # 4

Veronica's Secret: Bras, Lingerie and Nightwear

Veronicassecret.com

Welcome to your account, Magdalene:

Shopping Basket

Plunge push-up bra	£89
Waist cincher	£78
V-string panty	£62
Total:	**£229**

ITEM # 5

The Dragon of Wantly
Gastro-pub,
Barchester

Lamb shank	£16.50
Salmon en croute	£14.50
Eton Mess	£06.00
Local Cheeses and biscuits	£06.00
½ Bottle of Pouille Fume	£11.00
½ Bottle of Merlot	£12.00
2 x expresso	£05.00
Subtotal:	£71.00
Service at 15%	£10.50
Total:	£81.50

Date: 28/06/2012   Time: 14:16

ITEM # 6

The Beeches Motel
Boxall Hill

27 June 2012

For 1 double room,

Received from Mr Smith:

£70 paid in cash

Date: 28/06/2014   Time: 17:02

ITEM # 7

CARPHONE WAREHOUSE
Annesgrove

Pay as You Go Nokia 225 x 2

£29.99 paid in Cash

Date: 29/06/2012   Time: 15:26

ITEM # 8

CROWN SPA HOTEL
THE ESPLANADE
TORQUAY

11 JULY 2012

FOR 1 SUITE, £201

ROOM SERVICE:

BOLLINGER SPECIAL CUVÉE:	£65.00
SMOKED SALMON SANDWICHES:	£12.95
RECEIVED FROM MR SMITH:	£278.95
PAID IN CASH	

ITEM # 9

Hello, Jolyon, we thought you would like to know that we have dispatched your item(s). Your order is on its way and can no longer be changed.

Your estimated delivery date is: 13 July – 14 July

Your order was sent to:
Magdalene Dyer
Flat 1b,
Cosby Lodge,
33 Courcy Road,
Silverbridge.

Delivery Information: Jean Patou Joy Eau de Parfum Spray 75 ml: £110.

ITEM # 10

THE RIVERSIDE HOTEL
LONDON W I

Romance Package: £550 (inclusive of VAT) based upon two people sharing, including:

- One night's sumptuous accommodation in an Edwardian inspired guest room
- Flowers, fresh fruit and a bottle of Champagne in your room on arrival
- Rose petals on turndown
- English breakfast

ITEM # 11

MSSRS. HARTER AND BENJAMIN
OLD BOND STREET
LONDON

19 July 2012

White Gold Watch 18ct white gold and diamonds

♦ 0.18ct of round brilliant-cut diamonds
♦ White mother of pearl dial
♦ Alligator strap with pin buckle

£9,950

To be engraved: 'M mon amour J'

ITEM # 12

London to Paris

London St Pancras Int'l to Paris Gare Du Nord
Eurostar
Departs 09:17 on Tues, 07 Aug
Arrives 12:47 on Tues, 07 Aug
Business Premier
2 x adults (£245.00)
£490.00

Paris to London

Paris Gare Du Nord to London St Pancras Int'l
Eurostar
Departs 16:13 on Wed, 08 Aug
Arrives 17:39 on Wed, 08 Aug
Business Premier
2 x adults (£245.00)
£490.00

Total: £980.00

ITEM # 13

LE BRISTOL PARIS

112 rue du Faubourg Saint Honoré

8 August 2012

Suite de luxe: €990
Dom Perignon Rosé: €109
Total: €1099

ITEM #14

JAMES SCUTTLE MOTOR COMPANY LTD
Established 1977
27-39 West Street
Exeter

17 August

Vehicle Sales Invoice:
Mr Jolyon Sleep
Ullathorne House
Barchester

Vehicle	Porsche 911 Cabriolet
Colour	Red
New/Used	New

Invoice total: £80,169, incl. VAT

Deliver to:
Magdalene Dyer
Flat 1b
Cosby Lodge,
33 Courcy Road,
Silverbridge

ITEM # 15

www.credit-edelweiss.com/uk/en/private-banking.html

Discover how we can help you. Based in Zurich we have the expertise and experience to deal with all your banking needs.

Get in touch to arrange a meeting, speak to an Account Manager or request a login to access our Investment Research through My Credit Edelweiss.

Please note: the minimum investment for clients of Credit Edelweiss is £1 million.
Numbered accounts available.

ITEM # 16

Littlebitofeden.com

Idyllic Ocean View Home Sales Price: US$599,000

Ready for a new life style? Welcome to Paradise!

This 2 bedroom, 2 bathroom house has easy access to the beachside town of Santa Teresa, a luxurious pool measuring over 550 sq. ft., large open living spaces, and a manicured lawn.

Built-in A/C makes sure even the hottest Costa Rican days are cool and comfortable. It's a bargain you really won't want to miss!

Good connections from local airport to San José International Airport.

ITEM # 17

Barsetshire Bank
Crabtree Parva,
Barsetshire

29 August 2012

Dear Mr and Mrs Sleep,

We are writing to inform you that your joint current account is overdrawn by £213.86. This deficit cannot be made good from your other accounts, which we have closed as per your instructions. We would be grateful if you would remedy this situation at your earliest convenience.

Yours sincerely,

Matthew Todd, Branch Manager

ITEM # 18

HARRY'S HARDWARE

Scarington
Barsetshire

For All Your DIY Needs!
We're Here To Help!

Thick bleach 5 litre
Qty: 2: £16.58
Polythene Sheeting Black 4m x 25m 500g
Qty: 1 Roll: £25
Black gaffer tape 50 mm by 50m
Qty: 1 Roll: £2.30
Total: £43.88

Date: 30/8/2012 Time: 09.34

ITEM # 19

White Goods Warehouse
Greshamsbury Retail Park
Barsetshire
30/8/2012

- Chest Freezer, Capacity: 250 litres
- Energy rating: A+
- Width: 111 cm
- Suitable for outbuildings

One-year manufacturer's warranty

£229 paid in cash

Date: 30:8:2012   Time: 14:21

ITEM # 20

SELF-STORAGE UNITS
8 GRESHAMSBURY INDUSTRIAL ESTATE
GRESHAMSBURY

30/8/2012

One standard storage unit

£25 per week:
3 months paid in advance in cash: £300

ITEM #21

James Finney,
16 Knowle Road
Plumstead Epsicopi
Barsetshire

Private Investigations Undertaken
Absolute Discretion Guaranteed

26 September 2012

Re: Tracing their daughter, Mrs Laura James-Sleep, of
Ullathorne House, Barchester

Last contact 28 August 2012

Initial payment of £500 received from Mr and Mrs James.

ITEM #22

SILVERBRIDGE POLICE STATION
CUSTODY SUITE

3. 10. 2012

Received from Mr Jolyon Sleep:

- Wallet containing £160 in cash, one American Express card, one Visa
  Card, one Mastercard, one Barsetshire Bank credit card

- Loose change to the sum of £3.86

- One Rolex watch

- One bunch of keys

ITEM #23

Gumption, Gazebee and Gazebee Solicitors
6 Cathedral Close,
Barchester

Mr Jolyon Sleep
Ullathorne House,
Barchester

Our ref: FEG. PP.017566.1

4 October 2012

Dear Mr Sleep

We acknowledge receipt of your payment of £5000 as a retainer for our services. As I explained on the telephone we intend to employ Geoffrey Bonstock (QC) of Borleys & Bonstock, Barristers at Law, Gray's Inn on your behalf and will arrange a meeting at the earliest opportunity. My assistant will send you a formal engagement letter which will cover various issues including further payment of fees, which we require to be paid on a monthly basis.

Kind regards,

Yours sincerely,

Fiona E. Gazebee

ITEM # 24

HM PRISON WORMWOOD SCRUBS
DU CANE RD, SHEPHERD'S BUSH,
LONDON

30. 4. 2013

Receipt for clothes belonging to prisoner no. 1938394.

One suit (Gieves & Hawkes)
One white cotton shirt
One tie
One pair underpants
One pair lace-up shoes (Church's)

ITEM # 25

Gumption, Gazebee and Gazebee Solicitors
6 Cathedral Close,
Barchester

> Borleys & Bonstock
> Barristers at Law
> Gray's Inn Square
> Gray's Inn
> London

30 April 2013

Dear Geoffrey,

Just to inform you that a bank transfer of £25,000 to Borleys and Bonstock has been effected, being the balance outstanding in the case of Regina V. Sleep.

I've much enjoyed working with you again. My best regards to Mildred.

Ever yours,

Fiona

PS. You win some, you lose some. I didn't think the sentence was unduly harsh, did you?

ITEM # 26

THE GAZETTE
OFFICIAL PUBLIC RECORD
Bankruptcy Orders

Sleep, John Jolyon
Ullathorne House, BARCHESTER
John Jolyon Sleep, a self employed accountant, residing at and carrying on business at Ullathorne House, Barchester, lately residing at H M Wormwood Shrubs Prison, Du Cane Rd, Shepherd's Bush, London
In the County Court at Barchester
No 76 of 1015
Date of Filing Petition: 9 May 2013
Bankruptcy order date: 10 May 2013
Time of Bankruptcy Order: 10:40
Whether Debtor's or Creditor's Petition—Debtor's
A Prichart, 3 Paradise Walk, Barchester
Capacity of office holder(s): Receiver and Manager
24 May 2013

ITEM # 27

BUSINESSES FOR SALE IN SILVERBRIDGE

Popular patisserie and bakery located in Silverbridge,
Barsetshire • Town centre location • Healthy turnover and
profits • Excellent local reputation • Fantastic change of
lifestyle opportunity • Good mix of complementary businesses
nearby •.annual turnover £45,000

seller relocating, favourable price for fast sale,
offers in the region of £60,000

ITEM # 28

www.ebay.co.uk

PORSCHE 911 CABRIOLET RED ONE CAREFUL LADY OWNER
GREAT SPEC

£ 63,990

WHITE GOLD WATCH 18CT WHITE GOLD AND DIAMONDS
ALMOST NEW

£ 8,999

ITEM # 29

LUXURY TRAVEL
FIRST CLASS ALL THE WAY
WHEN ONLY THE BEST IS GOOD ENOUGH!

25.6.2013

Itinerary for
Miss Magdalene Dyer

Flight

SAT 25JUNE HEATHROW TO ZURICH DEP 1000; ARR 12.40. BUSINESS CLASS	£255
TUES 28JUNE ZURICH TO SAN JOSE DEP 07.30; ARR 15.50. BUSINESS CLASS	£6,446

Please note
NO RETURN FLIGHTS REQUESTED

ROSENLAUI

CONRAD WILLIAMS

I was stillborn, after a fashion.

Unable to speak, unable to move other than this blinking of the eyes. I was told my paralysis was due to a cerebro-vascular disease passed on to me by my mother. I come from poor genetic stock, you see. My mother was descended from a bloodline that barely deserved the name: it was diluted red juice, she always said. It was rusty tap water. Her grandparents had died in their forties; her parents had done the same. Her husband came from a family who seemed to suffer heart attacks for fun; he died when I was but a child.

My mind, at least, flourished while the flesh surrounding it withered. I did well at school, having been forced, from a very early age (thanks to my ever patient and guilt-ridden mother) into developing a means to communicate. This I managed via an alphabet-based system connected to the frequency of blinks I managed with either eye, a practice that consumed many hours of painstaking trial and error.

Though my sight is keen, I often suffer from a number of optically related problems: double vision, flashes, headaches and so forth. I cannot cough, spit or swallow with any degree of success. I do not eat solid food. I'm unable to control my emotions and find myself oscillating between bouts of laughter-induced hysteria and racking sobs. I am blessed to be in the bosom of a family that loves me dearly, and they have sacrificed a great deal to make me comfortable, to ensure a future, of sorts, for me. A great deal of money has been spent to adapt a room at my mother's hotel (she and her brothers, Pascal and Tobias, have run the Schilthorn since the 1870s) so that it is comfortable for me. A special, raised bed – very heavy, so I am told – needed to be built on site. Ramps had to be added to the hotel infrastructure so that my wheelchair – itself of a bespoke design – could be more easily pushed around the grounds. My gratitude knows no bounds. But for my mother's love and devotion to me, and the support and protection afforded to me by my uncles, I might well have been abandoned, destined to live a miserable life in the cold, cruel poorhouses in Bern or Lausanne.

Nevertheless, I wished I had died in childbirth. I did not want to live. As soon as I was able, I begged my mother to help me go to sleep for ever, to end my suffering. But she refused; she was horrified. It was a sign from God, she told me. If I had been meant to die, it would have happened in the womb. She begged me to put such thoughts out of my head – she was convinced that the mind, if focused on one particular subject for long enough, could achieve its ambition – scared rigid that I would be delivered straight to hell should I be granted my heart's desire.

My mother's paraenesis went unheard, I'm ashamed to say. Lying in bed or sitting, immobile in my fortress chair, was causing my muscles to atrophy. I once heard the doctor telling my mother that the heart might not escape the same fate. Though it was beating, and strong because of that, it was having to work extra hard to serve my failing body. The doctor suspected my heart might eventually be affected by the malaise of the flesh and either stop working so effectively, or stop working altogether.

I lay awake at night imagining my heart in my chest, perhaps deciding if it was time to give up. But such thoughts did not panic me. I knew death would be a release. I knew it was every parent's concern that they might outlive their offspring, but I couldn't imagine what life would be like once my mother was gone. I could only envisage misery, and the interminable, wretched pursuit of her to the grave.

Some nights, when my misery seemed to know no lower limit, and I felt stretched and on the brink of dissolution, like a drip of molten wax, I thought of my heart – imagined it in the prison of my ribcage – beating more and more slowly, until it trembled and stopped. I willed it to happen. I wanted it more than anything else. I would wake the next morning, feeling cheated by God, and convinced He wanted me to live so that He could be entertained by my travails.

It was after this episode that I began to really turn my focus inwards. I began to study my feelings and I realised that although I was an intelligent young man – given the limitations of my affliction – I was retarded in terms of experiencing the full gamut of emotions. I have already mentioned that I shifted between extremes, albeit without any discernible external stimuli to trigger it. My emotions were chaos. In short, I did not understand them. I could not interpret them. Like me, my feelings were inert, broken, paralysed. I had learned to 'talk', but there was no colour to my words. How could you develop a personality, how could you convey wit or spirit or character if you had never lived? My reaction to every situation was the same: dumb passivity. I could not engage unless I was engaged. I could initiate no kind of contact.

I thought more deeply. I thought of the broad issues of life; the crucial signifiers. I thought of death dispassionately, with a strange kind of curiosity. I thought of love with a greater sense of mystification. Mother, every day, before she turned in, would ruffle my hair, kiss my cheek and say 'I love you'. I never reciprocated. I didn't know what it meant. I didn't know then how important for her it would have been had I signed the words *I love you too.*

In my room, I watched, incessantly, the bend of the larch trees under stiff north-westerly breezes. I could stare for hours at the trees, and the sun and shade flickering across the mountains behind them, and the clouds. I was jealous, and fascinated by any kind of movement; my eye was fast upon it, wherever it might originate. These momentary distractions apart, I felt doomed. To die in my father's footsteps, relatively young from heart disease, meant that I was yet to spend over two more decades upon this Earth. Little was I to know how much my world would be changed over the course of a few days...

Who could have known that the events of those coming days would create ripples to be felt across the world? I can't help feeling that the reason for the ripples – the stone cast at the centre of it all – was me. If it weren't for me, then the dreadful business at Reichenbach would not have happened... could not have happened. I saved one man and sent another to his death – or at least that's what it looked like to me at the time. Everyone believed they both died that day, the light and the shade. The virtuous and the diabolical.

∾

And so the strangers came to our village. This is no great shock of course. I live in an agreeable part of the world, a beautiful place with fresh air and attractive scenery (we have mountains and meadows, alpine flowers and goats, a spectacular waterfall and, in the shape of Rosenlaui, a glacier of awe-inspiring note); we receive many visitors eager to partake of its rejuvenating qualities. I spend a great deal of my time in the small lobby of the hotel, people-watching. I suppose you could say I was attuned to the small fluctuations that occur in the general current of humanity that drifted through our hotel. Such as that created by the two fellows who arrived on the 3rd of May. I was drawn to them instantly. One was tall and rangy, the kind of fellow you know is aware of everything and everyone in a room without ostentatious scrutiny; his companion was somewhat shorter, more rotund, and reminded me of the pictures of walruses I had seen on the walls of the library in Zurich. He wore a perplexed expression that struck me as likely to be a permanent fixture. I watched them talk to my mother for a while, and she made little flip-flop gestures with her hands, a gesture I had seen many times before; it meant there were no rooms vacant. The shorter man's face lost its perplexity to a thunderstruck mien but the taller man – immaculate in his inverness cape – smiled congenially and bent to ask my mother a question. She pointed through the window in the direction of Innertkirchen and the men bowed slightly and readied themselves to leave. Just then, the taller man espied me and tapped his companion on the shoulder. The perplexed look returned, but he remained where he was standing. The taller man approached me, that convivial smile countered somewhat by the greedy curiosity in his eyes.

"Sherlock Holmes," he said, in a rich, sonorous voice, "at your service. Forgive me, but I couldn't help noticing your predicament. You are a C4 quadriplegic, are you not?"

I was taken aback, not only by his direct and pinpoint diagnosis (my mother would have never volunteered such intimate information), but that he had approached me at all. Though I spent a lot of time in the lobby only my family engaged me in conversation. This was, I persuaded myself, because I was unable to enjoy any interaction – brief or otherwise – with people who were unaware of the method of 'speech' I employed. But more likely it was because people didn't understand what they saw, and they feared me.

I decided to have some fun with Herr Holmes.

YOU WILL EXCUSE ME IF I DO NOT GET UP.

"Of course, young fellow," he replied, instantly. "It's heartening to see a man with a complete spinal injury who has retained a sense of humour."

He told me he admired my 'silent, sombre observation' of the lobby and that he sensed in me a kindred spirit, a man enthused and intrigued by the human condition. He only regretted the fact that he would be unable to stay at our hotel.

"I wonder if you might do me the enormous courtesy of a favour, for which I would pay you the princely sum of thirty francs."

I was stunned by his apparently instant deciphering of my code; doubly so now that such a promise of money had entered our conversation.

HOW CAN I HELP?

"I've noticed you are a keen observer, and you have probably picked up on a number of physical traits and behavioural peccadilloes displayed by your hotel guests. My colleague, for example, Dr

Watson. No doubt you've been struck by his seemingly perpetual aspect of befuddlement?"

I couldn't smile, but Mr Holmes detected humour in me; reflected it perhaps, in the twinkling of his eye.

"I'd like you to keep watch for a man who is… shall we say… looking for me. This man is very much like me, though it pains me to say so – he is tall, quite thin, and has a bookish air; he is after all a quite brilliant professor of mathematics. His name is Moriarty, but he might well be travelling under a different moniker. Boole, perhaps, or Wild, or Newcomb. Perhaps even Zucco or Atwill. But no matter which pseudonym he hides behind, you will know this if you see him: there is something of the devil in his make-up. He moves as if hell is at his heels."

HOW WILL I GET WORD TO YOU?

I had known him but five minutes and already I felt compelled to help him. There was something urgent about him; something infectious. His curiosity, I aver: I wanted to know more about him. Where he was from, where he was going, why he was so far away from his native country.

"We will be taking rooms at the Englischer Hof," he said. "I shall endeavour to send someone to receive reports from you every evening."

And with that, he stood up, thanked me, and placed thirty francs in my jacket pocket. He rejoined his companion (whose air of consternation deepened) and then they left, Mr Holmes turning to touch his hat and smile my way.

I never saw him again.

∽

I ate my supper – a thin broth pumped down my throat (I have never tasted food) – on the veranda overlooking the peaks of the Wetterhorn and the Eiger and the Rosenlaui glacier. I loved to watch the sun sink over the white crags, darkening and deepening the green alpine meadows. Away to the south I could see thunderclouds forming, clenching into fists that would batter our village within the next twenty-four hours or so. It was a regular occurrence in these parts, and one I looked forward to immensely. My mother hated these attacks of low pressure, but they afforded me the closest proximity to understanding what it meant to be alive. I could almost believe that I felt the sensation of skin tingling under that bracing net of wet electricity. Part of me imagined – invited, even – the catastrophic visitation of one of those blue forks upon my body. I imagined the fire and heat coursing through my veins, effulgent, reinforcing. The lightning would either reduce me to a cinder or serve the miracle cure. Either possibility was eminently preferable to this endless, silent stasis.

Mother removed the feeding apparatus from my throat and withdrew. She knew I sometimes liked to take a nap upon receiving nourishment. Sometimes she asked if I would like her to read aloud, but she tended to shy away from the suggestion these days: my tastes are dark, and hers are not. She did not like to read *Frankenstein* to me, nor *The Strange Case of Dr Jekyll and Mr Hyde*, which she recited only recently, and that with evident distaste colouring her narrative. She accused me of wanting her to read stories that would serve only to remind her of my plight, and I must admit that I received a certain amount of grim pleasure from watching her squirm.

The air this evening was warm and sweet, but the potential in that burgeoning storm could already be felt in the fingers of wind tousling my hair. Gradually, I succumbed, my eyelids becoming heavier. I saw him then, on the cusp of a dream, so that I could not be sure that he was real, or some shade conjured by somnolence. There was no question who this man was, though I was mired in torpor. He moved rapidly, a thin, tall man, his shoulders hunched by years of academic study. He resembled Holmes, to a point. But there was something predatory in his gait. There was something hungry about it.

I watched him keenly, anxiety flooding my mind. When would Mr Holmes send his emissary to query me? Why was he so keen to know the whereabouts of this man, unless he signified a very grave threat? I could believe it. I saw the beast in him. I saw –

The figure had stopped abruptly, as if someone had called his name. Or – the paranoid whisperer at my shoulder insisted – as if he had *read your mind*. His face, at this distance, seemed like a pale, inverted teardrop; I could see that the frontal lobes of his head were massive, could almost see within the diabolical machinations of his brain, churning like some confounded engine. His eyes were a furious, black area of shadow, like the cross-hatchings in a sketch by Hogarth. Did I feel the first frisson, then, of… well… what? Fear? Is this what fear felt like? A spike in the gut, in the vitals, the incipient juice of me? Some feeling that was no slave to the destroyed nerves in my body. Something primal and basic, borne of the will to stay alive.

I thought then that the will in me to die might very well be countered by this ancient instinct in the flesh to survive.

He was coming towards me. I considered bluffing, pretending I was asleep, but I just knew he would be the type of person to instantly see through such a charade. When he reached the wheelchair, he did not ask my name. Instead, he took hold of the handles, disengaged the brake, and began wheeling me down the path in the direction of the meadow.

Uncle Tobias, the previous summer, had grafted the thick tyres from a wheelbarrow on to the chair, so that he was able to push me across the unforgiving terrain, broaden my horizons, and give me a different view of the world. Moriarty – for it must be he – took advantage of that customisation now, putting distance between us and the hotel. Again I felt the unwinding of what must be fear in the pit of my stomach, like a nest of adders coiling against and around each other. Night was coming on; already the sun had descended beyond the mountains, limning their edges with golden fire. The blue of the sky was thickening. In the east, stars were beginning to make themselves known. He pushed me hard and fast, and I bounced in my seat like a bag of sticks, threatening to spill to the floor at every bump or swerve. We travelled for what seemed like hours. At one point I lost my blanket, and the cold leapt at me like a wildcat, turning my hands blue. The water from my eyes began to freeze on my cheeks, stiffening them. For once, I was grateful that I could not feel pain.

Did I fall asleep at one point? Or was I plunged into senselessness by the cold? Whatever it was, I emerged into calm. The sky was fully dark now, and the stars in all their countless billions seemed to be howling against their icy backdrop. I could make out the shape of the mountains where they blocked those pinpoints of light, but nothing else. He had taken me to the tongue of the glacier and left me here to perish. He had –

"I spoke with your mother," he said. He was somewhere behind me. "As *he* did. Oh, she was most forthcoming. It is amazing, sometimes, the wag of the tongue when confronted with the spectre of appalling consequence."

I have never felt so trapped within my own body. I wanted to scream and snarl and rage at him. I wanted to tear his face from his skull and send it to the hungry winds like a scrap from a standard born by a defeated army. IF YOU HAVE DONE SOMETHING TO MY MOTHER – I signed, impotently.

"I know where Mr Holmes resides, and that lapdog of his, Watson. He is not much longer for this world, and by God I am ready to depart it too, should it come to that.

"Your mother spoke eloquently about you, young man," he said. "She told me you spent a lot of time together, talking of life and death and all points in between. She said you were hell-bent upon ending your life, and would have done so by now if you were able to lift a finger against yourself. She told me that you didn't even know what life was about. You had no frame of reference. You could not feel, yet you believed life was about nothing but feeling."

I thought I heard the compress of snow underfoot. The ruffle of clothing in wind. I caught glimpse of him, a shadow, wraith-like, at my shoulder. And for a moment I thought I could smell him too. He smelled of books and leather and, as in me, I smelled in him the sickly sweet redolence of death. Whereas I was inviting it, he was admitting it, he was cozying up to it within the folds of his heavy coat.

"Your mother talked of you as a child. They would bring you here, to the glacier, determined that the cold, fresh air would be beneficial. Of course, it wasn't, but she kept bringing you. In blind hope. In stubborn belief. You became agitated, and she saw that as a good thing; she thought you were stirring from this pitiful state, this curse of being locked within yourself. She thought you might suddenly stand up, rejuvenated by the magic of frigidity, and be miraculously cured. But I suspect it was because you were distressed. You were brought to a place that seemed to only mirror your condition. The cold, cruel, still mass of ice. The suffocation of life beneath it. The smothering. The glacier mocked you. It, after all, enjoyed some minute advance. The incremental creep through the mountains. More movement than you could ever dream of.

"I could leave you here," he said. "Nobody would think to check this location. You would be dead within the hour, of exposure. But I am no monster, despite what *he* says."

I felt the charge of his gloved fists upon the handles once more. We turned away from the great mound of the glacier, pale under the night as if it were blessed with its own light source. "I ask you… no, sir, I *warn* you not to involve yourself in this affair. My issue with Mr Holmes is a private one. He has put you in jeopardy to serve himself, which goes to show you, I think, that the true nature of monsters is not such a subject given to black and white."

I think the cold was getting to me, though I could not feel it. I was no longer shivering, and I was drowsy, as if injected with sedatives. I had read somewhere that once you stop shivering, then the body is not far away from serious hypothermia, and that tiredness is a sign. But again it looked as if I would be cheated of death; Professor Moriarty was playing with me. When we got back within view of the hotel, I could see frantic movement in the grounds. Staff and guests were roving around with lanterns. I heard my name being called above the clamour of the wind.

"You can be a glacier," he told me. "Or you can be a waterfall. It is your choice, though you might not think it so."

I heard the snap of something behind me, and a rustling. He didn't say anything else. I smelled smoke, and a golden glow built, casting my shadow before me. I heard a cry: "There! Over there! Look. Fire!" And then many figures were dashing across the meadow towards me. Moriarty was long gone by the time they reached me. I was swaddled in blankets and my mother's scent was here, though I could not yet see her. She was crying. I heard her crying all the way back, and it followed me down into sleep.

When I awakened a man was sitting opposite me, peering at me as if I were an arresting specimen in a museum. He said: "I was sent by Mr Holmes. He said you might have a message for me."

MY JACKET POCKET.

The man stood up and reached for my jacket. He withdrew an envelope. It was the money Holmes had paid me to be his watchman.

"No message?"

I did not reply. I waited until he had left. I fell into a sleep so deep it was like sinking into the cold fathoms of a lake.

Word began to trickle through the following afternoon, like the first thaw waters of spring from the crags, that Sherlock Holmes and his nemesis, Moriarty, were dead. Evidence of a struggle had been found at Reichenbach at midday, and a few artefacts belonging to the eminent detective. I had seen the falls once, when I was very young, and I had been cowed by its power and fury. If you were driven underground by that torrent of water, you would never surface again. But it had excited me too. That movement. That ceaseless thrashing energy.

I saw Dr Watson, bereft, exhausted, being ushered with his suitcase to the train station where he would begin his journey back to London. I wanted to offer him some crumb of comfort, but others more able than I were doing that job already, and so much better. After he had gone – I watched the puffs of steam from the locomotive dissipate like my own thought bubbles in the boiling Meiringen sky – Mother suggested I take to my bed for a rest. My fingers and toes exhibited signs of frostbite, and she thought it would be injurious to my good health to remain outdoors, but I was firm. I WISH TO SIT ON THE BALCONY. I would not be diverted. After a while, she gave up trying to change my mind and left me alone. I'm sure she was thinking that I might be abducted once more, but Moriarty was gone, and Tobias had replaced the rugged wheels on my chair with the original casters. I was unlikely to be making any more unscheduled trips again.

The storm hit Meiringen an hour later, leaden cloud bringing artificial night to the village. I watched the skin on my arms pucker, the hairs rise as if in supplication to the power swelling in the sky. This time I felt it, an echo of the fear I had known in Moriarty's presence, as if he dragged its trickery around with him like a humour or a scent. Lightning flashed and the thunder it created was instantaneous. Rain dropped as if shocked out of the clouds by the sound; heavy, brutal, pummelling rain. I had never felt so alive, and for a moment I was grateful that I could never utter the name of the person who had triggered that in me. Fear was survival. Fear was life. I could feel. I could FEEL.

In the hiatus after a second lightning flash, I saw something different in the scenery imprinted upon the darkness behind my eyes. A figure was standing still to my left beneath the awning of the bakery a little way up the road from the hotel. The flash of lightning. A refreshed scene in acid white: the figure now closer. There was something wrong with its physique.

Flash. Everything remained the same: the great mass of the mountains, the reach of the trees, the wet template of buildings known to me as intimately as the pattern of freckles on the back of my hand. And this figure. Closer yet. Bent over and buckled like a child's model shaped from clay.

I tasted his name upon my tongue though I could not utter it. So much like some play upon the Latin phrase reminding us that we have to die.

Flash. A step nearer. Now I could see his face. The prominent lobes of his forehead split and bloodied. The cliff of his face blackened by bruises. An arm broken so badly it resembled a flesh scythe curling up around his back. Bone was visible in the soaked swags of his exposed skin, as if he were carrying some strange bag of splintered antlers with him, to ward off bad luck.

He looked at me with those massive gaping shadows deep in his face. In the next window of light, he had raised his good hand and let it fall haltingly, like a child's representation of rain, or, perhaps, the deluge of a waterfall.

When the lightning returned again, he was gone.

METHOD MURDER

SIMON BRETT

As an actor, Kenny Mountford yearned to be taken seriously. Since finishing at drama school, he'd done all right. A bit of theatre work, but mostly television, which was good news because it paid better. However, a continuous round of small parts in *The Bill*, *Heartbeat* and *Midsomer Murders* had left him, by the time he reached his early thirties, with a deep sense of dissatisfaction. It wasn't celebrity that he craved, it was respectability. He wanted to be able to hold his head high amongst other actors when the discussion moved on to the issues of the 'truth' and 'integrity' of their profession.

And really that meant doing more theatre. For the more obscure and impenetrable the theatre work, the higher the integrity of the actors involved. This meant, in effect, working with one of a small list of trendy directors, directors who didn't pander to the public by making their work accessible or simply entertaining. So Kenny Mountford set out to meet and ingratiate himself with such a director.

It was a good time for him to make the move. A stint playing the barman on a successful sitcom had bolstered his income to the point that he had paid off the mortgage on his Notting Hill house. And, besides, his live-in actress girlfriend Lesley-Jane Walden was not only a nice bit of arm candy to satisfy the gossip columns, she was also making a good whack as the latest *femme fatale* in a long-running soap opera. Her hunger for celebrity was currently satisfied, they weren't in need of money, so Kenny Mountford was in a position where he could afford to pursue art for art's sake.

The latest *enfant terrible* of British theatre was a director called Charlie Fenton. Like many of his breed, he had a great contempt for the written word, rejecting texts by playwrights in favour of improvisation. In the many television and newspaper interviews he gave, he regularly pontificated about 'the straitjacket of conformity' and derided 'the crowd-pleasing lack of originality demonstrated by the constant revival of classic theatre texts.' One somewhat sceptical interviewer had asked if this meant Charlie Fenton considered one of his improvised pieces to be better than a play by Shakespeare and, though hotly denying the suggestion, the director made it fairly clear that that actually was his view.

What Charlie Fenton was most famous for was his in-depth approach to characterisation. Though claiming to have developed his own system, he owed more than he cared to admit to the pioneering work in New York of Lee Strasberg, the originator of the 'Method'. This was a style of acting which aimed for greater authenticity, and its exponents had included Meryl Streep, Paul Newman, Robert De Niro and even, surprisingly, Marilyn Monroe. Rather than building up a character from the outside and assembling a collection of mannerisms, a 'Method actor' would try so to immerse himself in the identity of the person he was playing that he virtually *became* that person.

So if an actor were playing a milkman in a Charlie Fenton production, the director would send the poor unfortunate off to spend three months delivering milk. Someone with the role of a Muslim terrorist would be obliged to convert to Islam. An actress playing a prostitute would have to turn tricks in the streets around King's Cross (and almost definitely service Charlie Fenton too, so that he could check she was doing it properly). And one poor unfortunate had once spent three months in a basement blindfolded and chained to a radiator for a proposed production about hostage-taking. (It would only have been three weeks, but Charlie Fenton omitted to inform the actor when he abandoned the idea.)

Once his casts had immersed themselves in their characters, weeks of improvisation in rehearsal rooms would ensue, until the director edited what he considered to be the best bits into a script. After the production had opened, this text, based on the actors' lines, would then be published in the form of a book, for which Charlie Fenton took all the royalties.

The carefully leaked details of his rehearsal methods only added to the director's mystique, and very few people realised that ordering actors around in this way was just part of the Charlie Fenton's ongoing power trip. The lengthy build-up to his productions was nothing to do with the quality of theatre that resulted; it was all about his ego. Also the total control he exercised over his companies proved to be a good way of getting pretty young actresses into bed. (He had a wife and family somewhere in the background, but spent little time with them.)

Awestruck accounts of the director's procedures, tantrums and bullying ensured that any actor in search of theatrical respectability was desperate to work with Charlie Fenton. And so it was with Kenny Mountford.

They finally met after a first night of a National Theatre *King Lear*. The play wasn't really Lesley-Jane Walden's cup of tea, but it was a first night, after all. Any occasion when there was a chance of her being photographed and appearing in the tabloids suited her very well indeed (though she had been a little disappointed by the lack of *paparazzi* down at the South Bank). As soon as the final curtain was down Charlie Fenton was at the bar, surrounded by toadies, who hung on every word as he proceeded to list Shakespeare's shortcomings as a dramatist. Kenny and Lesley-Jane had gone to the performance with one of their actor friends who had once spent six months picking tomatoes and learning Polish in order to take part in a Charlie Fenton production about migrant workers. And the friend effected the coveted introduction.

The director, who sported a silly little goatee and grey ponytail, favoured Lesley-Jane with a coruscating smile. 'I've seen some of your work,' he said. 'It's amazing how a really good actor can shine even amidst the dross of a soap opera.'

She blushed and smiled prettily at this. Which wasn't difficult for Lesley-Jane Walden. She was so pretty that she did everything prettily.

Kenny Mountford felt encouraged. If Charlie Fenton had recognised his girlfriend's quality in a soap opera, the director might look equally favourably at his work in a sitcom. But that illusion was not allowed to last for long. Looking superciliously at him over half-moon glasses, Charlie Fenton said, 'Oh yes, I know your name. Still paying the mortgage rather publicly on the telly, are you?'

'Maybe,' Kenny replied, 'but I am about to change direction.'

'Towards what?'

'More serious theatre work.'

'Oh yes?' the director sneered. 'That's what they all say.'

'No, I mean it.'

'Kenny, I don't think you'd recognise "more serious theatre work" if it jumped up and bit you on the bum. You have clearly been destined from birth for a life of well-paid mediocrity.'

'I disagree. I'm genuinely committed to doing more serious work.'

'Really?' The director scrutinised the actor with something approaching contempt. 'I don't think you could hack it.'

'Try me.'

Charlie Fenton was silent for a moment of appraisal. Then he said, 'I bet you wouldn't have the dedication to work with me.'

'Are you offering me a job?'

'If I were, I'm pretty confident you couldn't do it.'

'Again I say: try me.'

Another long silence ensued. Then the director announced, 'I'm starting work on a new project. About criminal gangs in London.'

'What would it involve for the actors?'

'Deep cover. Infiltrating the gangs.'

Kenny was aware of the slight admonitory shake of Lesley-Jane's head, but he ignored the signal. 'I'm up for it,' he said.

'I'll phone you with further details,' the director announced in a magisterial manner that suggested the audience was at an end.

'Shall I give you my mobile number?'

'Landline. I don't do mobiles.' Clearly another eccentricity, which was indulged like all Charlie Fenton's eccentricities. He flashed another smile at Lesley-Jane, then looked hard at Kenny, his lips curled with scepticism. 'If you can come back to me in three months as a member of a London gang, you've got a part in the show.'

'You're on,' said Kenny Mountford.

⌇

Lesley-Jane wasn't keen on the idea. If Kenny was going to go underground, he wouldn't be able to squire her to all the premières, launches and first nights her ego craved. Their relationship was fine while he too had a high-profile television face, but she didn't want to end up with a boyfriend who nobody recognised. She also knew that her own work situation was precarious. Young *femmes fatales* in soap operas had a short shelf life. One of the scriptwriters had already hinted that her character might have a fatal car crash in store. There was a race against time for her to announce that she was leaving the show before the public heard that she'd been pushed off it. And then she'd need another series to move on to, and there weren't currently many signs of that being offered. At such a time she'd be more than usually dependent on the reflected fame of her partner. (She had always followed the old show business advice: if you can't be famous yourself, then make sure you go to bed with someone who is.) The last thing she wanted at that moment was for Kenny to disappear off the social radar for some months while he immersed himself in gangland culture.

But Lesley-Jane's remonstrations were ignored. Her boyfriend's mind was now focused on only one thing: proving his seriousness as an actor to Charlie Fenton.

And to do that he had to infiltrate a London gang. Which actually turned out to be surprisingly easy. He didn't have to hang around Shepherd's Bush Green for long before he was approached by someone with a heavy Russian accent and asked if he wanted to buy drugs. After a couple of weeks of making regular purchases of heroin (which he didn't use but stockpiled in his bathroom cabinet), he only had to default on payments twice to be hustled into a car with tinted windows, blindfolded and taken off to meet the organisation's frighteners.

They didn't have to hurt him to get their money. Kenny Mountford had the cash ready with him and handed it over as soon as his blindfold was removed. He found himself seated on a chair in a windowless cellar, loomed over by the two heavies who'd snatched him and facing a thin-faced man in an expensive suit. From their conversation in the car, he'd deduced that his abductors were called Vasili and Vladimir. They addressed the thin-faced man as Fyodor. All three spoke English with a heavy accent from somewhere in the former Soviet Union.

'So if you had the money all the time, why didn't you pay up?' asked the man in the suit, whose effortless authority identified him as the gang's leader.

'Maybe he enjoys being beaten to a pulp,' suggested the heavy who Kenny was pretty sure was called Vasili.

'Maybe,' said Kenny Mountford with a cool that he'd spent three years at drama school perfecting, 'but that's not actually the reason. I just thought this was a good way of getting to meet you, Fyodor.'

'Do you know who I am?' the man asked, intrigued.

'I only know your name, but it doesn't take much intelligence to work out that you're higher up this organisation than the two goons who brought me here.'

Kenny felt the men either side of him stiffen and was aware of their fists bunching, but he remembered his concentration exercises and didn't flinch.

Fyodor raised a hand to pacify his enforcers. 'You are right. I control the organisation.'

'And am I allowed to know what it's called?'

He smiled a crooked smile. 'The Simferopol Boys. From where we started our operations. Do you know where Simferopol is?' Kenny shook his head. 'It is in the Crimea. Southern Ukraine. Near to Yalta. I assume you have not been there?' Another shake of the head. 'Well, we did what we could over there, but the pickings were small, and there were a lot of… entrenched interests. Turf wars, dangerous. In London our life is easier.'

'And how many are there in the Simferopol Boys?'

'Twenty, maybe thirty, it depends. Sometimes people become untrustworthy and have to be eliminated.'

Kenny was aware of a reaction from Vasili and Vladimir. Clearly elimination was the part of the job they enjoyed.

'And do you just deal in drugs?'

Fyodor spread his hands wide in an encompassing gesture. 'Drugs… prostitution… protection rackets… loan sharking… The Simferopol Boys are a multifunction organisation.' Then came the question that Kenny knew couldn't be delayed much longer. 'But why do you want to know this? Curiosity?'

'More than just curiosity.'

'Good. If it was just curiosity, I think Vasili and Vladimir would have to eliminate you straight away.' The gang boss smiled a thin smile. 'They may well have to eliminate you straight away, whatever the reason for your enquiries. You could be a cop, for all we know.'

'I can assure you I am not a cop.'

'But that's exactly what you would say if you were a cop.'

'Well, I'm not.'

'Mr Mountford, I am not here to chop logic with you. I am a busy man.' He looked at his watch. 'I have a meeting shortly with a senior civil servant in the Home Office. He is helping me with some visa applications for members of my extended family in Simferopol. Now please will you tell me why you are here. And why I shouldn't just hand you straight over to Vasili and Vladimir for elimination.'

Kenny Mountford took a deep breath. There was no doubt that he had put himself in very real danger. But, as he had that daunting thought, he couldn't help also feeling a warm glow. Charlie Fenton would be so impressed by the lengths he had gone in his quest for authenticity.

'I'm here because I want to join your gang.'

'Join the Simferopol Boys?' asked Fyodor in astonishment. Vasili and Vladimir let out deep threatening chuckles at the very idea.

'Yes.'

'But why should we let you join us? As I said, you could be a cop. You could be a journalist. You could be a spy from the Odessa Reds.' The reactions from Vasili and Vladimir left Kenny in no doubt as to what Fyodor was talking about. They might sound like a breed of chicken, but the Odessa Reds were clearly a rival gang.

'How can I prove to you that I'm none of those things? What are the qualifications for most of the people who join your gang?'

'Most of them have family connections with me in Simferopol which go back many generations. At the very least, most of them are Ukrainian.'

'I can sound Ukrainian,' said Kenny, demonstrating the point. (He had made quite a study of accents at drama school.)

His impression didn't go down well with Vasili and Vladimir. They clearly thought he was sending them up. Two giant hands slammed down on his shoulders, while two giant fists were once again bunched.

But again a gesture from their boss froze them before the blows made contact.

'Anyone who wants to join the Simferopol Boys,' said Fyodor quietly, 'has to pass certain tests.'

'A lot of tests?' asked Kenny Mountford, maintaining his nonchalance with increasing difficulty.

The gang boss nodded. 'The big one's at the end. Not many people get that far. But if you want to have a go at one of the starting tests…'

Kenny nodded. Fyodor leant forward and told him what the first test was.

Like most actors, Kenny Mountford always felt a huge surge of excitement when he got a new part. However trivial the piece, hours would be spent poring over the script, making decisions about the character's accent and body language. The part that Fyodor had given him prompted exactly the same adrenaline rush, though in this case he had no text to work from. Kenny started reading everything he could find about the Crimean region, and Simferopol in particular. He also tracked down recordings of Ukrainians speaking English and trained himself to imitate them.

The new direction his career was taking still failed to raise much enthusiasm in Lesley-Jane. From an early age her main aim in life had been to be the centre of attention, so she didn't respond well to being totally ignored by the man she was living with. But Kenny was too preoccupied with his new role to notice her disquiet.

The first test he had been given by Fyodor was relatively easy. All he had to do was to sell drugs in Shepherd's Bush, just like the dealer who had served as his initial introduction to the Simferopol Boys. Apart from the work he was doing on his accent, Kenny also spent a considerable time sourcing clothes for the role, and was satisfied that the hoodie, jeans and trainers he ended up with had achieved exactly the requisite degree of shabbiness. He found it a welcome relief to be selecting his own clothes for a part, rather than having to follow the whims of some queeny costume designer as he would in television.

He needn't have bothered, though. The kind of lowlife he was peddling the drugs to didn't even notice what he looked like. The only thing they thought about was their next fix. But for Kenny Mountford as an artist – and a potential participant in a Charlie Fenton production – it was very important that he should get every minutest detail right.

After his first successful foray as a drug dealer, he got home early evening to find a very impatient Lesley-Jane Walden, dressed up to the nines and in a foul temper. 'Where the hell have you been?' she shrieked, almost before he'd come through the door. 'You know we're meant to be at this Tom Cruise première in half an hour.'

'I'm sorry. I forgot.'

'Well, for God's sake get changed into something respectable and I'll call for a cab.'

'I don't want to get changed.' Kenny Mountford hadn't really formalised the idea before, but he suddenly knew that he wasn't going to change his clothes until Charlie Fenton agreed to give him the part in his next production. He was going to immerse himself in the role of a Simferopol Boy until that wonderful moment. 'And don't try to change my mind,' he added in his best Ukrainian accent.

'What the hell are you talking about – and why the hell are you using that stupid voice?' demanded Lesley-Jane. 'If we don't leave in the next five minutes, we'll have missed all the *paparazzi*. And if you think I'm going to be seen at a Tom Cruise première with someone dressed like you are, Kenny, then you've got another think coming!' Her face was so contorted with fury that she no longer looked even mildly pretty.

'Listen,' Kenny continued in his Ukrainian voice, 'I've got more important things to do than to—'

He was interrupted by the phone ringing. Lesley-Jane turned away from him in disgust. He picked up the receiver. A seductive 'Hello' came from the other end of the line. The man's voice was vaguely familiar, but Kenny could not immediately identify it.

'Hello,' he replied, still Ukrainian.

The voice changed from seduction to suspicion. 'Who is this?'

Then Kenny knew. 'Charlie,' he enthused, reverting to his normal voice, 'how good to hear you.'

At the other end of the phone Charlie Fenton sounded slightly thrown. 'Is that Kenny?'

'Yes. What can I do for you?'

The director still didn't sound his usual confident self as he stuttered out a reply. 'Oh, I just… I was… um…' Then, sounding more assured, he said, 'I just wanted to check how you were getting on with your infiltration process.'

'I thought you weren't going to be in touch for three months.'

'No, I, er, um… I changed my mind.'

'Well, in answer to your question, Charlie, my infiltration is going very well. I'm already working for a gang.'

'That's good.'

'They're Ukrainian,' he went on, reassuming the accent to illustrate his point. 'And, actually, it's good you've rung, because there's something I wanted to ask you...'

'What's that?'

'How deep do you think I should go into this character I'm playing?'

'As deep as possible, Kenny.' With something of his old pomposity, the director went on. 'My style of theatre involves the participants in *total immersion* in their characters.'

'I'm glad you said that, because I've been wondering whether I should actually be living in my house while I'm doing this preparation work. A Ukrainian gangster wouldn't live in a Notting Hill house like mine, would he?'

'No, he certainly wouldn't.'

'So what I want to ask you is: do you think I should move out of my house?'

'No question. You certainly should,' replied Charlie Fenton.

He took a grubby room in a basement near Goldhawk Road and, as he got deeper into his part, Kenny Mountford realised that he could no longer be Kenny Mountford. He needed a new identity to go with his new persona. He consulted Vasili and Vladimir on Ukrainian names and, following their advice, retitled himself Anatoli Semyonov. He also cut himself off from the English media. He stopped watching television, and the only radio he listened to on very crackly short wave was a station from Kyiv.

He bought Ukrainian newspapers in which at first he couldn't even understand the alphabet.

Meanwhile, the tests set by Fyodor got tougher. On top of the dealing, Kenny was now delegated to join Vasili, Vladimir and other of the Simferopol Boys in some enforcement work. Drug customers dragging their feet on payments, prostitutes or pimps trying to keep more of the take than they were meant to... to bring these to a proper sense of priorities called for a certain amount of threatening behaviour, and frequently violence. In such situations, as with the drug dealing, Kenny – or rather Anatoli Semyonov – did what was required of him.

The thought never came into his mind that what he was doing might be immoral, that if he were caught he could be facing a long stretch in prison. Kenny Mountford was *acting*, he was researching the role of Anatoli Semyonov with the long-term view of appearing in a show created by the legendary Charlie Fenton. When such a conflict of priorities arose, Morality was for the petty-minded; Art was far more important.

As he got deeper and deeper under his Simferopol Boys cover, Kenny saw less and less of Lesley-Jane Walden. He didn't feel the deprivation. He was so focused on what he saw as his work, that his mind had little room for other thoughts.

At the end of an evening with Vasili, Vladimir and some baseball bats, which had left a club-owner who was behind on his protection payments needing three weeks' hospitalisation, the three Simferopol Boys – or rather the two Simferopol Boys and the one prospective Simferopol Boy – reported back to Fyodor.

The gang leader was very pleased with them. 'This is good work. I think we are achieving more since Anatoli has been with us.' Vasili and Vladimir looked a little sour, but Kenny Mountford glowed with pride. He had reached the point where commendation from Fyodor was almost as important to him as commendation from Charlie Fenton. 'And I think it is time that Anatoli Semyonov should be given his final test...'

Kenny could hardly contain his excitement. In his heavily Ukrainian voice, he asked, 'You mean the one that will actually make me a fully qualified member of the Simferopol Boys?'

Fyodor nodded. 'Yes, that is exactly what I mean.' He gave a curt nod of his head. Vasili and Vladimir, knowing the signal well, left the room. A long silence filled the space between the two men who remained.

It was broken by Fyodor. 'Yes, Anatoli, I think you have proved you understand fully the role that is required of you.'

Kenny Mountford could hardly contain himself. It was the best review he'd had since *The Stage* had described his Prospero as 'luminescently compelling'.

'So what do I have to do? Don't worry, whatever it is, I'll do it. I won't let you down.'

'You have to kill someone,' said Fyodor.

At first Kenny had had difficulty with the amount of vodka-drinking that being an aspirant Simferopol Boy involved, but now he could match Vasili and Vladimir shot for shot – and even, on occasions, outdrink them. They tended to meet during the small hours (after a good night's threatening) in a basement club off Westbourne Grove. It was a dark place, heavy with the fug of cigarettes. Down there in the murk no one observed the smoking ban. And, having seen the size of the barmen, Kenny didn't envy any department of health inspector delegated to enforce it.

He was always the only non-Russian speaker there, though his grasp of the language was improving, thanks to an online course he'd enrolled in. Kenny had a private ambition that, when the three months were up, he would return to Charlie Fenton not only looking like a Ukrainian gangster, but also speaking like one.

That evening they were well into the second bottle of vodka before either Vasili or Vladimir mentioned the task which they knew Fyodor had set Kenny. 'So,' asked Vladimir, always the more sceptical of the two, 'do you reckon you can do it? Or are you going to chicken out?'

'Don't worry, *tovarich*, I can do it.' He sounded as confident as ever, but couldn't deny to himself that the demand made by Fyodor had been a shock. Playing for time, he went on, 'The only thing I can't decide about it is *who* I should kill? Just someone random who I happen to see in the street? Would that be the right thing to do?'

'It would be all right,' replied Vasili, 'but it would be rather a waste of a hit.'

'How do you mean?'

'Well, if you're going to kill someone, at least make sure it's someone you already want out of your way.'

'I'm sorry, I don't quite understand you.'

'For heaven's sake, Anatoli,' said Vladimir impatiently, 'kill one of your enemies!'

'Ah.' Kenny Mountford tried to think whether he actually had any enemies. There were people who'd got up his nose over the years – directors who hadn't recognised his talent, casting directors who had resolutely refused to cast him, actors who'd stolen his laughs – but none of these transgressions did he really think of as killing matters.

His confusion must have communicated itself to Vladimir, because he said, 'You must have a sibling who's infuriated you at some point, someone's who's cheated you of money, a man who's stolen one of your girlfriends...'

'Yes, I must have, mustn't I?' Though, for the life of him, Kenny Mountford still couldn't think of anyone who was a suitable candidate for murder. He also couldn't completely suppress the unworthy feeling – which he knew would threaten his integrity as an actor in the eyes of someone like Charlie Fenton – that killing people was wrong.

The conversation became becalmed. After a few more shots of vodka, Vladimir announced he was off to get a freebie from one of the Bayswater working girls controlled by the Simferopol Boys. 'Got to be some perks in this job,' he said.

But Vasili lingered. He seemed to have sensed Kenny's unease. 'You are worried about the killing?'

'Well...'

'It is common. The first one. Many people find that. After two or three, though...' Vasili downed another shot of vodka '...it seems a natural thing to do. It might even seem a natural thing for an actor to do...'

Kenny was shocked. 'You know I'm an actor?' Vasili smiled. 'Do Fyodor and Vladimir know too?' Vasili shook his head. 'Only me.' Kenny Mountford felt a flood of relief.

There was a silence. Then Vasili leant forward, lowering his voice as he said, 'Maybe I could help you...'

'How?'

'There is a service I provide. It is not free, but it is not expensive... given the going rate.' He let out a short cynical laugh. 'There are plenty of Simferopol Boys who have got their qualifications from me.' Kenny Mountford looked puzzled. 'I mean that they have never killed anyone. I have done the killings for them.'

'Ah.' Kenny couldn't deny he was tempted. He knew that, for the full immersion in his character that Charlie Fenton required, he should do the killing himself. But he couldn't help feeling a little squeamish about the idea. And if Vasili was offering him a way round the problem… 'How much?' he asked, not realising that, now the danger of his actually having to commit a murder had receded, he'd dropped out of his Ukrainian accent.

Vasili told him. It seemed a demeaningly small sum for the price of a human life, but Kenny knew this was not the moment for sentimentality. And he did still have quite a lot of money left from the sitcom fees. 'So how do you select the target? Even more important, how do you make it look as if I've actually committed the murder?'

The Ukrainian dismissed the questions with an airy wave of his hand. 'You leave such details to me. I have done it before, so I know what I'm doing. So far as Fyodor is concerned, it is definitely you who has committed the murder. So far as the police are concerned, nothing ties the crime to you. All you have to do is to get yourself a watertight alibi for tomorrow evening.'

'Tomorrow evening?' Kenny was rather shocked by the short notice.

With a shrug, Vasili said, 'Once you have decided to do something, there is no point in putting off doing it.'

'I suppose you're right…'

'Of course I am right.'

'But I'm still not clear about how you select the victim.'

'That, as I say, is not your problem. Usually, I kill one of my client's enemies. That way, not only does Fyodor recognise there is a motive for the murder, the client also gets rid of someone who's bugging them. It is a very efficient system – no?'

'But if your client doesn't have any enemies...'

'Everyone has enemies,' said Vasili firmly. Kenny was about to say that he really didn't think he did, but thought better of it. 'So, Anatoli, have we got a deal?'

'Yes, we've got a deal.'

Having checked with Vasili the proposed timescale for the murder and handed over the agreed fee the next morning, Kenny set about arranging his alibi. It couldn't involve any of the Simferopol Boys, because Fyodor wasn't meant to know that he had an alibi. So, to keep himself safe from police suspicions, Anatoli Semyonov would have to, for one evening only, return to his old persona of Kenny Mountford.

He decided that a visit a fringe theatre was the answer. A quick check through *Time Out* led to a call to an actor friend, who sounded slightly surprised to hear him, but who agreed to join him in darkest Kilburn for an experimental play about glue-sniffing, whose cast included an actress they both knew. 'You're not going with Lesley-Jane?' asked the friend.

'No.'

'I'm not surprised.'

'What do you mean by that?'

'Nothing, Kenny, nothing.'

Normally he would have asked for an explanation of his friend's remark, but Kenny was preoccupied by his plans for the evening. Even if the audience was small, as audiences for fringe theatre frequently are, he would still have people to vouch for where he was at the moment Vasili committed his murder for him. Kenny Mountford felt a glow of satisfaction at the efficiency of the arrangements he had made.

The serenity of his mood was shattered in the afternoon by a call from Fyodor. 'Anatoli, I want you to keep an eye on Vasili. I'm not sure he's playing straight with me.'

'How do you mean?' asked Kenny nervously.

'I've heard rumours he's doing work on the side, not just jobs I give him for the Simferopol Boys.'

'What kind of work?'

'Contract killing. If you can bring me any proof that's what he's been doing, Anatoli, I will see to it that he is eliminated. And you will be richly rewarded.'

'Oh,' said Kenny.

He spent the rest of the afternoon trying to get through to Vasili's mobile, but it was permanently switched off. By the time he met his friend at the fringe theatre in Kilburn, Kenny Mountford was in an extremely twitchy state. There was no pretending that his situation wasn't serious. If Fyodor found out that he had actually paid Vasili to do his qualifying murder for him, Kenny didn't think it'd be long before there was a contract out on his own life. But he couldn't let anyone at the theatre see how anxious he was, so all his acting skills were called for as he sat through the interminably tedious and badly acted play about glue-sniffing and then, over drinks in the bar, told the actress who'd been in it how marvellous, absolutely marvellous her performance had been.

His friend had his car with him and offered to drop Kenny off. As they were driving along they heard the Radio 4 *Midnight News*. The distinguished theatre director Charlie Fenton had been shot dead in Notting Hill at ten o'clock that evening.

'Good God,' said his friend. 'If you hadn't actually been with me, I'd have had you down as number one suspect for that murder, Kenny.'

'Why?'

But his friend wouldn't say more.

Had Kenny Mountford not completely cut himself off from the English press and media, he would have known about the affair between Charlie Fenton and Lesley-Jane Walden. Their photos had been plastered all over the tabloids for weeks. He might also have pieced together that the director had never had any interest in him, only in Lesley-Jane – hence the request when they first met for their mutual landline, rather than Kenny's mobile number. How convenient for Charlie had been the actor's willingness to go undercover and leave the field wide open to his rival.

Vasili, however, read his tabloids and knew all about the affair. He recognised Charlie Fenton as the perfect victim. The guy had gone off with Kenny's girlfriend! Fyodor wouldn't need any convincing that that was a proper motive for murder.

So Vasili had laid in wait outside the Notting Hill house, confident that sooner or later Charlie Fenton would appear. As indeed he did, on the dot of ten o'clock. A car drew up some hundred yards away from Kenny Mountford's house and the very recognisable figure of the director emerged, blowing a kiss to someone inside. Vasili drew out his favoured weapon, the PSS silent pistol which had been developed for the KGB, and when his quarry was close enough, discharged two bullets into Charlie Fenton's head.

Job done. Coolly replacing the pistol in his pocket, Vasili had walked away, confident that there was nothing to tie him to this crime, as there had been nothing to tie him to any of his previous fifty-odd hits. Confident also that Fyodor would assume that the job had been done by Kenny Mountford.

What he hadn't taken into account was Charlie Fenton's tom cat nature. No sooner had the director bedded one woman than he was on the lookout for another, and his honeymoon of monogamy with Lesley-Jane Walden had been short. She, suspecting something was going on, had been watching at the window of the house that evening for her philandering lover to return. As soon as Charlie Fenton got out of the car she had started to video him on her camera, and thus recorded his death. The footage, when handed over to the police, also revealed very clear images of Vasili, from which he was quickly identified and as quickly arrested.

Lesley-Jane Walden was in seventh heaven. To be at the centre of a murder case – there were actresses who would kill to achieve that kind of publicity. In the event, though, it didn't do her much good. The police made no mention of the help she had given to their investigation in any of their press conferences. They didn't even mention her name. And all the obituaries of Charlie Fenton spoke only of 'his towering theatrical originality' and his reputation as 'a loving family man'. Lesley-Jane Walden was furious.

Her mood wasn't improved when Kenny ordered her to get out of the house. She moved into a girlfriend's flat and started badgering her agent to get her on to *I'm A Celebrity…Get Me Out Of Here!*

'You are a clever boy, Anatoli Semyonov,' said Fyodor, when they next met. 'To get rid of your girlfriend's lover and arrange things so that Vasili is arrested for the murder – this is excellent work. I have wanted Vasili out of the way for a long time. You are not just a clever boy, Anatoli, you are also a clever Simferopol Boy.'

'You mean I have qualified to join the gang?'

'Of course you have qualified. Now you will always be welcome here. You are one of the Simferopol Boys.'

So Kenny Mountford too thought: job done. Except, of course, having done that job was not going to lead on to the other job. Kenny had done what he promised – infiltrated a London gang – but the man to whom he had made that promise was no longer around. There would never be a Charlie Fenton production about London gangs. All Kenny Mountford's efforts had been in vain.

And yet the realisation did not upset him. No one could say he hadn't tried everything he could to achieve respectability as an actor, and now it was time to move on. Time to get back to being Kenny Mountford. All that 'Method', in-depth research approach to characterisation might be all right for some people in the business. But, for him, he reckoned he preferred something called 'acting'.

When he finally spoke to his agent, she revealed that she'd been going nearly apoplectic trying to contact him over the previous weeks. The BBC was doing a new sitcom and they wanted him to play the lead! He said he'd do it.

But Kenny Mountford didn't lost touch with Fyodor and the Simferopol Boys. As an actor, it's always good to have more than one string to your bow.

JUROR 8

STUART NEVILLE

M y name is Emmet McArdle. I am seventy-six years old, and
I feel every day of it. I don't sleep well. I don't pass water well.
I don't eat much. Which leaves me a lot of time to think. And I've
been doing far too much of that lately.

I wish I could say all this started after the trial, but that wouldn't
be true. I'm just an old man with old man complaints, and my
discomforts go back long before I did jury duty nine months ago in
August of '57. But now, when I can't sleep at night, it's the trial that
plays on my mind. The boy we saved from the chair.

That boy went free because of us twelve men.

You'd think that would be easier to live with than if we'd sent him
to burn. Probably should be. But ever since I left that courthouse,
he's nagged at me. Kept whispering in my ear, saying maybe you
were wrong, maybe I did kill my father after all. And maybe I'm
fixing to kill again.

Well, a week and a half ago, that's exactly what he did.

I heard the news on the radio. I didn't make the connection

straight away, mind you, but there it was. I was in the back room of the store, what used to be my store, and I guess on paper it still is. But my boy Eugene runs it now.

McArdle Musical Instruments of 48th Street.

When my father survived the boat trip from Ireland, escaping the poverty that devoured his own parents, he and his brother brought with them four piano accordions, two melodeons, three mandolins, and a suitcase full of D whistles. His brother, my uncle, also made it across, but he died within a week of landing. He coughed his lungs up from pneumonia. I don't know what they did with his body.

My father, Emmet Senior, found a room somewhere in the Bowery, probably sharing a floor with a gang of other Irishmen, all of them wondering where those streets paved with gold were located. He used the little money he'd brought with him, and what he'd taken from his brother's pockets, to rent a stall on Canal Street. As he told it to me, he wound up selling those fancy accordions for less than they cost him, but he made a killing on the whistles, snapped up by immigrants who wanted to hear a little 'Londonderry Air' to remind them of home. He made enough to buy more stock and establish a paying business.

A year later, he was making a profit on accordions, and mandolins, and banjos, as well as playing in a ceilidh band in the evenings. That was how he met my mother, a brown-haired girl from Clonmel, at a neighbourhood dance. I never knew her. She died giving birth to me, and my father never married again. Not unless you consider whiskey a wife.

I took over the running of the store at age sixteen. I never got much schooling, at least not the proper kind, learning everything I needed to know on the shop floor. How to tell what a customer wanted, how much he had to spend, whether he was good for credit. My father remained the boss, of course. We walked to the store together every morning from our apartment on the next block. While I opened up, Emmet Senior went to the back office, with its big old mahogany desk and the portrait of that brown-haired girl from Clonmel, and sat down. He'd leave it a decent time, maybe until noon, and then he'd open the right-hand drawer, remove the bottle of liquor, and start drinking.

I carried him home most evenings, his arm slung around my shoulder, his feet dragging on the ground. And the store takings in my pocket, ready to stow in the safe in his bedroom. I never saw the money again. I don't know what he did with it, whether he banked it or drank it. All I know was the rent got paid, and I got my salary. Weekends he'd go out and play at the local ceilidhs.

I was twenty-five when he died. He touched up some young woman at a dance, neither realising that her fiancé was only a few feet away, nor that said fiancé was in the habit of carrying a pistol.

I cried when I buried him, not that he deserved it.

Ten years later, I had a wife and five children of my own, and I'd made enough money that I could move the store from the Bowery up to 48th Street.

My two girls grew up to be schoolteachers, same as their mother. I met Mary at a dance, just like my father had met my mother, but I took better care of her. I paid for proper care when she gave birth to our children, rather than giving some backstreet witchdoctor a dollar for the job.

My eldest, Jarlath, became a police officer. Don't ask me where he got that from. All right, we're Irish, but that doesn't mean we're all born with badges.

Eugene had the music in him since he was a baby. I knew before his first birthday that he would take over the store for me. And he did, not long after he came back from fighting the Nazis in Europe.

His younger brother Columba was not so fortunate. He never made it off the beach, cut down by machine gun fire along with hundreds of other good men. I miss him too much to be proud of him, hold too much resentment in my heart to be glad of what he sacrificed. He was my son and it isn't fair that he died, no matter what for. I am angry about it, and that's that.

I still show up to work every day. I live with Eugene and his wife – Mary was taken by a stroke five years ago – and we both travel to the store every morning, just like me and my father did. We don't walk all the way, of course; some of the journey is by train, but we go together all the same.

And just like my father, I go to the back office. I took his desk with me when I moved the store, and it's still there now, along with that portrait of the girl from Clonmel, and another of my absent son. Sometimes I talk to my mother, as if we had known each other. I hope she'd be proud of me, proud of the life I'd made for me and my children. I talk to her more now than I used to. Perhaps the growing awareness that I'll see her before too long makes me want to know her better.

I only get called out of the office when someone's interested in an accordion, or they want one repaired. The store's ground floor used to be a gallery of pearloid, rows of Hohners, Paolo Sopranis, Victorias, big 120-bass monsters right down to little 12-bass tiddlers.

Not any more. Nowadays, everybody wants a guitar.

And not even real instruments, proper acoustic instruments with air in them to make a decent sound. Now the ground floor is full of these planks with strings on them, Fender, Gibson, Gretsch, and I don't know what. I swear it's a race to see how much paint they can put on a stick of wood and still get money for it. The Gibson rep came by last week, and he had a guitar with him that looked like an arrowhead. He called it a flying something or other. I asked him how someone was supposed to sit down and play the darned thing without it sliding off his knee.

Eugene took one even though I told him it was a damn fool thing to do. Mark my words, it'll still be hanging there five years from now.

Anyway, I spend my days in the back room, looking at that photograph of my mother, wondering how I'm going to get through the day. If I'm honest, I was relieved to get the letter calling me for jury duty. I grumbled about it to Eugene, but inside, I relished the idea of getting out and doing something that mattered.

And when I realised what the trial was, I felt good, I felt the importance of this burden I'd been given.

All twelve of us had the boy strapped down and wired up the minute the prosecutor opened his mouth. Not a chance in the world this young thug was innocent. They talked till I was dizzy, and not a word told me anything but this young man had stabbed his father in the heart in a fit of anger. They had two witnesses, a man about my age, and a woman in her forties. One saw the boy do it, the other heard him.

And yet, and yet, and yet.

The foreman held a ballot, and we all raised our hands to say guilty. All but one.

The man next to me, Juror 8.

Let's talk, he said.

And we talked.

We talked until God cracked the sky. We talked until every other man in that room had been reduced to a sweating pulp. That man, Juror 8, didn't stop until he'd broken every one of us.

I was the first to fall.

When he stood against the rest of them, saying let's talk, I'm not sure, let's go over it again – when he said that, when he made his stand, I listened.

Why?

Because I'm a contrary old bastard, that's why. Pardon my language. And I'm Irish. Show an Irishman a lost cause, and he'll fight to the death for it, just out of pure wickedness.

So I changed my vote. When all the rest of them protested, thought me an old fool, I dug my heels in and said I wanted to hear what Juror 8 had to say. If I hadn't, he would've let it go, and the boy would've got fried. And that young couple in the new Pontiac Star Chief would be breathing this morning.

The young man had called at his sweetheart's building on West 127th to take her to the movies. They were approached by two Hispanic males, threatened with a knife, ordered to hand over the keys to the shining new car. The young man resisted. He was stabbed in the heart.

They took the girl with them. Her parents found the young man's body on the sidewalk and called in the description of the vehicle. Lord alone knows what they went through, knowing their daughter had been taken by the same people who had killed her boyfriend.

The police caught up with them out in Queens. The two males didn't show their hands quickly enough, and they were shot dead right there in the car. The cops found the girl's body in the trunk.

She must have put up a fight, made too much noise. They'd killed her before they had a chance to molest her.

I shook my head when I heard the report on the radio the following morning, wondered at the state of the world. But that was all. It wasn't until Jarlath called by that night for supper that I learned the truth of it.

Jarlath had a wife at one time, but she couldn't hack being married to a cop. At least that's what he said. God forgive me, my eldest son has a mean streak in him, and he's hard to like. His brother barely tolerates him, only has him over for supper once a week in order to placate me.

'You hear about that double homicide last night, Pop?' Jarlath asked between mouthfuls of pork chop with applesauce.

Eugene and his wife Wendy exchanged a look. Their three girls remained silent as they ate.

'Not at the table, Jarlath, all right?' Eugene said.

Jarlath ignored him. 'You hear about it, Pop?'

'I heard something on the radio,' I said. 'Let's maybe talk about it after supper.'

I swear Jarlath is as thick in the skull as a gorilla. He kept right on talking.

'You heard the perps got shot over near Flushing Meadows, right?'

Eugene shook his head and rolled his eyes.

'Yes,' I said, deciding to humour Jarlath in hopes of finishing the conversation as quickly as possible.

He put his fork down, ran his tongue around his teeth, seeking stray morsels of pork.

'Well,' he said, sitting back in his chair, 'you've come across one of them before.'

'Oh?'

'Hugo Fuente,' he said.

My scalp prickled. I felt the hairs on my arms stand up like soldiers. A loose feeling low down in my stomach.

'Pop?' Eugene said.

Jarlath's crooked smile fell off his face.

They must have seen it on me. The horror. My fork fell from my fingers and rattled on Wendy's good china plate, taking a chip off it.

'Pop,' Eugene said once more, reaching for my hand. 'You're shaking. What's wrong?'

'Nothing,' I said. 'Please excuse me.'

I left the table and made for my room at the back of the house. The door hit the frame harder than I meant it to. I sat on the edge of my bed and chewed on my knuckle.

'Pop?'

Eugene calling from the corridor. I sprang to my feet, or as near as a man my age can manage, and turned the key in the door. The handle rattled, then he knocked hard.

'Pop? What's wrong? Open the door.'

'I'm fine,' I called. 'I just want to lie down for a little while.'

'Come on, Pop. You're scaring me.'

'I'm all right,' I said. 'Let me alone. Please.'

'Pop, you got me worried. C'mon, open the door.'

'Let me alone, dammit.'

I didn't mean to yell, but it did the trick.

'All right,' Eugene said. 'Wendy can warm your supper when you feel like eating.'

I returned to my bed, sat on the edge, my hands clasped together.

Hugo Fuente.

Just a kid, we'd said, all twelve of us. A boy. How could we send an eighteen-year-old to die? Some of us wanted to. Some of us fought hard. But Juror 8 ground them down.

This boy, he said, had been hit on the head every day of his life. I didn't doubt it. But he didn't look like a mean kid. I can still see him there in the courtroom, small, lean like a greyhound, and those frightened eyes.

I thought about the other eleven men. Had they heard the news? Had they dismissed it as they had all the other murders they'd read about in the papers? Just another couple of unfortunates caught up in the violence that haunted the darker parts of town. Nothing for them to worry about.

Had Juror 8 heard it?

I wondered, had he?

It was the day after we delivered the verdict that the worry set in, gnawing at my conscience like a woodworm. One part of me said Juror 8 was right. We were all pretty sure the boy had killed his father, but the law says pretty sure isn't enough. It's black or white, this or that, yes or no. That's all right. I can live with that.

The other part of me kept asking, is possibly innocent enough? Does it weigh more than probably guilty? I guess men have wrestled with that question since human beings first invented trials. And I guess many men have had tougher decisions to make than I had.

But few men could've had Juror 8 by their sides, pushing and pulling them, making them question every measure of their being. Making them turn on themselves. Turning them into children, shying from their parents' hands, nodding, red-faced, tears and snot on their lips, saying yessir, I'll behave.

I went to bed, but I didn't sleep a wink.

My belly growled with hunger, but I didn't get up to reclaim the dinner I'd abandoned. I just lay there, thinking. Thinking hard as I'd ever done in my life. But still no answer came. I'd have to go out for one of those, ask my questions out loud, not bounce them around inside my skull like it was a pinball machine ready to scream tilt.

I called by Jarlath's precinct early the following morning. I knew he always turned in an hour before he went on his beat. The desk sergeant watched me approach in much the same way a chimpanzee might watch a human through the bars in the zoo. A look on its face that says it'd tear you to pieces if it ever got the opportunity, but for now it's content to watch you pass.

'Jarlath McArdle,' I said, taking off my hat.

The desk sergeant seemed to look past me. 'What about him?'

'He's my son,' I said. 'I'd like to see him.'

The desk sergeant raised his eyes to really look at me for the first time.

'You're the Jar's old man? Jesus.'

'I'd like to talk to him, please,' I said.

He called over my shoulder. 'Mickey. Hey, Mickey. The Jar down in the locker room?'

'I think so,' a big man behind me said.

'Well get him up here. His old man wants him.'

'Thanks,' I said.

The desk sergeant didn't reply. He kept his eyes on whatever paperwork he had in front of him.

'Should I take a seat?' I asked.

He waved his fingers toward the wall, and the bench that leaned against it.

I sat down and waited. The man next to me fell asleep, his head on my shoulder, breath smelling of beer. The woman on the other side applied make-up. I believe fifteen minutes passed before Jarlath appeared.

'What's up, Pop?' he asked. 'I was just about to go out. Kenny's waiting for me in the car.'

'I could use your help with something,' I said.

'Sure, Pop, what do you need?'

I looked at the people either side of me. 'I need to talk in private.'

'Sure,' he said, taking me by the arm and helping me to my feet.

He held on to my elbow as he led me down a corridor. I shook him off.

'Easy, Pop,' he said. 'Just don't want you falling.'

I stopped, turned to him, and asked, 'Do you see me landing on my face?'

'No, Pop,' he said.

'All right,' I said. 'Where are we going?'

'The squad room should be empty,' Jarlath said. 'In here.'

He led me into a room that looked like it belonged in a schoolhouse. A dusty blackboard covering most of the wall at one end and a podium, a dozen desks facing it.

Jarlath sat me down at one of the desks, pulled a chair up next to me.

'So, what's up?'

I looked down at my hands and marvelled at how papery my skin had become, the blue of the veins, the dark liver spots.

'Pop?'

I took a breath and said, 'I want you to find some information on a man for me.'

'Who?'

I wet my lips. 'One of the jurors on the Hugo Fuente trial.'

Jarlath sat quiet for a few seconds. 'Why, Pop?'

'I have my reasons,' I said. 'He was Juror 8. He told me his name was Davis.'

'I don't know,' Jarlath said. He worried at his cap with his fingers. 'Maybe you need a private eye or something. There isn't much I can find out about a man. Least, not legally, and not with that little information to go on.'

'There must be a record,' I said. 'At the courthouse, or the district attorney's office. They must have kept a note of who he was, where he lived.'

'Yeah, sure, but what do you want with him?'

I'm not sure I knew the answer to that question.

'Just to talk,' I said. It was the best I could think of.

'All right, Pop.' He put his big hand on my shoulder. I felt the weight of it there and for the millionth time I wondered how I had begot such a hulk of a man. 'I'll see what I can do.'

We both stood. Jarlath looked at his feet. I looked at the door. Between us, the awkward static of men who love each other but don't know how to admit it.

'Well, I'll be going,' I said. 'You've got work to do.'

I made my way to the door, but Jarlath called from behind.

'You okay, Pop?'

I stopped at the doorway and turned to face him. Concern deepened the lines on his face.

'What I told you last night, about the Fuente kid, that rattled you, didn't it?'

'A little, I guess.'

A lot, I should've said. Enough that I hadn't slept all night.

He came closer, shuffling like a man unsure of his footing. 'Well, don't worry, you hear? Maybe he did that murder, and maybe he didn't. Plenty of juries get it wrong. You did the best you could with the evidence you had. Those kids he killed the other night, that had nothing to do with you. You know that, right?'

'I know,' I said.

I've lost count of the lies I've told in my life, even if God hasn't. I left Jarlath there in the squad room and made my way home.

I didn't expect to hear from him until he was due to call for supper the following week. Instead, he rang Eugene's buzzer the very next night. I knew it was him as soon as I heard it. Little rivers of chills ran across my skin.

Voices at the door, then Eugene's eldest, Colette, calling, 'Grandpa? Grandpa, it's Uncle Jarlath for you.'

He waited for me in the hall. Eugene arrived at the same moment I did.

'What's going on?' he asked.

'I need to talk with Pop,' Jarlath said.

'What about?'

'Nothing you need to worry about,' I said, more curtly than I'd intended. I grabbed my coat from the stand by the door and turned to Jarlath. 'Come on, I feel like an egg cream.'

Eugene watched us leave, irritation and worry on his face.

Jarlath and I took a couple of stools at the farthest end of the counter in the drugstore three blocks from Eugene's place. I ordered two egg creams, but Jarlath said, no, a Pepsi-Cola.

I guess he'd rather I'd taken him to a bar. He had that dry-lipped look about him, like he craved a beer or a whiskey, the same look my father used to get right around lunchtime every day.

A pretty young lady brought us our drinks then left us in peace. The chatter of teenage couples jangled in the air around us. Couples like the boy and girl who'd died a few nights ago.

No, they didn't die. They were murdered.

I shook the image away.

'I'm guessing you have something for me,' I said.

'Yeah, I got something,' he said, wiping cola from his lips. 'I got something all right.'

I waited.

Eventually, he said, 'Before I tell you this, Pop, you gotta promise me something.'

'Promise you what?'

'That you don't go near this guy. Okay? Just promise me that. Don't go near him, don't talk to him, just stay away. All right?'

I didn't hesitate. 'All right,' I said.

One more lie couldn't damn me any more than I was damned already.

'His name is Willard Davis,' Jarlath said. 'He's an architect, a partner in a firm on Madison. Reynolds & Waylan, they do big commercial stuff, skyscrapers, all that. A big shot. He's got a fancy apartment on Central Park West, around 68th or 69th, overlooking the park. A wife and two boys. A family man, a good career, a beautiful home, drives one of those little British sports cars.'

I nodded slowly. 'Sounds like a nice life. And it sounds like any second now, you're going to say "but".'

'Yeah,' Jarlath said. 'A big but.'

I took a swig of the egg cream, sickly sweet, chocolate syrup cloying at the back of my throat. 'Go on,' I said.

'When I got the name, I knew it sounded familiar. So I looked it up. I went down to records and ran him. This guy, Pop, he's bad news.'

'Tell me,' I said.

'About four years ago, a girl went missing, a secretary at that architecture firm. Marian Wallace, she was called. I mean, just gone, like in a puff of smoke. You know, one minute she was there, next thing she's gone and no one knows where to. Except…'

'Except what?'

'I know one of the detectives who worked that case. Paddy Comiskey, big guy, he was at me and Joanie's wedding. Got drunk and hit on Wendy. I had to stop Eugene from trying to lay one on him. Anyway, another girl in that office, she told Paddy about Marian, how she was getting friendly with one of the senior architects, how he'd taken her to dinner a couple times, maybe a club, maybe some drinks. And next thing, he's going to take her up to Vermont for a weekend.

'So, that was a Friday when Marian said this to her friend. Come Monday, Marian doesn't show up for work. It's three days before anyone thinks to report her missing.'

The egg cream felt cold in my stomach, oily and sugary on my tongue. 'And this senior architect,' I said.

Jarlath nodded. 'Yeah, it was Willard Davis. He denied it, of course. His wife said he never left the city that weekend. But Paddy didn't buy it. He interrogated this Davis guy. Said he was the coldest son of a bitch he ever come across, and believe me, Paddy's seen some cold fish in his time. But he told me he ain't never seen cold like this. He grilled Davis for eight hours straight, never got a goddam scrap out of him. Said Davis just kept looking him in the eye all the while, like he was daring him, saying, come on, catch me if you can. You got no body, you got no weapon, you got nothing but suspicion. Leading him on, like it was a game. And this guy can talk, Paddy says. Davis had him doubting his own mind.'

'Yeah,' I said. 'That sounds like Juror 8.'

'But here's the thing, Pop. The girl, the witness who said Marian had told her this stuff. A month or so after Paddy dropped his case against Davis, this girl is found drowned in her own bathtub.'

'A coincidence, maybe?'

Jarlath shook his head. 'Cops believe in coincidences like they believe in Santa Claus and the Tooth Fairy. Paddy had Davis for the killing. He didn't have a shred of real evidence, nothing physical, but he was sure Willard Davis killed that girl.'

'Why?' I asked. 'With no evidence, why did he think that?'

'He didn't think it,' Jarlath said. 'He knew it. See, Pop, there's two sides to nailing a perpetrator. There's knowing and there's proving. You understand?'

'I guess,' I said, but I really didn't.

'Anyway, Pop, stay away from this Davis guy. Just let the whole thing go. All right?'

'All right,' I said.

I finished my egg cream without saying another word, deaf to the clamour of the kids all around us, thinking only of what I would say to Willard Davis when I found him.

At breakfast the next morning, after another sleepless night, I told Eugene that I wouldn't be going to work at the store that day.

'What's up, Pop? Don't you feel well?'

'I'm a little tired, that's all. I might go back to bed, catch up on my sleep.'

Eugene nodded. 'You do that, Pop. Take it easy.'

I waited until Eugene had left, and his girls had gone to school, before I slipped back out of my room and made for the door. I heard Wendy humming in the kitchen, the clink of plates, the rattle of cutlery. Quiet as the dead, I let myself out, down the stairs and onto the sidewalk.

The stairs from the subway station on 68th and Lexington led up to the street beneath the towering grandeur of Thomas Hunter Hall, like a gothic castle that had sprouted up from the pavement, its battlements seeming too high off the ground. I had looked up Reynolds & Waylan in the Yellow Pages that morning, and walked southwest toward their building on the corner of 66th and Madison.

I brushed shoulders with young men in good suits rushing to meetings, wealthy housewives heading to coffee dates or shopping in the swanky stores, bags dangling from their elbows. Strange how I had shared a city with these people all my life, yet they seemed from a different world. The constant rumble of cars, blaring of horns, the thrum of it all.

I found the door to Reynolds & Waylan's building between a bridal shop and a chocolatier. Pushing my way through the revolving door, I entered the lobby, all pink marble, dull brass and moulded ceilings. I approached the desk, a hefty man in a uniform and a peaked cap sitting behind it.

'Who you looking for?' he asked with less courtesy than I expected.

I told him.

'On sixth,' he said, pointing to the row of three elevators.

A hard-faced woman gave me a forced smile as I crossed the lobby, extended her hand in the direction of the middle elevator, where a girl waited, ready to press whichever button I required.

We did not speak as the car rose through the floors, a bell ringing as each passed.

'Sixth,' she said eventually. 'Mind the doors.'

I stepped out onto a reception area that looked more like a hospital, all clean lines, black granite, white marble, glass everywhere.

A young woman behind the desk asked, 'Can I help you?'

I stood mute for a moment, suddenly aware of the foolishness of my actions. Suddenly, and quite reasonably, afraid.

'Sir?'

I removed my hat, gripped it in front of me. 'I... uh... I want to see Willard Davis.'

'Is Mr Davis expecting you?' she asked.

I shook my head.

'Who should I say is calling?'

'My name is Emmet McArdle,' I said. 'Tell him, Juror 9. He'll know.'

A small ripple of uncertainty on her face. She indicated a row of leather-upholstered chairs by the elevator.

'Please take a seat,' she said.

I did so. The chair was square-edged and uncomfortable. A modern design, I guess, the sort of thing young professional types like. I watched as she spoke into a telephone, her hand shielding her lips and the mouthpiece, as if she shared some conspiracy with the plastic and wires.

When she finally hung up, she called across the reception to me.

'I'm sorry, sir, Mr Davis is in a meeting right now. If you'd like to leave a telephone number, he'll be glad to get in touch.'

'I can wait,' I said.

'Mr Davis expects to be busy all day. Like I say, I can give him your number and he can contact you at another time.'

'I can wait all day,' I said.

A moment's pause, her smile faltering. 'Sir, Mr Davis will be busy all day. He will contact you when he can.'

My mouth dried. I felt the jangle of adrenalin and anger crackling out to my fingertips. 'I can wait all day,' I said. 'Mr Davis has to go to lunch some time. He has to leave when he's finished work for the day. I promise you, I won't take up any more of his valuable time than I have to.'

Her smile dissolved. 'Sir, again, Mr Davis won't be able to see you today. Our reception area is only for people who have business here, so I'm afraid I must ask you to leave.'

I sat there, silent, my heart bouncing in my chest.

The young woman's voice hardened. 'Sir, I must ask you to leave.'

I stood rather too quickly, and my head went light. I staggered a little.

'Sir, are you feeling all right?'

'I'm fine,' I said, steadying myself with a hand against the chair. 'Thank you for your help.'

I leaned against the elevator wall on the way down, sweat prickling my brow.

Willard Davis left the building, alone, at a quarter of six.

I expected him to perhaps visit a bar for an after-work cocktail with some colleagues, or maybe that receptionist. Instead he walked the block westward to Fifth Avenue, across, and into the park.

The day had passed slowly for me, wandering the pathways among the trees, touring the blocks around Lenox Hill. The owner of a coffee shop gave me angry looks every time I used his restroom without buying anything. By the time I took up position some yards further along Madison, a newspaper held open in front of me, I neared a state of exhaustion. But when Davis emerged and started walking, I ditched the paper in a trashcan and did my best to keep pace with him.

Early May is a fine time to take an evening stroll through Central Park, the place flooding with new green, the new-born leaves and flowers masking the smell of the exhaust fumes. The sun, now low in the sky, made glowing pools on the path as it twisted one way and another.

Willard Davis walked like he owned the world. Tall as I remembered him, and thin like a whip. Late forties, dark hair combed back, showing a little scalp on top. One hand carried a good leather briefcase, the other nestled in his pocket. His light grey suit clung to his lean body, the fabric rippling on the breeze.

I started to breathe hard as I struggled to keep him in sight. Cars rumbled and roared on the 65th Street Transverse, a few yards to my left. I heard the clip-clopping of horses, the rattle of the carriages they pulled. But Davis stuck to the small paths, the branches overhanging, loose stones stirred by his feet. I could not match his pace.

'Dammit,' I whispered as I lost him around the corner up ahead.

I dug deep inside myself for some reserve of energy, but found none. Defeated, I slowed as the splendid buildings of Central Park

West came into view. The evening had dimmed, the breeze a little cooler on my skin.

'God dammit,' I said aloud as I slowed to a stop, my shoulders rising and falling, air wheezing in and out of me.

After a minute or so, I had enough wind in me to go on. I crossed between the traffic on Central Park West, ignoring angry blasts of taxi horns.

Jarlath had said Davis lived around 68th or 69th. I headed north, but I don't know why I felt I had to. I had lost him, and that was that. I didn't believe he would have called me, even if I'd left a number with the receptionist. But still, I kept walking, looking up at the buildings as I passed, imagining him being greeted home by his loving family.

As I passed beneath the awning of a building, a voice said, 'Mr McArdle.'

My heart leapt in my chest. I spun around, my arm up in a defensive gesture, though I had no reason for it.

Willard Davis stood there, watching me, briefcase in his hand. A thin smile on his lips that didn't reach his grey-blue eyes.

I have never been more frightened in my life.

'Why have you been following me?' he asked.

'I... I... I wanted to...'

He interrupted my stammering. 'I would like to have been able to speak with you at the office, Mr McArdle, but as Hattie told you, I was busy all day. And now you've followed me home. Why?'

'I'm sorry,' I said, my fear giving way to a strange kind of shame, the shame of being caught in a despicable act even though I knew I had done no wrong. 'I just wanted to talk,' I said.

He studied me for a few seconds, like I was a bug on a pin.

'How did you know where I worked?'

'My eldest boy,' I said. 'He's a policeman.'

'I expect that's against the law. For a policeman to give out personal information like that.'

I nodded. 'I expect it is.'

'All right,' he said. 'You'd better come up.'

'Sarah, boys, this is Mr McArdle, an old friend of mine.'

The two boys, one around eleven, the other a year or two older, had been standing in the drawing room like soldiers awaiting an inspection.

'Pleased to meet you, sir,' they said in unison.

Clean-scrubbed faces, their clothes pressed and spotless. When my boys were that age, there was never a moment when they didn't look like they'd been pulled feet-first from a muddy ditch.

Sarah, the wife, didn't respond. She sat in an armchair, her gaze fixed on some far away place that I believe only existed in her mind.

'Sarah?' Davis said. 'Sarah, darling, this is Mr McArdle.'

She looked at me, startled, as if I had appeared in a flash of sparks and smoke. A smile visited her lips.

'Pleased to meet you,' she said, her words dull and thick.

I wondered what medication she was on to blunt her so.

Davis spoke to a coloured lady in a dark pinafore.

'Elizabeth, go ahead and serve Sarah and the boys dinner. Keep mine warm for later. Mr McArdle and I will be in my study. I'd like not to be disturbed.'

'Yessir,' she said, bending at the knee.

Davis showed me to a cavernous room lined with book cases, oil paintings on the walls, an antique desk at the far end, not unlike the one I'd moved uptown with my music store, but in far better condition. The room smelled of old paper and wood varnish.

He sat down in a leather swivel chair on one side of the desk, indicated the seat opposite. 'So what can I do for you, Mr McArdle?'

I took the seat, feeling very small in this room, like a fish in the belly of a shark.

'Maybe you heard the news a few nights ago,' I said. 'Or maybe you read about it in the papers. A double homicide. A young couple, not so very far uptown from here. They were killed by two Hispanic males.'

'Tragic,' Davis said.

He reached for a stack of mail that waited on his desk, lifted the first letter, and slipped the dagger-like blade of an opener beneath the flap.

'The two killers were shot by the police over in Queens,' I said. 'One of them was Hugo Fuente.'

Davis paused, the blade clear of the envelope, his stony eyes on me.

'The boy we let go,' I said.

He blinked. Nodded. 'Like I said, tragic.'

'That young couple would be alive if we hadn't saved that boy from the chair.'

'Maybe,' Davis said. 'Maybe not. We didn't try him for the murder of that couple. We tried him for the killing of his father. And we found him not guilty. Whatever he did before or after the trial, it has nothing to do with you, me, or any man on that jury.'

'I wish I could believe that,' I said. 'I wish I could turn away from this, convince myself that two young people didn't die because I changed my vote from guilty to not guilty.'

'There were ten men in that room besides you and me,' Davis said. 'Ten men who changed their votes. You have nothing to feel bad about.'

'Yes I do,' I said, my voice rising. 'Because I fell first. Because I allowed you to go on and take every other man down, one by one.'

He set the blade on the desktop, slid the letter from its envelope, and spoke as he skimmed the pages. 'All we did was talk. No one had a gun to his head. We reasoned it out. You know that.'

Davis looked up from the letter, fixed his gaze on mine, hard like flint.

'Now, here you are, wanting to talk some more. The time to talk was nine months ago. It's too late now.'

'That's right,' I said. 'It's too late. But I want to ask you one question.'

He dropped the pages on his desk. 'Go on.'

I took a breath and said, 'Why?'

'I don't understand.'

'Why did you do it? Why did you go on a crusade to save the boy?'

Davis shrugged. 'You know why. Because I didn't believe the evidence was strong enough to put him in the chair. Do you want to pick over it all again? The old man in the apartment below, the woman across the El track, the knife with the carved handle. Shall we do it all again, Mr McArdle?'

'No,' I said. 'I've gone over it enough times myself since that day.'

'Well, then. What more is there to say?' He got to his feet. 'If you don't mind, Mr McArdle, I have work to do tonight, and I'd like to take an hour with my family if I can.'

I remained seated and asked, 'You want to know what I think?'

Davis's face hardened as he lowered himself back into his chair. 'All right, what do you think?'

Leaning forward, I said, 'I think it was just a game to you. I think you didn't give a hoot if that boy was guilty or innocent. I think it mattered not one jot to you if he went to the chair or walked free.'

Davis sat quite still as I talked, his stare never leaving me, his face blank as an unmarked grave.

'I think you wanted to prove yourself better than any other man in the room. To be smarter than them, to outthink them, to outtalk them. I remember the look on your face when each one of them broke down, the pleasure, almost savage. And when one of us stood up to you, you mind him? Juror 3. The man with the messenger business. When he stood his ground, when he didn't allow himself to be beaten into submission by you, you went for him like a torpedo. You didn't let up till he was crying his heart out, you didn't stop until you'd humiliated him in front of the rest of us. It was just a game, wasn't it, Mr Davis? We were playthings to you. That boy's life was a ball for you to bat around the room, like a cat toys with a mouse before he gobbles it up.'

Davis watched from the other side of his antique desk, still, silent and dead-eyed as a statue.

'Am I right, Mr Davis?' I asked, breathless, my nerves carrying the charge like bell wire.

He picked up the letter opener, ran its edge along the pad of his thumb, leaving a string of tiny red beads. His tongue licked them away. He asked, 'Exactly what kind of man do you think I am, Mr McArdle?'

I'm not sure what rose in me then, I thought it was courage, but I realise now that it was not.

'I know what kind of man you are,' I said. 'My son told me. I know about the girl from your office who disappeared, and about the one who drowned in her own bathtub. I guess you'll never answer for those young women, or for the couple who died

315

because you talked eleven men into giving the wrong verdict. You'll get away with it, I suppose.'

I stood, wavered, gripped the edge of the desk, breathed deep.

'I just want you to know, Mr Davis, that your sin did not go unnoticed. I can see myself out.'

He did not speak as I left the room, as the heavy door closed behind me.

I walked to the apartment door, the one that opened onto its own private entrance hall, leading to the elevator. As I passed the drawing room, I saw his wife, Sarah, watching me from the doorway. She said nothing as our eyes met, but even now I wonder if, somewhere deep in her consciousness, somewhere behind the veil of whatever drugs Davis kept her on, I wonder if part of her mind begged me for help?

We buried Jarlath one week later.

Eugene took it worse than anybody. He had no time for his brother when he was alive. Now he's grieving so hard I fear it might unman him.

Jarlath left a bar on Charles Street at two in the morning, steaming drunk. One witness, a vagrant, saw a tall thin man with dark hair slip out of a doorway as Jarlath passed, slide a blade between his ribs three times, and walk on as if nothing had happened. Jarlath died on the sidewalk, his lungs filling with blood. No one to hold his hand as he faded. I hope there wasn't a great deal of pain or fear for him in those last minutes. I will carry the knowledge that I caused his death to my grave, that if I had heeded his advice and stayed away, my son would not be in the ground today.

I expect he'll come for me. When enough time has passed, when the receptionist has forgotten about the strange old man who wouldn't go away, I imagine I'll feel a hand on my shoulder, something cold and sharp in my side.

But I will keep my mouth shut.

I solemnly swear, so help me God, that I will never breathe a word about Juror 8, a man called Willard Davis, to another living soul.

A LONG TIME DEAD
A MIKE HAMMER STORY

MICKEY SPILLANE & MAX ALLAN COLLINS

Co-author's note: This story, found unfinished in Mickey Spillane's files, dates to the mid-1960s. I have completed it, using Mickey's notes to do so.   M.A.C.

Kratch was dead.

They ran forty thousand volts through him in the stone mansion called Rahway State Prison with eight witnesses in attendance to watch him strain against the straps and smoke until his heart had stopped and his mind quit functioning.

An autopsy had opened his body to visual inspection and all his parts had been laid out on a table, probed and pored over, then slopped back in the assorted cavities and sewn shut with large economical stitches.

One old aunt, his mother's sister, came forth to claim the remains and, with what little she had, treated him to a funeral. Kratch had left a fortune but it was tied up, and auntie was on his mother's side of the family, and poor—Dad had married a succession of showgirls, and Kratch's mom had been the only one to produce an heir.

Whether hoping for a bequest or out of a sense of decency her nephew hadn't inherited, the old girl sat beside the coffin for two days and two nights, moving only to replace the candles when they burned down. Her next-door neighbor brought her the occasional plate of food, crying softly because nobody else had come to this wake.

Just before the hearse arrived, a small man carrying a camera entered the room, smiled at the old lady, offered his condolences and asked if he could take a picture of the infamous departed.

There was no objection.

Quietly, he moved around the inexpensive wooden coffin, snapped four shots with a 35MM Nikon, thanked auntie and left. The next day the news service carried a sharp, clear photo of the notorious Grant Kratch, even to the stitches where they had slid his scalp back after taking off the top of his head on the autopsy table.

No doubt about it.

Kratch was dead.

The serial killer who had sent at least thirty-seven sexually defiled young women to early graves was nothing more than a compost pile himself now.

It had been a pleasure to nail that bastard. I had wanted to kill him when I found him, but the chance that he might give up information during interrogation that would bring some peace of mind to dozens of loved ones out there made me restrain myself.

I knew it was a risk—he was a rich kid who had inherited enough loot to bribe his way out of about anything—but I figured the papers would play up the horror show of the bodies buried on his Long Island Estate and keep corruption at bay.

So I'd dragged him into the Fourth Precinct Station, let the cops have him, then sat through trial where he got the death penalty, sweated out the appeal lest some soft-hearted judge drop it to a life sentence, then was a witness to his smoldering contortions in the big oaken hot seat.

Oh, Kratch was dead all right.

Then what was he doing on a sunny Spring afternoon, getting into a taxicab outside the Eastern terminal at LaGuardia Airport?

Damn. I felt like I was in an acid dropper's kaleidoscope—it came fast so fast, no warning...just a slow turn of the head and there he was, thirty feet away, a big man in a Brooks Brothers suit with a craggily handsome face whose perversity exposed itself only in his eyes, and the hate wrenched at my stomach and I could taste the bitterness of vomit. I had my hand on the butt of the .45 and almost yanked it out of the jacket when my reflexes caught hold and froze me to the spot.

Those same reflexes kept me out of his line of sight while my mind detailed every inch of him. He wasn't trying to hide. He wasn't doing a damn thing except standing there waiting for a taxi to pick him up. When one came, he told the cabbie to take him to the Commodore and the voice he spoke in was Kratch's voice.

And Kratch was a long time dead.

I flagged down the next cab and told the driver to take me to the Commodore, and gave him the route I wanted. All he had to do was look at my face and he knew something was hot and leaned into the job. I was forty-five seconds behind Kratch at the terminal, but I was waiting in the Commodore lobby a full five minutes before he came in.

At the desk he said his name was Grossman and they put him on the sixth floor. I got to the elevator bank before he did, went up to the sixth and waited out of sight until he got out and walked away. When he'd gone in his room, I eased past it and noted the number—620.

Downstairs I asked for something on the sixth, got 601, then went up to my room and sat down to try to put a wild fifty minutes into focus.

There are some things so highly improbable that any time considering them is wasted time. All I knew was that I had just seen Kratch and that the son of a bitch was a long time dead. So that put a lookalike on the scene—a possible twin or a relative with an exceptional resemblance.

Bullshit.

That *was* Kratch I saw. Not unless they had developed human clones, after all. I looked around the room I'd laid down eighty bucks for, wondering just what I had been thinking about when I registered. Been a long while since I'd taken off half-cocked on a dead run like this and I had damned near pushed myself into a corner.

Great plan I had—push his door button, then pull a gun on him, walk inside and do a dance on his head—maybe I'd pop those autopsy stitches. Only if I had the wrong guy my ass was grass. I'd had to drop a credit card at the registry desk and a halfway decent description would point a finger right at me.

Aside from a dead guy who was up and walking around, the basic situation wasn't a new one—I wanted to look around somebody else's hotel room. And after a lot of years in the private cop business in New York, I had plenty of options, legal and ill. I propped my door open enough to see anybody who might pass by, then dialed the Spider's number and got his terse, "Yeah?"

"Mike Hammer, kid."

It had been more than a year since I'd seen him, so I got a special greeting: "Whaddya want?"

"That gimmick you use for not letting a hotel door shut all the way."

"You goin' inta my business?"

"Don't get smart."

"Where are you?"

"The Commodore."

"And you can't rig something up your own self? Hell, you got wire in the furniture, and in the toilet bowl—"

"Look, I haven't got time. Just bring it over."

"Give me till tonight and I'll get you a pass key."

"No. Now."

"Mike—cut a guy a break. Security knows me there."

"Then send Billy. I'm in 601."

"You're a pain in the ass, Mike."

"Tell me that when yours is back in the can again."

"Okay." He let out a sigh that was meant for me to hear. "This better even up the books."

"Not hardly. But it's a start."

Twenty minutes later, Billy Chappey, looking like the original preppie, showed up at my door to hand me a small envelope, winked knowingly and strutted off. He sure didn't look like one of the best safe-crackers in the city.

After three tries on my own door, I had the routine down pat. Once it was in place, the little spring-loaded gimmick was hardly noticeable. I eased out into the hall, walked down to room 620, slipped the gizmo into the proper spot, then went back to my room again.

After two rings, he answered the phone with a pleasant, resonant, "Hello?" He sounded curious but not at all anxious.

I put something nasal in my voice. "Mr. Grossman?"

"Yes."

"This is the front desk, sir. When we entered your credit card in our machine, there was a malfunction and the printout was illegible. Strictly our problem, but would it be too much trouble for you to come down and let us do it over?"

"Not at all. I'll be there right away."

"Thank you. The management would like to send a complimentary drink to your room for the inconvenience."

"That's nice of you. Make it a martini. Very dry."

"Yes. Certainly, sir."

He was punctual, all right. His feet came by my door, and I waited until the elevator opened and shut, then went to his room and went the hell on in. Wouldn't be time to shake the place down. All I wanted was one thing and I lucked out: he had used the water glass in the bathroom and his prints were all over it. I replaced it with one from my room, after wetting it down, then took the gimmick off the door which I let close behind me.

The hall was still empty when I shut myself up in my own room. I pulled the bed covers down, messed up the sheets, punched a dent in the pillow and hung a DO NOT DISTURB sign on the doorknob.

When I got to the lobby, the guy calling himself Grossman was just leaving the bell desk with two no-nonsense security types. They both wore frozen expressions, having been through countless scam situations before. Grossman's face seemed to say someone was playing a joke on him, and nothing more.

My pal Pat Chambers was captain of Homicide and couldn't be bothered with chasing wild gooses.

"No it's *not* Grant Kratch's print," he growled at me over the phone, after running the errand for me. "Jesus, Mike, that guy is dead as hell!"

"I wish *I'd* made him that way. Then I could be sure."

"The print belongs to Arnold Veslo, a smalltime hood who hasn't been in trouble with the law since the mid-fifties."

"What kind of smalltime hood, Pat?"

"He had a couple of local busts for burglary, then turned up as a wheelman for Cootie Banners in Trenton. Did a little time and dropped off the face of the earth."

"Dropped off the face of the earth when? About the time the state fried Kratch?"

"I guess. So what?"

"Messenger over Veslo's photo and anything you got on him."

"Oh, well, sure! We aim to please, Mr. Hammer!"

"I pay my taxes," I said, and hung up on him.

Velda had been eavesdropping from the doorway, but now the big beautiful brunette swung her hips into my inner sanctum, pulled up the client's chair and filled it, crossing long, lovely legs. She could turn a simple white blouse and black skirt into a public decency beef.

"You want me to start checking on this Arnold Veslo?"

I shook my head. "We'll wait and see what Pat sends over. What about the aunt?"

Most people thought Velda was my secretary. They were right, as far as it went—but she was also the other licensed P.I. in this office, and my partner. In various ways.

"Long time dead," she said. "Some bitterness about that in the old neighborhood—seems Kratch didn't leave the old lady a dime."

I was trying to get a Lucky going with the desk lighter. She got up, thumbed it to life with one try, and lit me up. "Sure you aren't seeing ghosts?"

"Once I've killed this guy—*really* killed him—then maybe I'll see a ghost."

She settled her lovely fanny on the edge of my desk, folded her arms over the impressive shelf of her bosom, and the lush, luscious mouth curled into a cat-like smile. "That all it takes to get a death sentence out of you, Mike? Just resemble some long-gone killer?"

I grinned at her through drifting smoke. "That was Kratch, all right, doll. And I don't think there was anything supernatural about it."

I'd already filled her in on what I'd got at the Commodore. It wasn't the kind of hotel where engravings of George Washington could get you much information. But Abraham Lincoln still had a following.

"So you're stalking an insurance salesman from Lincoln, Nebraska," she said, her mouth amused but her eyes worried, "in the big city for a convention."

"Not just a salesman. He has his own agency. And he'll be here through Sunday. So we've got a couple days. And I hung onto my room on the sixth floor. So I have a base of operations."

"So there's no rush killing him, then."

"Shut-up."

"Remind me how this pays the overhead again?"

"Some things," I said, "a guy has to do just to feel good about himself."

The file Pat sent over on Arnold Veslo seemed an immediate dead end. During the war, young Veslo had been tossed out of the army for getting drunk and beating up an officer. As Pat indicated on the phone, the lowlife's stellar postwar career ran from burglary to assault, and notes indicated he'd been connected to Cootie Banner, part of a home invasion crew whose members were all either dead or in stir.

But where was Veslo now?

If that fingerprint was to be believed, he was an insurance broker named Grossman staying at the Commodore. But as far as the states of New York and New Jersey knew, Veslo had been released from Rahway a dozen years ago and done a disappearing act.

This time I was in Velda's domain, the outer office, sitting on the edge of her desk, which visually doesn't stack up with her sitting on the edge of my desk, but you can't have everything. I was studying the Veslo file.

"I can't find any connection," I said. "But I do have a hunch."

She rolled her eyes. "Rarely a good sign...."

"Stay with me." I showed her the mug shots. "You remember what Kratch looked like, right? Would you say this guy bears a resemblance?"

She squinted at the front-and-side photos I was dangling. "Not really."

"Look past the big nose and the bushy eyebrows. Check out the bone structure."

"Well...yeah. It's there, I suppose. What, plastic surgery?"

I shrugged. "Kratch had dough up the wazoo. It's Hollywood bullshit that you can turn anybody into anybody else, under the knife—but if you start out with a resemblance, and the facial underpinning is right...."

"Maybe," she said with a grudging nod. "But so what? You aren't seriously suggesting a scenario where Kratch hires Veslo to undergo plastic surgery, and then...take his place?"

"Kratch had enough dough to pull just about anything off."

For as beautiful as she was, she could serve up an ugly smirk. "Sure. Makes great sense. Here's a million bucks, pal—all you gotta do is die for me. And by the way, let's trade fingerprints!"

"There are only two places in the system where fingerprint cards would need switching—Central Headquarters and the prison itself—and suddenly Kratch's new swirls are Veslo's old ones."

She frowned in thought. "Just bribe a couple of clerks....It *could* be done. So what now, Mike?"

"Doll," I said, sliding off the desk onto the floor, "I got things I want you to check out—you'll need the private detective's chief weapon to do it, though."

"What, a .45? You know I pack a .38."

"That's an understatement." I patted the phone on the desk. "Here's your weapon. You walk your fingers. Mike has to follow his nose."

I told her what I wanted done, retrieved my hat from the closet and headed out.

⌒

George at the Blue Ribbon on Forty-Fourth Street had a habit of hiring ex-cops for bartenders. It wasn't a rough joint by any means, in fact a classy German restaurant with a bar decorated by signed celebrity photos and usually some of the celebrities who signed them. Still, a bar is a bar and having aprons who could handle themselves always came in handy.

Lou Berwicki was in his mid-sixties, and worked afternoons, six-two of muscle and bone and gristle, with a bucket head, stubbly gray hair and ice-blue eyes that missed nothing.

He was also an ex-cellblock guard from Rahway State Prison.

Lou got off at four-thirty, and I was waiting for him at my usual table in a nook around a corner. I had ordered us both beers and, as his last duty of the shift, he brought them over.

We shook. He had one of those beefy paws your hand can get lost in, even a mitt like mine.

"Great to see you, Lou."

"Stuff it, Mike—I can tell by that shit-eating grin, this is business. What the hell can an old warhorse like me do to help a young punk like you?"

I liked guys in their sixties. They thought guys in their thirties were young.

I said, "I need to thumb through your memory book, Lou. Need some info about Rahway, and I hate driving to New Jersey."

"Who doesn't?"

"You didn't work Death Row."

"Hell no. My God, it was depressing enough on the main cellblocks."

"But you knew the guys who did?"

"Yeah. Knew everybody there. Big place, small staff—we all knew each other. Paid to. What's this about?"

I lighted up a smoke; took some in, let some out. "About ten years ago they gave Grant Kratch the hot squat."

"Couldn't happen to a nicer guy."

"How well did you know the bulls working that block?"

"Enough, I guess. What's this about, Mike?"

"Any rotten apples?"

He shrugged. "You know how it is. Prison pay stinks. So there's always guys willing to do favors."

"How about a big favor?"

"Don't follow...."

"I have a wild hair up my ass, Lou. You may need another beer to follow this...."

"Try me."

"Say a guy comes to visit Kratch, maybe the day before he's set to take the electric cure. This guy maybe comes in as Kratch's lawyer—might be he's in a beard and glasses and wig."

"I think I *will* have that beer..." Lou gulped the rest of his down, and waved a waitress over. "I didn't know you were still readin' comic books, Mike."

"Hear me out. Say this guy has had plastic surgery and is now a ringer for Kratch—"

"This may take a boilermaker."

"So they switch clothes, and Kratch walks, and the ringer gets the juice."

Lou shook his head, laughed without humor. "It's a fairy tale, Mike. Who would do that? Who would take a guy's place in the hot seat?"

"Maybe somebody with cancer or some other incurable disease. Somebody who has family he wants taken care of. Remember that guy in Miami, who popped Cermak for the Capone crowd? He had cancer of the stomach."

The old ex-prison guard was well into the second beer now. Maybe that was why he said, "Okay. So what you're saying is, could you pull that off with the help of the right bent screw?"

"That's what I'm saying. Was anybody working on Death Row at that time that could have been bought? And we're talking big money, Lou—Irish sweepstakes money."

The beer froze halfway from the table to his face. Lou was a pale guy naturally but he went paler.

"Shit," he said. "Conrad."

"Who?"

"Jack Conrad. He was only about fifty, but he took early retirement. The word was, he'd inherited dough. He went to Florida. Him and his wife and kids."

"He was crooked?"

"Everybody knew he was the guy selling booze and cigarettes to the inmates. Legend has it he snuck women in. Whether that's true or not, I can't tell you. But I *can* tell you something that'll curl your hair."

"Go, man."

He leaned forward. "Somebody *murdered* Conrad—maybe…a year after he moved down there. Murdered him and his whole family. He had a nice looking teenage daughter who got raped in the bargain. Real nasty shit, man."

I was smiling.

"Jesus, Mike—I tell you a horror story and you start grinning. What's wrong with you?"

"Maybe I know something you don't."

"Yeah, what?"

"That the story might have a happy ending."

Velda was in the client's chair again, but her legs weren't crossed—her feet were on the floor and her knees together. Prim as a schoolmarm.

"How did you know?" she asked.

"I said it was a hunch."

She was pale as death, after hearing what Lou had shared with me.

"Arnold Veslo had a good-looking wife and child, a young boy," she said, reporting what she'd discovered. "Two weeks after Kratch was executed, Mrs. Veslo was found at home—raped and murdered. The boy's neck was snapped. No one was ever brought to justice. What kind of monster—"

"You know what kind."

She leaned in and tapped the fat file folder on my desk. "Like you asked, I checked our file on Veslo—it's mostly clippings, but there's a lot of them. And I put the key one on top."

I flipped the folder open, and they stared back at me, both of them—Arnold Veslo and Grant. Veslo in a chauffeur's cap and uniform, opening the car door for his employer, Kratch, who'd been brought in for questioning two weeks before I hauled his ass and the necessary evidence into the Fourth Precinct.

"You were right," she said, rapping a knuckle on the yellowed newsprint. "Veslo worked for Kratch. How did you know? What are you, psychic?"

"No. I'm not even smart. But I saw a murderer today, a living, breathing one, and I knew there had to be a way."

She shrugged. "So we bring Pat in, right? You lay it all out, and the investigation begins. If Grossman really is Kratch, then before his 'death,' Kratch had to find a way to transfer his estate into some kind of bank set-up where his new identity could access it. That kind of thing can be traced. You can get this guy, Mike."

"Velda, we know for sure Kratch killed and raped thirty-seven women over a five-year period. Mostly prostitutes and runaways. You remember our clients' faces? The parents of the last girl?"

She swallowed and nodded.

"Well, it's a damn sure bet that he also killed that prison guard's family *and* Veslo's, and got his jollies with a couple more sexual assaults along the way. And do you really think that's his whole damn tally?"

"What do you mean, Mike?"

"I mean 'Grossman' has spent the last ten years doing more than selling insurance, you can damn well bet. Think about it—you just *know* there are missing women in unmarked graves all across the heartland."

"God," she said, ashen. "How many more has he killed?"

"No one but that sick bastard knows. But you can be sure of one thing, doll."

"What?"

"There won't be any more."

Back in my hotel room, I was still weighing exactly how I wanted to play this. I'd been seen here, and a few people knew I'd been asking about Grossman, so even if I handled this with care, I'd probably get hauled in for questioning.

And of course Captain Pat Chambers already knew the basics of the situation.

With my door open, and me sitting in a chair with my back to the wall, I had a concealed view of the hallway. I wasn't even sure Kratch was in his room. I was considering going down there, and using the passkey I'd taken Spider up on, and just taking my chances confronting the bastard. I'd rigged self-defense pleas before.

Which was the problem. I was a repeat offender in that department, and the right judge could get frisky.

I was mulling this when the bellboy brought the cute little prostitute—because that's surely what she was—up to the door of 620. She had curly blonde Annie hair and a sparkly blue mini-dress and looked about sixteen.

I could see Kratch, in a white terry cloth Commodore robe, slip into the hall, give the bellboy a twenty, pat him on the shoulder, send him on his way, pat the prostitute on the bottom, and guide her in.

Knowing Kratch's sexual proclivities, I didn't feel I had much choice but to intervene. My .45 was tucked in the speed rig under my sport jacket, the passkey in my hand. It was about 10 p.m. and traffic in the hall was scant—too late for people to be heading out, too early for them to be coming back.

So I stood by that door and listened. I could hear them in there talking. He was smooth, with a resonant baritone, very charming. She sounded young and a little high. Whether drugs or booze, I couldn't tell you.

Then it got quiet, and that worried me.

What the hell, I thought, and I used the passkey.

I got lucky—they were in the bathroom. The door was cracked and I could hear his smooth banter and her girlish giggling, a radio going, some middle-of-the-road station playing romantic strings, mixed with the bubbling rumble of a Jacuzzi.

I got the .45 out, and helped myself to a real look around, this time—this was a suite, a sprawl of luxury. There was a wet bar and I could see where he'd made drinks for them. In back of the bar, I found the pill bottle, and a sniff of a lipstick-kissed glass told me the bastard had slipped her a mickey.

That wasn't the most fun thing he had in store for her—I checked the three big suitcases, and one had clothes, and another had toys. You know the kind—handcuffs and whips and chains and assorted S & M goodies. Nothing was in the last big, oversize suitcase.

Not yet.

So he had a whole evening planned for her, didn't he? But there's always a party pooper in the crowd....

When I burst into the bathroom with the .45 in hand, he and his big hard piston practically jumped out of the big deep tub. The hot bubbles were going, and more drinks sat on the edge of the tub, but I motioned with the gun for him to sit down and stay put. The girl didn't notice me, or anyway didn't notice me much. She was half-unconscious already, leaning back against the tub, a sweet little nude with hooded eyes and pert handfuls with tiny tips poking up out of the froth like flowers just starting to grow.

I held the gun on him as he frowned at me in seeming incomprehension and I leaned over and lifted the girl by a skinny arm out of the tub. She didn't seem to mind. She might have been a child of twelve but for the cupcake breasts. If I hadn't got here when I did, she wouldn't have ever got any older.

She managed to stand on wobbly feet, her wet feet slippery on the tile.

I took her chin in my free hand. "I'm the cops. You want to leave. Wake up! This bastard doped you."

Life leapt into her eyes, and self-preservation kicked in, and she stumbled into the other room. I left the door open as I trained the gun on Kratch.

He was a handsome guy, as far as it went. His hair was gray and in tight Roman curls, with a pockmarked ruggedness, his chest hair going white, too, stark on tanned flesh. His erection had wilted. Having a .45 pointed at you will do that.

And he frowned at me, as if I were just some deranged intruder— he didn't have to fake the fear.

"My name is Grossman. I'm an insurance salesman from Nebraska. Take my money from my wallet—it's by the bed. You can have it all. Just don't hurt the girl."

That made me laugh.

She stuck her head in. She was dressed now. Didn't take long with those skimpy threads.

"Thank you, mister," she said.

"I never saw you," I said. "And you never saw me."

She nodded prettily and was out of the door.

I grinned at him. "Alone at last. Are you really going to play games, Kratch?"

He smiled. "Almost didn't recognize you, Hammer. You're not as young as you used to be."

"No, but I can still recognize a piece of shit when I see one."

"No one else will. I'm a respectable citizen. Have been for a long, long time."

"I don't think so. I think Grossman is just the latest front for your sick appetites. How many young girls like that have you raped and killed in the past ten years or so, Kratch? I will go to my grave regretting I didn't kill you the first time around."

"My name isn't Kratch." The fear had ebbed. He had an oily confidence—if I was going to kill him, he figured, I'd have done it by now. "It's Grossman. And you will never prove otherwise. You can put all your resources and connections behind it, Hammer, and you will never, *ever* have the proof you need."

"Since when did I give a damn about proof?"

The radio made a simple splash going in, like a big bar of soap, and he did not scream or thrash, simply froze with clawed hands and a look of horror that had come over him as the deadly little box came sailing his way. I held the plug in and let the juice have him and endured the sick smell of scorched flesh with no idea whether he could feel what I was seeing, the all-over blisters forming like so many more bubbles, the hair on his head catching fire like a flaming hat, fingertips bursting like overdone sausages, eyes bulging, then popping, one two, like plump squeezed grapes, leaving sightless black sockets crying scarlet tears as he cooked in the gravy of his own gore.

I unplugged the thing, and the grotesque corpse slipped under the roiling water.

"*Now* you're fucking dead," I said.

THE PLATER

ANN CLEEVES

The land was east coast flat, washed by floods, so the ditches were full and the fields on either side of him greener than he could remember. It was a familiar road, long and straight and narrow. He'd picked up the Saab in Hull that afternoon and now he was on his way home. He'd spend the night at the cottage before delivering the car to a showroom in Coventry early the next day. He liked his own bed; it was better than sleeping in the vehicle or a cheap B and B and it didn't add much to the mileage. From Coventry he'd hitch-hike to Bristol, taking his trade plates with him, and collect an Audi for Liverpool. That's what he did for a living; he drove other people's cars from one end of the country to another.

It was July and hot. The ditches steamed as the water evaporated, and the road disappeared into a heat haze before it turned a corner so it seemed to go on for ever, straight and flat to the horizon. Way ahead of him was a small, squat bus, but there was no other traffic. The verges on each side of the road were lush and untreated. Reeds in the dykes and cow parsley so tall that it formed a hedge. He drove slowly. There was no rush. Since he'd lost Suzy there was nothing to hurry home to.

Ahead of him a small drama was being played out. The bus slowed to a stop and a couple of school kids jumped off. Lads with shirts hanging out and scruffy sports bags. As they chased up a farm track a woman appeared. The plater thought she must have come from one of the tarted-up cottages set back from the road, but the bright afternoon sun shone straight into his eyes and he couldn't be certain. Suddenly she was there, a black, mad silhouette, running and waving after the bus. It was clear to the plater that the driver hadn't seen her. He indicated and drove on. She stood for a moment looking after the bus, as if she could drag it back towards her, just with the power of her will. Then she gave up. In a single gesture of defiance she turned to face the on-coming traffic, planted one foot firmly ahead of her, and stuck out her thumb.

He would always stop for other platers. That went without saying. A rule as fixed as his contract with the agency. He needed the others to get him home on the dark, wet nights when he stood at motorway junctions, just as they needed him. But he never picked up anyone else. The students and the soldiers on leave and the motorists who'd broken down could find there own way home. He hated making conversation. He'd chosen this job because it had given him the chance to be on his own.

But this time he stopped. He was drugged by the heat and the sun in his eyes, and something of this woman reminded him of Suzy. Besides, he seemed to have no choice in the matter. Although he had already driven past her he stopped and reversed. For the first time he saw her clearly. She was older than Suzy, at least ten years older, smaller, more delicate. Her hair was fine as rabbit fur, faded blond, pinned up with a tortoise shell comb so her neck seemed long and thin enough for him to put one hand round. Her brown eyes had sparks in them. He leant across the passenger seat and opened the car door for her. Until then she'd made no move to get in.

'Where are you going?' he asked.

'Town?' A question. Or a riddle. Surely she knew where she wanted to be.

It was further than he'd intended taking her, past where he lived, but he nodded. When he'd opened the door he'd smelled the humid air – a mixture of cows and ditchwater – and then her perfume.

She got in quickly as if she were worried that he'd change his mind. Or that she'd change hers. She was wearing sandals and a blue, sleeveless dress printed with silver stars. There was pink polish on her toe nails, a scattering of freckles on her shoulder. The dress rode up when she stepped in and her leg was brown and smooth. No freckles there. She was clutching a bag made of purple velvet patchwork on her lap. It would have been big enough to contain everything *he* needed for an overnight stay, including a light-weight sleeping bag and a couple of maps. But he didn't think it would do for a woman. Even Suzy had needed a rucksack when she went on the road. The smallness of the bag confused him. He didn't understand what she intended. If she was planning to go all the way into the big town she wouldn't be back before night fall. She seemed to have left home in a hurry, without any thought.

'God,' she said. She shifted her hips so she was comfortable in the leather seat, lifting her buttocks and pulling down the dress. 'It was never that easy when I was young.'

He stared at her but she didn't move again.

'Hitching, I mean. I thought I wouldn't stand a chance at my age.'

'Aren't you worried?' he asked slowly. 'Hitch-hiking on your own?'

'It's not something I do every day. The last time was when I was a student. Twenty years ago. And the rest! But when the bus drove off I thought "Sod it. Why not?"'

'I saw you think that. That was why I stopped.'

She turned and looked at him. 'Did you? How very perceptive.'

He could feel his face prickle with a blush so he put the Saab into gear and pulled off. Still there were no other cars.

'I'm running away,' she announced. Her voice wasn't loud but it was clear. If you were at one end of a church and she was at the other, and she whispered, you'd still hear every word. He wondered what had made him think of churches because he hadn't been inside one since Suzy's funeral, and that was a whole year before, almost to the day. He allowed himself to take his eyes off the road for a moment to look at his passenger. Was she serious? He suspected she was laughing at him. Under the clear voice, he thought he heard laughter.

Then she did give a little chuckle out loud. 'I'm running away from my husband. He'll come home from work and no-one will be there. No one to pour him a drink or cook his dinner.'

He didn't say anything.

'You're shocked.'

'No.' Of course he was and she could tell.

'Perhaps you think you should drive me straight back.'

'Only if you want me to.' Part of him had wanted her to say yes. He was already regretting the impulse to stop. No more complications, he'd told himself after Suzy. But trapped by the car her perfume was stronger, heady. She played with the velvet of her bag, squeezing it into pleats with long, supple fingers.

'No,' she said. 'Really, I don't.' More gently she added 'I'll probably only run away for one day. Teach him not to take me for granted. Tomorrow I'll go back and cook the supper like a good little wife.'

It occurred to him then that perhaps Suzy had only meant to run away for one day and that she'd intended to come back to him. The thought winded him as if he'd been kicked in the chest. He fought for breath. The woman seemed not to notice his distress.

'One day of adventure,' she was saying. 'Time out. That's all I want.'

A tractor and trailer pulled out of a lane in front of him. He overtook it smoothly.

'What's your name?' he demanded. The question was too abrupt. He could hear that as soon as the words were spoken. The image of Suzy as she might have been, apologetic on the doorstep, stopped him thinking straight.

'Belle.'

'I had a girlfriend called Suzy.' Why had he told her that? Conversation didn't work this way. He'd got it wrong again. You had to talk about things no-one cared about, at first at least. And anyway it was dangerous to bring up the subject of Suzy. He wasn't sure he could remember the story.

The woman seemed not to notice he'd broken the rules. 'Did you? What happened to her?'

'She walked out one night.'

'Like me,' Belle said.

'But she never came back.'

'Oh,' she said in the whisper which would fill a church. 'I'm sorry. That's so sad.'

He looked at her again, expecting to find her mocking him, the smirk, the 'isn't he dumb?' pity he usually provoked. But she seemed moved by his loneliness. He thought she understood it. Perhaps she wasn't being frivolous in running away. Perhaps she didn't have a marriage worth saving. She touched his arm, a gesture of sympathy, and there was a sort of dreaminess in her eyes. He wondered fleetingly if he might feature in her adventure. He might make it more special for her.

'Town then, yeah?' He tried to keep his voice natural, though a croak had developed. He wished he was wearing something different. Not the jeans he'd bought in the market for a fiver and the checked shirt with the frayed collar. He wished he'd had a shower before leaving home.

'Why?' she asked. 'Where were *you* going?'

'Home.' The other words came as a mumbled rush. 'You could come if you like. I could make you some tea. I've got herbal. I'll take you into town later.' Suzy had liked herbal. It would still be alright, wouldn't it, wrapped up in its foil packet, even after a year? As he waited for the woman to reply he felt as if he were growing, that his limbs were getting longer and more awkward and clumsy, that he was taking up so much space in the car that there was no air left for either of them to breathe.

She hesitated and he knew she was thinking back to her young days, when she'd taken risks and gone hitching on her own and talking to strangers. He realised that was what he'd been banking on: her leaving her middle-aged wifely caution behind.

'Herbal tea,' she said gently. 'Why not?'

So he looked in his mirror to check the road was empty, and indicated and turned into the track.

Belle *adored* the cottage. That was what she said when she first saw it. He'd known that she'd like it. Suzy had been hooked by it too when she'd first wandered up the track. 'Wow,' she'd said. 'It's, like, really fairy tale. Hansel and Gretel.' Love at first sight.

It was made of old brick and flint. A red-tiled roof which came so low that he could easily reach the black, cast-iron gutter with his hand. Outside, a saw-horse and a pile of logs, a couple of feral hens, a place to park his cars. Inside, four rooms, unchanged pretty much since his mother's day, but tidy. He didn't like clutter. And a neat extension that he'd built on the back. He didn't invite Belle inside. Not yet, he thought. He'd have to be careful with her. They stood for a moment looking at the house. The low sun threw their shadows ahead of them. His seemed enormous in comparison with hers. Not Hansel and Gretel, he thought. Some other story.

'But it's magic,' Belle said. 'It can't have changed for a hundred years.'

'Of course it's changed.' He spoke more sharply than he'd intended but he felt defensive. 'There's a bathroom now. Suzy needed a bathroom.' He wanted to explain what a job that had been, the cesspit and the plumbing, but thought better of it. 'And there's a phone. I need a phone for work.'

'It's not just the building,' Belle said. 'It's the quiet.' He listened to sounds he didn't usually hear. Water in the field drain. The sandpaper scratching of a hen. A wood pigeon. She shut her eyes and he saw a spider's web of fine lines around them. As he watched the lids lifted and she looked out past the row of coppiced willow to where cows grazed. The quiet had bothered Suzy in the end, but it seemed not to trouble Belle.

'Tell me about your work.' She turned and smiled at him. He felt faint again like when he'd first smelled her, and stood up to compose himself.

'I'll make the tea first. That'll be best.'

It had been sunny when Suzy had arrived, but that had been a winter late afternoon sun in a pink and grey sky, with a frost starting to form. He'd been out to fetch logs and she'd appeared at the end of the track. He'd stopped, still bent over the barrow, and watched her come closer. She'd been dressed in black leather and carried a crash helmet under her arm and he was reminded of a film about aliens in space suits. It was *that* strange to see anyone there. But she was on her own and there wasn't a flying saucer in sight. He'd straightened as she came up to him.

'Can I use your phone?' she'd said. 'I came off my bike. Frozen surface water. The road's dead greasy.' But she wasn't looking at him. She was looking at the cottage, grey now that the sun had gone, icicles hanging from the eaves. That's when she made the comment about the fairy tale.

He'd invited Suzy in immediately because he couldn't keep her outside when it was freezing, and that was what she was there for, to use the phone. She'd reminded him of that as he stood holding the rubber grips of the wheelbarrow, staring at her. 'You do have a phone?' Stamping her fat leather boots up and down to tell him how cold she was. And besides, she was different from Belle, more confident, with her curious eyes and her voice demanding attention and answers.

He would have been shy in a stranger's house, but Suzy had wandered through it touching and probing, running her finger over the back of the chair where he sat in the evening, making him open the little gate in the bottom of the range to show where the fuel went, picking up a teacup to look at the pattern on the side.

'Is it just you here?'

'Since mother died.'

'Don't you mind being on your own?'

'Sometimes...' he'd hesitated. '...Sometimes I'd prefer the company.'

The next day she'd turned up with her stuff. He'd heard the motorbike coming down the track, so loud he could feel the vibrations through his feet and it was as if the foundations were shaking. It seemed she'd had a row with her boyfriend. She described it but the plater wasn't listening.

'You don't mind?' she asked. A challenge. 'I mean, you did sort of say...'

He hadn't been able to speak, dizzy with disbelief and delicious indecision. She'd stood on the square of carpet in the parlour. 'Of course I'll need a bathroom.' And softened the demand by taking his hand and tilting her head and standing on her toes to push her tongue between his lips. Then stroking his hair in a way that was almost tender. By then the indecision was over. He had no choice.

'Tell me about your work,' Belle said again, and he left winter behind and returned to the smells and the sounds of a July afternoon. She was sitting on a wooden bench set along the front wall of the house. One of the smells was of roasting wood preservative. He'd made the tea and put it on the bench beside her, then sat on the grass, not wanting to crowd her. He knew his size sometimes intimidated. She'd wanted to bring out the tray but he was still reluctant to let her into the house. If he'd left Suzy outside that first time, offered to make the phone call on her behalf, he wouldn't have this guilt which he carried round in his gut like a permanent bellyache. He tried to push Suzy out of his head but it was difficult because, despite their physical differences, the women had become blurred in his mind. Perhaps he had been more upset than he'd realised by the anniversary of Suzy's death.

He saw that Belle was waiting for him to answer. He stumbled into an explanation of what it was to be a plater.

'Do you enjoy it?'

'Oh yes,' he said. 'It's the cars. How could I drive a car like that otherwise? And it's the maps too. You move across the map in a different line each day.' He stopped, realising he was using almost exactly the same words as when he'd first described his work to Suzy.

'I've seen the platers,' Belle said. 'Men at motorway junctions carrying trade plates? They must have been. I didn't know what they were doing. You don't really take any notice do you? They all seem to look the same.' She was excited. It was as if she seldom came across a subject she knew nothing about. 'And so organised… It is a man thing, I suppose. Not really a suitable job for a woman.'

'There was one woman.'

'Was there?' Excited again. A pause, a flash of inspiration. 'Not Suzy?'

How could she have guessed? 'She enjoyed coming out with me,' he said slowly.

'She would. Of course.' Belle was looking out beyond the cows to the horizon. He waited for her to go on but she seemed lost in thought.

'At first that was enough. She loved the fast cars. She was wild about speed. I drove too fast for her because that was what she wanted. She sat beside me. Shouting "Faster. Faster". Like a kid on a ride at the fair. But it couldn't have been enough. Without telling me she contacted the agency. She fixed the insurance and the contract. Without telling me.' His voice sounded too loud, a sort of booming in his ears, and he tried to control it, to become reasonable. He didn't want to scare Belle away. 'I came in one night and she wasn't there. She'd left a note. She was delivering a VW to Wolverhampton and bringing back a people carrier. Working as a plater. I lay awake, listening for the engine, watching for the headlights on the bedroom ceiling. When she got in she said I was daft for being anxious.'

'Perhaps she felt trapped,' Belle said. 'She wanted her own life.'

'Her own life?' he demanded. 'What does that mean? It wasn't safe, what she was doing. My nerves were ragged with waiting for her night after night. And all the time I was working I was wondering where she was. In the end I told her: "If you work as a plater, you don't live here."'

'So she went?'

'She packed up her clothes and left while I was at work.' He hesitated. He didn't know how much more to say. But it was a story and stories needed endings. 'Two days later the police were here. Two of them. A grey-haired bloke and a girl so young she looked as though she should still be at school. I'd heard their car and I'd thought it might be Suzy, so it threw me, seeing the uniforms standing there. She was dead. Hit and run. She'd been hitching on the motorway. I'd always said she should get the train once she'd delivered the car...' He'd told it well, he thought. Well enough.

Belle touched his hand and squeezed it gently a couple of times, as she'd squeezed the velvet bag when she was sitting in his car.

'You can't blame yourself.'

'No? Maybe not.'

'Did they ever find the driver?'

The guilt got him again, weighed him down so it was a struggle to stand up. 'No,' he said. 'They never found out who did it.' He remembered the police officers, standing on the doorstep, looking round the yard for a car which had already been delivered to Stamford.

Now he was on his feet, looking down at the top of her head. He saw the stray hairs escaping from the comb, the long swan's neck. 'Look,' he said. 'Why don't you come inside?'

The next day the plater drove the Saab to Coventry, then stopped for an early lunch at a transport café close to the M4. Not part of the usual routine but the weather had changed. There was a blustery west wind and sudden squally showers. The café was an ugly house built of raw yellow brick with a concrete pull-in where trucks stopped overnight. Inside, it was all smoke and steam and the smell of fried food. Condensation ran in streams down the window. Someone had left a paper open with the mucky pots on the only empty table. The plater began to read.

The article, on an inside page, was about the search for a woman. She had last been seen by two school boys running for a bus on a country road. After that, it seemed, she'd disappeared. The police were anxious to trace her. Early the previous evening a neighbour had discovered the body of her husband in the cottage where they'd lived. The man had been strangled and by implication the woman was prime suspect in a murder enquiry. There was a photograph, which the plater studied carefully, even holding it up towards the flickering strip light, but it was grainy and blurred. It could have been of any middle-aged woman.

Belle folded the newspaper carefully, ran her finger along to straighten the crease and felt a stab of injured pride. She would have liked to tell the lorry drivers slumped over their sweet teas and ketchup splattered chips. To shout her cleverness out loud. Not one murder. Two. Thanks to the plater she'd disappeared, become invisible, nothing but a woollen hat and a waterproof coat.

And no-one would find his body for months. Who ever went to his cottage? Who cared about him? Not the agency when she'd phoned them and told them he didn't want to be considered for work for a while. Not after the Saab. The woman at the end of the phone had sounded relieved if anything. He would have been slow at the work and difficult to deal with. No loss.

Belle wiped the grease from her face with a paper handkerchief. The rain had stopped. She hoisted her velvet bag onto her shoulder, stuck the trade plates under her arm and made her way outside. She stood at the café entrance and stuck out her thumb. She only had to wait two minutes before a lorry pulled up.

WHAT YOU WERE FIGHTING FOR

JAMES SALLIS

I was ten the year he showed up in Waycross. It was uncommonly dry that year, I remember, even for us, no rain for weeks, grass gone brown and crisp as bacon, birds gathering at shallow pools of water out back of the garage where Mister Lonnie, a trustee from the jail, washed cars. And where he let me help, all the while talking about growing up in the shacks down in Niggertown, bringing up four kids on what he made doing whatever piecemeal work he could find, rabbit stew and fried squirrel back when he was a kid himself.

I'd gone round front to fetch some rags we'd left drying on the waste bin out there and saw him pull in. Cars like that—provided you knew what to look for, and I knew, even then—didn't show up in those parts. Some rare soul had taken Mr. Whitebread's sweet-tempered tabby and turned it to mountain lion. The driver got out. He left the door open, engine not so much idling as taking deep, slow breaths, and stood in the shadow of the water tower looking around.

I grew up in the shade of that tower myself. There wasn't any water in it anymore, not for a long time, it was as baked and broiled as the desert that stretched all around us. A few painted-on letters, an A, part of a Y, an R, remained of the town's name.

I could see Daddy inside, in the window over the workbench. Didn't take long before the door screeched in its frame and he came out. "Help you?" Daddy said. The two of them shook hands.

The man glanced my way and smiled.

"You get on back to your business, boy," Daddy told me. I walked around the side of the garage to where I wouldn't be seen.

"She's not handling or sounding dead on. And the timing's a hair off. Think you could have a look?"

"Glad to. Strictly cash and carry, though. That a problem?"

"Never."

"I'll open the bay, you pull 'er in."

"Yes, sir."

"Garrulous as ever, I see."

I went on around back, wondering about that last remark. Not too long after, Mister Lonnie finished up and headed home to his cell. They never locked it, and he had it all comfy in there, a bedspread from Woolworth's, pictures torn from magazines on the wall. You live in a box, he said, it might as well be a *nice* box. I went inside to the office, which was really just a corner with cinder blocks stacked up to make a wall along one side. Daddy's desk looked like it had been used for artillery practice. The chair did its best to throw you every time you shifted in it.

I was supposed to be studying but what I was doing was reading a book called *The Killer Inside Me* for the third or fourth time. I'd snitched it out of a car Daddy worked on, where it had slipped down between the seats.

Everyone assumed I'd follow in my father's footsteps, work at the tire factory maybe, or with luck and a long stubborn climb uphill become, like he had, a mechanic. No one called kids special back in those days. We got called lots of things, but special wasn't among them. This was before I found out why normal things were so hard for me, why I always had to push when others didn't.

They got to it, both their heads under the hood, wrenches and sockets going in, coming out. Every few pages I'd look through the holes in the cinder blocks. Half an hour later Daddy said the man didn't need him and he had other cars to see to. So the visitor went on working as Daddy moved along to a '62 Caddy.

After a while the visitor climbed in the car, started it, revved the engine hard, let it spin down, revved it again. Got back under the hood and not long after that said he could use some help. Said would it be okay to ask me and Daddy grunted okay. "Boy's name is Leonard."

"You mind coming down here to give me a hand with this engine, Leonard?" the man said.

I was at a good part of the book, the part where Lou Ford talks about his childhood and what he did with the housekeeper, but the book would always be there waiting. When I went over, the man shook my hand like I was grown and helped me climb in.

"I'm setting the timing now," he said. "When I tell you, I need for you to rev the engine." He held up the timing light. "I'll be using this to—"

I nodded just as Daddy said, "He knows."

To reach the accelerator I had to slide as far forward in the seat as I could, right onto the edge of it, and stretch my leg out straight. I revved when he said, waited as he rotated the distributor, revved again. Once more and we were done.

"What do you think?" the man asked Daddy.

"Sounding good."

"Always good to have good help."

"Even for a loner, yeah."

The man looked back at me. "Maybe we should take a ride, make sure everything's tight."

"Or take a couple of beers and let the boy get to *his* work."

Daddy snagged two bottles from the cooler. Condensation came off them and made tiny footprints on the floor. I was supposed to be doing extra homework per my teachers, but what was boring and obvious the first time around didn't get any better with age. Lou and the housekeeper were glad to have me back.

Daddy and the man sat quietly sipping their beers, looking out the bay door where heat rose rose in waves, turning the world wonky.

"Kind of a surprise, seeing you here." That was Daddy, not given to talk much at all, and never one for hyperbole.

"Both of us."

Some more quiet leaned back against the wall waiting.

"Still in the same line of work?"

"Not anymore, no."

"Glad to hear that. Never thought you were cut out for it."

'Thing is, I didn't seem to be cut out for much else."

"Except driving."

"Except driving." Our visitor motioned with his bottle, a swing that took in the car, the rack, the tools he'd put back where they came from. "Appreciate this."

"Any time. So, where are you headed?"

"Thought I might go down to Mexico."

"And do what?"

"More of the same, I guess."

"The same being what?"

Things wound down then. The quiet that had been leaning against the wall earlier came back. They finished their beers. Daddy stood and said he figured it to be time to get on home, asked if he planned on heading out now the car was looking good. "You could stay a while, you know," Daddy said.

"Nowhere I have to be."

"Don't guess you have a place…"

"Car's fine."

"That your preference?"

"It's what I'm used to."

"You want, you can pull in out back, then. Plenty of privacy. Nothing but the arroyo and scrub trees all the way to the highway."

Daddy raised the rattling bay doors and the visitor pulled out, drove around. We put the day's used rags in the barrel, threw sawdust on the floor and swept up, swabbed the sink and toilet, everything in place and ready to hit the ground running tomorrow morn. Daddy locked up the Caddy and swung a tarp over it. Said while he finished up I should go be sure the man didn't need anything else.

He had the driver's door open, the seat kicked back, and he was lying there with eyes open. Propped on the dash, a transistor radio the size of a pack of cigarettes, the kind I'd seen in movies, played something in equal parts shrill and percussive.

"Daddy says to tell you the diner over on Mulberry's open till nine and the food's edible if you're hungry enough."

"Don't eat a lot these days."

He held a beer bottle in his left hand, down on his thigh. The beer must have been warm since it wasn't sweating. Crickets had started up their songs for the night. You'd catch movement out the corner of your eye but when you looked you couldn't see them. The sun was sinking in its slot.

"Saw the book in your pocket earlier," he said, "wondered what you're reading," and when I showed him he said he liked those too, even had a friend out in California that wrote a few. Everything about California is damn cool, I was convinced of that back then, so I asked a lot of questions. He told me about the Hispanic neighborhood he'd lived in. Billboards in Spanish, murals on walls, bright colors. Stalls and street food and festivals.

Years later I lived out there in a neighborhood just like that before I had to come back to take care of Daddy. It all started with him pronouncing words wrong. Holdover would be *ho*lover, or noise somehow turn to nose. No one thought much about it at first, but before long he was losing words completely. His mouth would open, and you'd watch his eyes searching for them, but the words just weren't there.

"Everyone says we get them coming up the arroyo," I said, "illegals, I mean."

"My friend? Wrote those books? He says we're all illegals."

Daddy came around to collect me then. Standing by the kitchen counter we had a supper of fried bologna, sliced tomatoes and leftover dirty rice. This was Daddy's night to go dancing with Eleanor, dancing being a code word we both pretended I didn't understand.

That night a storm moved toward us like Godzilla advancing on poor Tokyo, but nothing came of it, a scatter of raindrops. I gave up trying to sleep and was out on the back porch watching lightning flash behind the clouds when Daddy pulled the truck in.

"You're supposed to be in bed, young man," he said.

"Yes, sir."

We watched as lightning came again. A gust of wind shoved one of the lawn chairs to the edge of the patio where it tottered, hung on till the last moment, and overturned.

"Beautiful, isn't it?" Daddy said. "Most people never get to see skies like that."

Even then I'd have chosen *powerful, mysterious, angry, promise unfulfilled*. Daddy said *beautiful*.

It turned out that neither of us could sleep that night. We weren't getting the benefits of the weather, but it had a hold on us: restlessness, aches, unease. When for the second time we found ourselves in the kitchen, Daddy decided we might as well head down to the garage, something we'd done before on occasion. We'd go down, I'd read, he'd work and putter or mess about, we'd come back and sleep a few hours.

A dark gray Buick sat outside the garage. This is two in the morning, mind you, and the passenger door is hanging open. What the hell, Daddy said, and pulled in behind. No lights inside the garage. No one around that we can see. We were climbing out of the car when the visitor showed up, not from behind the garage where we'd expect, but yards to the right, walking the rim of the arroyo.

"You know you have coyotes down there?" he said. "Lot of them."

"Coyotes, snakes, you name it. And a car up here that ain't supposed to be."

"They won't be coming back for it."

"What am I going to see when I look under that hood?" Daddy glanced at the arroyo. "And down there?"

"About what you'd expect, under the hood. Down there, there won't be much left."

"So it's *not* just more of the same. I'd heard stories."

"I'm sorry to bring this on you—I didn't know. It's taken care of."

Daddy and the man stood looking at one another. "I was never here," the man said. "*They* were never here." He went around to the back. Minutes later, his car pulled out, eased past us, and was gone.

"We'd best get this General Motors piece of crap inside and get started tearing it down," Daddy said.

We all kill the past in our own way. Some slit its throat, some let it die of neglect.

Last week I began a list of species that have become extinct. What started it was reading about a baby elephant that wouldn't leave its mother's side when hunters killed her, and died itself of starvation. I found out that ninety percent of all things that ever lived on earth are extinct, maybe more. As many as two hundred species pass away between Monday's sunrise and Tuesday's.

I do wonder. What if I'd not been born as I was, what if I'd been back a bit in line and not out front, what if the things they'd told us about that place had a grain of truth. Don't do that much, but it happens.

"When the sun is overhead, the shadows disappear," my physical therapist back in rehab said. Okay, they do. But only briefly.

And: "At least you knew what you were fighting for." Sure I did. Absolutely. We steer our course by homilies and reductive narratives, then wonder that so many of us are lost.

A few weeks ago I made a day trip to Waycross. The water tower is gone, just one leg and half another still standing. It's a ghost town now, nothing but weightless memories tumbling along the streets. I pulled in by what used to be my father's garage, got my chair out and hauled myself into it, rolled with the memories down the streets, then round back to where our visitor had parked all those years ago. Nothing much has changed with the arroyo.

You always hear people talking about I saw this, I read this, I did this, and it changed my life.

Sure it did.

Thing is, I'd forgotten all about the visitor and what happened that night, and the only reason I remember now is because of this movie I saw.

I'd rolled the chair in at the end of an aisle only to be met with a barrage of smart-ass remarks about blocking their view from a brace of twenty-somethings, so I was concentrating on not tearing their heads off and didn't pay much attention to the beginning of the movie, but then a scene where a simple heist goes stupid bad grabbed my attention and I just kind of fell through the screen.

The movie's about a man who works as a stunt driver by day and drives for criminals at night. Things start going wrong then go wronger, pile up on him and pile up more until finally, halfway to a clear, cool morning, he bleeds to death from stab wounds in a Mexican bar. "There were so many other killings, so many other bodies," he says in voiceover near the end, his and the movie's.

After lights came on, I sat in the theater till the cleaning crew, who'd been waiting patiently at the back with brooms and a trashcan on rollers, came on in and got to work. I was remembering the car, his mention of Mexico, some of the conversation between my father and him.

I'm pretty sure it was him, his story—our visitor, my father's old friend or co-worker or accomplice or whatever the hell he was. I think that explains something.

I wish I knew what.

THE PRICE OF LOVE

PETER ROBINSON

Tommy found the badge on the third day of his summer holiday at Blackpool, the first holiday without his father. The sun had come out that morning, and he was playing on the crowded beach with his mother, who sat in her striped deckchair smoking Consulate, reading her *Nova* magazine and keeping an eye on him. Not that he needed an eye kept on him. Tommy was thirteen now and quite capable of amusing himself. But his mother had a thing about water, so she never let him near the sea alone. Uncle Arthur had gone to the amusements on the Central Pier, where he liked to play the one-armed bandits.

The breeze from the grey Irish Sea was chilly, but Tommy bravely wore his new swimming trunks. He even dipped his toes in the water before running back squealing to warm them in the sand. It was then when he felt something sharp prick his big toe. Treasure? He scooped away the sand carefully while no one was looking. Slowly he pulled out the object by its edge and dusted it off with his free hand. It was shaped like a silver shield. At its centre was a circle with "METROPOLITAN POLICE" curved around the top and bottom of the initials "ER." Above this was a crown and a tiny cross. The silver glinted in the sunlight.

Tommy's breath caught in his throat. This was exactly the sign he had been waiting for since ever his father died. It was the same type of badge he had worn on his uniform. Tommy remembered how proud his dad had sounded when he spoke of it. He had even let Tommy touch it and told him what "ER" meant: *Elizabeth Regina.* It was Latin, his father had explained, for The Queen. "That's our Queen, Tommy," he had said proudly. And the cross on top, he went on, symbolized the Church of England. When Tommy held the warm badge there on the beach, he could feel his father's presence in it.

Tommy decided not to tell anyone. They might make him hand it in somewhere, or just take it off him. Uncle Arthur was always doing that. When Tommy found an old tennis ball in the street, Uncle Arthur said it might have been chewed by a dog and got germs on it, so he threw it in the fire. Then there was the toy cap gun with the broken hammer he found on the recreation ground—"It's no good if it's broken, is it?"—Uncle Arthur said, and out it went. But this time Uncle Arthur wasn't going to get his hands on Tommy's treasure. While his mother was reading her magazine, Tommy went over to his small pile of clothes and slipped the badge in his trouser pocket.

"What are you doing, Tommy?"

He started. It was his mother. "Just looking for my handkerchief," he said, the first thing he could think of.

"What do you want a handkerchief for?"

"The water was cold," Tommy said. "I'm sniffling." He managed to fake a sniffle to prove it.

But his mother's attention had already wandered back to her magazine. She never did talk to him for very long these days, didn't seem much interested in how he was doing at school (badly), or how he was feeling in general (awful). Sometimes it was a blessing because it made it easier for Tommy to live undisturbed in his own elaborate secret world, but sometimes he felt he would like it if she just smiled at him, touched his arm and asked him how he was doing. He'd say he was fine. He wouldn't even tell her the truth because she would get bored if she had to listen to his catalogue of woes. His mother had always got bored easily.

This time her lack of interest was a blessing. He managed to get the badge in his pocket without her or anyone else seeing it. He felt official now. No longer was he just playing at being a special agent. Now that he had his badge, he had serious standards to uphold, like his father had always said. And he would start his new role by keeping a close eye on Uncle Arthur.

Uncle Arthur wasn't his real uncle. Tommy's mother was an only child, like Tommy himself. It was three months after his father's funeral when she had first introduced them. She said that Uncle Arthur was an old friend she had known many years ago, and they had just met again by chance in Kensington High Street. Wasn't that a wonderful coincidence? She had been so lonely since his father had died. Uncle Arthur was fun and made her laugh again. She was sure that Tommy would like him. But Tommy didn't. And he was certain he had seen Uncle Arthur before, while his father was still alive, but he didn't say anything.

It was also because of Uncle Arthur that they moved from London to Leeds, although Tommy's mother said it was because London was becoming too expensive. Tommy had never found it easy to make friends, and up north it was even worse. People made fun of his accent, picked fights with him in the schoolyard, and a lot of the time he couldn't even understand what they were saying. He couldn't understand the teachers, either, which was why the standard of his schoolwork slipped.

Once they had moved, Uncle Arthur, who travelled a lot for his job but lived in Leeds, became a fixture at their new house whenever he was in town, and some evenings he and Tommy's mother would go off dancing, to the pictures or to the pub and leave Tommy home alone. He liked that because he could play his records and smoke a cigarette in the back garden. Once he had even drunk some of Uncle Arthur's vodka and replaced it with water. He didn't know if Uncle Arthur ever guessed, but he never said anything. Uncle Arthur had just bought his mother a brand new television, too, so Tommy sometimes just sat eating cheese and onion crisps, drinking pop and watching *Danger Man* or *The Saint*.

What he didn't like was when they stopped in. Then they were always whispering or going up to his mother's room to talk so he couldn't hear what they were saying. But they were still in the house, and even though they were ignoring him, he couldn't do whatever he wanted, or even watch what he wanted on television. Uncle Arthur never hit him or anything—his mother wouldn't stand for that—but Tommy could tell sometimes that he wanted to. Mostly he took no interest whatsoever. For all Uncle Arthur cared, Tommy might as well not have existed. But he did.

Everyone said that Tommy's mother was pretty. Tommy couldn't really see it, himself, because she was his mother, after all. He thought that Denise Clark at school was pretty. He wanted to go out with her. And Marianne Faithful, who he'd seen on *Top of the Pops*. But she was too old for him, and she was famous. People said he was young for his years and knew nothing about girls. All he knew was that he definitely *liked* girls. He felt something funny happen to him when he saw Denise Clark walking down the street in her little grey school skirt, white blouse and maroon V-neck jumper, but he didn't know what it was, and apart from kissing, which he knew about, and touching breasts, which someone had told him about at school, he didn't really know what you were supposed to do with a girl when she was charitable enough to let you go out with her.

Tommy's mother didn't look at all like Denise Clark or Marianne Faithful, but she wore more modern and more fashionable clothes than the other women on the street. She had beautiful long blonde hair over her shoulders and pale flawless skin, and she put on her pink lipstick, black mascara and blue eye-shadow every day, even if she was only stopping in or going to the shops. Tommy thought some of the women in the street were jealous because she was so pretty and nicely dressed.

Not long after they had moved, he overheard two of their neighbours saying that his mother was full of "London airs and graces" and "no better than she ought to be." He didn't know what that meant, but he could tell by the way they said it that it wasn't meant as a compliment. Then they said something else he didn't understand about a dress she had worn when his father was only four months in his grave, and made tut-tutting sounds. That made Tommy angry. He came out of his hiding place and stood in front of them red-faced and told them they shouldn't talk like that about his mother and father. That took the wind out of their sails.

Every night before he went to sleep, Tommy prayed that Uncle Arthur would go away and never come back again. But he always did. He seemed to stop at the house late every night, and sometimes Tommy didn't hear him leave until it was almost time to get up for school. What they found to talk about all night, he had no idea, though he knew that Uncle Arthur had a bed made up in the spare room, so he could sleep there if he wanted. Even when Uncle Arthur wasn't around, Tommy's mother seemed distant and distracted, and she lost her patience with him very quickly.

One thing Tommy noticed within a few weeks of Uncle Arthur's visits to the new house was that his father's photograph—the one in full uniform he was so proud of—went mysteriously missing from the mantelpiece. He asked his mother about it, but all she said was that it was time to move on and leave her widow's weeds behind. Sometimes he thought he would never understand the things grown-ups said.

When Tommy got back to his room at the boarding house, he took the badge out of his pocket and held it in his palm. Yes, he could feel his father's power in it. Then he took out the creased newspaper cutting he always carried with him and read it for the hundredth time:

POLICE CONSTABLE SHOT DEAD:
BIGGEST HAUL SINCE THE GREAT TRAIN ROBBERY
AUTHORITIES SAY.

A police constable accompanying a van carrying more than one million pounds was shot dead yesterday in a daring broad daylight raid on the A226 outside

Swanscombe. PC Brian Burford was on special assignment at the time. The robbers fled the scene and police are interested in talking to anyone who might have seen a blue Vauxhall Victor in the general area that day. Since the Great Train Robbery on 8th August, 1963, police officers have routinely accompanied large amounts of cash....

Tommy knew the whole thing off by heart, of course, about the police looking for five men and thinking it must have been an inside job, but he always read the end over and over again: "PC Burford leaves behind a wife and a young son." *Leaves behind.* They made it sound as if it was his father's fault, when he had just been doing his job. "'It is one of the saddest burdens of the badge of office to break the news that a police officer has been killed in the line of duty,' said Deputy Chief Constable Graham Brown. 'Thank God this burden remains such a rarity in our country.'"

Tommy fingered his badge again. *Burden of the badge of office.* Well, he knew what that felt like now. He made sure no one was around and went to the toilet. There, he took some toilet paper, wet it under the tap and used it to clean off his badge, drying it carefully with a towel. There were still a few grains of sand caught in the pattern of lines that radiated outwards, and it looked as if it was tarnished a bit around the edges. He decided that he needed some sort of wallet to keep it in, and he had enough pocket money to buy one. Uncle Arthur was still at the pier, and his mother was having a lie down, having "caught too much sun," so he told her he was going for a walk and headed for the shops.

Tommy went into first the gift shop he saw and found a plastic wallet just the right size. He could keep his badge safe in there, and when he opened it, people would be able to see it. That would be important if he had to make an arrest or take someone in for questioning. He counted out the coins and paid the shopkeeper, then he put the wallet in his back pocket and walked outside. The shop next door had racks of used paperback books outside. Uncle Arthur didn't approved of used books—"Never know where they've been"—but Tommy didn't care about that. He had become good at hiding things. He bought *The Saint in New York*, which he hadn't read yet and had been looking for for ages.

The sun was still shining, so Tommy crossed over to the broad promenade that ran beside the sands and the sea. There was a lot of traffic on the front, and he had to be careful. His mother would have gone spare if she had known he hadn't looked for a zebra crossing but had dodged between the cars. Someone honked a horn at him. He thought of flashing his badge but decided against it. He would only use it when he really had to.

He walked along the prom, letting his hand trail on the warm metal railing. He liked to watch the waves roll in and listen to them as they broke on the shore. There were still hundreds of people on the beach, some of them braving the sea, most just sitting in deckchairs, the men in shirtsleeves and braces reading newspapers, knotted hankies covering their heads, the women sleeping, wearing floppy hats with the brims shading their faces. Children screamed and jumped, made elaborate sandcastles. A hump-backed man led the donkeys slowly along their marked track, excited riders whooping as they rode, pretending to be cowboys.

Then Tommy saw Uncle Arthur on the prom and froze.

∽

He was wearing his dark blue trousers and matching blazer with the gold buttons, a small straw hat perched on his head. He needed a haircut, Tommy thought, looking at where the strands of dark hair curled out from under the straw. It wasn't as if he was young enough to wear his hair long like The Beatles. He was probably at least as old as Tommy's mother. As Uncle Arthur walked along with the crowds, he looked around furtively, licking his lips from time to time, and Tommy hardly even needed the magic of his badge to know that he was up to something. Tommy leaned over the railings and looked out to sea, where a distant tanker trailed smoke, and waited until Uncle Arthur had passed by. As he did so, he slipped his hand into his pocket and fingered the wallet that held his badge, feeling its power.

He could see Uncle Arthur's straw hat easily enough as he followed him through the crowds along the prom away from the Central Pier. Luckily, there were plenty of people walking in both directions, and there was no way Uncle Arthur could spot Tommy, even if he turned around suddenly. It was as if the badge had given him even extra power to be invisible.

Shortly before Chapel Street, Uncle Arthur checked the traffic and dashed across the road. Tommy was near some lights, and luckily they turned red, so he was able to keep up. There were just as many people on the other side because of all the shops and bingo halls and amusement arcades, so it was easy to slip unseen into the crowds again.

The problems started when Uncle Arthur got into the backstreets, where there weren't as many people. He didn't look behind him, so Tommy thought he would probably be OK following, but he kept his distance and stopped every now and then to look in a shop window. Soon, though, there were no shops except for the occasional newsagent's and bookie's, with maybe a café or a run-down pub on a street corner. Tommy started to get increasingly worried that he would be seen. What would Uncle Arthur do then? It didn't bear thinking about. He put his hand in his pocket and fingered the badge. It gave him courage. Occasionally, he crossed the street and followed from the other side. There were still a few people, including families with children carrying buckets and spades heading for the beach, so he didn't stick out like a sore thumb.

Finally, just when Tommy thought he would have to give up because the streets were getting too narrow and empty, Uncle Arthur disappeared into a pub called The Golden Trumpet. That was an unforeseen development. Tommy was too young to enter a pub, and even if he did, he would certainly be noticed. He looked at the James Bond wristwatch he had got for his thirteenth birthday. It was a quarter to three. The pubs closed for the afternoon at three. That wasn't too long to wait. He walked up to the front and tried to glance in the windows, but they were covered with smoked glass, so he couldn't see a thing.

There was a small café about twenty yards down the street, from which he could easily keep an eye on the pub door. Tommy went in and ordered a glass of milk and a sticky bun, which he took over to the table near the window, and watched the pub as he drank and ate. A few seedy-looking people came and went, but there was no sign of Uncle Arthur. Finally, at about ten past three, out he came with two other men. They stood in the street talking, faces close together, standing back and laughing as if they were telling a joke when anyone else walked past. Then, as if at a prearranged signal, they all walked off in different directions. Tommy didn't think he needed to follow Uncle Arthur any more, as he was clearly heading back in the direction of the boarding house. And he was carrying a small hold-all that he hadn't had with him before he went into the pub.

"Where do you think you've been?"

Tommy's mother was sitting in the lounge when he got back to the boarding-house. Uncle Arthur was with her, reading the afternoon paper. He didn't look up.

"Just walking," said Tommy.

"Where?"

"Along the front." Tommy was terrified that Uncle Arthur might have seen him and told his mother, and that she was trying to catch him out in a lie.

"I've told you not to go near the sea when I'm not with you," she said.

"I didn't go near the sea," Tommy said, relieved. "All the time I was on the prom I was behind the railings."

"Are you certain?"

"Yes, mummy. Honest. Cross my heart." At least he could swear to that without fear of hellfire and damnation. When he had been on the prom, he *had* been behind the railings at the top of the high sea wall, far away from the sea.

"All right, then," she said. "Mrs. Newbiggin will be serving dinner soon, so go up and wash your hands like a good boy. Your Uncle Arthur had a nice win on the horses this afternoon, so we'll be going out to the Tower Ballroom to celebrate after. You'll be all right here on your own reading or watching television, won't you?"

Tommy said he would be all right alone. But it wasn't watching television that he had in mind, or reading *The Saint in New York*.

The boarding house was quiet after dinner. When they had cleared the table, Mrs. Newbiggin and her husband disappeared into their own living quarters, most of the younger guests went out, and only the two old women who were always there sat in the lounge knitting and watching television. Tommy went up to his room and lay on his bed reading until he was certain his mother and Uncle Arthur hadn't forgotten something, then he snapped into action.

Ever since he had been little, he had had a knack for opening locks, and the one on Uncle Arthur's door gave little resistance. In fact, the same key that opened his own door opened Uncle Arthur's. He wondered if the other guests knew it was that easy. Once he stood on the threshold, he had a moment's panic, but he touched the badge in his trouser pocket for luck and went inside, closing the door softly behind him.

Uncle Arthur's room was a mirror-image of his own, with a tall wardrobe, single bed, chair, chest of drawers and a small wash-stand and towel. The flower-patterned wallpaper was peeling off at a damp patch where it met the ceiling, and Tommy could see the silhouettes of dead flies in the inverted lampshade. The wooden bedframe was scratched, and the pink candlewick bedspread had a dark stain near the bottom, as if someone had spilled tea on it. The ashtray on the bedside table was overflowing with crushed-out filter-tipped cigarettes. The narrow window, which looked out on the Newbiggins' backyard, where the dustbins and the outhouse were, was covered in grime and cobwebs. It was open about an inch, and the net curtains fluttered in the breeze.

First, Tommy looked under the bed. He found nothing there but dust and an old sock. Next, he went through the chest of drawers, which contained only Uncle Arthur's clean underwear, a shaving kit, aspirin and some items he didn't recognize. He assumed they were grown-ups' things. The top of the wardrobe, for which Tommy had to enlist the aid of the rickety chair, proved to be a waste of time, too. The only place remaining was inside the wardrobe itself. The key was missing, but it was even easier to open a wardrobe than a door. Uncle Arthur's shirts, trousers and jackets hung from the rail, and below them was his open suitcase containing a few pairs of dirty socks and underpants. No hold-all.

Just before he closed the wardrobe door, Tommy had an idea and lifted up the suitcase lid. Underneath it, on the floor, lay the hold-all.

He reached in, pulled it out and put it on the bed. It was a little heavy, but it didn't make any noise when he moved it. There was no lock, and the zip slid open smoothly when he pulled the tab. At first, he couldn't see what was inside, then he noticed something wrapped in brown paper. He lifted it out and opened it carefully. Inside was a gun. Tommy didn't know what kind of gun, but it was heavier than any cap gun he had ever owned, so he assumed that it was a real one. He was careful not to touch it. He knew all about fingerprints. He wrapped it up and put it back. Then he noticed it was lying on a bed of what he had thought was paper, but when he reached in and pulled out a wad, he saw it was money. Five pound notes, crumpled and dirty. He didn't know how much there was, and he wasn't going to count it. He had discovered enough for one evening. Carefully, he put everything back as it was. What he had to work out next was what he was going to do about it.

❦

That night as Tommy lay in bed unable to sleep, he heard hushed voices in his mother's room. He didn't like to eavesdrop on her, but given what he had just found in Uncle Arthur's room, he felt he had to.

It was almost impossible to hear what they were saying, and he only managed to catch a few fragments.

"Can't… money here… wait," he heard Uncle Arthur say, and missed the next bit. Then he heard what sounded like, "Year… Jigger says Brazil," and after a pause, "…the kid?" Next his mother's voice said, "…grandparents." He missed what Uncle Arthur said next, but distinctly heard his mother say, "have to, won't they? …"

Tommy wondered what they meant. Was Uncle Arthur planning a robbery, or had he already committed one? He certainly had a lot of money. Tommy remembered the three men talking outside the pub. One of them must have given Uncle Arthur the hold-all. What for? Did it represent the proceeds or the means? Were Uncle Arthur and his mother going to run away to Brazil and leave him with his grandparents? He didn't believe she would do that.

The bedsprings creaked, and he thought he heard a muffled cry from the next room. His mother obviously couldn't sleep. Was she crying about his father? Then, much later, when he was finally falling asleep himself, he heard her door close and footsteps pass by his room as if someone were walking on tiptoe.

The next day at breakfast his mother and Uncle Arthur didn't have very much to say. Both of them looked tired, and his mother had applied an extra bit of make-up to try to hide the dark pouches under eyes. Uncle Arthur's hair stuck up in places, and he needed a shave. The two old ladies looked at them sternly and clucked.

"Stupid old bags," muttered Uncle Arthur.

"Now, now," said Tommy's mother. "Be nice, Arthur. Don't draw attention to yourself."

The conversation he had overheard last night still worried Tommy as he ate his bacon and eggs. They had definitely mentioned the money. Was his mother about to get involved in something criminal? Was it Uncle Arthur who was going to involve her? If that was so, he had to stop it before it happened, or she would go to jail. The money and the gun were in Uncle Arthur's room, after all, and his mother could deny that she knew anything about them. Tommy had heard his mother insisting before they came away that they would have a room each. Uncle Arthur hadn't liked the idea because it would cost more money, but he had no choice. Tommy knew what it was like when his mother made her mind up.

The bag and gun would have Uncle Arthur's fingerprints all over them. Tommy was certain that Uncle Arthur must have handled the bag and the items in it since he had picked them up at the pub, if only to check that everything was there and to take out enough money for their trip to the Tower Ballroom last night. But his mother would have had no reason to touch them, or even see them, and Tommy himself had been careful when he lifted and opened the bag.

"Pass the sauce," said Uncle Arthur. "What we doing today?"

Tommy passed him the HP sauce. "Why don't we go up the Tower?" he suggested.

"I don't like heights," said Uncle Arthur.

"I'll go by myself, then."

"No you won't," said his mother, who seemed as concerned about heights as she was about water.

"Well what *can* we do, then?" Tommy asked. "I don't mind just looking at the shops by myself."

"Like a bloody woman, you are, with your shops," said Uncle Arthur.

Tommy had meant bookshops and record shops. He was still looking for a used copy of *Dr No* and hoping that the new Beatles single 'Help!' would be released any day now, even though he would have to wait until he got home to listen to it. But he wasn't planning on going to the shops, anyway, so there was no sense in making an issue of it. "I might go to the Pleasure Beach as well," he said, looking at Uncle Arthur. "Can you give me some money to go on the rides?"

Uncle Arthur looked as if he was going to say no, then he sighed, swore and dug his hand in his pocket. He gave Tommy two ten shilling notes, which was a lot of money. He could buy *Dr No* and 'Help!' *and* go on rides with that much, and still have change for a Mivvi and five Park Drive tipped. But he wasn't sure that he should spend it because he didn't know where it had come from. "Cor" he said. "Thanks, Arthur."

"It's Uncle Arthur to you," said his mother.

"Yeah, remember that," said Uncle Arthur. "Show a bit of respect for your elders and betters. And don't spend it all on candy floss and toffee apples."

"What about you?" Tommy asked. "Where are you going?"

"Dunno," said Uncle Arthur. "You, Maddy?"

"You know I hate being called that," Tommy's mother said. Her name, Tommy knew, was Madeleine, and she didn't like it being shortened.

"Sorry," said Uncle Arthur with a cheeky grin.

"Do you know, I wouldn't mind taking the tram all the way along the seafront to Fleetwood and back," she said, then giggled. "Isn't that silly?"

"Not at all," said Uncle Arthur. "That sounds like a lot of fun. It looks like a warm day. We can sit upstairs in the open. Give me a few minutes. I've just got to get a shave first."

"And comb your hair," said Tommy's mother.

"Now, don't be a nag," said Uncle Arthur, wagging his finger. "Maybe we'll see if we can call in at one of them there travel agents, too, while we're out."

"Arthur!" Tommy's mother looked alarmed.

"What? Oh, don't worry." He got up and tousled Tommy's hair. "I'm off for a shave, then. You'll have to do that yourself one day, you know," he said, rubbing his dark stubble against Tommy's cheek.

Tommy pulled away. "I know," he said. "Can I go now? I've finished my breakfast."

"We'll all go," said his mother. And they went up to their rooms. Tommy took a handkerchief from his little suitcase and put it in his pocket, because he really was starting to sniffle a bit now, made sure he had his badge and the money Uncle Arthur had given him, then went back into the corridor. Uncle Arthur was standing there, waiting and whistling, freshly shaven, hair still sticking up. For a moment, Tommy felt a shiver of fear ripple up his spine. Had Uncle Arthur realized that someone had been in his room and rummaged through his stuff, found the money and the gun?

Uncle Arthur grinned. "Women," he said, gesturing with his thumb towards Tommy's mother's door. "One day you'll know all about them."

"Sure. One day I'll know everything," muttered Tommy. He pulled his handkerchief from his pocket to blow his nose, and it snagged on the plastic wallet, sending his badge flying to the floor.

"What have we got here, then?" said Uncle Arthur, bending down to pick it up.

"Give me it back!"' said Tommy, panicking, reaching out for the wallet.

But Uncle Arthur raised his arm high, out of Tommy's reach. "I said what have we got here?" he repeated.

"It's nothing," Tommy said. "It's mine. Give it to me."

"Mind your manners."

"Please."

Uncle Arthur opened the wallet, looked at the badge and looked at Tommy. "A police badge," he said. "Like father, like son, eh? Is that it?"

"I told you it was mine," Tommy said, desperately snatching. "You leave it alone."

But Uncle Arthur had pulled the badge out of its transparent plastic covering. "It's not real, you know," he said.

"Yes, it is," Tommy said. "Give us it back."

"It's made of plastic," said Uncle Arthur. "Where did you get it?"

"I found it. On the beach. Give it to me."

"I told you, it's just plastic," said Uncle Arthur. And to prove his point he dropped the badge on the floor and stepped on it. The badge splintered under his foot. "See?"

At that moment, Tommy's mother came out of her room, ready to go. "What's happening?" she said, seeing Tommy practically in tears.

"Nothing," said Uncle Arthur, stepping towards the stairs. He gave Tommy a warning look. "Is there, lad? Let's go, love. Our carriage awaits." He laughed.

Tommy's mother gave a nervous giggle, then bent and pecked Tommy on the cheek. He felt her soft hair touch his face and smelled her perfume. It made him feel dizzy. He held back his tears. "You'll be all right, son?" She hadn't seen the splintered badge, and he didn't want her to. It might bring back too many painful memories for her.

He nodded. "You go," he said. "Have a good time."

"See you later." His mother gave a little wave and tripped down the stairs after Uncle Arthur. Tommy looked down at the floor. The badge was in four pieces on the lino. He bent and carefully picked them up. Maybe he could mend it, stick it together somehow, but it would never be the same. This was a bad sign. With tears in his eyes, he put the pieces back in the plastic wallet, returned it to his pocket and followed his mother and Uncle Arthur outside to make sure they got on the tram before he went to do what he had to do.

"You ready yet, Tommy?"

"Just a minute, Phil," Detective Chief Inspector Thomas Burford shouted over his shoulder at DI Craven. He was walking on the beach, the hard wet sand where the waves licked in and almost washed over his shoes, and DI Craven, his designated driver, was waiting patiently on the prom. Tommy's stomach was churning, the way it always did before a big event, and today, 13th July, 2006, he was about to receive a Police Bravery Award.

If it had been one of his men, he would have called it folly, not bravery. He had thrown himself at a man holding a hostage at gunpoint, convinced in his bones, in his every instinct, that he could disarm the man before he hurt the hostage. He had succeeded, receiving for his troubles only a flesh wound on his shoulder and a ringing in his ears that lasted for three days. And the bravery award.

At his rank, he shouldn't even have been at the hostage-taking scene—he should have been in his cubicle catching up on paperwork or giving orders over the police radio—but paperwork had always bored him, and he had sought out excitement whenever he had the chance. Now he walked with the salt spray blowing through his hair trying to control his churning bowels just because he had to stand up in front of a crowd and say a few words.

Tommy did what he usually did on such occasions and took the old plastic wallet out of his pocket as he stood and faced the grey waves. The wallet was cracked and faded with time, and there was a tear reaching almost halfway up the central crease. Inside, behind the transparent cover, was a police badge made out of plastic. It had been broken once and was stuck together with glue and Sellotape. Most of the silver paint had worn off over the years, and it was now black in places. The crown and cross had broken off the top, but the words were still clearly visible in the central circle: "METROPOLITAN POLICE" curved around "ER". *Elizabeth Regina*. "Our Queen," as his father had once said so proudly.

In the opposite side of the wallet was a yellowed newspaper clipping from July, 1965, forty-one years ago. It flapped in the breeze, and Tommy made sure he held on to it tightly as he read the familiar words:

> **SCHOOLBOY FOILS ROBBERS.** A thirteen year old schoolboy's sense of honour and duty led to the arrest of Arthur Leslie Marsden in the murder of PC Brian Burford during the course of a payroll robbery last August. Five other men and one woman were also arrested and charged in the swoop, based on evidence

and information given by the boy at a Blackpool police station. Also arrested were Madeleine Burford, widow of the deceased constable, named as Marsden's lover and source of inside information, Len Fraser, driver of the getaway car, John Jarrow...

Tommy knew it by heart, all the names, all the details. He also remembered the day he had walked into the police station, showed his badge to the officer on the front desk and told him all about the contents of Uncle Arthur's hold-all. It had taken a while, a bit of explaining, but in the end the desk sergeant had let him in, and the plainclothes detectives had shown a great deal of interest in what he had to say. They accompanied him to the boarding house and found the hold-all in its hiding place. After that, they soon established that the gun was the same one used to shoot his father. The gang had been lying low, waiting for the heat to die down before daring to use any large quantities of the money—a year, they had agreed—and they had been too stupid to get rid of the gun. The only fingerprints on it were Uncle Arthur's, and the five hundred pounds it was resting on was just a little spending money to be going on with.

The one thing the newspaper article didn't report was that the "boy" was Tommy Burford, only son of Brian and Madeleine Burford. That came out later, of course, at the trial, but at the time, the authorities had done everything within their power to keep his name out of it. Every time he read the story over again, Tommy's heart broke just a little more. Throwing himself at gunmen, tackling gangs armed with hammers and chains and challenging rich and powerful criminals never came close to making the pain go away; it only took the edge off for a short while, until the adrenalin wore off.

His *mother*. Christ, he had never known. Never even suspected. She had only been twenty-nine at the time, for crying out loud, not much more than a girl herself, married too young to a man she didn't love, for the sake of their imminent child, and bored with her life. She wanted romance and glamour and all the nice things that his father couldn't give her on a policeman's wage, the life she saw portrayed on posters, in magazines, at the pictures and on television, and Arthur Marsden had walked into her life and offered them all, for a price.

Of course Tommy's father had talked about his job. He had been excited about being chosen for the special assignment, and had told both his wife and son all about it. How was Tommy to know that his mother had passed on the information to Marsden, who was already her lover, and that he and his gang had done the rest? Tommy knew he had seen her with Uncle Arthur before his father's death, and he wished he had said something. Too late now.

Whether the murder of Tommy's father had ever been a part of the master plan, or simply an unforeseen necessity, nobody ever found out. Uncle Arthur and Tommy's mother never admitted anything at the trial. But Tommy remembered the look his mother gave him that day when he came back to the Newbiggins' boarding house with the two plainclothes policemen. She came out of the lounge as they entered the hall, and it was as if she knew immediately what had happened, that it was all over. She gave Tommy a look of such deep and infinite sadness, loss and defeat that he knew he would take it with him to his grave.

"Hurry up, Tom, we'd better hurry up or we'll be late!" called DI Craven from the prom.

"Coming," said Tom. He folded up the newspaper clipping and put it away. A wave rolled in and touched the very tips of his polished black shoes. He stepped back. How upset his mother would have been if she had known he had stood so close to the water. Brushing his hands across his eyes, which had started watering in the salt wind, he turned away from the sea and walked towards the waiting car, thinking how right they had all been back then, when they said he was young for his age and knew nothing about girls.

COPYRIGHT

ABOUT THE EDITOR

Maxim Jakubowski is a noted anthology editor based in London, just a mile or so away from where he was born. With over 70 volumes to his credit, including *Invisible Blood,* the 13 annual volumes of *The Mammoth Book of Best British Mysteries,* and titles on Professor Moriarty, Jack the Ripper, Future Crime and Vintage whodunits. A publisher for over 20 years, he was also the co-owner of London's Murder One bookstore and the crime columnist for *Time Out* and then *The Guardian* for 22 years. Stories from his anthologies have won most of the awards in the field on numerous occasions. He is currently the Chair of the Crime Writers' Association and a *Sunday Times* bestselling novelist in another genre.

For more fantastic fiction, author events,
exclusive excerpts, competitions, limited editions and more

VISIT OUR WEBSITE
titanbooks.com

LIKE US ON FACEBOOK
facebook.com/titanbooks

FOLLOW US ON TWITTER AND INSTAGRAM
@TitanBooks

EMAIL US
readerfeedback@titanemail.com